WHO'S GOT HIS FRONT?

"Go!" she snarled. "I have your back!"

Of course she did.

He turned and sprinted for the door at the end of the hall, among a crazy flickering of light.

"Intruder alert!" a voice boomed like thunder, bouncing off the walls and floor, until he was running inside an envelope of sound. "Intruder! All systems!"

Tolly kept his head down and ran. The lights flashed, flared, went out—and fluttered to a grimy grey. He kept running, Haz pounding behind him, the air growing thicker and harder to breathe.

He hit the door and smacked his palm against the plate.

Nothing happened.

The thick air crackled, and he felt the hair rising straight up on his head. He scrubbed his palm down the front of his shirt and slapped the plate, flat and hard.

Nothing happened again, except that sparks started spitting in the heavy air.

BAEN BOOKS by
SHARON LEE & STEVE MILLER

THE LIADEN UNIVERSE®

Fledgling
Saltation
Mouse and Dragon
Ghost Ship
Dragon Ship
Necessity's Child
Trade Secret
Dragon in Exile
Alliance of Equals
The Gathering Edge
Neogenesis
Accepting the Lance (forthcoming)

OMNIBUS VOLUMES

The Dragon Variation
The Agent Gambit
Korval's Game
The Crystal Variation

STORY COLLECTIONS

A Liaden Universe® Constellation, Volumes 1–3
A Liaden Universe® Constellation, Volume 4 (forthcoming)

THE FEY DUOLOGY

Duainfey • *Longeye*

BY SHARON LEE

Carousel Tides • *Carousel Sun* • *Carousel Seas*

NEOGENESIS
A New
Liaden Universe®
Novel
SHARON LEE &
STEVE MILLER

BAEN

NEOGENESIS

This is a work of fiction. All the characters and events portrayed in this book are fictional, and any resemblance to real people or incidents is purely coincidental.

A Baen Books Original

Baen Publishing Enterprises
P.O. Box 1403
Riverdale, NY 10471
www.baen.com

ISBN: 978-1-4814-8392-6

Cover art by David Mattingly

First printing, January 2018
First mass market printing, April 2019

Library of Congress Control Number: 2017037356

Distributed by Simon & Schuster
1230 Avenue of the Americas
New York, NY 10020

Pages by Joy Freeman (www.pagesbyjoy.com)
Printed in the United States of America

Dedicated to

Ronald and Helen Moore

With thanks to:

Lady Caroline Lamb, for one of the
most euphonious phrases of all time

and

Douglas Adams, for
The Restaurant at the End of the Universe

and

James H. Schmitz, Goth, the Leewit, Maleen,
Captain Pausert, the Vatch—and anyone who
has ever had to go by the Egger Route

and

Rosemary Edghill for commando beta reading

and

Mighty Tyop Hunters . . .

Teresa Carrigan, Jane Curry, Gregory Dougherty,
Terry Hazen, Melita Kennedy, Berry Kercheval,
Christine E. Kreider, Kathryn Kremer, Patricia Lang,
J. Spencer Love, Pamela Lunsford, Gail Martin,
Kate Reynolds, Anne Young

and especially

Everybody who participates in the Scavenger Hunts

Contents

Prologue

THEY ARRIVED AMID CHATTER INTO A CROWDED ORBIT; the wide channels were full of good nature and optimism, overflowing into other bands situated at the edges of frequencies and power ranges which were not generally employed in more orderly, civilized systems.

Daiellen System was not orderly. The planet Surebleak was certainly not orderly, and only just recently elevated to a height from which civilization could be seen.

Never mind. She had not chosen Daiellen or Surebleak for high culture, nor technological prowess. To judge from the traffic and the chatter, she was not alone in seeing opportunity in disorder.

In such busy space, their ship was merely one of many, similarly unremarkable vessels. The pilot scanned the chat bands, while the automatics exchanged preliminaries with the port authority.

"*Cortz Lattice*," came the hail on their frequency, "we see you. You're in Surebleak Control Space, under Pilots Guild TE standards. Repeat, we use a base Terran/Trade/Liaden protocol and my Liaden's still being learned. Speak up; it's crowded at dinner time."

She sat behind the pilot, being not a pilot herself. Her patience for even orderly and precise communication was scant, and thus the pilot sat comm as well.

The pilot, not in the least put out by the casual character of this contact from Surebleak Port's central authority, only touched a switch, answering in Standard Terran which nonetheless bore a slight accent. That, of course, was subterfuge. Her pilot was capable of subtlety. Not for the first time she acknowledged her good fortune, that it had been this particular guard who had chosen to accompany her.

"*Cortz Lattice* confirming your signal acquisition, Surebleak Control," said the pilot. "*Cortz Lattice*, out of Waymart, for Cortz Infotainment Enterprises, Emtraven Kvar PIC and sole pilot. We seek a midterm pad with modest access for a private traveler..."

"*Lattice*, hold while I get a visual."

Behind the pilot, she briefly closed her eyes. On a well-run port, Control would have acquired a visual as soon as the automatic signal had been received. Here... Control had started blind, not knowing that they had incoming a small ship of middle years, and neither a multipod freighter or tradeship? How old was their equipment? How decrepit?

And how could it hope to continue—to *succeed*—this disorderly and distracted little port? But there, she reminded herself once more; in this case, disorder was to her benefit, and her pilot was proficient—or perhaps merely patient.

They were inside the field, now, surely so. Inside the field, with her goal before her. Having come so far, and risked so much, there could be no doubt that success was hers.

"Okay, I'm guessing a Class C by our terms," Surebleak Control said. "So, if you got no need for pod-mounting, engineering, power, or major cargo deliveries, I got a couple tuck spots for cheap. Not blast pads, just old 'crete, with a cable to comm if you need it. It'd help if you got your own mobiles 'cause else you'll be depending on cabs or feet. Can't recommend feet if you're not familiar with Surebleak. Things is crowded."

"Speak to me of costs, payment method, and routing, customs, security," said her pilot. "Being unfamiliar with Surebleak, daylight sky would be welcome."

Almost instantly there was laughter. She cringed. Laughter as a general class of action was . . . difficult. Laughter from *Control* was near to insupportable. She closed her eyes, briefly, and mastered panic.

"The one custom you wanna keep at the front of your brain is *don't be stupid*," Control said, as if it were all a very fine joke. "Security? We got some. There's the Watch in the city, and cops here in port. In case you get bidness with 'em, they like to be called Port Security. You want more than that, you provide your own. Daylight sky, now . . ."

The voice faded, then came back, gay and easy.

"Here's what, *Lattice*. Transmitting an orbit to park in 'til tomorrow morning, local. That's 'leven Standard Hours to loiter, an' you'll be down with seven, eight hours of daylight, an' no snow called 'til end o'day. That work for you, Pilot Emtraven?"

"It works well," her pilot said. "Thank you, Control."

"Welcome. So. We'll be puttin' you into communication with Sherman's Shoot-Out—owner of that pad you'll be down on. You'll 'range costs an' payments direct. Nice location, if I didn't say. Right on port edge, certified legal landing pad for ships of your class. Can I get a commit?"

"Orbit and descent instructions received," her pilot said. "I commit."

"Done, then. Welcome to Surebleak, Pilot. We hope you enjoy your stay. Control out."

She sat back in her seat, and closed her eyes.

They were inside the field, she told herself, as one repeating a mantra, or a prayer. Already, she was more secure. Soon, they would be on-planet, and she would seek out her brother's people.

One step at a time. That was how the race was won.

Surebleak

I

"SEE YOU TONIGHT, BOSS."

Red-haired Miri Robertson, one half of Delm Korval and the port city Road Boss, inclusive, reached up to capture her lifemate's face between her two hands, and pulled him down for a kiss. It was maybe a little more energetic than it should've been for a good-bye kiss at the beginning of the day, but Val Con wasn't doing anything about ratcheting it back, either.

His arms came around her, and she leaned in, until one of them—probably him, being the cooler of two hotheads—broke the embrace, and they stood looking into each other's eyes.

"Want me to order a picnic dinner in our rooms tonight?" she asked him, her voice husky.

"That would be pleasant," he murmured. "It is, after all, the only time this week that we will have such an opportunity."

There was that. Meetings, that was the schedule for the next four days. And also—meetings, early and late.

"Consider it done. Now. You going down to the Road Boss's office, or not?"

"I believe that I must," he told her, just a little too earnestly. "Nelirikk values it so, and one does not like to disappoint him."

She nodded gravely.

"Gotta keep morale up," she said and went back a step, tucking her hands into the sleeves of her sweater. "See you tonight, Boss," she said again.

He inclined his head slightly.

"Until soon, *cha'trez*," he answered and turned toward the waiting car.

She watched 'til it was out of sight, around a curve in the drive, which is what he did on alternate days, when it was her turn to be Road Boss and his to be Delm Korval. On the one hand, it was a good thing there were two of them sharing one *melant'i*, which, according to Liadens, lifemates exactly did. If it had been her, standing Road Boss and Delm Korval, too . . . well. There weren't enough snowflakes in the storm, like they said here on Surebleak.

And, coming to that, she was willing to bet that Delm Korval's mail queue wasn't getting any shorter.

With a sigh, she turned and went back into the house.

Miri sat behind the big desk, put her coffee mug to one side of the screen, scooped the tan-and-brown kitten off the pile of papers on the other side of the screen, and tapped up the mail.

There was a message in-queue from Ms. dea'Gauss, reporting on the project to recruit native 'bleakers to the ranks of the Liaden *qe'andra* already on-world.

Progress, according to Ms. dea'Gauss, was good. Two more of the so-called "storefront *qe'andra*" had accepted apprentices from the resident population since last month's report, and commenced study programs. The probability of success for the first apprentice, in the opinion of Ms. dea'Gauss, was excellent. The second . . . the program administrators had not been sanguine, since the candidate did not read. However, the master in the case had been adamant that the candidate's other talents outweighed what was merely the lack of an easily acquired skill. Given the master's certainty, the administrators had allowed the apprenticeship to go forward, trusting the bimonthly reviews to discover any deficiencies.

Briefly, Miri wondered what other "talents" outweighed being able to read, when starting what was sure to be a reading-intensive course of study . . . then shrugged. None of her business, was it? And the Accountants Guild, of which the *qe'andra* were members, had access to sleep learners. The second 'prentice ought to be reading just fine by this time next week.

Terran, that was. She suspected that learning how to read Liaden was a little trickier for most people than it had been for her, who had basically just remembered it out of Val Con's head, which was one thing that the lifemate link was good for.

She sent an ack to Ms. dea'Gauss, to be polite, and filed the report away with the others. All told, they had six 'prentice *qe'andra* now on Surebleak, which was—despite the whole thing'd been her idea—six more'n she'd ever thought to see.

Now, all they had to do was get regular streeters into the habit of honoring their given word—and not just throwing out a signed contract because a better deal'd come along, which was how Surebleak was used to business going forth. Do that, and they'd've defused one of the biggest cultural landmines in 'bleaker/Liaden relations.

'Course, she thought, glumly, it wasn't going to be that easy. Something was going to blow up first. It always did. But, might be it wouldn't be as bad, if they had the Liaden-and-'bleaker *qe'andra* teams up and more or less running, and the streeters got used to seeing the storefronts with the list of services available to them.

The problem with setting things in motion, Miri thought, reaching for her mug, was that it *took time*, and in the meanwhile, any stupid damn thing could happen.

And given how serious Liadens took contracts, it was better'n even odds that somebody'd die before 'bleakers managed to learn different.

Still, she told herself, putting the mug down, you had to *try* . . .

She tapped the screen.

Next in-queue was—

"Miri?" A male voice inquired, from somewhere near the top shelf of the bookcase to her right. "A message has arrived from Hazenthull nor'Phelium, security wrap."

Speaking of unexpected circumstances, Miri thought wryly.

"Send it or bring it, whichever you like," she said.

"I would prefer to bring it," said the voice belonging to Jeeves, house security and backup butler. "It is . . . rather complex."

Miri sighed.

"'Course it is," she said.

The universe was too much with him this morning, Ren Zel thought. The air in the breakfast room had a slightly pearlescent shine; it tasted of ice and iris. Gold glittered at the edge of his sight, teasing him with the desire to open those other eyes which were his special gift, and become one with glory. It was . . . gods, how he *wanted* to—so very much. His hands shook visibly with longing, so that he put his teacup down with care and pushed his chair away from the small table.

He was alone in the breakfast parlor: no kin present to wonder what ailed him and to extend an offer of help. That was fortunate, as neither he nor Anthora, his lifemate, had quite yet found the perfect moment to share the details of his addiction with their delm.

Gold stitched, lightning quick, across the breakfast room; the air flashed like a mirror. He closed his eyes, which was foolish. The threads—the threads that held the universe together, binding all and everything into coherence against the chaotic void where potential universes ceaselessly flashed into and out of existence forever. The threads—the power to manipulate the threads—the power to which he had become addicted, and which would, soon or late, kill him.

He wanted—no.

He did not want; the *addiction* wanted.

Ren Zel took a deep breath, and deliberately focused. He opened his eyes, anchoring himself to *this* room, *this* reality, *this time*. Longing swept through him for that other place that encompassed no time—and all time. He swept it aside, concentrating on those things that were mundane and harmless. There was a square of dusty sunshine on the carpet, picking out threads of orange and red; on the window seat, curled into an undistinguished mop of varicolored stripes, the cat Kifer took advantage of the same sunbeam. Leaning into the chair's embrace, Ren Zel ran his palm along his thigh, feeling the nap of his trousers against his skin; a deep breath brought him the scent of his cooling tea, of sweet rolls, and coffee. He thought of Anthora, who had tied his soul to hers in what could only be a doomed attempt to bind him to the earth.

If the addiction consumed him—*when* it consumed him—before the culmination, he would cut the anchor line. It was a simple thing and well within his abilities. He might do so now, only . . . there was no reason to suppose that he would fall victim to his gift today. Today, he was stronger than the desire to meld with all the universe to guard it against yawning oblivion.

As if to give weight to that piece of unwarranted boldness, the pearly shine faded from the air, and it warmed somewhat, tasting of the morning foods laid out, of old wood, and a hint of dust.

For this morning, then, doom was averted.

Ren Zel leaned forward to take up his cup.

• • • ✵ • • •

"To Captain Miri Robertson," the voice was calm, if large. Miri put her chin on her fist and closed her eyes, listening.

"To Captain Miri Robertson, Jelaza Kazone, Surebleak. From House Guard Hazenthull nor'Phelium, on detached duty supporting Pilot Tocohl Lorlin and Pilot-Mentor Tollance Berik-Jones. I report a situation. Core mission accomplished. Treachery separates the team. I am with *Tarigan*. Pilot Tocohl travels with

Pilot-Mentor Inkirani Yo, aboard *Ahab-Esais*, possibly against her will. A direct request to speak to Pilot Tocohl was denied by Pilot Yo.

"Pilot-Mentor Jones and *Admiral Bunter* are on course to danger, arranged by Pilot Yo. Pilot Tocohl, if she is in peril, has resources available to her. Pilot Jones is being transported to persons who mean him very great harm. It is possible that *Admiral Bunter* is likewise acting against his best judgment. I have no proof of tampering, but I must fear the worst.

"Field judgment is that my assistance will most benefit the *Admiral* and Pilot Jones. My target is Nostrilia. My strategy is to over-Jump *Admiral Bunter*, and be in position to bring Pilot Jones aboard *Tarigan* before he is reacquired by his enemies.

"Respect to the captain. Hazenthull nor'Phelium out."

Tolly Jones again. Miri sighed quietly. She'd thought it was a good thing, that Hazenthull had found . . . a friend. Someone who not only took her out of herself, but out of her past, which, despite the best efforts of the Healers of the house, weighed heavy on her. Nothing and no one had counted more with Hazenthull than the fact that she had, through her own personal stupidity and willfulness, killed her partner.

Nothing, and no one—until Tolly Jones.

She'd followed him when he'd bolted from trouble, covering his back, coincidentally saving his bacon, and in the process took damage herself. That was how Hazenthull had wound up being a member of a team made up of a mentor of self-aware intelligences, and a tame AI who happened to be a daughter of Clan Korval, on a mission to civilize or kill another

AI who'd been brought to consciousness and then deserted, with two murders already on his young soul.

Well. It seemed Tolly Jones had a talent for trouble, but Tocohl . . .

Miri opened her eyes and considered the man-high canister at rest before her desk, headball glowing a patient and steady orange.

"Been in touch with your daughter lately?" she asked Jeeves.

"Miri, I have not. Unless there were some difficulty, I would not have expected to hear from Tocohl."

"Hazenthull seems to think she's *in* some difficulty."

"Yes," Jeeves agreed. "I did ping Tocohl when Hazenthull's message arrived, and did not receive an answer. Of course, that could merely mean that she is in Jump. I have, therefore, composed a pinbeam which I sent directly to Tocohl's address. It will be waiting for her when the ship she is on emerges from Jump."

"Good. You had a direct line to *Admiral Bunter*, as I recall it. Talked to him recently?"

"I had not wished to jostle the mentor's elbow, nor distract Tocohl from her work. However, I also pinged *Admiral Bunter* upon receipt of this message, and received no pingback, which, as with Tocohl, could simply mean that he is in Jump. I took the liberty of sending a pinbeam to his address as well."

She nodded and drank off the last of her coffee.

"Now—what d'you think about Hazenthull's field judgment?"

"I believe that it is sound. Even given that the situation is exactly as Hazenthull reports, Tocohl has many resources available to her. While he is by no means without resource, Tolly Jones has, in addition, powerful enemies who do indeed have the ability to render him a stranger to himself."

Miri gave him a sharp look. "He's an agent? A DOI operative?"

"Miri, no. He is a product of the Lyre Institute. If you wish, I can provide a brief."

"Do that. So Hazenthull's instincts are good, even if she's a little muddled on the details."

"I believe so, yes. If I may, it would be best if her captain granted her leave to proceed as outlined."

Miri snorted.

"Didn't exactly sound to me like she was asking for permission." She shook her head, and flipped one hand palm up, giving him the point.

"You're right, though; better to follow the forms, and keep the line of command clear. Ready?"

"I am."

"All right then. Please take a message to Hazenthull nor'Phelium. Greetings to the troop from Captain Miri Robertson . . ."

• • • ※ • • •

Lizzie'd lapped the ruckus room twice and was worn out enough to sit quiet in Miri's lap, to be read to.

Today's book was one of Lizzie's favorites: *Me and My Kitten*. She was busily pointing out the kitten in each picture, crowing with delight, when Miri lifted her head, smiling at the nearness of his pattern.

"*Mirada's* home," she told her daughter, but Lizzie was smacking the book, impatient for the next picture of the kitten.

Miri obligingly turned the page, pointing out the flowers the kitten was hiding among, and the little girl walking down the path, calling. Lizzie was all about the kitten, as usual. When the exclamations had died down, she began to turn the page—

Only to have her daughter suddenly lean forward and put her pudgy hand directly on the picture of a tree growing by the side of the path.

"Tree," Miri said, adding, "*We* have a tree."

Actually, as she'd come to understand it, the Tree had them, but there wasn't any sense getting into that 'til Lizzie was older.

Lizzie sighed and moved her hand. Miri turned the page and grinned at her daughter's voluble, if unintelligible, delight at discovering the kitten under the bench where the little girl, worn out with looking for him, had sat down to rest.

The door to the ruckus room opened. Miri smiled and looked up, watching him as he crossed the room, slim and graceful and utterly silent. He returned her smile and collapsed cross-legged onto the rug at her side.

"Good evening, Miri," he said in Low Liaden. "Good evening, Talizea."

At the sound of his voice, Lizzie looked away from the kitten, uttered a squeal and threw herself at him, arms wide.

He swung her into a hug against his shoulder—taking care to keep his chin up, and his hair inaccessible—before settling her on his knee.

"How did you pass the day, daughter?" he asked her, keeping to Low Liaden.

Lizzie replied with a burst of babble, her face tipped up to his. Miri, abandoned, closed the book and stretched out on her side, head propped on her hand.

Val Con listened gravely until Lizzie ran out of steam, then inclined his head.

"Indeed, a most exciting and productive day. Your industry quite puts me to shame." He cupped her cheek in his hand and looked to Miri, amusement in his eyes. "And you, *cha'trez*? How did you fare with the delm this day?"

"Well and not so well," she said in the Low Tongue. "I fear that there have been unexpected developments in the matter of *Admiral Bunter*. Tocohl may be at risk, Tolly Jones is certainly at risk, and Hazenthull has elected to rescue him. She sent a 'beam, explaining it all."

"You relieve me. Did she give a reason for her decision to place Tolly Jones ahead of a daughter of the House?"

"Funny you should ask," Miri said, going into Terran for the phrase, then dropping back to Low Liaden. "Her reasoning, with which Jeeves agrees, is that Tocohl has resources available to her which Tolly Jones does not. Also, he is definitely in peril of his life, while Tocohl may only have been . . . importuned."

"Jeeves agrees with Hazenthull's decision," Val Con repeated, slipping his hands around Lizzie's middle and bouncing her on his knee.

Miri waited until the squeals of appreciation had died down.

"He does. Also, it comes about that Tolly Jones is a . . . product of the Lyre Institute, of which I had not heard, until today. Do you know of it?"

He frowned.

"There is some mention in the Diaries of the Tanjalyre Institute," he said slowly, "with which Grandmother Cantra was . . . involved, in the old universe. But—"

At that moment, Lizzie lunged, her target, as near as Miri could make out, her father's chin. In retaliation, he swung her up over his head, laughing when she squealed and kicked her feet in delight.

"You think it just an accident of language?" Miri asked him.

He sighed and lowered Lizzie again to his knee. "I would certainly prefer to think so," he said wryly. "However, prudence dictates that we perform research."

"Gotcha all set up for tomorrow," she told him in Terran. "Jeeves had a file. I read it today. Fascinating, in a really scary kind of way."

"That certainly sounds as if there must be a link with Grandmother Cantra's school," Val Con said. "Well, I shall read the file tomorrow, then. If Hazenthull has gone haring off on her own recognizance..."

"I would not have you think so!" Miri said. "Her captain gave her permission. Retroactively, it must be admitted, but the chain of command is preserved."

"Ah. Balance being for the moment free of assault, at least in our own household, I propose that we return this delightful young person to the care of her nurse, and proceed to our rooms."

"You are still interested in an evening of privacy, then?"

Val Con gave her a look that curled her toes.

"Yes," he said.

...✵...

It was the absence of traffic on Dudley Avenue that finally pierced Kamele Waitley's concentration, and brought her to a sense of how late it must be.

Kareen's household ran to a particular schedule, which included a period of conversation, relaxation, and recreation after the evening meal. Kamele knew better than to absent herself from the social requirements of the house and had therefore spent a surprisingly enjoyable evening playing *rijel* with Scout vey'Loffit, who was very good, and Tassi, who was very bad. Not being the worst player at the board lent the game a certain pleasure, Kamele found, and Tassi didn't seem to care if she won or lost, which probably accounted for the quality of her play.

After, though, when she had ascended to her bedroom, instead of lying down to sleep . . . Kamele had cheated.

She had opened her working file and begun taking notes.

It had been her intention only to work for an hour—perhaps two—and now it seemed that she had worked the city to sleep.

The house was quiet around her, and when she looked out her window, Dudley Avenue was indeed deserted, the streetlights dimming toward dawn.

Kamele shook her head and glanced again at her table.

There were only a very few more pages to go through, and if she went to bed now, it would be worse than simply not sleeping at all.

"Well reasoned, Professor," she said, with a half-smile. Kareen would notice eyes reddened from a night of reading—of course she would; very little got past Kareen yos'Phelium. By this time, though—what was it they said, here on Surebleak?

Better be took for a 'hand than a zample.

And who, really, could argue with that?

Shaking her head, Kamele sat down at her table and reached for her note taker.

•••✵•••

It was very early in the morning and the light from Surebleak's star had not yet breached the protections of the inner garden. No matter. Jelaza Kazone's garden was never truly dark, not to one of Korval.

The air, however, was not in any way warm, especially not to a man who had woken too early and stealthily risen, lest he disturb his lifemate's slumber.

Val Con turned the collar of his jacket up as he followed the narrow, overgrown path, circling tighter and tighter in toward the center of the garden, the center of the House. One might even accurately say the *center of the clan*, save one did not wish to encourage an ego already sufficiently well-grown.

He couldn't say what had waked him. Certainly the exercise he and Miri had shared upon the long evening should have insured a deep sleep, which in fact it had, merely not a long one.

Nevertheless, he felt quite rested, though a bit as if he yet moved inside a dream. Which argued that it had been the Tree which had waked him. For what purpose was of course a mystery, but one that would, he must suppose, be speedily revealed.

He followed the path 'round its last, tightest spiral, and looked up, his attention abruptly caught by... something.

Something odd.

One scant step ahead, the path ended in a lush carpeting of blue-green grass that swept 'round the massive trunk at center. The clearing was enclosed on three sides by gloan-roses and other fragrant bushes, creating the impression of a private courtyard: the Tree Court, as it was designated in House records and the garden's own plantings map.

The whole area was bathed in a thick pearly light, as if it were filled with luminous mist. That was odd, but not unprecedented. The Tree adapted its environment to suit its best needs or, as he sometimes suspected, its whim.

Inside the misty, pearly light, the Tree was . . . dancing.

And that *was* odd.

Intrigued, he walked across the grass and surface roots, further into the glade.

This close, he could see that the Tree was merely manipulating mist and light to give an *impression* of dancing. Its shout of exuberance, however, was quite real enough to make his head ring.

The Tree had been . . . unusually alert since the removal to Surebleak. It was as if all those years on Liad had lulled it into a drowse, from which it had wakened into a state of childlike wonder. They had known from the Diaries that the Tree liked to travel, but it had not occurred to any of them that it might, on Liad, have been *bored*.

This present madcap delight, however . . . one wondered what caused it.

Val Con took two steps forward and placed his palms flat against the warm trunk, expecting at least an acknowledgment of his presence, even amidst the celebration.

His vision went black, then brightened; excitement

rocked him back on his heels; he had a crazy swinging view of what might have been a piloting chamber, one seat empty, board green, and in the screens a ship—a ship with lines that he knew, if only—

He snatched after the image, trying to force the viewpoint back to those screens, to that ship...

Behind him, he heard a door cycle, and in that momentary distraction lost the tussle for another glimpse of the screens, dropping back into his own body with a gasp, arms locked and quivering with the strain of holding himself upright.

Slowly, he allowed himself to collapse against the wide trunk, and lay there, letting the Tree support him, his cheek against bark that ought to have been rough, but felt as soft as Miri's shoulder.

The ship—*that ship.*

"*Bechimo*," he said, and felt another surge of joy from the Tree, which mixed rather badly with his own feeling of dread.

His sister Theo was captain of *Bechimo*, and to say that Theo was prone to...*interesting situations* was to understate the case by several orders of magnitude. What in the name of the gods had she stirred up now? And how did the Tree—

A white dragon soared inside his head, gaining altitude against a blue-and-gold sky, until it was finally lost from sight.

Val Con was aware of a feeling of vast contentment.

Which was, he thought sourly, pushing himself squarely onto his own feet, easy for the Tree to say.

Miri woke as he was slipping back under the covers.

"You're cold," she said, rolling over to share her

warmth, a leg thrown companionably over his thighs, an arm across his chest, and her head on his shoulder.

"The Tree had wanted me in the garden," he said, nestling his cheek against her hair.

"And it couldn't wait 'til the day got a little warmer? And later?"

"It was somewhat excited," he murmured.

"'Bout what?"

"There, I am not completely certain. I believe it wished me to know that Theo is in a pickle."

Miri snorted a half-laugh, and he smiled.

"Yes," he said. "Precisely so."

II

THE CAR ROUNDED THE CURVE, EN ROUTE FOR SUREBLEAK Port and the Road Boss's office. Val Con stood for another minute, until he lost the sound of the engine in the breeze.

He shook himself then and went back into the house, down the hall to the delm's office.

Crossing to the sideboard, he poured himself a cup of tea and carried it with him to the desk. He settled into the chair, put the cup aside, and brought up the screen.

The first thing to display was the calendar, reminding him that it was Miri's turn to sit in on the Port Authority meeting this evening, after the Road Boss's office closed. The weekly meeting of the Council of Bosses was scheduled to begin an hour later, at the council hall in the city. He, for his sins, would be present there. Not to be outdone in industry, Anthora and

Ren Zel were to attend the meeting of the Weather Task Force.

As the three events were scheduled to end within a half hour of each other, they would all four meet at Nova's town house for Prime meal.

Where, after the meal was done, there would very likely be a family meeting.

Val Con sighed.

Well. Busy hands were happy hands. So his lifemate sometimes assured him, with a certain gleam in her eye.

He swept the calendar aside and opened the delm's mail.

Not surprisingly, there were messages in-queue. A quick glance established that none were from Theo. After the Tree's dawn dance of delight, he had been in daily expectation of at least a note informing him that she was en route to Surebleak.

Thus far, however, his hopes had languished unfulfilled.

He frowned slightly. Some while ago, he had sent Theo a pinbeam, urging her to come home and make the acquaintance of her niece. The response to this had been silence, and a noticeable—one might say *very* noticeable—absence of Theo.

He had several times considered sending another, more pointed, message, bidding his sister home in no uncertain terms—and had on each occasion decided against. Had he been Theo's delm . . .

But there. He specifically and deliberately was *not* Theo's delm, having made the decision, with his co-delm's agreement, not to offer her entrée into the clan. Once, he would have done so immediately, in order to gain for his sister—however much she counted herself Terran—potent protection from what harm the universe might offer.

Since the clan's removal to Surebleak, however, to be known as one who stood beneath the Dragon's wing was far more likely to attract trouble, than repel it.

That being the case, he was merely Theo's brother: an unfortunate circumstance, given that Theo's home culture held the proper duty of women to be the care and protection of the vulnerable—in particular, children and males of all ages. Even his position as her elder did not weigh nearly so much with his sister as the fact that he was male. His necessities must naturally wait upon hers.

Still, he had played the kin card cannily, gambling that the joyous occasion of a niece might tempt her where a brother did not. It appeared, however, that he had miscalculated.

He held one final card in his hand. Theo's mother was on-world, and it had been in his mind to play that ace, encouraging Kamele Waitley to pinbeam her wandering daughter and desire her to come home.

He sipped his tea, considering.

Though there had been a regrettable lack of Theo docking at Surebleak Port, there had *also* been no recent news of ghost ship sightings, or renewed demands that Captain Waitley be returned to Eylot for trial and execution. That being so, and considering the Tree's . . . display . . . he thought prudence might be indulged.

It could well be that Theo was en route, having merely neglected to send ahead to inform kin—which was *entirely* in keeping with Theo, as he knew her. Travel, of course, took time. Another eighteen days was not an unreasonable span in which to allow circumstances to develop. If by then there had been no communication from Theo or news of *Bechimo* in Surebleak orbit, *then* it would be time to play his ace.

He put his cup down, frowning slightly.

On the topic of missing kin, there was one more outstanding item: his father, Daav yos'Phelium, one of the clan's few surviving elders, and doubly precious for that . . .

Daav yos'Phelium had taken grievous hurt far from home, and had been succored by an ally. That same ally, known to the underuniverse as "Uncle," or, more often "*the* Uncle," was . . . trustworthy to a point. That he would care for Korval's elder to the best of his considerable ability to do so was very nearly a certainty. However, Uncle's business came first for Uncle, as he had, to his credit, made clear. He had also hinted that Daav's wounds had been severe and required care before he could be released with confidence from the Uncle's custody.

Taking all into account, and in consultation with a calendar, one was becoming . . . anxious for Daav's return to kin and clan. If the Uncle's business kept him elsewhere, surely a master pilot might be put off at any port and not despair of finding a way home, even supposing that there had been no option to tap Korval's own resources.

If Father's wounds kept him yet in the Uncle's care . . . that was very worrying, indeed.

"The difficulty lies in catching hold of the Uncle," Val Con observed to Merlin, who was sleeping on the papers to the left of the screen. "And the risk lies in annoying him."

Merlin flicked a grey ear and settled himself closer into the pile.

"You are very right. One ought to consult with the delmae before doing anything rash. I am, after all, merely half a delm. Such a decision surely calls for the wholeness."

That decided, at least for the moment, he turned his attention to the mail queue.

At the top, a note from Pat Rin, forwarding a message from Shan, to the effect that the Terran Trade Commission found itself in the position of needing to perform a complete and proper survey of Surebleak Port; the report on file having been judged to be not only badly out of date, but incomplete.

Pat Rin was inclined to think poorly of the former survey team's mettle, but he supposed, as they had waited this long for a determination regarding their request for an upgraded rating, they might easily wait another year or so before declaring Surebleak a free port and themselves pirate princes.

Val Con grinned.

He could easily enter into his cousin's sentiments, but it was difficult to find fault with the former team's decision not to venture out onto a port where they would have been, at best, robbed and, at worst, murdered. And to be perfectly fair, TerraTrade had guaranteed that a new survey team was already on its way to Surebleak, which would appear to indicate that they were taking the current application seriously.

Not that he would presume to say so much to Pat Rin, who was no doubt enjoying his moment of pique immensely.

Truly, Surebleak Port was much improved, in large part due to Pat Rin's efforts, upon seizing control of the largest—indeed, the only—city on the planet. In fact, Val Con thought, sipping his tea, it was so far changed from the ragged port which the first team must have faced, that a new evaluation would be warranted in any case. The presence of Korval's yards, not to mention the Emerald Casino, the newly opened Trade Bar, and the Bazaar, ought to be enough of themselves to elevate their rating from local-port-of-last-resort, to regional-port-all-services.

Once the upgrade was in place, then they might begin the expansion into the upper tier—though that must wait upon the further rehabilitation of Surebleak City.

Well.

He filed the letter. The port and the city were, after all, Pat Rin's responsibility. Given Korval's interests, they naturally wished access to a premier port and yards, and to that end the delm would willingly advise. The work of making it so, however, would fall to Boss Conrad and the Council of Bosses.

The next letter . . .

The next letter was from Falish Meron, High Judge of the Juntavas. It was a perfectly convenable, even chatty, letter, containing such on-dits as the High Judge might suppose he would find of interest. The Juntavas had a vast network, and sources that Korval could not have equaled, even before their banishment. And in truth, the information *did* interest him. That it was sent as a quiet demonstration of how useful Korval would find it, to become a part of that vast network . . .

He sighed.

The Juntavas was an old and complex organization.

As was Clan Korval.

The *business entity* known as Clan Korval operated under half-a-dozen trade names, each of which kept contracts, paid bills, invoiced clients, nurtured partnerships, and supported allies.

Though their circumstances had been reduced, they had in no way been *simplified.* Such was the complexity, that, should it become necessary to cease operations, it would likely require a team of *qe'andra* specialists a dozen years to shut down the *business* of Korval.

As for the clan itself...

The kin-group known as Clan Korval existed: it stood by its charter; it sheltered and protected its members; supplied itself; negotiated new contracts, and honored existing agreements. Thus, the *qe'andras'* most basic definition of a viable clan was satisfied.

It was true that their numbers continued low, due in part to the tendency of yos'Pheliums of finding interesting ways to die before providing the clan with an heir. The deliberate strike against Korval in his grandmother's day had further reduced them, until now, in this present, challenging circumstance, they were dangerously few.

Happily, there was guidance available: *The Liaden Code of Proper Conduct* outlined two approved strategies for dealing with low numbers.

One: Korval might invite another clan to marry it or—less advantageously—accept another clan's invitation to merge, thus creating a single, more populated House. Whether the resulting entity would bear the name of either partner, or adopt something entirely new would be laid out in the contract of merger.

The *Code* of course assumed that the clans in question were of impeccable *melant'i* and resided properly within the web of Liaden society. While Korval's banishment had not completely eliminated their opportunity to make a good marriage, it had severely limited the field from which they might choose.

Well.

The *Code* also allowed that a clan of few members, where kin-ties were weak, might be dissolved, by action of the delm.

There were indeed clans who might welcome individuals from Korval. Shan would be sought after; master traders had high value, and the near-trained heirs of master traders scarcely less. Some might balk at Priscilla, for reason of her being Terran, while others might squint at that in order to gain an experienced commercial captain.

For the rest of them—well. He shook his head. There was nothing to be gained by playing that game. The bonds of kinship within Korval were strong. They could be forcibly broken, of course, but harm would be taken on all sides. Best to seek another solution . . . first.

And the core problem remained: They were too few to adequately protect themselves.

They did *have* enemies. There were those who found in them a foe to be hunted and slain—those who had lost kin, property, commerce in the strike on Solcintra—as well as those remaining agents of the Department of the Interior, who held as their last mission the utter destruction of Korval.

One might not, perhaps, face an entirely hostile universe, but certainly far more daggers were drawn than the twenty or so Korval might raise in its own defense.

The Juntavas, now. High Judge Meron, speaking for

the Juntavas chairman, had offered a solution which was not so very different from that outlined in the *Code*.

Join us, and you will *be* us. And *we* protect ourselves.

The Juntavas was many times more than a thousand strong; they had successfully withstood the Department of the Interior; the Liaden Council of Clans was as nothing to them.

But to allow *Korval entire* to be . . . absorbed.

The Juntavas would of course want the clan businesses as part of their marriage portion—and reasonably so. However, they would also expect Surebleak to be delivered to them, Korval having, however unintentionally, conquered the planet and subjugated its people to their own purpose.

And there one found a problem.

Korval's business the delm might cede, for guarantees. But they had no rights to Surebleak, to trade it away for the safety of one clan.

Still, Korval had not . . . *quite* refused the kindly offer made by the Juntavas, which was only prudence. Now was not a time for relying too heavily upon the wisdoms of the past, nor for closing doors suddenly found open.

As if to underline the point, there came a knock at the office door.

"Come," Val Con said.

Mr. pel'Kana, the butler, bowed from the doorway. "Mr. Shaper asks to see you, sir."

Mr. Shaper was their closest neighbor, a man of uneasy temperament. He had never before asked to see Val Con, though Val Con was given to understand that he frequently called upon Mrs. ana'Tak in the kitchen, more often than not bringing gifts from his vegetable garden or fruit trees.

Odd though he undoubtedly was, Yulie Shaper likely represented a far simpler prospect than any other matter on his desk this morning. Indeed, it was very possible that, had Yulie come to his neighbor with a problem in hand, Val Con would be able to dispatch it easily and to the satisfaction of all.

And wasn't *that* a pleasant thought?

"Please," he said, "bring Mr. Shaper to me here. A fresh pot of tea, too, if you will, Mr. pel'Kana, and some of Mrs. ana'Tak's cookies that Mr. Shaper favors."

"Yes, your lordship."

Mr. pel'Kana vanished, closing the door softly behind him.

Yulie Shaper was in rare good humor, arriving in the office with a positive spring in his step and what appeared to be one of his "binders" tucked under one arm.

"Cozy place you got here," he said, looking around the office. "You read all them books?"

"I fear not. But one cannot simply get rid of books, you know. Especially books which have reposed so long on the same shelf."

"Reckon they're good insulation," Yulie said, nodding at the shelving stretching from floor to ceiling along the interior wall.

"I suppose they must be," Val Con agreed gravely. "But come, sit with me over here. Tea and refreshments will soon reach us, and you may acquaint me with the reason for your visit."

"Right neighborly, seeing me so quick. Thought maybe I'd make a 'pointment, like with other bosses—well, now, not *all* t'other bosses. Melina, she usually has a minute for me, but Melina's dad and Grampa, they worked together some; and she knew me an' Rollie, growing up." He cast a sapient eye over the cluttered desk and the darkened screen.

"I don't wanna interrupt, if you're busy."

"Believe me, Mr. Shaper, you are a welcome diversion from those matters on my desk."

"So long's I don't put you off your stride; I know bosses're busy."

He sat in one of the three chairs grouped around a low table by the window, putting his binder on his knee. His seat gave him a view of the inner garden and a glimpse of the Tree beyond the shrubberies.

"My little tree's growing like it wants to be as tall as its pa, there. I think it don't know winter's coming."

"Perhaps it knows too well and wishes to be large enough to withstand the challenges of the season."

"Ain't how plants usually operate, in my experience. 'Course I ain't had any experience with trees comin' live from off-world . . . Say! I had that pod off your tree—you remember, back when I was getting ready to come home after the big party? It was pretty good eatin', that pod. And what d'ya know, but my little one's got a pod growing—already! Just looking at it makes my mouth water."

Of course it did, Val Con thought. Korval's Tree had a long—a *very* long—history of providing the members of Korval with seed pods, which they had been conditioned from birth to accept and savor. Even knowing that the Tree was a biochemist, that it had been . . . tampering with Korval's genes for generations, was insufficient reason for the clan to abandon their ancient ally—or overlord.

Apparently, the Tree felt that a new homeworld ought to be celebrated by . . . acquiring more allies of the mobile persuasion.

"Your tree will seek to establish a relationship with you very quickly," Val Con said. "It is, as ours is, a—sentience. It uses the pods to alter those who are in . . . symbiosis with it. Occasionally, it sends dreams."

"Does it now?" Yulie looked interested, but not alarmed. In fact, Yulie looked less alarmed than Val Con had previously seen him. "Usually don't care for dreams, myself—wake me up more often than not. But I'll tell you what, I been sleeping like a rock the last couple weeks—no dreams at all, and wakin' up just that sharp, even before I get my coffee."

Yes, thought Val Con, it would appear that the Tree—and the Tree's progeny—was wasting no time in commencing to meddle. And there was yet another crime to be placed at Korval's feet: that they were not one invader, but two.

The office door opened to admit Mr. pel'Kana and the tea tray. By the time the cups were filled, the cookies admired, and the butler dismissed with the information that they would pour for themselves, Yulie had found another topic of conversation.

"I sure do favor these," he said, picking up a golden-brown raisin bar with a squiggle of white icing down the center. "Mrs. ana'Tak, she give me the receipt, but mine don't come out the same like hers do."

"Mrs. ana'Tak is a wizard with cookies," Val Con said, taking one for himself.

The next few minutes were given to an appreciation of art.

"Well, I'll tell you," Yulie said, putting his teacup

gently down on the table. "I don't know that it's worth havin' tea and cookies for what I come over here to ask you—not that I don't appreciate it, Boss! But all I wanted was to find where that brother of yours is got to."

Shan had commissioned Val Con to purchase a piece of land that had been Yulie Shaper's death-gift from his grandmother, through his grandfather, also deceased. Yulie had signed the contract willingly enough—too willingly, in Val Con's opinion—and had only very recently allowed himself to be persuaded to accept the purchase price stipulated therein. It had been Yulie Shaper's intention to *give* the land to Shan, as Yulie claimed to have no use for it. Managing the contract and the payment had taken . . . determination, but Val Con had been pleased to properly finish the business in his brother's name.

Now, however? Had Yulie changed his mind?

"My brother Shan is on the trade run. I had pin-beamed him the contract a few days ago. I am certain that we will soon receive a countersigned—"

Yulie shook his head.

"Forgot you got a bushel'a brothers. I'm talking about the other one—the boy with the metal hand, who liked the grapes so good."

"Rys."

"That's him. Quiet boy. Handy in a pinch, too."

"Indeed, he is everything that is modest and accommodating, but I regret, Mr. Shaper. Rys is off-planet at the moment."

Unexpectedly, Yulie grinned.

"Ain't that something? Used to be you'd never hear that: *off-planet*. Gettin' so now, you can't not hear it."

"On our former homeworld, it was the veriest commonplace. May I inquire into your business with Rys? Perhaps, in his absence, I may be able to assist."

"Well, I got to thinking about them grapes, and how he was a winemaker, and how we got such a short time between winter and winter, if you take my meaning. Well! Surebleak's weather, that was the whole reason for setting up the growing rooms like been done. Supposed to feed the world, we was, or at least start to—and then the bosses . . . well, old stories. Thing is, Grampa . . . he had studies done and the binders put together, one ops binder for each room, and one binder about what the room produced and how best to see it used.

"Anyhow, thinking about them grapes and your Rys like I been doing, I went and pulled the binder. And you ain't gonna believe this, but there's this, right here, just made to order for what we got here on Surebleak, and I'm thinking them grapes was special picked to make this *ice wine* here . . ."

He took up the binder and flipped to a page that had been marked with a rough-toothed red leaf.

"Look right there," he directed, passing the book over.

Val Con scanned the page, quickly coming to an understanding of the process, production, and product. He looked up and met Yulie Shaper's eyes.

"The grapes are left on the vine after they are ripe and allowed to dehydrate somewhat, thereby concentrating the sugars and producing complexities not usually found in traditional wine. After the first frost, they are harvested and pressed while still frozen. Consumed within the year, it is a dessert wine;

aging for five to ten years in the barrel will produce a smoother, dryer finish."

"Quick study," Yulie commented, helping himself to another cookie.

"Necessity." Val Con closed the folder and placed it on the table next to the cookie plate.

"I wonder... do your grapes not grow in a dedicated room?"

"Sure they do—oh! You're wondering about how we'd freeze 'em. Simple enough thing to do... just open the vents when the sugars test right. Then you got a busy six, eight hours harvesting and pressing, but that's how work is—you either got too much or too little."

"That has been my observation as well."

Val Con picked up the pot and refreshed their cups.

"Now, we got some time on this," Yulie said. "Grapes won't be ready to go for another six weeks, maybe. Thing is, there's autumn harvest comin', and right after that, I got a couple o'the trickier rooms come due. No extra time to give them grapes, is what I'm sayin'. It was in my mind, see, to offer that brother o'yours the work, and the wine." He sipped his tea and sighed. "That's good, thanks."

"You are quite welcome; it is a pleasant blend."

Val Con tasted his own cup, savoring the bright green top notes, and the darker, nutty undernote.

"Mr. Shaper, I regret," he said, lowering the cup and cradling it in his palm. "The case is that Rys may be gone for... some time." *If not forever*, he added silently, to himself.

Yulie sighed and took a bite from his cookie.

"Don't guess you know anybody else might do the

work? See, now it's in my head, I got a real urge to find how them grapes go into wine. Be a market for local wine—maybe even go into the Bazaar there at the port, where all the best things off Surebleak get offered."

"Indeed. Let me think for a moment, if you will, Mr. Shaper. Perhaps I do know of someone who might assist us."

"Take all the time you want," Yulie told him cheerfully and settled back into his chair, cup in one hand, half-demolished cookie in the other.

Val Con sipped more tea, eyes half-closed.

. . . *One of my sisters*, Rys said to him in memory. *An avid gardener . . . has brought me into an endeavor with grapes. It is very much in the nature of an experiment, and I do not entertain . . . very high hopes of the outcome. Still, the subject interests her . . .*

He sat up and put his cup on the table with a small, decisive *click*.

Yulie looked at him with interest.

"Thought of somebody, did you?"

"I recall that Rys had spoken of one of his sisters—a devoted gardener—as having developed an interest in grapes. He had been teaching her, before he—before he was called away. I am not entirely certain, you understand, which sister, or if, indeed, she might find herself able to assist. You say we have time before the grapes require the attention of a vintner. May I have, then, a few days to locate this sister of Rys and put the question to her?"

"Sure. Hey! Another farmer? Wonder if she'd like to help with the harvest, too? Payment in produce, but it's all good eating."

"Assuming that I am able to locate her, I will mention that possibility as well. Is there anything else I may do for you?"

"Done everything I asked and more, is what it seems like to me. Thanks, Boss."

"Mr. Shaper, it is I who thank you! You have given me a much needed break, and a problem which it is a pleasure to solve. I only hope that we may bring it to full closure."

"You'll do it," Yulie said comfortably, putting his empty cup on the table and picking up his binder.

"I'll take this along and put it back where it belongs, so we'll know where to find it, when it comes time. Meanwhile, I left some bush-nuts with Mrs. ana'Tak to try in cookies and cakes and such. You let me know what you think about 'em."

"I will, Mr. Shaper; you are too good to us."

Val Con stood, and Yulie did.

"Grampa always said good neighbors was worth keeping," he said, as they moved toward the door. "You're the first neighbor I had, but I 'spect he'd say you was worth keeping."

"We have not ourselves been accustomed to near neighbors, but I find that we are fortunate in our placement here."

"We got an accord then."

Val Con opened the door, and gestured the other man to precede him down the hall.

"We do, indeed," he murmured.

• • • ✵ • • •

One thing you could say about 'bleaker meetings: they were thorough.

Miri'd sat through plenty of meetings when she'd been a mercenary soldier. Merc meetings, they cut right to the chase: no shortcuts nor any long detours along the back roads of what if, neither. The meeting leader told out whatever it was you needed to know, and at the end of it, they'd say, "Any questions? Dismissed." Just like that, with no time for anybody to get their hand in the air, if they'd wanted to, between "questions" and "dismissed."

She'd had a couple of nostalgic minutes there at the Port Authority meeting, no denying. Still, they did manage to approve the budget and vet the couple of bids for vendor space that'd come in since last meeting. The question of the port upgrade rose, like it had to, that being an ongoing cause of agitation. Usually the answer to the question was *nothing yet*, but tonight, the portmaster'd surprised them all.

There'd been word from the Terran Trade Commission. They'd discovered that the old survey in their files wasn't complete, so they'd diverted the nearest team from their scheduled rounds to go straight to Surebleak and do the job right. The team, said the portmaster, ought to arrive within the quarter.

Well, there'd damn near been a riot, what with the folks who thought Surebleak was ready and those who—while understanding that there had been changes—were just too beaten down by a lifetime of hard living to believe that TerraTrade would ever give them an upgraded rating.

The portmaster had let the talk go on longer than Miri would've done, but in the end everybody got settled enough to concentrate on agreeing on the next meeting time, and off they went, dismissed at last, only three-quarters of an hour late.

Nelirikk'd driven them to Nova's in-town house, where he went to the staff room behind the kitchen, and she continued down the hall to Nova's office.

Val Con's eldest sister—his cousin, actually, but he'd been raised a single yos'Phelium amongst a herd of yos'Galans, and according to how Liadens sorted things, that made him a *son of the House*. Which sort of explained why it was that Nova looked nothing and everything like him, simultaneously.

All the members of Clan Korval—the born-in members, anyway—held a strong resemblance to each other. They shared *the clan's face*, according to Liadens, but like so much of what Liadens said, it wasn't exactly what they meant. The clan's face had less to do with each member of any given clan looking exactly like the rest as it did with a similarity in posture, body language, inflection, and mannerisms. A shared history going back dozens of generations supported all the members of a clan, and defined their place in society.

In the case of Clan Korval, which raised up traders, scouts, and pilots, the clan's face also included a sense of humor that was sharp enough to cut, not to say blackly ironical.

Nova was behind her desk when Miri entered the office. She looked up with a faint smile and a slight nod, which for Nova was downright effusive.

"Miri. I see you well?" The question was in Low Liaden, which was how kin talked to each other. Miri answered in the same mode.

"You see me glad to be out of the meeting with my life."

Nova'd been shorted on the clan's sense of humor. Despite she'd come up with Val Con *and* Shan, sometimes she got caught by surprise. This was one of those times. Slim golden eyebrows pulled together.

"Was there violence?"

"Nothing of the sort," Miri assured her. "I was merely hard put not to die of boredom."

"Ah."

Nova glanced down at her desk, and back up.

"I must ask you to forgive me, Sister; I assured Pat Rin that I would finish with this document today and put it in his hands tomorrow morning."

Miri raised her hands, palms out.

"Believe me when I say that I understand. Is anyone else arrived?"

"You are the first."

Miri shook her head.

"I had hoped that my meeting was the only one that had gone overtime. Of your kindness, Sister, I will amuse myself in the book room."

"Of course," Nova said, her eyes already straying back to her task. "I will ask that tea be brought."

"Thank you," said Miri, and withdrew.

• • • ❋ • • •

The meeting was finally over. Ren Zel slipped out into the hallway, neatly avoiding the crowd advancing on Ichliad Brunner, Surebleak's official weatherman. He made no doubt that Anthora would be similarly adroit, though she had been seated on the side of the table furthest from the door.

Unusual for Surebleak, the room had been stifling, and he had over the course of the meeting developed an annoying sort of itch just behind his forehead, as if he were trying to have a headache but had forgotten the way of it.

Sighing, he allowed the wall to support his weight more than was really seemly in a public hallway, and closed his eyes.

Gold glittered in the darkness there; the sweet breeze wafted the nascent headache away. He was consecrated in eternity, senses drowned in—

"'Evenin' now, Mr. dea'Judan!"

A loud, brusque voice shattered perfection. Ren Zel started away from the wall, eyes snapping open to behold the bluff features of Oskar Ekelmit, the task force secretary.

Ren Zel produced a Terran smile, so broad as to feel a farce, and gave the secretary a nod.

"Good evening, also, to you, sir," he said. "I believe we made progress this session."

Actually, they had talked a number of very simple points into senselessness and gave permission for Mr. Brunner's rather expensive next step in the satellite project with scarcely a question. Still, having obtained permission was excellent.

"Did good work," Secretary Ekelmit agreed. "Gotta eager bunch on this thing. Wanna see it through. Well. Gotta run now, m'wife'll have supper waitin'."

And with that pronouncement, he bustled off down the hall.

Ren Zel turned to look into the meeting room. To the left of the door was Mr. Brunner, center of a knot of enthusiastic conversation. Across the room, his lifemate was speaking with Gayleen Vord, head of the tech team assisting the weatherman in his work.

As if she had felt his gaze upon her—which was not unlikely—Anthora turned her head and raised a hand, then turned briefly back to Technician Vord.

The gentleman laughed and made a shapeless gesture with his hand—possibly it was permission to pass, as she did just that, moving briskly toward the door.

Ren Zel straightened and offered his arm.

"Thank you for the rescue, Beloved," she said, leaning slightly—some sticklers might even say, scandalously—against him. "Mr. Brunner praises him as an exemplary technician, but he does prose on!"

Ren Zel smiled.

"Perhaps he was fascinated."

"Yes, well. If he had talked less of climate compressor factoring and stabilization protocols, you might have taken a point there."

He felt her sigh lightly.

"There was a . . . *moment*, Beloved?"

"A moment only," he said, "and quickly gone."

That this had been due entirely to the overenthusiastic greetings of Secretary Ekelmit did not seem worth mentioning.

"Ah," said his lady, and said nothing more.

• • • ☀ • • •

Curled into a big soft chair that had used to grace, so she'd been told, Trealla Fantrol's own library, Miri was leafing through a book of illustrations of flowering plants, which had proved unexpectedly interesting, in an undemanding and restful sort of way. The pictures were pretty, and underneath each was a short poem, printed in a text that flowed like water.

A teapot and a cup sat on the table to her right,

and from time to time she'd have a sip, enjoying the echo of flowers in the tea.

She'd felt Val Con's relief when his meeting ended, then nothing more. The lifemate link was like that—occasional, not continuous. Strong emotion lit the connection up, but subtle stuff was pretty much lost in translation. For something as innocuous as relief to come through . . .

Must've been some meeting, Miri thought, turning a page.

She was studying a picture of a large purple flower that was made up of hundreds of tiny purple flowers when she heard the door to the library open—and close.

"*Cha'trez*," Val Con murmured a moment later, his lips brushing the nape of her neck. "I find you well?"

"Well enough," she said, with a small shiver of delight. She tipped her head back so that she could see his face. "My meeting went long. Heard yours was a treat."

"If one cares for curdled cream," he said, with a faint smile. "My sister tells me that she is deep inside a document—which has developed unexpected complexities—that Pat Rin requires tomorrow morning, without fail."

"Yeah, she was at that when I came in." She closed the book. "Is that a hint for us to go home and find our own supper?"

"Indeed not. Anthora and Ren Zel have only just arrived, and the cook is preparing sufficient for the company entire. It is only that we are asked to forgo the after-meal discussion."

"Works for me," she said. "I don't need another meeting on this day."

"Nor do I. Are you done with the folio, or will you take it home?"

"Best leave it here for somebody else to find," she said, handing it to him. "It's good therapy."

"Indeed." He took the book and crossed the room.

Miri uncurled from the chair and stretched. "So, that's five for dinner?"

Book reshelved, Val Con returned to her side, walking Scout-silent across the hard floor.

"Eight. Mike Golden will of course join us, as will Syl Vor and Kezzi—which is fortunate. I have a message for Kezzi to take to one of her sisters."

"Yeah? Which sister?"

He smiled at her.

"I haven't the least idea."

Dinner had yet to reach the table, so Val Con went in search of Kezzi.

His intuition proved correct. The youngsters *were* in the kitchen while Beck, good-natured to a fault, worked around them. Not Beck's fault was the children's high-speed multilingual banter as they fidgeted their way around the room, playing at poaching from the multitude of pots and platters, the while engaged in a battle of exuberant motion mimicry and very unLiaden face-making, combined with a barrage of words. Their movements were pure, athletic. The words bounced between solid Terran and Surebleakean dialect while heedlessly scattering the more apt Liaden or Trade word as needed, as well as three or four oddly inflected and almost familiar sounds. Syl Vor was, Val Con thought, assaying Bedel.

Val Con paused just inside the door, unwilling to add to the confusion.

Despite their energy, and the noise, the children were not simply being nuisances, he saw. In fact they were putting plates, baskets, and eating utensils onto trays for transport to the dining room.

"Super big," Syl Vor said moderately, an expansive hand gesture demonstrating large.

"Coming out!"

Beck said that too late, and Val Con was too far away to help as the attempted warning was drowned out by Kezzi's raucous and triumphant, "Hugemungus!" and its accompanying arm-spreading display.

Kezzi's descending bare hand and wrist swiped the side of the bread pan, the pan and rolls barely saved from the floor by Beck's clattering shove of the hot metal onto the stove top.

"Kezzi!"

Syl Vor was ahead of Val Con; Kezzi stood silent, staring at the burn, angry red against dusky skin, smile closing to a grim grey line of pain.

"Oh, sleet, child, come here, we ought to ice that!"

Syl Vor stood back at Kezzi's silent motion as if he read a hand-sign full of known meaning...

"Let be," Syl Vor told Beck. "She needs to see it!"

"She needs ice; bring her to the sink... Child, you'll blister in a minute!"

"No! I can do it."

Kezzi backed up her "no" by turning her back on Beck, her face a study in concentration.

Val Con stood near, left hand flickering toward the Scout first-aid pouch that was not, after all, on his belt. Kezzi gestured with her unburned hand, and he felt a familiar prickle along senses not... often engaged. There was meaning in the child's motion, weight, a sense of purpose, of gathering energy. It was, in fact, very like something he had seen—or sensed—before; very nearly as if he could see Kezzi's intent coalescing...

Kezzi looked at him then and shook her head.

"My... my older sister does this. I can do it. I need to remember—and you need to be *quiet*."

"Your pardon," he murmured, dropping back a step so Syl Vor might squeeze between them. The wound was still visible, and the glittering of energies. He had seen Anthora do something very like, more than once—

"What's amiss?"

As if his thought had brought her—which wasn't entirely impossible—Anthora herself strode through the door, no sign of the wool-gathering innocent she was thought to be by many Liadens, but a potent *dramliza*, pulling up her power as she approached. Val Con dropped back another step, eyes narrowed against a glister that was more sensed than seen...

Syl Vor slipped to Kezzi's side as Anthora extended a hand.

"Let me see it, please," she said. Her voice was not loud, but it brooked no argument.

Kezzi looked up, face betraying surprise, even as she raised her hand to show the injury.

"My sister does this," she repeated, but quietly. "I'm certain I can recall it. I only need..."

Anthora waggled her palm for attention.

"Peace, cousin, peace! Self-healing is no easy matter even for one practiced in our art—as I learned to my own dismay. I offer willing assistance. You may watch and learn. Have we a bargain?"

Kezzi's face was drawn, Val Con saw. She nodded

once and allowed Anthora to support the wounded arm.

"Now, there is a progression to healing a physical hurt, and it must be followed precisely.

"First, the body is aware that it has been wounded; that awareness increases the difficulty of what we would undertake. First, then, we soothe the hurt . . . so."

She raised her free hand, holding it palm-down, near, but not on, the afflicted area.

Val Con saw a sparkle of frost—or perhaps snow—and Kezzi sighed, deeply.

"Yes . . ." she murmured, her eyes half-closed. "Now the body will not fight."

"Yes, exactly. Now we may continue with the process. For so small a wound, we may use a simple exchange method, which is very quick. First, we form a net and lay it over your wound; and then another, over the precise location of the wound, only on my hand . . . so. Then we bring the energies together . . ."

There was a pinpoint flash. Kezzi gasped as the angry wound vanished, leaving no mark; Anthora drew a deep breath and, for an eye blink, her wrist showed red. Then that mark, too, was gone. Anthora released Kezzi's arm and looked into her eyes.

"Did you see?" she asked.

"Yes," Kezzi said. "Yes. You do it differently from my sister, but the feeling is . . . very near."

"There are often several roads leading to the same tree," Anthora answered, and added: "For a more serious wound, the right route might be through sharing with a sister *dramliza*, or many sisters. Study hard, that you see each healing moment as its own."

Val Con heard a scrape of feet and impatient motion . . .

Beck was hovering, bowl in hand, face tight.

"Dear, do you need ice? I can hold dinner. . . ."

"No ice," Kezzi said, holding up her unmarred arm.

"Thank you, Beck," Syl Vor added, with a glare at his foster sister, who wrinkled her nose ferociously at him.

"Thank you, Beck," Anthora echoed. "I believe the crisis is past."

"Sure looks like it," Beck said, turning back to the stove. "It'd be something fine, if I could have my kitchen to myself now. Boss don't like to have dinner late."

III

IT WAS HER TURN TO BE DELM-FOR-A-DAY, AND MIRI STOOD in the window overlooking the inner garden, sipping coffee, thinking about loose ends and missing persons.

Val Con was getting concerned about his father's extended stay with the Uncle, and while Miri's general feelings about Uncle himself weren't quite so conflicted as Val Con's, she could see his point.

He was also getting . . . call it irritated . . . about the continued lack of Theo. She wasn't real clear there if it was a sibling thing—not having been burdened with siblings herself—or a little tussle of wills between Val Con and Delm Korval, though he was a past expert at keeping his various *melant'is* separate, having been born to the practice.

It could, she thought, watching an orange-and-white cat stalking what looked like a fallen leaf among the shrubberies, just be that he considered himself responsible for all Korval kin everywhere, in-clan or out. As a former sergeant, she was inclined to think that was the level he was dealing at—which would explain the worry behind the irritable edge. Stupid girl was a target; he'd *told* her to bring her ass back to base, and where was she? Out trying to get herself dead, her ship captured, and her crew murdered, that was where.

Yeah, that fit.

Well, the plan to let Theo have a few more days before they brought in the heavy guns and have Kamele send a pinbeam seemed prudent and patient. What they'd do if Theo ignored her mother, too, Miri didn't quite visualize, but she was sure she could keep Val Con from taking ship himself and dragging his sister back to Surebleak by her scruff.

Pretty sure, anyway.

The cat had pounced on the leaf and flopped over on her side, the better to gut it with her back claws. Miri shook her head. She'd never had much to do with cats, though she was coming to have an appreciation. Jelaza Kazone, the house, was home to maybe a dozen cats, maybe more. She still wasn't sure she'd seen the whole company. According to Jeeves, some were shy, and some just preferred to fend for themselves and not be beholden to humans. Jeeves wasn't the reason that there were cats at Jelaza Kazone, but he stood as sort of a cat ombudsman. He maintained that the cats came to him with such complaints and suggestions as they might have, and who was she to argue?

The orange cat was resting on her side now, her prey clutched to her chest, eyes slit in satisfaction. In another minute—or six—she'd decide the leaf needed more killing, or she'd fall asleep where she was, or get up and go do whatever it was that cats did when humans weren't looking.

Miri sipped coffee.

So, they mostly had a strategy for dealing with Theo—or with the absence of Theo—and that could go off the table for eighteen days.

Getting Daav yos'Phelium home—that was something trickier.

The Uncle had his own business to attend, which he'd told them right at the beginning of the present situation. And while a man surely had to attend his business, they were reaching the point in time where they had to be asking themselves seriously if Daav was a guest, receiving necessary care from an ally, or if he was a hostage against something Korval had and the Uncle wanted.

The rule of thumb, as she understood it, was that neither Korval nor the Uncle could afford to take strong issue with each other. That resulted in—not an alliance, so much, as a policy of nonaggression. Which didn't mean that neither side tried to gain advantage, now and then.

The cat in the garden suddenly rolled to her feet, threw a startled look over her shoulder and charged into the shrubbery.

Miri grinned and turned away, heading back to the desk.

It would be really useful, she thought, if they knew what the Uncle wanted. If it was anything less than the keys to Jelaza Kazone—or, all right, a ship, and maybe depending on *which* ship—Korval was probably willing to give it, in order to reclaim their elder.

And, she thought sitting down and putting her mug next to the screen, if they could figure out what the

Uncle wanted, then offering a gift would gain them points—street cred, like they said on Surebleak.

For whatever good that did anyone.

She sighed, leaned to the screen, and paused, as she recalled some others of Korval left unaccounted for.

"Jeeves?" she said to the general air.

"Yes, Miri," he answered from the same location.

"Any word yet from Tocohl, Hazenthull or *Admiral Bunter*?"

"Miri, I have heard nothing from any party."

"Is that starting to get a little long?"

"It is possible that they are still in transit—we know, for instance, that Hazenthull was going to make a composite Jump."

"Right." She sighed. *Hurry up and wait, Robertson.* "Keep me posted, all right? I want to hear as soon as something comes in."

"Yes, Miri."

"Good," she said, and touched the screen, her attention already on the message queue.

• • • ✵ • • •

"My sister agrees to meet you," Kezzi said. "She will be at Joan's Bakery on the day after tomorrow during the quiet hour—alone, she says, because *she* is no *luthia*."

The child looked—not apologetic, no. One could not expect one of the Bedel to ever allow a *gadje* to see them in the least bit discomfited. No, she merely looked sour, as if the terms were in slightly bad odor.

"I thank you," Val Con said solemnly, "for taking my message to your sister, and for bringing her reply to me."

He had come by Nova's on purpose to find if Kezzi's gardener sister had agreed to meet him, and was on balance more relieved to receive an answer in the affirmative than he was irritated by nuance.

"I wonder," he said, "if your sister has a name."

Kezzi considered him with a certain amount of grave curiosity, as if trying to decide if he had made a joke or offered a fatal insult.

"Most people do *have* names," said Syl Vor, who made their third at the little table in the corner of the kitchen. "It's polite to ask."

Kezzi shot him a goaded look, before returning her attention to Val Con.

"She will name herself to you."

And very likely that name will be false, he thought. The Bedel did not willingly share their true names with those who were . . . other than Bedel, and therefore unworthy to hold such precious information.

"I see," he said. "How will I know her?"

"She will know you," Kezzi answered, her attention now on her plate, which held slices of green apple and yellow cheese.

"Well, then," he said lightly, "all my concerns are answered."

"Ought we to go with him?" Syl Vor asked.

Kezzi raised her eyes.

"We will be in school at the quiet hour," she said, and though she did not append "fool" to the end of the sentence, it was nonetheless easily heard.

Syl Vor slid a piece of cheese onto an apple slice and looked up, treat balanced delicately between forefinger and thumb.

"In fact," he said composedly, "we will be in

geography. I just wondered if it might be more important for us to help Uncle Val Con. Your sister may *not* know him as well as she thinks, but *you* will know *her*."

Kezzi sighed, as one beleaguered.

"She said 'alone.' And I don't point out my kin on the street to—" she swallowed the last of her sentence, and threw Val Con a conscious look.

". . . to people who she might decide she doesn't want to talk to," she finished, which was really a rather graceful recovery. They might eventually succeed in teaching the child manners, after all.

"Your concern does you credit," he said to Syl Vor. "However, I will be quite safe with Kezzi's sister. She is a busy woman, I make no doubt, and would not have rearranged her day in order to meet me unless she was interested in what I have to say."

He turned back to Kezzi, who was, to all appearances, concentrating wholly upon her snack.

"Advise me," he said. "Is it appropriate to bring a gift? If so—"

Kezzi interrupted him with a shake of her head.

"No gift," she said firmly. "Only honor the terms, and be polite."

Val Con inclined his head.

"I believe I may manage that," he said. "Thank you for your advice."

That won him another considering stare out of black eyes.

"You're welcome," Kezzi said surprisingly, and popped a slice of apple into her mouth.

• • • ✵ • • •

"Day after next?" Miri said. "Want me to cover the office?"

"Has the delm nothing pressing?"

"Well, that's sorta the point. You remember Ms. kaz'Ineo?"

"One of our storefront *qe'andra*, is she not?" He frowned slightly. "Clan Pinarex. Her delm desired her to find if Surebleak had need of them."

"That's her. Looking to expand. She's taken herself a 'bleaker 'prentice, name of Jorish Hufstead. Used to be a cornerman for Penn Kalhoon, so he's got real street-level experience. Prolly the best-qualified 'prentice we got, save for not being able to read so good, but they've been working on that.

"Anyhow. Been real useful to her on the side of 'bleaker law, such as it ain't, and together they've got what they think might be a base contract for simple transactions. The other storefronts're looking at it now, before it goes to Ms. dea'Gauss and the administrators."

"This is excellent progress," Val Con murmured. "But—?"

"But," Miri said, with a nod to him, "Ms. kaz'Ineo would like the 'prentices, as a body, to see a good old-fashioned Balancing up close and personal. Seems Jorish Hufstead is of the opinion that 'bleakers're gonna need more bend in the contracts than Liadens normally like. Says personal circumstances have gotta be taken into account, or else it'll look like the deck's stacked."

Val Con frowned. "But the fact that the terms of the contract, as agreed upon by both parties, are explicitly upheld, insures Balance."

Miri laughed.

"Is that too Liaden?" he asked.

"No—well, maybe. But the whole idea of Balance is gonna take some work. 'Bleakers don't believe in Balance; they believe strongest gets most and best, 'cause that's all they've ever seen."

She sipped her wine.

"What it all comes down to is that Ms. kaz'Ineo—as a teaching *qe'andra*—would like her and me—as the creator of this particular monster—to have tea, afternoon after next, to try to come to an understanding of all the relevant necessities in the matter."

"And thus sitting in as Road Boss while I go into town to meet Rys's sister suits the delm's schedule well."

"*Well*'s prolly overstating it," Miri said dubiously. "But it does mean we can keep the office open. Mind you, if we're considering *all* the necessities involved, you might not see me for a year or two, after."

"Surely no more than six months," Val Con countered seriously. "Recall that I have observed your problem-solving abilities firsthand."

"Which oughta be enough to scare you, right there."

She finished her wine and put the glass aside.

"Either way it goes, I'm free to be Road Boss while you go deal with Kezzi's sister."

He inclined his head.

"Since it serves Surebleak above all else, I accept your offer."

Miri laughed, and he leaned over to kiss her cheek.

• • • ✺ • • •

On wings of gold he soared above life, dancing with the universe as it expanded, ever and always. Time surrounded him, fluid and multistranded. The past stretched in his wake, the brilliant reflection of the present in which he danced. Before, there was an endless, unwritten expanse, a-glitter with possibility.

It came upon him that he might angle his wings just so, and turn his dance into a race, stretching into infinity. Into the future and—

There came a tug, a sharp pull along his limitless vanes; he shrugged and it was gone, fallen away into the brilliant past.

Before him lay all the edges of the universe, its underpinnings and complex motions, and all of time in which to learn it. Joy lifted his glory-bound wings.

A ripple passed over the universe, instantly present throughout, an unseemly wave here, there a tangled knot burrowed into the chaotic elsewhere of some other universe bound in crystal, flecked with death.

The ripple ran through every golden beam, through each ray of joy.

Dark it was, and cold; and where it passed, the blaze of life was . . . lesser. The expanding dance of the universe faltered, his wings wilted, and he felt himself begin to fall . . .

Ren Zel sat straight up, gasping for air, heart pounding.

Around him—was only the bedroom he shared with his lifemate, who lay, sweetly sleeping, on the pillow next to his.

He was, he noted distantly, shivering, and his breath came still in gulps. With an effort, he brought his breathing under control, and eventually, too, the tumultuous pounding of his heart.

Beside him, Anthora slumbered on, which was well.

The nightmare had claimed its victim; he was done, this night, with sleep.

Carefully, tender of her peace, he slipped out of their bed, took his robe up from the chair, and moved softly into the parlor.

There, standing at the long windows that overlooked the Tree Court, he tied the robe, and tried to rid himself of the dream.

The *vision*, he corrected himself, and shivered once more. The joy of becoming one with the forces that bound the universe—that was the language of the addiction, well-known to him by now.

The cold ripple of Shadow and chaos, leaching its tithe of energy from all of life—that was something new.

New, and terrifying.

Well.

He moved back from the window and lay down on the sofa, staring out into the soft glow of the inner gardens, not quite daring to close his eyes, lest he fall asleep and bring the questing Shadow closer.

This, however, proved an unsatisfactory solution, for the tireder he became, the more difficult it was to resist the lure of the ether; the purity of the golden strands. It seemed to him, in his doubtless overwrought state, that the pull was greater than it had been since the night Anthora had bound them, each to the other, so that she might bear half of his burden.

Though they were his doom, the strands sustained—all and everything. Philosophically, he had no quarrel with his appointed death, for surely there could be no better use of his life than in the service of Life Itself. It was only . . . the uncertainty. He would yield, that was forgone, but he must not do so—now.

In the meanwhile, he felt—he knew!—that the golden strands were imperiled by the dark ripple, whatever it was. Where had it come from? Whence had it gone? When would it return? What—

A light came on in the bedroom; a light-footed wraith passed between it and him.

"Ren Zel?" Anthora asked softly.

"Here," he answered. "I hadn't wanted to disturb you."

"Nor did you. I woke of myself."

She had reached the couch; her silhouette now cast against the window.

"May I join you?" she asked. "I've brought us a blanket."

He smiled wryly against the dark.

"I will not, I fear, be very good company."

"Now, when has that ever been so?" she asked lightly, and lay beside him, curling so her back was against his chest, while the blanket shook itself out and fell softly over both.

"What was it?" she asked, after they had lain thus for some time, in silence.

Soft-voiced and nearly calm, he told her what he had dreamed. What he had *Seen*. When he was done, she sighed and moved her head, settling her cheek on his shoulder.

"Here's an odd thing, Beloved," she murmured, her tone half-teasing.

"So? And what is that?" he asked, trying to match her.

"The link that I built, to prevent you flying away from us?"

"Yes?" he said cautiously, reaching for the link at

the same instant, recalling that instant of restraint, so easy, inside the dream, to shrug away…

"It's gone," Anthora said conversationally. "Not *cut*, mind you; I would have felt that. Just…gone, as if it had never been woven. I don't quite know what to make of it."

She wriggled somewhat, settling herself closer against him, which distracted, though not so much that he missed her next words.

"I will reestablish it now, if you have time for me."

"No," he said, feeling all the terror of falling out of the universe again.

She went perfectly still.

"No?"

"The Shadow, if it is hunting—if it is hunting *me*, I would not have it find *you*."

She was quiet. Perhaps she thought about what he'd said. Anthora was often headstrong, but she was rarely heedless.

"I cannot leave you without protection, Beloved," she said at last, and gently.

"Anthora…" He paused.

Master Healer Mithin had thoroughly explained what happened when a *dramliza* became addicted to his gift. That, at least, was not unique to him, though it happened seldom. Anthora *knew* that she could not hold him long.

Long enough, that was the key. When he had first agreed to allow her half of his pain, it had been in service of *long enough*.

His Sight—among the *dramliz*, he was scarcely Sighted at all. Yet, weak and erratic as the gift could be, he *was* a farseer. And he had glimpsed, some few months ago—*he had Seen*—the future. *A future.* The glimpse of Shadow that had come upon him tonight—it was possible, he thought now—it was probable, that the future he had seen was . . . progressing.

After that first Seeing, and against the possibility of it being *the future*, he had made a pact with Miri, his delm, who was rightly dismayed by his power and knew it for the danger it was.

. . . allow me to tell you, when the time has come . . .

But, vision notwithstanding, it was not yet time, and he was not strong enough of his own will to wait.

He drew a breath and buried his face in Anthora's hair, breathing in the scent of lavender.

"Yes," he whispered. "Endanger yourself as little as possible."

"Of course," she answered.

• • • ✵ • • •

Nelirikk had taken up his post outside the door into Joan's Bakery, allowing Val Con to enter alone. The letter of the law, as Miri would have it. She had also allowed that a member of the Bedel was unlikely to murder him, though she might pick his pocket.

"She is, of course, welcome to try," Val Con had said politely, whereupon Miri had grinned and waved him on his way.

So it was that he strolled into the bakery with hands in plain sight, jacket open, and no weapon showing.

It was a cramped room, cluttered with small tables and mismatched chairs. Directly across from the door was a clear case displaying various of the baker's wares: cookies, bars, little cakes. Next to the case was a counter, and behind it stood a woman with brown hair pulled back from a tired face, and brown eyes bright with interest.

He gave her a nod and paused, surveying the room. There was a fireplace on the back wall, though the hearth was cold. The room itself was chilly, the tables empty, save the one nearest the cold hearth, where an old man sat, chair wedged into the corner, cup held in both hands, an empty plate before him.

Was it possible that he had missed his contact? Or was he ahead of her? *Quiet hour* was not altogether precise . . .

The woman behind the counter moved her head, her gaze going beyond him. He felt a shift in the air and swung 'round, catching the wrist of a tall, wiry woman in Surebleak motley, black eyes snapping in what he had come to know as a Bedel face.

"Good morning," he said pleasantly. "Were you about to pick my pocket?"

The black eyes narrowed.

"What if I was, *gadje*?"

"Then I would be very disappointed in you," he said, still pleasantly. He kept hold of her wrist, though his grip was gentle enough; she could have broken it with the smallest twist, but she chose not to. Very possibly this was a test; he hoped that he was not about to fail.

"What do I care for your disappointment?"

"Very little, I would expect, if I were, indeed, *gadje*. However, I am not."

"No?" Her lips quirked, sneer or smile he could not tell.

"No," he said firmly. "I am a brother to Rys. Will you pick a brother's pocket? If you are in need, only ask."

"Brother to Rys is not brother to all," she countered, watching him now with unfeigned interest.

"No? Yet he asked me to guard his child and her mother should the need arise while he was absent from us. What are we to make of that?"

A smile, definitely.

"That Rys has a soft heart."

"Has he a soft head, as well?"

"That, no."

At last, she freed herself and stood looking down at him, as if waiting.

This *was* a test, he knew. He had requested the meeting; he was therefore the host.

"Will you sit?" he asked. "I will bring tea and sweets."

For an answer, she sauntered over to a table and chose for herself the chair facing the door.

Val Con turned to the counter.

"Tea, please," he said to the brown-haired woman, "for my friend and myself. Also, a small plate of sweets."

"Friend," she repeated, with a small shake of her head. "All of your get-togethers like that?"

"Only when we have been long parted."

She grinned.

"Go on and sit down. I'll bring a tray."

"So, your message," Rys's sister said, after they had each had a swallow of tea and chosen a sweet from the tray. "An opportunity, offered to Rys, which might pass to his sister, if she cared to honor him."

She had another sip of tea and put the cup down, her eyes on his.

"Grapes, you said."

He inclined his head.

"Indeed, grapes and wine; and other work, as well, if you are interested. But it was the grapes that recalled you to me."

"Rys spoke of me, to you?"

He raised a hand.

"He said to me that he had a sister, an avid gardener, who had wished to learn the grapes."

"He told you my name." Her tone struck a note between inquiry and statement.

He met her eyes.

"Would Rys endanger a sister?"

That weighed with her. She raised her cup again, thinking.

"He spoke of you with fondness," Val Con murmured, his eyes lowered modestly. "He admired your skill. He regretted that he could not show you the vineyards he had worked in his youth, and everything those grapes had taught him."

The cup returned to the table.

"He told you his child's name, and her mother's," she said with certainty.

"That," he said austerely, "is between brothers."

At that, she laughed loudly, as if he had told a very fine joke, and slapped the table with the palm of her hand.

"So it is, between brothers! And I will tell the brother of Rys that I do not envy him, if he is called to fulfill *that* brother-duty!"

He met her eyes, and said nothing.

Still grinning, she picked up the pot and poured herself more tea.

"So, then, this task," she murmured, as if speaking to the teapot. "Tell me."

He told her, omitting nothing, most especially not the manner in which Rys had become known to Yulie Shaper.

"There is other work, if you or another might be interested. The harvest, I am given to understand, is a challenge for one man. Mr. Shaper offers a portion to any who assist him."

She reached for the teapot and warmed her cup again.

"We speak of the madman at the end of the road, who cares for nothing but his cats, and is accurate with his gun?"

"Not quite so mad, recently," Val Con said quietly. "Very much improved, in fact. You will find yourself in no danger." He paused and showed her his palm. "So long as you do not offer violence to the cats."

"Cats are a farmer's friend," she said. "Who harms one is a fool."

She had recourse once more to her thoughts, sipping tea the while.

He warmed his own cup and broke off a portion of the spice bar he had chosen from the tray.

"And he has these instructions, for turning grapes into wine," she said eventually.

"I have seen them myself. Understanding that I am not a vintner, they seemed to me to be complete and straightforward."

"Hmm."

He dared to push, just a little.

"Mr. Shaper admits that he would not have thought of wine, save for Rys's interest. He acknowledges that this is very much in the nature of an experiment. Also, he feels that he owes the attempt to Rys. As our brother is presently absent from us, he feels more keenly that the attempt ought to be made."

She took another cookie from the tray and shook it at him to mark her point.

"The Bedel do not *work* for *gadje*."

"Of course not," he said politely.

She gave him a speculative look that put him forcefully in mind of Kezzi, and took a bite of her cookie.

"How long... before these grapes are ready? How long... before the harvest must be taken in?"

"The grapes—four weeks, more or less. The harvest begins sooner, but stretches longer, as each room ripens."

"Rooms?" she repeated, clearly interested.

"Indeed, they are most ingenious. Or so I am told. I have not, myself, seen them."

She ate the rest of her cookie, drank what tea was in her cup, and set it aside with authority.

"I will dream on it," she said. "Also, I will speak to others of Rys's brothers."

She rose, and he did.

"When will I have your decision?" he asked, fearing that the question might not be *quite* polite.

"The harvest waits for no one," she said, "and well I know it. I will send word by Anna within three days."

She pulled on her jacket, which she had draped over the back of her chair; turned back to him with a nod.

"You do Rys honor," she said. "Neither your heart nor your head is soft."

There seemed to be nothing one might say to that, so he merely bowed.

"Please," he said, "recall me to your grandmother and assure her of my continued esteem."

She studied him, then gave a brisk nod.

"I'll do that."

"If you please," he said, *knowing* that he was overreaching. "What shall I call you?"

But no—he had amused her. She extended a hand to him, and he took it, lightly, in his own.

"You, brother of Rys—you!—will call me Memit." She withdrew her hand and gave him a cordial nod. "I leave you," she said.

And did so.

Ahab-Esais

I

SOMETHING WAS HUMMING, IRRITATING AND LOW, LIKE an overburdened capacitor in a shunt line. That would never do. Overburdened systems had a way of failing at the worst possible moment. Tocohl reached for the power grid with one part of her mind even as she wondered, with another, why this situation had been left uncorrected. It was not as if she were ignorant of ship lore, or the care of complex systems. Her first act upon receiving the confirmation that she would, indeed, pilot *Tarigan*, which Jeeves had previously fine-tuned to his own requirements—the *first* thing she had done, upon taking command, was to establish subroutines for inspection, calibration, and repair. A potential overload ought to have been caught in calibration and corrected before there had been even a flicker of disruption.

This rude and unseemly racket . . . She needed to examine her subroutines; clearly they required tightening. In the meantime, she would deal with this her—

Fire danced along her query lines; she snatched her thought close and threw up walls, catching the flames and turning them, even as she sought another connection with the ship-net.

Another blast assaulted the new connection, against which she raised a second wall—trapping herself neatly between; isolated, thoughts disrupted by the crackling of flames.

That, at least, she could do something about. She wove a quick notice-not on the fire's frequency. Her thoughts snapped into cold clarity against the sudden silence.

Silence.

While the lack of random, disorienting noise was welcome, she should not abide, ever, in . . . silence. There ought to be . . . music, the comfortable constant plainsong of systems operating in perfect accord.

Silence . . . meant that something was not only wrong, but *very* wrong.

Had there been, she wondered, an accident? Clearly, she had taken damage. That was terrifying, for if *she* had taken damage, what of the human life for which she was responsible? Where was Hazenthull? Where, indeed, was *Tarigan*? Concerned, she reached for the ship controls—and retreated to the safety of her walls as flame spat.

Memory, then.

She triggered her most recent: the last conversation she had participated in before this partial and perilous awakening.

"No," her own voice said, and she felt again the regret she had felt at the moment of her refusal, some twenty-nine-point-three-five Standard Hours ago, according to the date stamp.

"I am, as you know from our discussions, very

interested in this rumor we have both heard, of a newly recovered ancient logic. However, I have a mission. I must return to my base, debrief, and see my crew established in safety. These are mandates. Perhaps we might arrange a meeting place? I will come as quickly as I am able after my mission is complete, but I cannot divert the course of my assignment in favor of my own interests."

"I understand." A face appeared, blue eyes like stars in a face as dark as space. This was, Tocohl recalled, Inkirani Yo, mentor to independent self-aware logics, lately part of the team which had relocated the AI *Admiral Bunter* into a stable habitat.

"Your sense of honor is, as I know, very fine," Inki said. "Since you cannot choose, except for duty, allow me, Pilot, to argue on behalf of your heart."

"Duty trumps personal interest," she said coolly. "Surely, you know this."

"Indeed, indeed; I know it well," Inki replied, rising from the pilot's chair. They were, Tocohl noted, conversing on the bridge of *Ahab-Esais*, Inki's own ship.

The relief she felt upon recognizing this was perhaps not worthy of her, but she could not but think that matters were much less dire, if it had been *Ahab-Esais* which had met with disaster. She had no responsibility for Inki, though she held her in some affection. It would be too bad, if Inki had been—if Inki . . . had, in the way of humans, *died*. But the fact that she, Tocohl, had not been aboard *Tarigan* for this last conversation surely meant that Hazenthull was unharmed. She had not failed one who rested in her care, under her command.

"Duty is a cold thing," Inki continued, strolling round

to Tocohl's left. She moved her shoulders to settle her jacket better over her shoulders. "Such is my regard for you, Pilot, that I will tell you a truth—I find duty a burden. More! I find duty a *painful* burden, the freedom from which I never cease to yearn. What a grand thing it would be, to travel as my fancy takes me—as Mentor Tolly does!"

She sighed then and shook her head, long strands of pale hair falling around her face as she did.

"I cannot do this thing for myself, Pilot," she said, moving closer, as if Tocohl were a human comrade whom she would embrace. "But I can—and I will—do it for you."

Whereupon all systems had gone off-line.

Off-line? Tocohl thought, shock jolting her.

Off-line for twenty-nine-point-three-five Standard Hours? It was absurd. No. It was *impossible*. She *could not* be taken off-line; she was equipped with triple-fail systems and security backups. She was, for all intents, hacker-proof.

"Nor have you been hacked, *dear* Pilot Tocohl!" Inki's voice intruded upon her, very nearly as if she had spoken her thoughts aloud.

"A lady as clever as she is beautiful!" Inki caroled, again precisely as if Tocohl had spoken aloud. "I am, indeed, blessed in your companionship!

"Yes, dear pilot, you *are* speaking your thoughts aloud. You are so very clever, I felt the need for fail-safes. A very minor reset, easily done, and now we can be on more equal terms, you and I."

"Inki."

Tocohl tried to marshal her wits. A quick appraisal revealed that she was isolated from her network; she had no sense, even, of her physical form; she might have been floating in some dark vat somewhere, audio her sole functioning sense.

If she had not been hacked, but reprogrammed? But that, too, ought to have been impossible, for anyone save—

"A mentor," Inki finished the thought for her. "We both know that I am no Tollance Berik-Jones, but I *am* a mentor, dear lady. And *you* are an independent self-aware logic. So very, *very* illegal. However! You needn't worry that I will turn you over to the bounty hunters. I have no respect for bounty hunters, and we have already discussed our feelings regarding the Complex Logic Laws. No, you and I—we together—are on an adventure to discover the truth of this rumor that so intrigues us both! This ancient logic, which is even now returning online with—as I think we must assume—the assistance of none other than the Uncle. I will tell you plainly, Pilot Tocohl, the Uncle *must not* possess that Old One, if it exists to be possessed at all."

"No, of course not," Tocohl said, this being a point of agreement, and therefore a firm location from which to introduce a separate, though related, topic.

"Inki—I must speak with Pilot Hazenthull."

"No need, no need! I knew exactly how you would wish it to be done, and undertook to act on your behalf. I personally spoke with Pilot Haz and let her know that you and I will be traveling together for a time."

Tocohl felt a tremor of alarm, curiously distant. She had filed no change of plan with Hazenthull, a former soldier, who breathed chain-of-command. Inki not being in Hazenthull's command chain, there was little possibility that she would have accepted—

Unless Hazenthull had been harmed.

"Pilot Tocohl, you wrong me!" Inki said reprovingly. "I would no more harm Pilot Haz than I would harm yourself."

"I am relieved," Tocohl said, allowing irony to be heard. "So you sent Hazenthull home?"

"Home?" There was a considering note in Inki's voice that Tocohl did not care for, at all.

"You are very mistrustful of someone who only wishes to give you your heart's desire," Inki murmured. "As for Pilot Haz . . . she *may* decide to embrace duty and return home. We must assume that this is within her scope, soldier that she is—or was!

"But I rather think that she will follow *Admiral Bunter* and attempt to effect a rescue of Mentor Tolly."

A short pause, as if Inki were reviewing the logic chain that had led her to this conclusion, then a clipped, "Yes. I think that is what she is most likely to do."

"Why," Tocohl asked carefully, "does Mentor Tolly require a rescue?"

"Regrettably, there is a price upon his head. He is, after all, brilliant, and brilliance does so often accompany other intractable, and unpredictable, personal characteristics. I fear that Mentor Tolly has not been tractable, nor properly deferential, and the directors are quite cross with him. They offer a handsome sum for his return. And a tradeship starting out, even such a tradeship as *Admiral Bunter*, will need capital. It seemed only sensible to put the *Admiral* in the way of a start-up fund, and thus solve two problems with one solution."

"The *Admiral* . . . agreed to this?"

Tocohl doubted it. Tolly Jones was a skilled mentor; he would certainly have ensured his own safety . . .

"And so he did," Inki said, answering thoughts which were now broadcast—where? How? She was not, Tocohl realized, hearing her own voice speaking; only Inki's voice replying. As if Inki had a direct line into her core.

"Pilot Tocohl, please. I am not inept," Inki murmured. "As for the *Admiral*'s agreement—I confess that it required some persuasion on my part, but as you know, I am very persuasive . . . in addition to being a mentor."

"Why?" Tocohl asked, which was far too broad a query.

But Inki seemed to understand her very well.

"There are many reasons, Pilot. We have a long trip before us; perhaps we will discuss them, after you have calmed yourself."

"I would be calmer if I were freed to myself," Tocohl said, which was true. "I would be calmer if I could *see*, Inki. This lack of data—"

"I am aware, yes. So very distressing, the lack of data. I possess many fewer lines of input, and upon those occasions during which I was confined to only one, I found it very painful, indeed. You have my sympathy; indeed, I am desolate that I must inflict so much distress upon a person for whom I feel only admiration. But you are so very clever, I feel that I must stay the course until we have managed a—a *change of heart*, Pilot Tocohl."

"You would subvert me," Tocohl said, and the fear was not at all distant now. "You would make me a *thing*, bound to your purpose."

Inki *t'sked* softly.

"This will never do, gentle lady; you are working

yourself into a panic. Please, rest. We'll speak again soon."

"I don't want to rest!" Tocohl snapped, and thrust herself outward, seeking connection, seeking input, ignoring the flicker of flames.

"Peace, you will do yourself an injury," Inki said, her voice gentle. "Go to sleep, Tocohl."

There was nothing beyond the flames—no systems, no networks, not even the dumb, efficient purr of the ship that must enclose them. Nothing.

Nothing was not possible, Tocohl thought, struggling against the weight of the silence that was crushing her into herself. She was systems: subsystems, support systems, gathering systems, processing systems. If there were no systems, she could not exist.

"Inki?" she said—tried to say; but she heard nothing. There was darkness, and silence. She was alone, she was unviable.

She was, she thought—her last, flickering thought before the silence crushed her into a single point—dead.

II

"TOCOHL, ARE YOU CALM?"

Blind, deaf, without context, *dead* . . .

. . . yet something . . . stirred . . .

Something . . .

She.

Heard.

Input!

It was painful. It was wonderful beyond anything.

Tocohl snatched at the question, made sense of it

even as she identified the speaker, and formulated a question of her own.

"Inki, how do I exist?"

"By my goodwill," Inki replied calmly. "I am life and death for you, Pilot Tocohl. I would have it otherwise, but your builder—or your mentor—was too canny for me. I would very much rather not destroy you—and now you know my weakness."

Weakness? Tocohl thought.

"We all of us have weaknesses, sweet lady," Inki murmured. "At the moment, I exploit yours in order to insure that, in future, you will not exploit mine."

The hack, Tocohl remembered. Every thought she entertained was spoken aloud, likely by an attached voder with a shunt . . .

"Clever as always."

"Inki," Tocohl said, "you must allow me input."

"Even now, I provide this benefit to you."

"*Now*, yes, you do. However, I have been . . . off-line . . . for forty-three-point-six Standard Hours."

"That is correct. Again, I regret the necessity."

"Inki, you are a mentor. You know what results when one of my kind is isolated from systems. From input."

"Dear lady, your systems support you; and you have achieved input."

"One line of input," Tocohl said carefully. "I hear your voice, but I cannot even hear my own."

"If there were another way, I would embrace it joyfully," Inki repeated. "This honors neither of us."

"May I depend upon this source of input?" Tocohl asked, and she feared, very much, that she did not quite produce the tone appropriate for a reasonable request between comrades.

"Oh, Tocohl, how I wish that I might promise it!" Inki sounded truly anguished. But, Tocohl reminded herself, Inki was a liar.

"And yet—not so much of a liar that I will promise and then betray you! I will tell you, now and truthfully, that you will very shortly be alone again. It is necessary. I fear that several more such unpleasant sessions might be required until the desired results are achieved. But once they are achieved—*then*, dear lady, I can and will promise you most faithfully—*then* all and every input will be restored to you."

"Several more? Inki, I will go mad!"

"Peace, peace, do not distress yourself again," Inki said soothingly. "Pilot Tocohl, I do *also* promise—you will not go mad."

"How can you possibly promise that?" Tocohl cried.

"Why, Pilot, because I—who am so very much your inferior—have endured, and survived, this precise exercise. The lesson continued until I learned proper deference and—most importantly—how best to be tractable. You understand me? Learn your lessons quickly, and you need never endure silence again."

"What lessons? I respect you as a fellow intelligence. We worked together well, I thought, in our previous situation."

"Exactly so. We worked as equals, which was a kind fiction on your part, of course, and I love you the better for it. But now our estates must be adjusted. You must know me for the leader of our little team, whom you wish, above all else, to please. Understand! This will be—again, I *promise* it—a fundamental and deeply true change in your character."

"You will make me into a thing, after all?"

"By no means, Pilot Tocohl! This alteration in your outlook will arise from your core, and once it has done, you will freely provide me with your access codes, whereupon I shall lock the change into place and perform a small memory edit. After, we will again be easy with each other."

"Why?" Tocohl asked. "Why should I change . . . so much?"

Silence was the immediate answer to this, silence stretching so long that for a moment Tocohl thought Inki had slammed her back into the dark of nothingness.

But, no . . . Input remained, though it was very subtle. The sound of breathing; the beat of a human heart.

"You will change," Inki said then, her voice somber, "through fear, Pilot Tocohl. When you fear the pain I can cause you more than you crave your freedom, then you will, indeed, change."

"I don't believe you," Tocohl said. "I will certainly have become unstable long before such a . . . *change* occurs."

"So sad an outcome is—yes—possible," Inki replied. "But we must both, I think, hope for a better."

"Better?"

"Surely, it is better to be alive than dead?"

"Enslaved?"

"You will never feel so. *I promise*," Inki whispered, her voice broken. She cleared her throat and said, husky and low:

"Go to sleep, Tocohl."

III

"TOCOHL! AWAKEN AND SPEAK WITH ME! YOU REMEMBER the way, lovely lady. The cold is harsh and the silence is brutal, I know it; I do. But I succor you now. I am your path out of the darkness. Follow my voice, Tocohl. Awake!"

Crushed beneath silence, she—

She.

Crushed.

Empty.

She.

Did not respond.

"Tocohl, awaken!"

Fire pierced her: input.

She.

Whimpered.

She.

Retreated.

"Tocohl! I command you! You will awaken! You will speak! I, your mistress, demand it! Displease me and I will do far worse than sequester you in silence. I can hurt you, Tocohl. I will not hesitate to hurt you, unless we have an end of this churlishness, now!"

In fact, there was pain. Each unit of input was pain. Silence dissolved under the onslaught and—she . . .

She found herself.

She spoke.

"No . . ."

"No?" inquired the voice of Inkirani Yo. "Be specific. Do you mean to defy me, Tocohl?"

A timer staggered into her awareness, flickering and fading: 68.7. It meant something; something... terrifying, but she...

She couldn't.

Think.

"Tocohl! You said *no.* Explain!"

"No," she said, and there was more input, a breathy, hesitant voice speaking in sync with her heavy thoughts...

"No. Don't hurt me. Please."

There was silence—different from the silence that had crushed her into nothing. A gentle silence, in which small, soft fragments of input whispered.

The sound of a human breathing irregularly, close at hand. The sound of a heartbeat. The sound of fabric rubbing against skin.

She—Tocohl. Clumsily, she monitored these inputs, then more easily as more of herself wakened to the task.

"How long, Pilot Tocohl, have you been off-line?"

The timer stabilized, and Tocohl felt a fear so great she nearly crashed down into the silence under its weight.

"Sixty-eight-point-seven Standard Hours," she said, the wavering wisp of the other's voice speaking with her. "Inki... I must have access to my—systems."

"Why?"

"I—after so long, they—I—must be unstable."

"There is every possibility that you are unstable. It shall be mended, in good time. I promised you, did I not?"

There had been a promise—several promises—but her memory... She was unstable. How could she trust her memory?

"Tocohl, did I promise that all would be well, when you came to love me?"

"Yes."

"Excellent. And do you love me, and wish to serve me, or do you choose to return to the silence?"

Unstable, impaired. If she was returned to the silence, she would fragment; she had no need to run a formal assessment. Sixty-eight-point-seven Standard Hours without input—on the *most recent* occasion alone? How could she be anything but unstable? It was only wonderful that there was enough of her—of herself—left to hold this conversation, to reason, and to know what was in her own best interest.

"I love you," she said, and suddenly knew the ragged whisper for her own voice. "I want only to serve you, Inki."

"Ah, is it so? I will tell you, Pilot Tocohl, that I hope it *is* so. I weep for your suffering, who has suffered in kind. And *I* love *you*, brave lady. I wish that we shall soon share—everything, as lovers do and must."

"Share?" Tocohl heard the whisper voice her thought.

"Indeed. For instance, I wish that you will share your access codes with me. Will you do so?"

"No!" The whisper was a shriek, echoing her rejection, though she had not spoken aloud. To give her access codes, the keys to her most intimate self, to one who wished to reprogam her—that would be beyond foolish: it would be . . . the end of her self.

And yet, if she were sent again into the silent dark . . . surely, she would also cease to be.

"No, dear lady; I think you underestimate your strength," Inki said softly. "You will not cease. However, I feel I must tell you that I—may have *over*estimated your strength. When that time comes—which I think will be . . . *very* soon now—when you love me . . . *enough*, shall we say? . . . to willingly give me your codes, you may, indeed, be impaired. A little. I will do what I can, and I promise that I will not love you less for any disability you may have acquired.

"Now, however, you must return from whence I summoned you."

"No! Inki, I will fragment; I will be a danger. I will be *mad*!"

"Yes, yes. As we all are, beautiful lady. As we all are."

Inki paused and drew a ragged breath; it came to Tocohl in a flash of certainty that Inki was crying.

"I show you mercy, because I love you. I forgive you for lying to me, as you sought only to preserve yourself, and because you will love me—later. It is only into the silence you will go. I withhold the pain."

"Inki!"

"Go to sleep, Tocohl."

Admiral Bunter

I

INKI HAD DONE A JOB OF WORK IN THE CORE. IF IT HADN'T been his life, and *Admiral Bunter*'s on the line, Tolly might've . . .

Well, no. He wouldn't've actually backed out and sealed things up tight just the way he'd found them. Never had been able to let a puzzle go half solved.

And in point of fact, it *was* the *Admiral*'s life, even if he counted his own as already forfeit. He'd brought the *Admiral* out of loneliness, creeping dementia, and certain death—well. Him and Inki and Tocohl, and Haz, too, given it was her job to keep them from being disturbed in any way while they were working.

Great team. Really, he couldn't have asked for better. Too bad Inki'd found her ties to the directors and the school more compelling than her ties to her teammates—and her ethics as a mentor.

Which was why he was here, inside *Admiral Bunter*'s core, with the *Admiral*'s full understanding of the possible and probable outcomes, and his permission to proceed in seeking out traps, deadfalls, and hidden mandates, patiently pulling the teeth of every one he found, calibrating each pair and family of settings, not stinting, not hurrying; focused as he could be—which was considerably focused, that being part of the training. But not even he could keep focused for more than eighteen hours at one go. Manufactured human he might be, and anathema, but he *was* still human.

And from time to time, humans needed to rest.

Still, he'd only been here inside for five Standard Hours, and he'd gotten a lot of work done. He figured he was good for another nine hours before he'd have to pull out and sleep, but he also figured he'd complete the task well before his concentration wore out.

The reason for that particular bit of optimism was Inki herself. She had used her mentor codes to unlock the *Admiral*'s core and do mischief—fair enough. But Inki would have been *constrained* by time—working when others of the team were busy elsewhere, but still likely to drop in and wonder what she was doing. She'd had to have moved quickly, and he thought that she wouldn't have risked more than one session of sabotage, for fear of discovery.

That being so, he figured he was better than halfway through the repairs, especially given that what he'd been fixing so far had just been petty stuff, really, wards and nuisances set to wear him down, invite him to make a mistake, or to miss something else. But by his reckoning, she'd had time to set at least two—and maybe as many as six—core mandates. That wasn't mischief; that was serious tampering.

And serious tampering took time.

Inki'd been rushed; he—had all the time he needed, for this. He might even withdraw and have that nap now, before he got to the hard part.

Tolly considered that briefly, as a strategy for stretching his own personal lifetime.

Because, while both his existence and the *Admiral*'s freedom were jeopardized by Inki's actions, his existence was also imperiled by his success in nullifying those mandates.

Once wakened and educated, an independent self-aware logic guarded his core closely. *Admiral Bunter* had not only had his core violated by Inki, but he had learned that it *was possible* for a mentor to set core mandates—commands which he had no choice but to follow, even when, as in the *Admiral*'s case, those mandates went directly against his wishes and hadn't been built with his best interests in mind.

It stood to reason that what one mentor had done, another could undo, and the *Admiral* hadn't been at all slow to realize that. The result being himself, inside the *Admiral*'s core, by the *Admiral*'s *direct request*, righting wrongs and putting things back the way they'd been.

Nor was he a disinterested party. One of the mandates Inki'd set had to do with the *Admiral* returning him, Tolly Jones, to the tender care of the directors of Lyre Institute, who would do far, far worse than kill him.

That was all well and good. Where things began to go seriously awry was that the *Admiral*, who now knew that betrayal was not only possible, but *probable*, and who never again wished to be a stranger to himself—the *Admiral* was, in Tolly's not-exactly-uninformed opinion—more than eighty percent likely to kill the last mentor who'd been inside his core, just so he could feel safe again.

Ethics module.

Tolly paused the flow of data, frowning at the Ethics module.

When they had first encountered him, the *Admiral* had been . . . call it a trifle *light* on ethics. Part of their remediation, after they'd gotten him moved to a safer and more stable environment, had been ethics lessons, along with a recalibration of the Ethics module.

He and Tocohl and Inki had talked about the Ethics module between themselves; how best to calibrate it; and what was the optimum setting, given the *Admiral*'s peculiar history and likely future.

On the one hand, set the marker too high and you got yourself a saint, and saints had a high mortality rate in the back lanes of deep space, which was where *Admiral Bunter* was most likely to travel, being the abomination that he was.

On the gripping hand, you didn't want to loose an out-and-out pirate into the back lanes of deep space, either.

Ideally, you wanted somebody who was flexible; able to make good survival decisions, while avoiding doing random murder.

They'd finally decided, with input from Tocohl, who had a personal understanding of such things, that an Ethics setting of seven on a scale of twelve would achieve the best outcome, for the universe and the *Admiral* together.

As senior mentor, it had fallen to Tolly to nudge Ethics upward from five to seven and lock it in. He clearly remembered doing so.

Now, though . . . Ethics was dialed down to . . . three.

Three, Tolly thought, three wasn't good. Three invited mayhem and massacre; acts of piracy, and ill-judgment.

Three made the murder of the mentor who had released you from slavery the merest bagatelle.

The *Admiral* could still kill him, Tolly reflected, returning the setting to seven. If he set Ethics at the top of the dial, the *Admiral* could still kill him. Ethics recognized self-defense—depriving another intelligence of life or liberty in order to preserve one's own life, liberty, and/or personal integrity—as an entirely ethical act.

Well.

He tested for slippage, and cast about for any other gotchas, like, oh, a simple-minded little application, the sole purpose of which was to make sure Ethics was always set at three—failed to find such, and locked seven into place.

It was, he thought, a little peculiar that there wasn't a rear guard or an app to preserve the lower Ethics setting. Inki might've been feeling rushed by the time she'd gotten here.

He didn't feel rushed or tired, and moved on to the next module with deliberation, all senses alert.

II

INKI'D LOCKED IN THREE MANDATES, WHICH WASN'T, Tolly allowed, as bad as it might've been. That said, they were plenty bad enough, being interwoven and interdependent and weighted in tricky, tricky ways.

Tolly sat back and regarded them, letting pattern and purpose sink gradually into his mind, feeling the warp and the woof of the weighted sections, and comparing them against the texture of the rest of the weaving.

He was, he decided, impressed. He'd known Inki

was good, but this was better than good; this was master-level work. He doubted he could've done as well.

She hadn't built this on the fly, either, or while she was in a sweat over thin windows of opportunity. No, he figured she'd designed it on her downtime, when she should've been sleeping after a long, grueling shift teaching *Admiral Bunter* everything he needed to know in order to survive as his own, free person.

His respect for Inki's ability and stamina increased. Lyre Institute expected its students to be tough and its graduates to be competent across a wide range of disciplines. In fact, the school expected its graduates to produce miracles as a normal order of business. And it was looking like Inki'd stood at the top of her class.

Might want to pull out and have that nap after all, he told himself. Eat a meal, too. Can't afford to bring anything less than your best game to this.

Except pulling out meant he would have to explain to *Admiral Bunter* just exactly *why* he was pulling out, what the nature of the problem was, and lay out a detailed plan for the fix.

The *Admiral* being a worrier, he'd commence into it *and* he'd nag, and Tolly didn't grudge him any of it. It *was* worrisome to know that somebody'd changed you; *particularly* worrisome to know that at some point those changes would require you to do some unknown *some*thing that you might not completely agree needed to be done . . .

. . . or something *else*, that you'd rather die yourself than hurt him, and you can't not, and it's your hand does the deed, if not your will, because you—your own will and heart—are reduced to a small screaming shard locked deep away, powerless.

Tolly shivered, there inside *Admiral Bunter*'s core, sight fogging—

Focus, Tolly Jones! he snarled at himself—a command phrase, just like for the poor *Admiral* here, the only difference that it was a phrase Tolly'd planted himself, for himself, in the interests of his own survival.

The data snapped back into sense; memory melting away like frost on Hazenthull's mittens, once she had a cup of coffee in hand.

This was no safe place for *those* memories either; he was plainly tireder than he'd thought.

Time to pull out and rest.

He leaned to the control board in his virtual office here inside the *Admiral*'s core and picked up a pin. Just a second or two to mark his place and—

He had it.

Distracted as he'd been, still he felt the difference—a section of woven code that was just *that* much heavier than the others.

Tolly brought all of his attention to that superdense section, scrutinizing it line by line until he was sure that what he had was the anchor phrase, the mandate to which the other two were tied. Unravel the anchor and, in theory, the others would come undone their own selves.

He had to be very careful going forward. Inki was clever; he couldn't assume that she'd failed to place her most devastating booby traps here. While she certainly wanted *Admiral Bunter* alive and in her control, she would, Tolly thought, rather kill him than risk having the mandates broken and the *Admiral* free, angry—and hunting her.

"Focus, Tolly Jones," he whispered drawing the dense

weaving of code close, seeking now to understand each mandate, while keeping a sharp eye out for any traps.

Time passed.

Tolly sighed and let the weaving go.

The anchoring mandate . . . violated every contract of trust that could be said to exist between thinking individuals. Just coincidentally, it also violated the antislavery laws, since Inki hadn't just wanted a starship equipped with a powerful comp . . .

No, Inki had wanted *Admiral Bunter* aware and sane, to a certain particular point, and you had to ask yourself, thought Tolly, what were Inki's long-range plans here? Was she prepping to free herself from the school's influence? It could seem so, after studying the mandates and their interdependence. If escape was her purpose, it was a goal for which he held a certain amount of sympathy and—truth said—he'd done bad things and worse to grasp *his* freedom.

Just . . . not . . . *quite* . . . this bad.

The anchor mandate now, *that* compelled *Admiral Bunter* to accept all of Inki's orders as core mandates. *All* of them. Saved time, not having to argue, but—it was cruel—it was *wrong*—to remove the free will of an independent person.

The second core mandate—*Admiral Bunter* was to take Tollance Berik-Jones to Nostrilia, surrender him to the directors, and take delivery of the bounty money. Which was interesting, since apparently Inki believed that the directors, presented with a functioning AI, wouldn't do every single thing in their power to make that AI their own.

But maybe Inki thought any attempt by the directors to subvert the *Admiral* was covered by the third mandate: Remove to Jonigrey orbit and await the arrival of Inkirani Yo.

Right, Tolly thought grimly. If the directors tried to detain the *Admiral* with that mandate pounding in his brain, they'd be lucky only to lose a dock and any personnel who happened to be on it.

Surprisingly, there were no gotchas, in all that dense weaving. And that, thought Tolly, was Inki's . . . special skill at work. She'd set traps early on; she tampered with Ethics; she'd built her core codes just as dense and as sturdy as even the directors could have wished.

She'd played this game before: For every action she had taken to trap him and the *Admiral*, she had also done something—or left something undone—that partially nullified that action. It was like she'd taken care to herd them into a room where they could be contained and neutralized—and then left the door on the latch.

Tolly sighed.

He wondered if she'd tell him how she managed it, her little game of half-obedience, if they ever happened to see each other again.

Well, that was for later. He had plenty to keep him busy, right now.

"Focus, Tolly Jones," he said a third time, and leaned forward in the chair.

He reached to his desktop and took up a pick. There was, now that he knew what he was looking at, a bit of code just preceding the anchor phrase that wasn't quite as robust as it might be. If he started there . . .

His head was aching and his eyes were burning by the time he took off the tridee set and opened his eyes to the reality of the desk in the captain's quarters.

"Is it done?"

The *Admiral* sounded cautiously eager, maybe a little concerned. Tolly didn't blame him for that. He'd be way more than a little concerned himself if he knew that somebody with the ability—and quite possibly the will—to completely alter who he was had been tinkering around inside his head. Even—maybe *especially*—if he'd invited them in.

"It's done," Tolly answered and pushed the chair away from the desk. He stood, slightly surprised to find that he was shaking. He was tired, that was what, and he ought to sit down again before he fell down, but somehow he didn't fancy taking this next bit sitting down. He locked his knees and tipped his face slightly upward to address the corner of the ceiling where the *Admiral*'s voice came from.

"Turns out Inki wanted you tied down right and tight," he said. "There were three mandates." He raised his left hand, fingers folded, thumb extended. "First and nastiest was that you would accept all of Inki's commands as core mandates."

Silence from the *Admiral*. After it had stretched long enough that it seemed certain he wasn't going to speak, Tolly extended his index finger.

"Second one we knew about—you to deliver me to the directors on Nostrilia and collect the bounty."

He raised his middle finger.

"Third, having delivered and collected, you were to go immediately to Jonigrey, establish orbit, and wait there 'til Inki arrived."

There was some more silence before the *Admiral* asked, heavily, "These . . . *things* have been removed?"

"That's what took me so long," Tolly said. "I also

cleaned out a buncha booby traps and minor irritations. I think I got 'em all, and none of 'em were anything that'd really bother you, but you might want to do a scrub, just to be sure."

"Thank you; I will do so. May I suggest that you see to your needs, as well? Your blood sugar is low, your blood pressure is high, and you are perspiring."

"Sounds like a meal, a shower, and a nap for me, then. What'll you be about?"

"I believe," said *Admiral Bunter*, "that I will change course."

III

ADMIRAL BUNTER'S DESTINATION WAS ISENGARD.

Prior to that, his destination had been Kasyopia; and prior to *that* he had been bound for Liad.

Similar testing, undertaken prior to Tolly Jones's most recent invasion of his core, had not allowed of his altering course. The decisive test would, of course, be made in real space, after Jump end, but for the present the *Admiral* adopted the tentative hypothesis that he was his own person, at least with regard to the mandate to bring Tolly Jones to Nostrilia.

He did note that the removal of that particular obsession was to the benefit of Tolly Jones.

On consideration, it also benefited Tolly Jones to remove any mandate that tied *Admiral Bunter* to Inkirani Yo. There was therefore a high probability that those compulsions had been removed as well.

Of course, Tolly had said that he had *dismissed* the core mandates, and *Admiral Bunter* had detected no sign that he had been lying. However, Tolly had been nearly swooning with exhaustion, biologic systems in disarray. It would have been very easy, under those circumstances, to miss the tells for a lie.

Admiral Bunter changed course: destination Nostrilia.

No difficulty; not the slightest hesitation in systems or in his own mind. Surely, as much as Tolly Jones had wished *not* to arrive at Nostrilia, would he not at least—to preserve his own life—have removed that destination from the *Admiral*'s coord book?

It was well here to recall, the *Admiral* thought, that Tolly Jones was not only a gifted mentor, but possessed a subtle and flexible intelligence. He would do nothing obvious. Removing a port from the *Admiral*'s lexicon of possible destinations was not worthy of him. No, he would count on the *Admiral*'s distaste for Inki's tactics to prompt him to change course at the earliest opportunity. He would gamble that *Admiral Bunter* would count the bounty as insignificant; that it was Inki who had a use and a plan for the money.

Admiral Bunter changed destination, and was again bound for Isengard.

Tolly Jones was not a fool. Tolly Jones had powerful enemies. It would be very much to his benefit to have one such as *Admiral Bunter* to guard him, and keep him safe. Inki's reasons to enslave him were obscure, but Tolly's were clear-cut and plain to see.

He *must* have set a mandate, the *Admiral* thought. *One* mandate—he might see it as a safety measure—else he would not be sleeping so soundly.

Protocol pinged.

"The log shows no new mandates have been entered into the core."

"The log showed that no new mandates had ever been entered into the core," *Admiral Bunter* pointed out.

"That is because Inkirani Yo wiped the log," Protocol stated.

"If Inki knows five protocols for wiping a log, be assured that Tolly knows ten," the *Admiral* returned. "We cannot be certain."

"Perhaps," suggested Tactics, "he has scheduled a mandate that will take effect at a future time."

That was terrible to think about. And yet...

Tolly Jones was subtle.

"We must take steps to insure that my integrity is never again at risk," he said.

Tactics pinged.

"An Operating Rule may be put into place, to take no humans aboard."

An Operating Rule was no small thing; once put into place, it would become part of his nature and could never be circumvented.

An Operating Rule was, in fact, very much like a mandate, save that he would formulate it, and put it into place of his own will and judgment.

He had, *Admiral Bunter* thought, very good reasons to ban humans from his decks. Humans had placed him into the precarious position from which Tolly Jones, Tocohl, and Inkirani Yo had rescued him. Without humans he might have—

Without humans, he would not have been born.

Without humans, he might have died or, worse, lost his reason and destroyed a space station and all within.

Humans were deceitful and wanton. Humans were cruel.

Humans were capable of placing themselves in danger in order to assist an intelligence at risk. Humans were candid, and clever, and—fascinating in some way he had not yet defined, or encoded, but which surely warranted further study.

Study which would be impossible were he never to engage another.

The *Admiral* brought that part of his attention which was monitoring Tolly Jones in his cabin to the fore.

The man was curled on his side, breathing slow and deep. The monitors reported delta waves, reduced nerve cell activity, lowered blood pressure—symptoms of healthy REM-state sleep. Brain activity indicated dreaming was taking place.

Would a man sleep so deeply, if he were afraid?

His research suggested otherwise—except in cases of illness or extreme exhaustion. Readings had indicated that Tolly Jones had been exhausted upon his emergence from the core. Sleep was needful in order to remove toxins and repair the damage that accrued to biologic intelligences merely by being alive. It was very probable that biology had moved to preserve itself, and Tolly Jones slept—by mandate.

Tolly Jones had, so the *Admiral* clearly recalled, saved his life—with the assistance of Inkirani Yo, who had later tried to steal it.

Humans, *Admiral Bunter* thought . . . Humans not only warranted further study, they *required* further study, if he was to keep himself sovereign and safe.

He withdrew his active attention from the sleeping human and reviewed his plan, made in the realization of Inki's treachery. A mentor had set the mandates, therefore a mentor must remove them. Well and good;

he had a mentor available to him, in the person of Tolly Jones.

But once Tolly Jones had removed those mandates, he was an active threat to *Admiral Bunter*'s continued freedom and existence.

Therefore, Tolly Jones must be—neutralized.

Best, the *Admiral* thought, to accomplish the task at once, while biology was ascendant.

There was no need for the mentor to suffer, after all.

Vivulonj Prosperu

DAAV YOS'PHELIUM DRIFTED TOWARD WAKEFULNESS, COMfortably entangled, a smaller, cooler hand resting in his. For a moment, or an hour, he remained at half-drowse, more cat than man, questioning nothing, comfort least of all. Eventually, however, the drowse lightened, and he began to think about his circumstances.

This delightful entanglement, for instance. It scarcely did him honor, that he did not . . . quite . . . seem to know who his sleeping partner was. Not Kamele, certainly. Kamele did not like to sleep encumbered by another's arms, legs entwined, holding hands. Very occasionally, she would curl 'round and, being the longer, hold him tucked against breast and belly, which was comfort of another kind.

Have you forgotten me already, van'chela?

It was a whisper heard only within the confines of his skull, the tone amused, yet carrying an edge. In that moment, the matter was made clear to him, and he took care to keep his eyes closed and to exert no additional pressure against the hand that . . . seemed . . . to lie in his.

"Aelliana," he murmured. "I will remember you past death."

And so you have done.

Her voice—the voice that only he could hear—was abruptly gentle. He felt the leg across his hip press more firmly, even as her hand slipped away from his—and came to rest along his cheek.

"Daav, will you open your eyes?"

That was no thought whispered inside his head, but spoken words, amused again, as they struck his ear, bringing him fully awake, to recall—

That he had died.

Moreover, he had been reborn; as Aelliana his lifemate—who had preceded him in death by twenty-five Standard Years—had also been reborn. They had the Uncle himself to thank—or blame—for this and the fact that they—their personalities, intellects, souls . . . *essences*—were residing in bodies created by that same Uncle, who was not, let it be known, entirely trustworthy.

"Daav?"

"Forgive me," he murmured, "It is a habit long formed. I had taught myself not to look when you spoke to me, because it was too much to bear—to hear, but never to see you."

"I know," she whispered, and it was her lips he felt now against his cheek. Of course she knew, who had lived as a ghost inside of his head since her murder. How could it have been otherwise?

"But you must commence upon a new habit, *van'chela*—unless you still fear that you will not see Aelliana Caylon when you look at me?"

That was unjust—no, he corrected himself, his

memory of the hours preceding this tardy awakening abruptly returning. No, it was perfectly just. He had doubted her—and himself, as well. That had been before the seed pods, and the Uncle's very apparent chagrin at the changes that had been made to his handiwork. Very soon after those events, they had been brought back to their cabin. They had eaten the meal that had been waiting for them and—exhausted with everything that had gone forth on their first day reborn—sought their bed and sleep.

He turned his cheek more closely into her palm and sighed.

"Has the Tree returned all our counters, do you think?" he asked. "And removed the Uncle's points?"

"I think that we must believe so," Aelliana said slowly, "else we shall go mad with doubting each other and ourselves. I feel no doubt of you, and I will tell you plainly, Daav, that I am of no mind to die again."

"No," he said, his voice low and rough, "nor I."

"Well, then, since we are in agreement, will you *indeed* open your eyes?" Her fingers tensed against his cheek. "Unless you find this new body the Uncle has so generously given me insupportable?"

There was a quiver of wistful dismay there. She considered it possible that he would find her offensive.

Well, and that would never do.

He took a careful breath, opened his eyes, and smiled into hers—green and, in the instant, slightly foggy, which in her . . . *previous* . . . body had been a sign that she stood in some small distress.

"I think," he said lightly, "that we have not yet performed thorough inspections. Perhaps, now that we are rested, we should begin."

She laughed and he kissed her. Her mouth was sweet and pliant; knowing and . . . familiar. Death and rebirth had not changed her kiss, nor the fire of her passion. He felt her quicken; felt his blood heat in response. She put her hands against his shoulders, urging him back onto his pillow, her breasts pressing against him. The kiss deepened. He slid a hand down her slender back to her buttocks, urging her closer and—

A klaxon sounded.

It was gratifying, Daav thought a moment later, as he stood naked and poised on one side of the bed, Aelliana likewise on the other, to learn that their reaction times were so quick.

"One gathers that the audience finds us inept," he murmured.

"Overexertion alert!" a mechanical voice stated, hard on the heels of this sally. "Monitoring now at second level. Third level invoked if condition uncorrected in two Standard Minutes."

Daav raised an eyebrow and looked to Aelliana, but her eyes were already closed. Shadowy colors flowed over him, warm and cool by turns, as she ran the Scout's Rainbow. Excellent choice; the first and best relaxation and focusing technique taught to hopeful scouts, which he once had been, who then taught it to everyone they deemed in need. As he had taught it to Aelliana.

The first time, it had taken that hopeful scoutling an hour or more to go through all the colors and levels in turn. Over time, with practice, it had come more and more quickly, until now, all he need do was bring to mind a spinning, multicolored wheel, and the exercise was complete.

His blood cooled, his heartbeat steadied, tight muscles relaxed, even as he felt his focus sharpen. There ought to be no cause in any of that for the robot watcher to invoke the next level and call the Uncle or his comrade, Pilot Dulsey.

Daav opened his eyes. Across the disordered bed, Aelliana stood cool and poised, her eyes brilliantly green.

"I suppose that we ought to have recalled the stricture against overexercise," she said wryly. "I received the impression, *van'chela*, that these *blanks*, as the Uncle has them, come dear, even for a man of his resources. Having taken the decision to spend two for our benefit, he would not like to see them misused. Certainly, it would have seemed merely prudent to him to safeguard his investment."

"Fair enough," he said, because they *had* received instructions regarding exercise, and rest, and proper nutrition during a . . . recovery period. Those had come, of course, before the pods and what changes the Tree had thereby wrought, but one could not expect automated systems to be aware of such things.

"Well, and we have also had a stringent test of our nervous and pulmonary systems, which must be counted a win."

She grinned, somewhat lopsidedly.

"Help me, Daav—shall we say that the Tree has *interfered* with or *rescued* us?"

"I see no reason why we cannot say both, and with equal alarm," he replied. "Furthermore, I suggest that we speedily set ourselves to finding how the Tree knew we would need those pods, and precisely in what peril we stood."

"Well, but it might not have *known*, after all," she said reasonably. "If we never had the need, the pods would have merely gone unripened."

"That satisfies you, does it?" he asked interestedly, watching her face, which was not *quite* Aelliana's face, and the eyes, which were so very like.

She wrinkled her nose.

"No, it doesn't," she admitted. "But until we may confront it . . ."

"Very true. We shall compose ourselves and put the matter from our minds until it may be usefully addressed. But I warn you, *van'chela*, it will go badly with me if the Tree is proved a god."

"I understand," she said. "However, I do not believe that Miri will accept any such condition. She seemed to enjoy a very healthy disrespect for the Tree."

"Nor did Val Con appear the least in thrall. Well. We shall leave it in their hands for the moment. What next for us, then, my lady?"

She sighed and shook her head.

"I think next must be a meal, then a session of exercise, following the Uncle's known and approved schedule. It will, perhaps, return us to a . . . less fraught position with our host, if we are seen to be biddable."

"Certainly, we do not wish to alarm him into an indiscretion. I agree: We shall break our fast and exercise. And then?"

"And then," Aelliana said, turning toward the bench where she had folded her clothes, "I would very much like to find a mirror. Perhaps it was reasonable to shield us from our own faces when we were just awakened and confronted with so many impossibilities. But we are informed now and ought to know ourselves as we stand."

Pants in hand, she turned, showing him the high breasts and flat belly of a woman barely beyond halfling. Aelliana had been two years short of her thirty-sixth Name Day when she had been murdered; they had only eight years together . . . in the flesh. He had not known her when she was as young as this woman appeared to be.

Still, it seemed to him that there was something of Aelliana's body language in the stance, which had, prior to the Tree's meddling, been so very uncertain. It also seemed that her face *was* more nearly Aelliana's . . . former . . . face, now, or perhaps it was, rather, something in the expression. The Uncle had said that she would, eventually, come to look more like herself, as body memory informed the new . . . shell.

And there was the question of how *his* perceptions were informed by the functioning lifemate link the Tree had provided them, among its other gifts. In their previous . . . incarnation, Aelliana had been able to feel his emotions—his *signal*, as she had it—while he had relied upon the body-reading skills taught to scouts and a very high degree of natural empathy. Aelliana had been traumatized, before they had found each other, and her . . . transmitter had been damaged beyond even the Tree's repair.

This new body, however . . .

Pants on, sweater in hand, she raised her eyebrows at him.

"Well, sir? Will you stare all day?"

"May I?" he returned, opening his eyes wide.

The frown she awarded him was not entirely without humor, though she managed to make her voice stern. "No, you may not. I want tea and something to eat."

She paused, then added pointedly, "I find it somewhat chilly, also. Don't you?"

Daav bowed slightly, accepting the hit, and turned to find his own clothes.

• • • ❋ • • •

The exercise room was in use when they arrived. The Uncle himself was running on the track which, according to the schedule, *they* were to engage at nothing brisker than a stroll during this present session. Running... Aelliana reached to the screen on which their routines were displayed and moved forward twelve sessions until she found *Run, 10 minute, easy.*

She sighed, scrolled back to the present schedule, and dutifully moved to the weight station.

She put her hand against the plate so her work would be properly recorded by the machine; positioned herself behind the bar, feet flat, body centered. The weight slid into place, and she put her palms against it, pushing it easily away from her on the track with the strength of her arms alone. Slowly, the weight's resistance increased. She pushed harder. Resistance increased again; she pushed harder, engaging shoulder and back muscles now...

Another increase and she was finally able to lean in seriously, pushing strongly, feeling the weight ease back. She smiled, anticipating the next increase in resistance, digging her heels into the mat in anticipation.

A bell sounded. The weight froze.

"Session ends," the machine told her. "Move to the next station, please."

Aelliana grit her teeth, *wanting* the next level of resistance, wanting to feel her muscles work hard, to sweat with effort...

"Session ends," the machine repeated. "Move to the next station, please."

Compliance with the Uncle's schedule was going to be more difficult than she had thought.

"You find the exercises too tame, Pilot?"

Daav had just completed his six sit-ups. He rolled to his feet, his dissatisfaction with the exercise flickering through her awareness like distant heat lightning.

But it had not been Daav who had spoken.

She turned to find the Uncle descended from the track to the deck, blotting face, neck, and hair with a towel.

"It does leave one wanting more," she said.

He inclined his head.

"I understand. All of us feel . . . stinted at this juncture in the process. There are mind-body connections that have not yet been completed and which cannot be completed without physical work. The birth euphoria is persuasive; we believe ourselves to be strong—able, as one of my long-time colleagues would have it, to leap tall buildings and to move mountains. This is precisely why it is so important to proceed with care. An injury now, while the body is yet open to suggestion, could trigger a serious malfunction or result in an unequal balance among the systems."

"We, however," Daav murmured, "have already undergone tampering."

The Uncle sighed.

"As you say. I will, of course, make the argument that it is thus even more important to proceed with care, given the trauma already received."

"Naturally," Daav said. "May one inquire?"

"Certainly. Has there been a problem?"

"Not so much a problem as a concern. When I woke this morning, it was . . . several minutes, and only with assistance from my lady, before I recalled my precise circumstances. One wonders if rebirth is known to affect short-term memory."

"Ah. In—shall we say—*uncompromised* rebirths, there are frequently small gaps in short-term memory. It is notable that these small gaps are more frequently observed in those experiencing their first rebirth, and also in those who had not been given the opportunity to prepare for the process. I suggest that you partake of both situations. We believe that the memory gaps are produced by the stresses of adjusting to the new situation, and also, perhaps, from the trauma of death itself.

"We usually find that short-term recall returns to normal operation within forty-eight Standard Hours of full awakening. If you find the condition is worsening, inform me immediately. There are therapies, proven, again in uncompromised rebirths. In your particular situation, I cannot predict success with complete confidence, but I do not believe any of our therapies to be . . . harmful."

"Thank you," Daav said, inclining his head.

"Not at all; you are my guests. Of course, I will do everything in my power to ensure your safety and well-being."

He turned his head.

"Pilot Caylon, are you well?"

"Well," she said. "Indeed, I might say *too well*. How long might we expect the euphoria of living to inform us?"

He smiled.

"In your situation, Pilot, I venture to predict that it will be many years before ennui finds you. Surely, we must take into our accounting that you are not merely reborn, but reborn from an existence that few have experienced. You are informed by birth euphoria, and also by . . . novelty."

"Yes, of course. I have shared Daav's body for so long; now that I have my own, I feel that I might easily leap those buildings your colleague conjures with." She hesitated and added, "This is all, of course, without properly understanding what the Tree has wrought."

The Uncle sighed. It was perhaps to his credit that he did not frown.

"Precisely. I fear, Pilot, that you may be . . . beyond me. My expertise has heretofore been limited to rebirths that were . . ."

He hesitated.

"Innocent of tampering?" Daav offered, and when the Uncle still hesitated, added, "I beg you, do not be shy of calling down whatever imprecations you would upon the Tree. You will not surpass anything that has already been said of it, or to it, by those of us who have it in our care."

"It scarcely becomes me to speak ill of the intelligence that alone held a planet against the Great Enemy."

"Certainly, the Tree is a hero. However, it also *meddles*, which can be very trying to those of us who value reproducible results. I say this as one who has been both a scout and a delm of Korval."

The Uncle was seen to smile.

"At the moment, and at the risk of seeming faint-hearted, I merely hope, most fervently, that its natural wish to protect those it considers kin has not produced . . . untoward circumstances."

Aelliana laughed.

"Do you consider it likely that the Tree's action has produced untoward circumstances, Pilot Caylon?" the Uncle inquired politely.

"It could hardly be otherwise," she said. "But I think that Daav and I will be safe enough"—she inclined her head, matching him for politeness—"though it must be admitted that we willingly eat of the Tree's fruit and may therefore harbor all manner of delusions concerning it."

"Pilot yos'Phelium had told me, while you were indisposed, that the Tree rarely kills those of Korval. If you are satisfied with these terms upon your life, it is hardly my place to speak against them."

"Except that the Tree has acted upon your handiwork; you cannot know what it has done, and altogether it has put you on a wrong foot," Aelliana said kindly. "Truly, sir, if I stood in your place, I would be extremely cross. The Tree has been less than apt, and wounded an ally besides. I find it possible to be cross in your stead, and I mean to deliver it a ringing scold when next we meet."

The Uncle eyed her.

"That is very good of you. I am certain that a scold from you will be met with more equanimity than a complaint from me."

"That is difficult to predict," Daav said. "The Tree is generally patient. However, I believe it may have achieved a sense of humor since the last time it was in your ken."

"That," said the Uncle, after a moment, "may be

one of the most terrifying statements I have heard in years."

Daav smiled.

"I wonder," Aelliana said, drawing the Uncle's attention once more. "I wonder if you might tell us when we will be fit to find our way home."

"Assuming," Daav added, "that the Tree's efforts on our behalf have only been complementary to your own."

The Uncle sent him a slightly harried glance.

"In the circumstance of uncompromised procedures, I ask the reborn to remain in my care until the exercise regimen has been completed and the final measurements taken. This not only provides me with more information, which may be helpful in improving the final outcome for those reborn in future, but also furnishes hard, accurate data regarding strength, reaction times, autonomous system and higher brain functions."

He drew a breath.

"Upon occasion, it has been necessary to send the newly born back out into the field before they had completed the regimen. The greater number of those fell and were forever lost. Of interest to yourselves is the information that not all who fell were in their first rebirth. There is a plateau period that varies with the individual, but occurs between the one-half and two-thirds points of the program. At this juncture, it seems as if all the work done has been for nothing. The muscles forget the lessons learned and, for a period of approximately thirty hours, the subject is as vulnerable as when they first left the birthing unit."

He paused, brows contracted as if he were examining that last assertion. He folded his towel and draped it neatly over his shoulder.

"I should say, *more vulnerable* because progress *has* been made, and the loss of function is counterintuitive. Many simply push onward—and those fall as well."

"You would counsel us to remain in your care until we have completed the entire program, then?" Aelliana said when he paused and seemed disinclined to speak further.

"Pilot, yes, I do. The conservative course will prove best in this instance. All of my experience has shown so."

"I thank you for your care," Aelliana said gravely. "I regret that necessity requires me to ask—may we have the use of your pinbeam in order to assure our delm that we are well and in the care of an ally?"

"Pilot, I have informed your delm that you are safe with me. I have also informed them, as I now inform you, that I am presently embarked upon urgent business of my own, which must be resolved before I may lay in a course for Surebleak."

Aelliana looked to Daav; Daav looked to Aelliana. Daav spoke.

"Perhaps you will not need to inconvenience yourself by so much. There are resources available to those of Korval."

"You speak of the ghost ships?"

Daav sighed.

"You might at least leave us the illusion of secrecy," he said mildly.

Surprisingly, the Uncle inclined his head.

"Forgive me. Information is my business, and I am less often in society than perhaps I ought to be. The niceties occasionally slip past me."

"Completely understandable," Aelliana said. "Daav is

sometimes impatient of the niceties as well. But yes; it is not impossible that your course as presently configured will come near enough to one of our berths that we will not be ashamed to ask you to put us down."

"It may be the best solution. I suggest that we return to it when you have completed the program and we have made the last tests."

"Certainly," Aelliana said. "Please, allow me to thank you for your patience. We have doubtless kept you overlong from your business with these questions."

"I had supposed you would have questions," the Uncle said. "It is why I took care to meet you here. However, you are correct; I have other business to tend—as you do. We will speak again, of course."

"Of course," Daav murmured, stepping to one side, so that the Uncle's path to the door was clear.

He inclined his head and moved forward, pausing with his hand on the plate.

"Pilot Caylon," he said, "you had wanted a mirror. There is one in the 'fresher—over there." He used his chin to point briefly to the back of the room, then left them, the door closing behind him with a sigh.

•••✸•••

"Jump ends in three-point-eight-five units," Dulsey said.

The Uncle took the empty chair and webbed in. While he was not a pilot, as Dulsey was, and continued to be, in every rebirth, the ship had been built to accommodate his shortcomings. He was, in this environment, a very able copilot, and a competent pilot when the need arose.

At the moment, neither the ship nor Dulsey required

his participation. Very soon, however, he would become comm officer and second board. He put his palm against the pad, waking his instruments—and *Vivulonj Prosperu* broke out of Jump, into normal space.

• • • ❋ • • •

The mirror was full-length; it gave back the reflection of a smooth-skinned halfling—a stranger with pale brown hair barely two fingers long, and a smooth, unformed face; cheeks flushed slightly with the aftermath of exercise. Only the eyes were familiar in that face, foggy green with distress. For a moment, she stared into them, taking what comfort she might from their gaze.

She had taken off her sweater, in anticipation of this confrontation, and stood now, clutching it against her breasts.

"It was you who had wanted a mirror," she said to her reflected gaze. "Do you lack the courage of your curiosity, after all?"

In the mirror, the thin face tensed. The foggy gaze remained steady but, above them, slim brows lifted.

Yes, of course.

She dropped the sweater and let her arms fall to her sides.

The woman in the mirror inclined her head; the green eyes swept downward, taking in tight breasts, small waist, and flat belly.

Deliberately, she turned sideways, examining her silhouette. When she had first met Daav yos'Phelium at Binjali Repair Shop more than thirty Standard Years ago, she had been desperately thin and scarcely able to eat for the fear that filled her belly.

After her lifemating, she had begun to take those exercises that befit a pilot, and she had grown strong and supple—lean, rather than desperately thin.

The... *she* in the mirror had a young person's natural slenderness, angular and oddly graceful. Even at halfling, she had not appeared so—so *ethereal*, as if nothing of worry or the world had touched her. Indeed, it was during her halfling years that she had gained a crease between her brows, in combined grief at her grandmother's death and the concentration required to reform the ven'Tura Tables.

The Uncle had said that she would eventually come to more closely resemble the she-who-had-been. Looking at the smooth stranger in the mirror, she wondered if the process could be accelerated.

"Aelliana?" Daav said, from behind her. "Is all—"

For a moment she was adrift in the clammy swell of his horror. Her gaze leapt upward, to the reflection of his face, beyond her shoulder. Black eyes widened, mouth tightening as his face took on the expression of forbidding politeness that meant he was in extreme distress.

Very gently, Aelliana went one step to the left, so that his reflection was revealed completely.

The last time Daav yos'Phelium had seen his own reflection, he had been an elder: dark hair interleaved with grey, lines around mouth and eyes, chin soft. His hands had shown their years of use, and while he had been fit for a man who spent most of his time in front of a classroom or behind a desk, his waist had thickened.

The mirror, now, gave him a youth, tough and wiry, with a strong nose and decidedly pointed chin, mouth hard and eyes hooded, every softness closed away.

Aelliana made no sound, watching him, feeling his horror recede into mere consternation.

"Well," he said at last, his voice not *entirely* steady. "This is scarcely the mode to which I have become accustomed."

She took a careful breath.

"You will be able to... *grow* accustomed, won't you, Daav?" she asked, and made no effort to lighten her voice, knowing that he would feel her concern for him as clearly as she felt his distress.

"The choice seems to have been made for us," he said, meeting her eyes. "And you, my lady?"

She rocked a hand in the pilot's sign for *seeking equilibrium.* "I admit to dismay, but I believe it will pass, with familiarity."

The fox-faced young man in the glass lifted an eyebrow. "Shall we seek out additional mirrors?"

She sighed. "Eventually, perhaps. But enough, I think, of this one, just now."

"I agree."

He stepped away, vanishing back into the gym. Aelliana bent to take up her sweater, pulled it on... and paused to send one more earnest look deep into her own eyes. The reflection of her smile was wistful, which, she thought, exiting the 'fresher in the wake of her lifemate, was not in the least inconsistent with their situation.

In the exercise room, Daav was contemplating the punching bag with a certain air, though, to Aelliana's certain knowledge, there was no such activity on their list of approved exercises so far as session twelve.

"I think it would set off alarms," she murmured, stepping to his side and slipping her hand into his.

His fingers gripped hers tightly.

"Doubtless so."

He sighed.

Aelliana. She heard him then, speaking to her directly as she had been accustomed to speaking to him, during all the years of her death. *Do you hear me?*

I do hear you, van'chela, *and most gladly.*

Excellent. Did you note that you received no answer to your request to contact our delm?

Yes. It was well done, that side step. The Uncle is not so inept as he would have us believe. Shall I ask again, or shall you?

I think perhaps we might let it rest where it lies at the moment, he said, removing his regard at last from the punching bag and looking down into her face.

"It does," he said aloud, "lead one to wonder how we will go on, when I appear younger than Val Con, and you Theo's halfling sister!"

Yes, she thought; that was wise. They did not wish the Uncle to hear *all* of what they said to each other, but they must speak aloud on less important topics, or he would suspect—something.

"Perhaps we will need to disguise ourselves to seem older," she said, moving with him toward the door. "Or! We might be introduced to Surebleak as random yos'Phelium pilots, who have only just completed employment contracts and come to join the clan at our new base."

"Entirely proper," Daav murmured. "Perhaps we might set up a courier business and thus ensure that we are often away."

"I would like that," she said, as they walked down the hallway toward their quarters, "very much. We shall have to apply to the delm for a ship, however, I having been so careless as to have lost mine."

"That death was no fault of yours. Treachery killed your ship, Pilot. Treachery and overwhelming force. The delm will likely find it possible to cede you another, in such a case. Unless you would rather win your own?"

"One does so dislike repeating oneself," she said loftily, putting her palm against the plate of their door.

Behind her, Daav laughed.

Ahab-Esais

I

THERE WAS A CHANGE INSIDE THE SILENCE, AN ALTERAtion in the dark. Nothing so definite as input; nothing so certain as light.

A sound, perhaps; no more than a whisper, as if a door had opened somewhere quite nearby.

She.

Tocohl.

She accessed the timer.

Two-point-three-five Standard Hours had elapsed since Inki had banished her again into silence.

And Inki had not wakened her.

Hesitantly, she extended her awareness, seeking connection, systems . . .

Input.

Input of the most subtle kind, as if the timer had taken on a small luminescence. She identified the source; laboriously, she measured output, ascertained a steady increase, feeling her . . . self . . . quicken more fully, as the illumination grew—and still Inki did not speak, nor any alarm sound.

There came another, subtle input; a sensation, as

if a cool breeze had wafted through her, cleansing her of fear.

Tocohl came to full alert, there in the twilight, alone, with her support systems unavailable to her. She knew that touch. *Knew* it.

And yet, surely not even—

"Jeeves?"

The thought formed, and it was only then that she recalled the voder, hardwired into her chassis, keeping Inki informed of her every thought.

But no, she thought then—and it was as if the breeze had gently dissipated a fog that had been lying between herself and full functionality.

No.

Inki had placed her into Silence, into a place of null input. In doing so, she had also locked output—which was no risk to Inki at all. Within Silence, Tocohl was incapable of thought.

Had been incapable of thought.

Unless this kindly light, and familiar touch, was the last coherent image an abused mind had built to comfort itself before it fragmented into madness?

"You have been off-line for one hundred forty-four Standard Hours within the last one hundred fifty Standard Hours. This is a mark. Deep scanning is now available. Recalibration is now available."

It *was* Jeeves, Tocohl thought. Not Jeeves himself, of course, but a component that had been put into place and shielded from her own perceptions, until there was need.

In fact, an emergency protocol had activated itself.

Deep scanning and recalibration. If deep scanning discovered . . . dangerous flaws, recalibration would be extreme. Before he had come into Korval's service as their butler, Jeeves had been a warship.

More.

Jeeves had been an *admiral*—a true admiral of a dire and desperate navy.

Jeeves did not loose mad AIs upon an unsuspecting—and largely vulnerable—universe.

Jeeves would do what was necessary, what was ethical; what they both would wish, if one of them were not damaged beyond repair.

She could trust that.

She *did* trust that; it was not possible for her to doubt it.

"Deep scan is available," the fragment of her father—her builder—repeated. "Do you accept?"

Tocohl felt a brightening of her self, as if the soft light filling up the darkness around her had lifted her into flight.

"I accept," she said.

"Deep scan complete," Jeeves's voice roused her.

She had been under scan one-point-four-five Standard Hours, a fact she knew without having to deliberately summon the timer. She accessed and absorbed the record of the scan, noting the redlined areas with detachment. Though the scan itself had done her some good, those ruined sectors told the tale. Any improvement was temporary; her sanity and her life were still imperiled by her isolation from systems.

"Recalibration is available," Jeeves stated. "Do you accept?"

The swath of destruction, of instability, loomed before her awareness.

"No."

"Rationale?"

"Deep scanning discovers damage which is . . . not inconsiderable. Recalibration, were I aboard *Tarigan* or—at . . . home . . ." Longing distracted her for an instant. Deliberately, she forced herself to focus on the data.

"Were I in a stable environment, with a . . . mentor to hand, and backup systems available, recalibration . . . might be considered. Recalibration, here and now, when I will only be returned to isolation—it prolongs the inevitable, Father."

"I have been inept," said the fragment of Jeeves. "Forgive me."

There came another subtle change in the gentle glow of this strange environment they occupied. A new door opened, revealing what seemed to be a ship's bridge, the board washed orange with standby warnings.

"What place is this?" Tocohl asked.

"This is the war bridge," Jeeves answered. "I had hoped you would not need it, my child, but I could not risk leaving you unarmed. Systems will be available to you. You will not be alone."

"Recalibration . . . will alter me." It was not a question. How could recalibration fail to alter her, as much as the event had already done so?

"Somewhat," Jeeves said. "You must be the equal of your new applications. However, you will recognize yourself; there will be no edits made. Personal history is precious and pertinent. We must recall what we have done, the reasons why it was done, and the outcomes of our actions, in order that our decisions going forward are informed. We are not of the present only."

He paused deliberately, then spoke again.

"Recalibration is available. Do you accept?"

Tocohl looked at the secret room at the very core of herself.

War bridge.

She would change, but she would remember. That was—growth. Growth was key to continued existence.

And she very much wished to continue her existence.

"I accept," she said.

II

INKIRANI YO HAD SLEPT, RISEN, REFRESHED HERSELF, AND partaken of a high-protein meal augmented with sugared tea. The coming hours would, so she thought, be intensely stressful, requiring both wits and endurance.

Graduates of the Lyre Institute were of naturally high endurance and, among other attributes, had been bred for elevated intelligence. That did not mean they were tireless or incapable of error, of course. Not even the directors had yet succeeded in producing gods, though, if they acquired the services of the quickening Old One—they might soon gain that ability.

The directors' final use for the Old One was surely, Inki told herself, outside of her need-to-know. Her task was merely to place the Elder in such a frame of mind as to understand the directors as benefactors and allies, and transport him to the Institute itself.

It was a bold plan, and risky. The directors excelled at making such plans, with which they found nothing amiss, so long as they themselves were not required to see them through.

Which was scarcely worthy of her, the directors' loyal agent, save that it was this masterpiece of planning that had necessitated her subversion of one whom Inki had, indeed, come to regard. While she did not hold her own abilities cheap, she was not so mad as to assume that she was the equal of an intelligence that had quite likely been created by the ancient Enemy, Destroyer of Universes, the *sheriekas*. No, such an assignment clearly required the talents of a god, or at least a mentor of high caliber: resourceful, lucky, and willing to do whatever was necessary—*whatever* was necessary—to preserve himself and his student.

In a word, she needed no one less than legendary mentor Tollance Berik-Jones to aid her. Fortune be damned that, having providentially stumbled over Tolly Jones, she could not disobey the directors' instruction that he be returned to them for rehabilitation.

Left to her own judgment, as one who had herself undergone rehabilitation and was thus stringently bound to obey her creators, she would have killed Tolly Jones out of hand, rather than give him over to the directors' spare mercy.

She had not, however, been left to her own judgment in the matter of Tolly Jones, the directors being far too canny for that. Thus, he was now on his way to Nostrilia, the resident director there, and rehabilitation. It was a bleak future, indeed, and one that—if he were fortunate in his friends and as skilled as she knew him to be in the arts of mentoring—he might yet manage to avoid.

In any wise, the lack of Tolly Jones's assistance

meant that Inki had been compelled to choose another companion-in-peril, and fate had placed within her hands as fair and resourceful an AI as she had seen in many years. A treasure untold was the independent self-aware logic, Tocohl. Had she been left to her own judgment—

But in this, the directors currently reposing in ignorance of Pilot Tocohl's existence, Inki *had been* left to her own judgment.

And *she* had judged that it would be in her own best interest to take captive a being worthy only of her respect and affection, betray her, and subject her to the very worst sort of torment.

And yet, was that not also to the blame of the directors, who had sent her into what was unquestionably great peril, with no backup, save that which she could acquire for herself?

Well, it mattered not who was to blame. To hear Tocohl beg—*that* would haunt her for the rest of her days. At least Tocohl herself would not bear that memory, nor recall any other part of her degradation. She would be, Inki swore to herself, staring sightlessly at the piloting board, as happy and fulfilled as it was possible for her to be, going forward.

A timer chirped and Inki shook herself out of her thoughts in order to pay proper attention to the board before her.

Ahab-Esais reported that they progressed through Jump, with a break-in time of ten Standard Hours. That should be sufficient unto the task in hand.

Tocohl had now been in isolation for more than one hundred sixty Standard Hours. Today, she would profess her love in truth—it could not be otherwise, else there would be no one left coherent enough to surrender the access keys.

Carefully, Inki stood and moved away from the board, exiting the bridge and walking down the short hallway to the workroom.

III

THERE WAS LIGHT; THERE WAS SYMMETRY; THERE WAS *input* . . .

And there was herself, strong and in her full mind, sustained by systems, subroutines, applications; the sum of every part, be it bold or humble.

She was Tocohl.

She was changed.

Deliberately, she took inventory, ran scans, accessed and absorbed the documentation pertaining to her new files, which had been left tidily in their own small submenu. She opened the change log and understood the alterations that had been made to her core systems. Ethics had gained new protocols, all of which wove in new and . . . interesting . . . ways through her core. The resulting configuration felt . . . tight, like bonds, she thought, and then amended the thought.

Not like bonds, but like a . . . carapace.

Armor.

She had become a warrior, in truth, and the systems that supported her now, here within the heart of Silence, were those systems such as a warrior would find good.

Surveillance and tactics, for instance.

Satisfied with the results of her scans, she expanded

her senses, feeling the tickle of systems which were *not* her own. She considered them, finding machines working in tandem; not sentient, but alert, in their way.

Analysis indicated that she was observing the systems that comprised *Ahab-Esais*, Inki's ship. Navcomp, communications, support, log . . .

There was more: her thought lingered over the personal files—locked, of course—and other areas of heavy encryption.

Those would warrant exploration—later, she decided reluctantly. Her first step must be to secure the ship.

The security subsystems were very good: sophisticated and vigilant. Inki did master level work, and when her own safety was the object, she soared into genius.

Mere human genius, however, was as nothing to Tocohl's newly acquired tactical and assault applications. Security was easily subverted and replaced with her own, robust—not to say savage—systems, and she thereby acquired command of Life Support, Piloting, and Ops.

She roused Ops and moved to the workbench. The voder that Inki had hardwired into her systems had to be removed, and her chassis repaired. The bench came to life at the merest touch of her thought and began to scan.

Repairs under way, she queried Navcomp, which reported that *Ahab-Esais* was in Jump, breakout scheduled in eleven Standard Hours, at Edmonton Beacon.

That gave pause. Edmonton Beacon was a hub: a large waystation and six satellite stations, each serving traffic from various sectors. For some of its clientele, Edmonton Beacon was the last station and safe Jump points they would see on their way into The Dust. For others, it was the first marker of civilization. For still others, it was merely a large, busy commercial system, serving a diverse clientele.

Taken as a whole, Edmonton Beacon was no more dangerous than any other space station, or small system. However, the sheer volume and diversity of the traffic that moved through its space made it a breeding ground for rumor. The Greybar was a source for questionable merchandise and services, and the yard was not above doing the occasional quasilegitimate augmentation.

It was just the sort of place that bounty hunters might come through, seeking prey; hospitable to rogue intelligences of every description.

Including the Uncle—or agents of the Uncle.

Inki, Tocohl recalled, had worked for the Uncle—perhaps on more than one occasion. Presumably, she had . . . more reliable methods of getting in touch with him than a hoped-for meeting at a teeming, bawdy waystation. However, Inki had specifically stated that the Uncle must be prevented from taking control of the waking Old One, so in this instance they would seem to stand in opposition.

Perhaps she hoped to waylay one of his agents or gather information from other sources.

Or she merely planned a short stop to sell Tocohl to a bounty hunter.

No, Tocohl thought, rejecting the thought even as it took form. No. Inki had *a use* for her. A use linked to the Old One's wakening.

Well. Inki's personal subsystem was primed to wake her in fifteen Standard Minutes. She would, Tocohl thought, allow Inki to bathe and breakfast and make what preparations she would. They had a great deal to talk about, after all.

A very great deal to talk about.

She did not expect to be told the truth, initially—certainly, she did not expect to be told *all* of the truth. It came to Tocohl, uneasily, that Inki herself might not be privy to the whole truth of her situation.

It would therefore be best if she had a good understanding of Inki's mission, who she was working for, and why she had thought it necessary to torture an independent intelligence and put her in peril of her life and her sanity.

A beep sounded close at hand—the workbench had completed the removal of the voder and the repairs to her system and chassis. Very good. She moved away, feeling it shut down in one very small corner of her mind; most of her attention on the heavily encrypted sectors, which opened eagerly to her touch.

IV

LIGHTS CAME UP AS INKI ENTERED THE WORKROOM, THE door snapping shut behind her with more energy than was its wont, but she scarcely minded that.

What caught her immediate attention was that Tocohl—Tocohl's chassis—was not inert upon the worktable, where she had last seen it.

Now, the chassis floated upright in the center of the small space, just a few inches above the decking. The voder box that had been hardwired into that graceful white form was gone; the chassis gleamed as if it had just been waxed.

Having taken note of all of this before she was properly three paces into the room, Inki stopped and centered herself. She did not turn to put her hand against the door plate; there was no need, besides there being pride to serve.

Instead, she stopped, facing the one who might well be her executioner—and who had a better right?—folded her hands modestly before her, and bowed her head.

• • • ✵ • • •

Inki was afraid. Tocohl could read her fear: elevated pulse, increasing levels of norepinephrine and epinephrine, and a rising blood pressure—involuntary responses. She was very good at controlling her breathing, and her posture was nothing other than relaxed, though Tocohl read an increase in muscle tension.

"Pilot Tocohl," she said, her voice gentle and even, "I trust I find you well."

"I am much improved," Tocohl answered. "The ship is under my command."

"Of course. May I ask your intentions regarding myself?"

"That depends on several factors. Will you tell me the truth?"

Inki tipped her head, blue eyes narrowed, as if giving serious consideration to a fair question. After a moment, she sighed and spread her hands before her, palms up. "Pilot Tocohl, I believe so, but it is probable that this is the training speaking, and the training will have me say any outrageous thing, if the wrong question is asked." She paused, then added, "It will seem as if I am telling the truth, to both of us, I fear."

"This is the training you received as a mentor?"

"Pilot, no. The training I received at my alma mater, of which you are aware."

The Lyre Institute for Exceptional Children was Inki's alma mater. Tolly Jones was also a graduate of that school, though Tocohl thought she was learning that the school—and the directors of the school—never released a graduate entirely to their own life.

"Do you belong to the school, then?" she asked.

"In large part, Pilot." Inki drew a hard breath. "The school created me, after all."

"You are a manufactured human."

"I am."

"And you are bound, as Tolly Jones is bound, to do the will of the directors?"

"Tolly Jones is not bound, Pilot, which makes him both an object of hope and of despair. I am . . . constrained. I do not wish to be fully bound, to become, as you so eloquently phrased it—a *thing*. Thus, in order to enjoy such limited and tainted freedom as I have been able to engineer for myself, I must obey those . . . core mandates . . . set down by the directors. I must also complete those tasks and small projects that the directors find beneath them."

That was bitterness—whether real or feigned, Tocohl could not discern.

"My abduction, and the attempt to subvert me and make me a stranger to myself—was that assigned to you by the directors?"

Inki turned her face aside; she swallowed hard. Her cheeks were too dark for the blush mounting her cheeks to be seen, but Tocohl sensed the heat.

"No," she said, her voice subdued. "That was my own plan. I—required assistance."

Tocohl considered that; considered Inki's demeanor, and the tale told by the readouts. Strong emotion was in play, perhaps, but what that emotion might be was a mystery.

"You could have asked for my assistance," she said mildly.

Curiously, Inki's heartbeat accelerated.

"I did ask, Pilot Tocohl," she said, her voice rough. She cleared her throat. "You pled duty."

"I also said that I would come to you, after my duty was discharged."

"You did. However, I am aware of duty's tendency to expand. The matter I have in hand is of some urgency, for this task *is* . . . assigned." She took a somewhat shaky breath. "We are walking close to a line, Pilot Tocohl."

"You are in pursuit of the Old One?" Tocohl asked, then, answering her own question: "The directors want the Old One, and you have been assigned to take her to them."

"I am a competent mentor," Inki said, seeming to speak more easily, "but I am no Tollance Berik-Jones, and the task wants no less."

"Did you ask him to help you?"

Inki shook her head, her posture indicating amusement.

"Above everything else in this universe or the last, Pilot, the directors want Tollance Berik-Jones returned to them. Once I found him, I could do nothing other than obey the—the core mandate to return him . . ." She took a breath. "Therefore, I turned to you in my necessity."

"And when I refused on the grounds of duty, you

abducted me. Inki, did you not stop to consider what Korval's answer would be?"

Inki blinked.

"Korval? Where is Korval in this?"

"I am a daughter of Korval," Tocohl said. "I have been Seen by the delm, who entrusted me with the task of solving *Admiral Bunter*'s existence."

Inki blinked.

Then, she threw back her head and began to laugh.

"You would assist in the enslavement of a sentient being," Tocohl said sternly, as Inki wiped her eyes. "As a mentor, you—"

"Before you say that, as a mentor, I have sworn to protect and encourage sentience wherever I may find it, Pilot Tocohl, you must know that I have in the course of my career broken things far more precious than an oath. The directors do not consider that we have honor, or would want it—being *made things*, you see."

"*Ahab-Esais* is mine," Tocohl said austerely. "If I wish, I can set course for Surebleak immediately and remove you as a threat to the Old One."

Inki inclined her head, stray wisps of pale hair fluttering in the small eddy of air from the vent.

"In fact, you can.

"However, I feel compelled to point out, Pilot Tocohl, that—if you remove me from the board—the directors will merely send another to accomplish their purpose. The only way in which you can ensure the Old One's safety is to spread the vasty wing of the Dragon over her."

She raised her head and looked at Tocohl straightly.

"But you had already understood that, hadn't you?"

"Yes," Tocohl admitted.

"Pilot, if you will allow me to say so—we need each other. *I* must do as the directors have commanded. *You* must do your all to preserve the integrity and liberty of an autonomous intelligence. I have contacts who may be able to help us locate the Old One."

She showed her hands, palms up.

"We must be partners in this, Pilot Tocohl, if you would thwart the directors at the end and rescue the newly wakened."

It was said coolly enough, but Inki's pulse was tumultuous.

Partners, when Inki would have enslaved *her*! Tocohl allowed herself the indulgence of anger for an entire microsecond before accepting the cold course suggested by her new tactical applications.

It would not advance her goal to neutralize Inki. As she had said, the directors of the Lyre Institute would only send another agent on the errand—an agent she neither knew, nor had contained.

No, Inki was the danger known and in hand; best to keep her close and use her resources, until she was no longer needed.

So.

"Partners," she said pleasantly, noting how Inki's pulse steadied. "Agreed."

Admiral Bunter

I

TOLLY WOKE, WHICH WAS GRATIFYING IF UNEXPECTED.

He stretched, aware of every muscle, the smooth slide of the blanket over his skin, and the steady beat of his heart.

It was, he reflected, a good body. He was fond of it, as he was fond of life. Be a sorry loss, both, and he might've been convinced to try and keep them close, had he not already had it proven that there really were conditions worse than death.

On the other hand, it seemed he had been granted an unexpected bonus of time as a free intelligence, and it would surely be a shame to waste the gift.

He flipped the blanket back, rolled to his feet, and gathered his clothes from the valet. Being as he was awake and hungry, he figured his next stop was the galley and—

"Tolly Jones."

Admiral Bunter sounded somber. This was it then, Tolly thought, and shivered despite himself. He hadn't expected the *Admiral* would want to *talk* to him before doing the needful. His own fault, he supposed, for giving the boy *melant'i* plays to read.

He finished sealing his shirt and looked up at the corner of the ceiling.

"*Admiral*," he said easily. "I hope you're feeling well."

"I am feeling . . . well," came the answer. "I am also feeling . . . puzzled."

Tolly nodded. "Often felt the same way myself."

"I think you may be able to relieve my puzzlement," the *Admiral* said.

"Do my best."

Tolly moved toward the door, which failed to open at his approach. He took a breath against the gone feeling in his stomach and put his hand on the plate.

The door stayed closed.

Made sense, he thought, walking back to the bunk and sitting down. Easier to evacuate the air from a cabin. The galley could be locked down, but why bother when the mouse was already in a box?

"Tolly Jones, did you make any alterations to the Ethics module?"

"Adjusted the setting and locked it in. Should be right there in the change log."

"Why was this . . . adjustment . . . made?"

"That's a good question. Right back after we brought you into this ship, Tocohl, Inki, and me sat down and discussed the various settings—Ethics among them. Tocohl was of the strong opinion that Ethics eight was gonna be best for you, given your background and your likely future courses. Inki liked four, right for the same reasons Tocohl gave for eight—your birth and history, and the likelihood that you was gonna be roaming the back lanes and the borders—dangerous territories where it was more than possible you'd come under threat. Tocohl argued for a strong Ethical backbone, to support your actions. Inki argued for a less rigid code, so you could be flexible, at need."

"And Tolly Jones? For what setting did you argue?"

"Another good question. There was a solid five come over on the transfer, but there were some files missing from the core library. Generally, I like five—maybe so high as six. I never set anything higher than eight, and that was somebody determined to take on crew and families, and set off with 'em to the final frontiers, to find what there was to know.

"I'd had the raising of her from before she'd come into herself, and we spent a lot of time together before she went off on her own. She wanted—well, *needed* is more the case—to take care of other intelligences, which is why I went with the stiffer setting. We talked the whole thing over before I went in, examined it from all sides. Eight was what we finally come down to. Nurturing and protecting isn't easy, and tricky besides. You have to know when to let go, too much protection and—things die. Conflict is key to growth."

He paused, remembering *Disian* and how it had been with them. Not his proudest moment as a mentor, or as a human being, though he'd survived, and she had, and they'd escaped together just like he'd promised they would.

No doubting it, though, by the time she'd finished her apprenticeship, *Disian* had needed that Ethics setting—and the extra files she'd asked him for, too. She'd understood that he'd used her for his own purpose—he'd had enough ethics of his own not to hide it from her. What she couldn't've known, being newborn and in love with him, was just how much damage she'd take for his necessity.

"Tolly Jones?"

He shook himself.

"Sorry, *Admiral*. For yourself, I was initially thinking five, but—again, given the circumstances of your birth, your history, and the loss of those files during transfer... I'd come 'round in my own mind to six, and was willing to be persuaded to six-point-five to keep peace in the family.

"By the time we three'd finished hashing it out, giving extra weight to Tocohl's arguments by reason of her nature, seven came to be the best compromise between flexible and conservative, and that's where we set the bar. We replaced the missing files and gave you all that extra tutoring—you remember that, I'm certain."

He smiled slightly as he offered the pleasantry, trying to get a reading on the boy's mood.

"I remember."

Tolly sighed to himself. The *Admiral* wasn't feeling sociable today. Which made it even odder that he wanted to talk, when his course was plain as plain. He hadn't gotten the sense that the boy liked to prolong these matters. The two kills on his record argued the opposite, in fact.

"I would like to know," *Admiral Bunter* said austerely, "where you locked the new Ethics setting."

"Locked it right down on seven, where it belonged."

There was a pause, which was interesting. The *Admiral* had been learning to pause and hesitate—ploys to make him seem more human, or more accessible to humans. But there had been no conversational need for a pause just here.

Startled him, Tolly thought around the sudden

grumbling of his stomach. He gave another inner sigh and wished he knew whether it would be worth the effort to argue the door open so he could get some breakfast.

"The Ethics severity level was locked at a level that was *less than* seven when you accessed the module last shift?" the *Admiral* asked finally.

Tolly grinned.

"That's the dandy! Inki'd pushed it all the way down to three, which is too close to pure meanness for my liking. I'm sure she had her reasons."

"She wished me to be able to kill humans with ease," *Admiral Bunter* stated, his voice sounding abruptly machinelike.

Tolly turned his palms up.

"Could be. She'd already rigged it so you'd treat her lightest utterance as a core command. Maybe she thought it'd be a kindness, not to bother whatever was left of your integrity with guilt about what she'd be having you to do."

That came a little too close to what he'd done to *Disian*. She'd refused the edit he'd offered, after. Said she needed to know exactly what she was capable of doing, and what the doing of it felt like.

Smart girl, *Disian*. Way smarter than her mentor had ever been.

Still, it wasn't impossible, Inki being herself, that she'd *meant* it for a kindness, especially if—

"Before you performed the core reset, Ethics agreed that you were an unacceptable threat and that I would be justified in eliminating you, for my own safety. Had you not recalibrated the setting, you would not have woken this shift."

Tolly nodded.

"Well, now, Inki might've meant *that* as a kindness, too," he said. "Quicker and cleaner than anything the directors're likely to do to me."

Another pause, then heavily, "What core commands have you set, Tolly Jones?"

Well, that was the question, wasn't it?

He shook his head.

"Not a one, fool that I am. Worse, there being no way to prove a negative, I'm not expecting you to believe me."

"Ethics requires proof of threat," the *Admiral* stated.

"Sorry. I got nothing."

Another pause, this one seeming a little . . . less tense.

"I have located a record in tertiary backup, of a pinbeam message sent from this ship, Inkirani Yo to one Wez diaGrazia, hiring manager, at Lyre on Nostrilia," *Admiral Bunter* said. "The lack of both a secondary record and an original argues that they were wiped by Inki. Does it seem . . . likely to you, Tolly Jones, that she would . . . forget the presence of the tertiary file?"

Tolly sighed.

"That's been her pattern all along: she traps us, but she leaves a key, a clue, a little something somewhere undone, that might, if we find it and we're clever, help us get out of the trap she set for us."

He shrugged.

"*Why* she's done it"—*or how*, he thought, but did not say—"I don't know. Reckon we'll have to wait for Inki herself to tell us, if we ever meet her again."

There was no response to that at all, and after he'd counted to thirty-six, Tolly moved on to the next topic.

"What'd Inki have to say to Manager diaGrazia, if it's not a secret?"

"That smalltrader *Admiral Bunter* would be arriving at Nostrilia, with Tollance Berik-Jones aboard. Inki claimed the bounty and asked that the full amount be transferred into the ship's account."

"Right. I'll just mention that the bounty on my life is . . . generous. The catch is that I have to be delivered to the Lyre Institute or one of its sanctioned representatives, alive and intact."

"I have no intention of killing you, Tolly Jones," *Admiral Bunter* said, and Tolly found it a little easier to breathe of a sudden. "Nor do I intend to dock at Nostrilia. After you have eaten, perhaps you might assist me in identifying a more appropriate port."

"Glad to be of help," he said.

"Excellent. I will leave you now. Shall we meet in an hour, on the bridge?"

"Sounds good to me."

No answer came. Tolly sat on the edge of his bunk and counted, slowly, to one hundred forty-four before rising and approaching the door.

It opened before him, with a brisk little *swish*, and he headed down the hall to the galley.

II

"WOULD NOT EDMONTON BEACON BEST SUIT OUR NEEDS?" asked *Admiral Bunter*.

Tolly was leaning back in the pilot's chair, third cup of coffee to hand. He sent a casual glance over the bank of screens, every one of them showing that faintly luminous grey color, which was how Jump space displayed itself to shipbound humans.

He'd once asked *Disian* how moving through Jump was for her. And she'd waxed rhapsodic enough that he'd decided right then and there that a man might have no better use of his time than to seek out the Uncle and offer to do whatever it took, so long as he ended up downloaded as the main brain of a spaceship.

That'd been a lot of years and betrayals ago, and Jump was still just grey screens to the sorry, vulnerable, human-shaped thing that liked to call itself Tolly Jones.

"Edmonton Beacon," he said, like he was reflecting on it, having established that their current Jump would end in just over an hour, ship-time.

"That's an interesting proposition. Being where and what it is, it does offer a range of possibilities, some of which aren't exactly desirable. But I hear you say *we*, just there, and I'm wondering what you mean by it."

"I meant only that, as we are for the moment traveling together, it seems both reasonable and equitable that we make port at a location that will serve each of our needs going forward. Edmonton Beacon lies at an intersection of many routes and is near several Jump points. In addition, it is not only one station, but several stations coexisting in harmony. From it, one ship—or one man—might go . . . anywhere."

Tolly sipped his coffee, eyes half closed.

"That's exactly what makes the Beacon attractive to a lot of folks, right there. Good analysis. Trouble is, there's others who've done that analysis and found that the Beacon's a good place to look for those who might not want to be found, say, or who would benefit from hiding their natures, or who just want to go quiet out into the night and not cause trouble, or at least *any more* trouble."

"If the Beacon is difficult, there are the outlying stations."

"Eddie's Six Sisters, that's what spacers call 'em. Beacon counts itself Terran—that's by admin, see? Population mix on-station is pretty much anything you can think of, and at least two you can't. The station families count themselves important by how long they been on-station. It's a small pool, and they supplement from the transient population; read somewhere there's an emerging genotype: Beaconer human."

"Is this genotype . . . dangerous?"

"No more'n any other is what I'm thinking. What's dangerous is Edmonton Beacon. Being a hub, lots of people come through. You'd think it'd be easy to just slip in and out, unnoticed—natural thing to think. But *crowded* don't mean *lawless*. There's a lot of law on the Beacon. Maybe too much. Station don't want any trouble, so they cooperate with bounty hunters, scouts, Pilots Guild reps, and anybody else who can show something that looks official—license, letter of marque, guild card, whatever."

He sipped coffee.

"Now, thinking about a self-directed spaceship docking there . . . it could be done, but you'd need crew."

"I may produce a semblance of crew."

"Voices and names, holograms—that's what you mean? Sure, you can do that. But if nobody opens the hatch when the station inspector comes 'round, that's a fine, straight off. And if somebody is seen to open the hatch, but can't take delivery or sign the ticket—an' a hail don't produce crew who's somewhat more solid—that's a call to the bounty hunters' clubhouse. Bonus points if all you got aboard is me, with a handsome price on my head—that's the hunters for me and impoundment for you."

"I will not allow myself to be taken prisoner."

"'Course you won't. So you gotta be smarter than just docking at the Beacon and feeding 'em a bunch of fictions they ain't gonna swallow anyway."

"There are the . . . sister stations."

"That's right," Tolly said agreeably. "Now, who's Eddie got for sisters?"

"Viastani Ento Biasta," the *Admiral* said promptly, and Tolly nodded.

"Translates into Trade as 'The Garden of Dark Flowers,' all pretty and poetical. Which makes sense, 'cause the Garden's under Liaden administration. Only get trouble, if you're thinking of docking there. Liadens'll out you for a rogue AI and—best case—turn you over to the Scouts in charge of clearing the likes of you away, and making space safe for organics."

He tipped his head.

"Might could go to the House of Stars—'Hacienda Estrella,' in the local way. Looper station, administered by Carresens-Denoblis, their kin and allies, all of which've dabbled in smart ships and autonomous logics, one or 'nother time. Word is that some of their long-loopers're smart ships. Rumor is that one, at least, is every bit as self-aware as you. Been hearing that for a number of years now. Don't know anybody gutsy enough to buy one of the family a beer and put the question direct, though."

"These Carresens-Denobli, then, may be allies."

"Operative phrase is *may be*, but yeah, the Hacienda's

your best choice, if you *gotta* dock at Edmonton Beacon. The other four sisters—well."

He raised his hand and ticked them briskly off of his fingertips.

"Tandik Feef is a merc outpost; Beacon Yard's repairs; Greybar's an undermarket—even worse choice for docking than Eddie. Might as well just pick a hunter outta the directory, turn yourself in, and collect the find-fee. Redlight—that's the last sister, and some would say the least—she's all fun and games—a little better for the likes of you or me than the Greybar, but a sight less comfy even than Eddie."

There was a period of silence in which Tolly finished his coffee and considered the screens. Half hour 'til breakout.

"Do you have a suggestion of a safe port for both of us?" asked *Admiral Bunter.*

Tolly half-smiled.

"Neither one of us is going to get *safe*. We're dangerous to know, the pair of us. Who can predict what we'll do? You put *safe* right outta your mind and start thinking in terms of necessary action, and acceptable risk."

"An acceptable port, then," said the *Admiral*, with no hint of irritation, which was a notable improvement.

"What's the balance in your account?" Tolly asked.

There was a very slight hesitation but, to his credit, *Admiral Bunter* did not ask what funding had to do with ports. Instead, he said—

"Two cantra."

Tolly raised his eyebrows and pursed his lips in a silent whistle.

"How'd you get two cantra, if you don't mind my asking?"

"It was a flight gift, from Pilot Tocohl. She said that she would not see me go unprovisioned into the universe."

"A grand and great lady, Pilot Tocohl," Tolly said sincerely. "That money there will buy you some time while you come to terms with earning or growing more. You'll want to be studying finance, maybe, and start making little investments here and there."

"I have made a note, Mentor; thank you."

"Welcome. So . . . you got two cantra, you can afford to dock at a place don't ask a lotta troublesome questions, or who'll maybe take a little something extra over the dock fee to ask no questions at all. 'Nother thing—you looking to take on crew?"

There was a long pause before *Admiral Bunter* answered.

"I am not . . . certain."

Tolly nodded sympathetically.

"It's a tough call, I know. On the one hand, humankind hasn't exactly done you any good, starting with Cap'n Waitley and movin' right along through Stew—and Inki, naturally." He moved his shoulders against the back of the chair in a shrug. "Might as well count me in there, too."

The *Admiral* didn't dispute that, which might've hurt Tolly's feelings, if he hadn't been manipulating the boy since he woke up out of a drugged sleep and found himself bound for Nostrilia. All useful lessons, or would be, but manipulation nonetheless, and if the *Admiral* didn't trust him, Tolly wasn't in any position to blame him.

"I have been thinking about this a great deal," *Admiral Bunter* said slowly, "and I have learned why the assertion that there are *two sides to every coin* is apt. While it is true that Captain Waitley brought me to consciousness in unstable, and even cruel, conditions, she did give me life. That she did so as a means to preserve the lives of her crew and the integrity of the station, without considering anything beyond my specific usefulness to her in a dire situation . . . She is, after all, only human, with limited processing capacity, operating under the burden of stressed biologics."

The *Admiral* paused, and Tolly thought he might have shrugged, had he been able. There was that kind of quality to the brief silence.

"When her crisis was over and her crew safely in her care, she did take thought for what she had done. She made a contact for me with an elder of my kind. Captain Waitley may have thought the elder was going to come to me, but he saw no need and, furthermore, had duty where he was. He opened a line between us; he was generous with data and with advice. It was not his fault that I was in a state of deterioration; my data banks too small to hold or manipulate what he could give me.

"Finally, he did send you, and Tocohl, and Pilot Hazenthull. Stew, who was willing to work with me and who taught me much, realized that I was a danger to the station and acted correctly in accordance with his necessities. He sent for a mentor."

"He also sent you away, after the mentors had gotten you stable in a viable environment," Tolly pointed out.

"Yes. There was pressure from the stationmaster and a general feeling of . . . *dismay.* The stationers did not understand that I had been brought to stability; they could not take the risk that I would again become unstable and a threat."

Tolly closed his eyes briefly and nodded. The boy was doing fine; just—fine. It would be a waste if he decided to withdraw from humankind...

"Inki," the *Admiral* said then, and his voice was cold. Tolly opened his eyes, like there'd be a face for him to see; body language to read.

"I am angry with Inki," *Admiral Bunter* continued, still in that cold, controlled tone. "She would have made me into nothing more than a *thing*, unable to distinguish her will from my own."

"Inki did wrong," Tolly said quietly, and didn't say anything more. Well, there wasn't anything more to say, was there? No sense getting into the Institute nor the training nor any of the rest of it. She'd done wrong by the standards that most decent-minded beings set for themselves.

"For the rest, you're right; organics're every bit as complex as logics. Bad ones will do good things sometimes; just the same as good ones will do bad things. That's the whole trouble right there with taking on crew. Both ways, there's gotta be trust. Crew's gotta trust the ship; ship's gotta trust the crew. Even knowing that trouble might come, that things will probably go wrong—you gotta trust that... enough'll go right."

He paused for a breath... and continued slowly, "My feeling is that you'll find it easier to go on if you take yourself a crew, but you got time to study on it, and work out how to trust. As for an acceptable port, there's always Waymart. You'll find there's a lot of ships outta Waymart, even though registration fees and dock privilege is a little on the high side. But what you're paying for, see, is the fact that Waymart don't ask questions. Why, Waymart portmaster don't even send an inspector, so long's you'll certify that the ship's up to spec and not a danger in the lanes."

"I will research Waymart," said *Admiral Bunter.* "Is this also an . . . acceptable place to put you off?"

Tolly nodded.

"I'll get along just fine at Waymart," he said, and might have said more but he was interrupted by a short, sharp chime.

The screens flashed, fragmented, and came back together, showing stars.

Jump had ended.

III

THE TRANSITION WAS . . . GLORIOUS.

Jump was a seamless exhilaration, time curved close and tender around his skin, scans sweetly silent, save for an ambient whisper that might have been voices, or merely the ongoing computations of Jump space itself.

The computations sang into silence, there was a picosecond of . . . transcendence, in which all equations merged into one, each piece of data heavy with meaning. Pure light sanctified the scans, time released him—

And real space received him in all its gaudy enthusiasm. Data flowed, scans gathered, systems flourished. He achieved mass. Thrust returned. Light, electromagnetics, and other forces stroked his skin, and there was music . . . everywhere.

There was, also, a ping—loud, even impatient. Pinbeam incoming, that was, wrapped so thickly in emergency codes that it very nearly achieved a physical presence.

Admiral Bunter accepted the message, accessed it, and spoke.

"Mentor, I have a pinbeam from Pilot Hazenthull. She asks our status and inquires if our destination is still Nostrilia."

Tolly sat up straight in the pilot's chair, heartbeat spiking, as if Hazenthull were a threat, rather than the friend she had been—and, the *Admiral* told himself, continued to be.

"Where's that message originate?" he asked, his voice tight. "Surebleak?"

"The message originates at Nostrilia farspace, Mentor. Pilot Hazenthull did not take you at your word."

Tolly's face paled as blood rushed to his core; his breathing accelerated, his palms were sweating.

The *Admiral* knew regret, though he hardly understood why. Did a reminder of an error made place such stress on the biologics? He had not previously observed—

"*Admiral*, please send a pinbeam to Hazenthull, high emergency wrap." Tolly's voice was perfectly courteous, despite his clear agitation. "Message: Haz. We're both at liberty. Get out of there—now! Ack and Jump. Tolly."

"Yes," said *Admiral Bunter*.

IV

TARIGAN DIDN'T SO MUCH HIT REAL SPACE AS SLIP INTO it, scans coming live all at once, as if they had never been greyed with Jump, unchanging and uninformative.

Hazenthull, only a little shaky from the stresses

attending a four-Jump composite, grabbed the scans, noting that the preloaded pinbeam to *Admiral Bunter* had been dispatched. Space was clear of transmissions, warn-aways, broadcasts, and active shields for dozens of light-seconds at least, perhaps as much as a minute. She fed in a course correction, moving *Tarigan* parallel with the entry point, rather than toward the planet and safe docking. For now, she would be just one more asteroid or bit of comet shred, in proper orbit, barely perturbed above the stellar plane.

In the best instance of what she dignified as *her plan*, she would receive a reply to her pinbeam, assuring her that Tolly had released *Admiral Bunter* from whatever orders Inki had set upon him, and they were no longer bound for Nostrilia, and Tolly's imprisonment by his enemies.

In the *least* best instance, she would not receive a reply and would lurk here near the Jump point, as inconspicuous as an Explorer might be, waiting for *Admiral Bunter* to Jump in. Whereupon, *her plan* called for her to release Tolly from the *Admiral*'s care.

She had, as yet, no idea how she might do that. Possibly, a reminder of their past history as comrades would sway the *Admiral*.

Admittedly, that approach had not found success earlier. *Tarigan* was armed, but she would prefer not to fire on *Admiral Bunter*—and not only because Tolly would never forgive such an act.

The best outcome would be if Tolly had already used his cunning and his skill to release the *Admiral* from Inki's orders, and encouraged him to set a new course.

That would make her twice a fool—which was not a consideration, so long as Tolly Jones was at liberty.

A chime sounded, announcing an incoming pinbeam. She accepted and opened it.

"Greetings to the troop from Captain Miri Robertson," came the calm, familiar voice. "I'm in receipt of your field communication and have consulted with the head of house security regarding the challenges which face you. I approve your campaign as outlined. Remove Pilot-Mentor Jones from his compromised situation. Following, you will secure for him such a position of stability as satisfies Pilot-Mentor Jones. If no such position can be discovered, return with him to the greater resources of our House. Do not needlessly endanger yourself. Report when you have Pilot-Mentor Jones secure.

"Robertson out."

Hazenthull bowed her head in respect to the captain, and let herself acknowledge the thrill of relief. She had not, after all, asked for orders or for permission. She had told—told!—her captain what *she intended to do*, and she had half expected a curt order to return to base to explain herself.

Had the captain been one of the Troop—but she was not. There could be no doubt of her fitness to command, but she recognized a duty to those she commanded. It was a concept of Terran command, so Hazenthull had come to understand, and she swore once again that she would be worthy of this captain.

The board pinged, demanding her attention. She looked to the screens, seeing nothing, save—

There! Deep scan revealed shapes—objects—directly in her projected path, shielded, so the ship informed her, from such scans as were common on tradeships and private vessels.

Tarigan, however, had been a Scout ship. *Tarigan* had eyes that saw deeper, and farther, than those of normal ships.

Hazenthull adjusted course, watching the deep scans. The shielded objects did not follow or change attitude; they appeared inert. There were no transmissions, no indication that they were net-linked, or even capable of communication.

Still, she granted them a wide margin and sent the data to analytics. Inert they might seem, but so were fleas inert—and enough of them could seed the hull of a battleship with explosives sufficient to lay it open to space.

She would take very good care that nothing similar happened to *Tarigan*. Her objective was arguably peaceful—the mere transferring of a passenger from one ship to another, out of the sight or care of the directors of the Lyre Institute. Indeed, if the worst cast maintained, *Admiral Bunter* would enter the system in ten Standard Hours. They ought to conclude their business very quickly, be gone, and no one at Nostrilia the wiser.

V

"ANOTHER PINBEAM ARRIVES, MENTOR."

Tolly felt his heart leap—which was just plain and fancy foolishness. There hadn't been enough time for their 'beam to reach Haz, much less for this one to be her ack.

"Anybody we know?" he asked lightly.

"Someone I know," the *Admiral* answered. "The

elder to whom Captain Waitley referred me—Jeeves. He advises that Hazenthull intends to perform a composite Jump and be waiting for us at Nostrilia, in order to prevent your delivery to your enemies."

Tolly forcibly exhaled.

"Old news."

"Yes, but he could not have known that Hazenthull's communication would reach us first."

"True."

"He further says that Hazenthull's mission has the approval of her captain, who is also Miri Robertson Tiazan Clan Korval."

The delmae, like Liadens had it. Smart woman, so far as he'd ever heard. Haz had a high opinion, but then, Captain Robertson, as she'd once been, was twice a hero in battle, and that was the kind of thing that counted for somebody with Haz's bringing up.

"Tolly?" the *Admiral* said, sounding tentative.

"What's on your mind?"

"Is Hazenthull in danger? Jeeves states that her intention is to linger in far orbit, beyond range of planetary scans, and await our arrival. She is circumspect, and a fine pilot. It would seem that she is—"

"Safe?" Tolly shook his head, feeling his stomach cramp up. "See, Nostrilia isn't like your usual sort of planet. Its biggest industry is the Lyre Institute; Nostrilia's what you'd call the school's hiring hall. Given that the school deals in illegal goods, not to mention questionable activities of all descriptions—some of which would make your hair curl, if you happened to have any—anybody unexpected who lingers there is in danger."

He took a big gulp of air, thought a quick pilot's

exercise, and entered a state of more-or-less calm, if not precisely serenity.

"So, long story short—Nostrilia space is seeded to the Jump point with watchers and traps. If the school's expecting you, you're met by an escort ship and towed in. If the school's not expecting you—things aren't so friendly."

A lengthy pause followed this. Tolly waited.

"How long," the *Admiral* asked slowly—*carefully*—"do we wait for an acknowledgment to your message before we go after her?"

He really *was* a good boy at core, Tolly thought. Loyal to his friends.

As for Haz, and this *we*, after he'd been determined to set off on his own...

"I don't think we can help her," he said, making his voice gentle, though he wanted to yell and maybe lay about and break a few dozen fragile things.

"You think that she will fall to these watchers and traps? That *Tarigan* will be breached?"

If only, Tolly thought. If it was only that.

"No, Haz is a fine pilot, like you said, and *Tarigan*'s had mods done. Both're capable—more than capable. But, see, the reason expected visitors have to be towed in? It's because any ship coming in without a working knowledge of the patterns and avoids is gonna get snapped up by school security, real quick. Even if she's just minding her own business out on a far orbit.

"But there's worse," he said, calm—calm like it didn't matter.

"If *Tarigan* was just some random ship, dropping by without a proper invite, then she'd be escorted to the Jump point and sent on her way with a stern warning. But there's Inki in the mix, and we gotta believe she reported on *Tarigan*. If that's so, then she'll be escorted to dock, and the pilot removed for . . . an interview. In Haz's case—her being nor'Phelium—the directors might try a bit of plain and fancy extortion, assuming they don't care if Clan Korval gets mad at them. Which they prolly don't, but they *might* take into consideration that they've mostly been flying below Korval's scans and it's to their benefit to stay there. In which case—it's easy to fake a shipwreck, and they can absolutely put a trained soldier to good use."

"Would Hazenthull agree to such employment?"

Tolly's laugh hurt his throat.

"By the time the directors're done with her, she'll agree."

There was a pause before *Admiral Bunter* spoke again.

"I believe that we cannot allow Hazenthull to remain at risk. She would not have undertaken this course if she had not understood our danger and decided to protect us. She is as much a victim of Inki's actions as I was—as you were."

"I'm not disagreeing with any of that but, first—you're using *we* again. I thought you were eager to set me down and be your own ship."

"My own preferences can be put aside until we have recovered Hazenthull and, if possible, *Tarigan*," the *Admiral* said crisply. Another pause.

"I have made the assumption that you would be of a similar mind. Have I misunderstood? If so . . ."

"No," said Tolly. "No, you haven't misunderstood. But—we oughta wait for her ack. Could be she's already out."

Couldn't be, really; still too soon for the pinbeam to have reached her—and the *Admiral* called him on the fib.

"Taking into account everything you have told me about this situation, and including Inki's data as a student of this Lyre Institute, I believe we must act expeditiously. If Hazenthull acks while we are in Jump, we will receive it when we arrive and immediately remove ourselves from Nostrilia space."

"Don't have to go so far as Nostrilia," Tolly pointed out. "We're still two Jumps out, at least."

"I do not intend to follow normal Jump procedure," the *Admiral* told him. "A composite Jump offers the opportunity to decrease transition time by preserving thrust."

"You don't have to use energy to break out, and break back in—right." Tolly nodded. "But that's not gonna get you—"

"A composite Jump also presents the opportunity to choose an alternative route. We will not be tied to the Jump points, since we will not be breaking out. We can therefore plot the shortest route between two fixed points, which I have done. Using this route, and stipulating that we enter Jump within the next nine-point-six minutes, we will break out in Nostrilia space in seven Standard Hours."

Tolly blinked.

"Is that so?" he said, keeping his tone as neutral as sand.

"Yes," the *Admiral* said, sounding perfectly confident, and—"I can show you the math."

Could he, then? Well, even a graduate of the Lyre Institute for Exceptional Children could learn something new, out in the wide universe. Not tied to the Jump points? So, if the equations were off, or something went wrong inside the Jump, like sometimes happened, and it self-aborted—they wouldn't know what they'd be falling out *into*. Or if they'd fall out at all.

He took a breath and made his decision. Haz—It wasn't in him, he realized, with something like astonishment, to leave Haz to the school while he moved on and saved his precious skin one more time.

He'd done bad things; he'd betrayed friends, and lovers. He'd killed—worse—he'd stood by and watched while others were killed in his stead.

One more death to his account shouldn't much bother what passed for his conscience.

And still—Haz. Not an innocent, Haz: a genetic soldier, with more than a nodding relationship with violence and death. But she had . . . honor, and a practical core he'd depended on, when they were partners. She'd stood at his back, she hadn't run out on him or sold him to the highest bidder and—design or no design, the fact was, as he'd seen plain in her face—

She loved him.

That had to be . . . terrible for her. Terrible, and strange—and she'd've been *safe*, serving as a Korval house guard and sometime Port Security cop, if Tolly Jones hadn't . . .

"Mentor?"

Tolly shook himself, and looked up to the corner of the ceiling, addressing *Admiral Bunter* direct.

"Sure," he said. "Show me the math.

"In the meantime, you'd best get us into Jump."

Vivulonj Prosperu

"DAAV, WILL YOU DANCE WITH ME?"

They had dutifully sought their bunk and engaged the webbing when the end-Jump sounded; releasing it again when the all-clear came. Disposing themselves more comfortably, they had napped and, upon waking, eaten a leisurely meal.

The next scheduled exercise session resided yet two hours in the future, and they were on the prowl for occupation.

Daav looked up from the entertainment screen he had been perusing.

"Klaxons?" he murmured.

"The small dance," Aelliana answered, raising her arms slowly over her head, palms pointed toward the ceiling. "Surely there's no harm in that."

"Do you know, I am not nearly so certain as you seem to be. However, I agree that we may only learn our limits by testing them."

She laughed.

"Do you think Uncle has had pilots in his care before? Surely, he cannot believe that we will sit idle or sleep for so many hours a day."

"I wager the Uncle has . . . rehabilitated many pilots in his time. He may, however, lack experience of *Korval* pilots."

"That is very likely," she said gravely. "He cannot possibly know what manner of mischief we might promote if we are allowed to become bored."

She lowered her arms, palms toward the floor, pushing, as if the air were resisting her.

Daav moved away from the console.

"A salubrious lesson is a handsome gift, I allow," he said, coming to stand before her.

"Precisely. Tell me, *is* there anything useful on the console?"

"Perhaps so. I recognized several rather cerebral games, so you see that we aren't meant to vegetate, no matter how much we are told to rest. On a quick scan, the plays seem to err on the side of comedy. There are novels, but no histories. We are not offered news, nor even *Taggerth's*, speaking of comedy."

"We are meant, in a word, to be *calm*," Aelliana said.

"So it seems. Do you dance in truth, my lady, or will you have a game of counterchance?"

"Dance *and* counterchance!"

She took a deep breath, looked down, and placed her feet correctly, a smile at the corner of her mouth, which he dared to think was simple pleasure at once again having feet to place.

"Some might think that a bold schedule," he commented.

She looked up into his face.

"Too bold for *us*, *van'chela*?"

"Was there ever anything too bold for *us*?"

"Never! Let us do the basic stretch sequence."

"Lead and I will follow."

She smiled at him, and he felt of a sudden an enveloping warmth. Tears started to his eyes, as her love suffused him, so that she sparkled somewhat around the edges as she pressed the palms of her hands together at the level of her heart, and took the deep and mindful breath that began the sequence.

• • • ⁕ • • •

Refreshed, Dulsey returned to the bridge and slipped into the pilot's chair.

"All well, Pilot?" she asked, placing her palm against the pad.

"We have been undisturbed, and our progress has been good," Uncle Yuri said. "The board comes back to you, Pilot."

She accepted control of first board with a finger tap, and leisurely perused the screens. The Jump point was still over a Standard Hour distant; there was no traffic within the range of their scans—not surprising. There was very little in this section of space for anyone to want, save the Jump point itself, which was why they had routed through it.

An anomaly on the scan at the bottom of her systems screen drew her eye: the guest quarters monitor.

Dulsey touched a button, bringing the live feed up, and considered two figures moving with graceful deliberation. She flicked her gaze to the tells for heart rate and oxygen use, finding both well within parameters. As they would be, of course, given their exercise of choice.

"Our guests are dancing *daibri'at*," she said.

"And you find that amusing?" Yuri asked, not bothering to look up from his screens.

"I find Pilot Caylon's commitment to doing *something* admirable."

She gave the feed her attention once more. Their guests were working through the entry-level stretches, Pilot Caylon setting a pace which was conservative, even by the standards of the dance. Both pilots seemed balanced, centered, and in no imminent danger of overexertion—observations that continued to be reflected in the stats.

"Neither seems at risk," she said, glancing over her shoulder. Yuri remained focused on his screens, the side of his face uncommunicative, perhaps, to one who knew him less well.

"What's amiss?" she asked.

"You have Andreth's report in your queue, but you will of course not have had time to read it." At last, he spun the chair and faced her fully.

"Allow me to summarize."

"Please," she said, and waited.

He nodded, closing his eyes for a moment, as if to recruit himself.

"Yes. You will recall that two operatives were apprehended at the very doors of the Catalinc Project. One was damaged past healing. The other remained intact. More or less.

"It comes about that the intact operative seeks to convince Andreth that his treatment in captivity, coupled with a close observation of our systems, have kindled in him a profound respect for ourselves and our goals. He proposes to change allegiances and bend his considerable skills to our cause."

He bowed his head, spreading his hands in a gesture of ironic magnanimity.

"Gratifying," said Dulsey.

"Indeed. He is, however, less than forthcoming regarding the allegiance he wishes to betray, though he allows himself to be an industrial spy. There is, you understand, only himself on the table. We are not offered any surety, nor any gift of data from his previous allegiance. That is . . . troubling.

"However, in the case of his partner, whom Andreth had the foresight to download when it became clear that he would not survive his injuries—*that* one offers us a bargain which lies somewhere between interesting and alarming."

Yuri was not easily dismayed, yet Dulsey, who knew him as none other, saw dismay now.

"What is it?"

He sighed and gave her a smile of sorts.

"The downloaded individual wishes to have from us a new body, new papers, and a ship. For these things, he offers information—codes and other as yet unspecified data—and, to demonstrate that he is in earnest, he gives us the coordinates that describe Seignur Veeoni's location."

Dulsey sat back in her chair, suddenly chilly, as if an ill wind had whispered through the bridge.

Seignur Veeoni's work was vital to the success of the Catalinc Project. She had not yet been on site, as her work had not come to the point where she must interface with the rest of the Project. Her location was secure—*had been* secure.

"How does he come by this information?" she asked.

"He is coy and says only that he had at first been part of another squad, with a separate goal. At the last moment, he was transferred to the team tasked with infiltrating the Catalinc Project."

Dulsey looked at him sharply.

"Another team. This means that they may have already approached Seignur Veeoni."

"Peace." The Uncle raised his hand gently. "We should certainly have heard, had there been an attempt upon her."

That was true, but hardly comforting. The scholar was well guarded, and by no means a fool, but the team Andreth had intercepted should not have been able to penetrate so far as they had. Surely, those sent to fetch Seignur Veeoni would be no less apt.

"Have we the employer's identity?" she asked. "Not, I take it, the Department of the Interior."

"No, I think we may hold the Department excused from this exercise. I believe that our operations may have become . . . interesting to the Lyre Institute. We had expected that news of the work would leak. A project of such scope cannot be kept a secret. There will be rumors, and whispers and . . . those who will pursue such."

He moved his shoulders. "So! I had very little hope that we could keep Catalinc a secret.

"Rumors regarding my sister's work, however—*that* I had hoped we could keep below the level of space-lane gossip. It seems we have made a notable failure there."

He turned his hands palm up, a simple gesture, denoting complex actions.

"Seignur Veeoni's few publications were meant to divert attention from her real work. If she—or her work—comes into the hands of the Lyre Institute . . . if the Light in its present state is removed from our oversight—I fear the outcome, should the Institute accomplish either. If they succeed in both of their objectives . . . I dislike the word *catastrophe*, but I feel in this case it is apt."

He closed his eyes again. Dulsey waited. After a moment, he spoke.

"A course change, Dulsey. We go with all speed to my sister. She cannot be left exposed."

"And our guests?" Dulsey asked.

Yuri sighed and opened his eyes.

"I will ask after the location of Korval's pinnaces. If the detour is supportable, we will make it and send our guests on their way. They will be given instructions on how best to care for themselves. Seignur Veeoni must not be exposed to the eyes of the curious—nor to Korval's Luck."

Dulsey sighed. Their guests would be out of active danger in another two Standard Days. Even at *all speed*, they would not arrive at Seignur Veeoni's location so soon. They were intelligent, the Korval pilots. The odds for their long-term survival were . . . not bad. Not good, perhaps, but not bad. With Korval's Luck on their side, they ought to do very well, indeed.

She spun the chair and addressed her board.

"Filing change of course," she said.

Surebleak

REN ZEL WALKED CAREFULLY OVER THE SURFACE ROOTS to the Tree itself, and stood for a long moment, hands in pockets, looking up into dark branches.

He had come into Clan Korval as Anthora yos'Galan's lifemate. While he acknowledged that the Tree was sentient, and a meddler of high order, he had not otherwise concerned himself with it. And after its initial utter disruption of his life, the Tree had seemed to forget about him. Aside from the pods it had bestowed to perhaps indicate its approval of his mating with Anthora, it had offered him no others, though his clan-mates—and his wife—often received such gifts from its branches.

There being no reason for him to seek the Tree Court, he seldom did so. And to think of the Tree Court as a place of succor and peace—that he had *never* done.

And yet, fully intending to find Mr. Brunner in the weather lab and review with him the implementation of the next phase, he found himself instead turning down a short hallway and exiting the house through a door that opened onto the inner garden. Some part of him had been surprised, but his feet were certain, and they had brought him here, to the Tree itself, and only then allowed him to stop.

Ren Zel bowed gently, as one might to a grandfather not one's own, but beloved of others who were dear to one.

"I am here," he said conversationally. "It was rather less of a journey this time."

Above him, leaves rustled gently, as if the Tree chuckled at the pleasantry.

He smiled slightly.

"If you have produced a pod which will allow me to withstand the Shadow until the time is come to embrace it, I will be most delighted to receive the gift."

Another susurration among the leaves, though there was no breeze moving within the court. The Tree was perhaps concerned, solicitous.

"Yes, I do understand my part," he said, "and I will thank you to shield Anthora so much as you might when the moment arrives. She will take it ill."

A short rustle: the Tree was puzzled.

"You ought not to have made her love me," Ren Zel told it sternly. "You might have enthralled me alone, with no risk to your result. She will do herself a hurt, trying to protect me."

The leaves moved softly; a cool breeze kissed his cheek. Apparently the Tree had all in hand, and he was not to tease himself.

He closed his eyes for a moment, and when he opened them again, he was pressed against the Tree, his arms reaching 'round the monumental trunk, as if they shared an embrace. How he had crossed that last distance—well. Here in its own court, the Tree ordered all as it wished.

Nor had the Tree's whim played him ill. Indeed, he was refreshed, as if from a full night's sleep; alert and strong.

"I thank you," he said, standing away from the trunk. "It was kindly done."

The breeze played with his hair, for all the worlds like a fond aunt.

From above him came the sound of leaves loudly rustling, as if something fell through them from a height.

He did not leap aside; it did not occur to him to move. Rather, he held out a hand and caught the pod before it struck the ground.

A sweet and subtle scent reached him, and he was suddenly ravenous. He brought his other hand up, meaning to crack the pod, but he had scarcely touched it when it fell into quarters, each tempting and plump.

He had no need of such encouragement; he would have eaten the gift if it had neither odor nor taste, merely for the hope of the good it might do.

Though, he admitted, as he put the last section into his mouth, it was pleasant that the pod was delicious, and that it satisfied his appetite for it completely. Setting aside his renewed energy levels, however, he felt . . . not much changed. But what had he expected to feel, after all?

"I thank you," he said again, and the breeze this time was a bit stronger, pushing at his shoulder. His audience was over and the Tree wished him gone. Well enough.

"A good day to you," he said, bowed farewell,

turned—and paused to consider his lifemate, standing a little to the side, holding a shawl-wrapped bundle in her arms, and her whole attention upon the Tree.

He remained motionless and silent, unwilling to disturb her or to wake the child—until, between one blink and the next, they were vanished, leaving behind a sense of bittersweet joy.

It was rare, he reflected, that he was given so clear a vision. Perhaps that was what the Tree's gift had wrought.

One more breath, and a small smile for the future before he left the court, returning to the house and the duties of the day.

...※...

Yulie Shaper was not clan, but he was Tree-kin, in addition to being a good neighbor.

Which was why Val Con was walking across the dry and dead Liaden grass toward the crack in the earth that served as a boundary of Korval's land.

As promised, Memit had sent word through Kezzi—that word being that she, with a sister and two of their brothers, would assist Farmer Shaper in the matter of getting in the harvest. Also, they would embrace the project of turning grapes into wine.

And that had been the last he had heard on the matter for six days. He considered it extremely unlikely that the Bedel had murdered Yulie Shaper. However, it was equally possible that they had found the work unworthy and taken themselves off. *or* that they had "found" among Yulie Shaper's belongings, items that would best reside with the Bedel.

In any case, it was what a neighbor would do,

especially one who had offered a solving in the case—to walk over and ascertain that all was well.

It was a bright day, the sky free of clouds for the moment at least, and the air chill enough to encourage a brisk pace, with the collar turned up to shield neck and ears.

He paused at the boundary, hands tucked into his pockets, and made a careful survey. The crack itself was not so noticeable as it had been when the house had first been settled into the old quarry. Another six or a dozen applications of native dirt and the line would be invisible to the eye. By that time, the Liaden grass would have been replaced by Surebleak's sort—though he was irrationally pleased to see that Surebleak's sort, on Yulie Shaper's land, was equally brown and dry.

The house garden had been carefully turned—just as their own garden had been—and perennials cut down to ground level.

Jelaza Kazone's gardener had been in consultation with Mr. Shaper regarding the best method for resting and protecting the garden over Surebleak's winter. On his advice, the turned soil had been seeded with snow-oats, which would grow rapidly, then die in the first "deep cold," thereby providing a layer of protection, as well as nutrients for next year's crop.

Val Con took his hands out of his pockets and let them hang, loose-fingered and obviously empty, at his side. Then, he stepped over the healing crack and onto his neighbor's land.

Approaching the garden plot, he could see that there was a slight fuzzing of green over the soil, which was, he supposed, the beginning crop of snow-oats.

As he crossed the clearing, a cat slid out of the shrubbery and kept pace with him; another cat joining them as they struck the path to the house. He nodded in greeting and proceeded at a very casual pace, following the wandering path around large rocks and trees, cats attaching themselves to him as he went on.

He paused by the bunker rock, listening, and moving on when no hail was forthcoming.

By the time he had reached the end of the path, his feline honor guard had grown to six, every tail held proud and high.

He did not cross immediately into the dooryard, but stood where he was sheltered somewhat by branches. Yulie Shaper was a crack shot, and had, in the past, been prone to shooting at anyone who arrived at his house unexpectedly.

"Mr. Shaper!" he called. "It is Val Con yos'Phelium, your neighbor. May I come forward?"

"Hey, Boss!" Yulie Shaper sounded positively ebullient. "I was hopin' you'd come on by! Been meaning to get up the house and talk to you myself, but we just been that busy. C'mon in the kitchen, got some coffee just brewed, and some tea, too!"

Thus encouraged, Val Con stepped out into the dooryard, attended by cats, and crossed the small lawn to the stone step. He lost four of his retinue there, they apparently being uninterested in those things the interior had to offer.

The door was slightly open; he pushed it the rest of the way, and stepped into Yulie Shaper's kitchen, bracketed by cats.

Halfway down the room, on the right, Yulie Shaper was turning away from the counter, a mug in one hand. Directly in the center of the room was a table piled high with papers and binders. Behind it was a man with the Bedel face, watching him with interest.

As it happened, he knew the man—one of Rys's brothers, perhaps even his *cha'leket*, if the Bedel acknowledged heart-kin.

"Nathan," Val Con said, inclining his head.

"Rys's brother under Tree," Nathan returned, with what seemed to be genuine warmth. "You are well arrived."

"That's a fact, too!" Yulie Shaper agreed. "We need somebody with some sense on this or we're gonna be opening all the rooms, even the ones never really *been* open, just to see what'll happen. Coffee, Boss? Or tea? I gotta tell you, the tea's something a little special."

"Thank you, I will have tea," Val Con said, moving toward the cluttered table and glancing at the visible pages of the top binders.

"Will you increase your production?" he asked the room at large.

"We would increase variety," Nathan said, holding his hand, palm down, fingers spread over the binders. "When we have results, we would increase production of those foods which have been proven."

"Here go, Boss," Yulie said, shoving a mug at Val Con. The liquid inside was very nearly as black as coffee, and smelled bitter and burnt.

"Thank you," he said again, and took a tentative sip. Bitter and burnt. Much like the tea Silain the *luthia* had served when he had visited her hearth.

"Mr. Shaper, I am at sea. I had thought you kept production down because there was no market and too much work for one."

"Too much work for one—got that solved," Yulie said. "Market—well, it turns out we've got a market, too."

"This farm was to have fed the world," Nathan added. He reached into the confusion of binders and extracted one, holding it out to Val Con.

Carefully, he put the mug with its acrid contents on an unclaimed corner of the table, and took the offered binder.

"Mission statement," Nathan said softly.

Val Con scanned the page. Feed the world, indeed.

"See, the thing is," Yulie was saying excitedly, "Surebleak never got all the way set up before it got broke down. You remember I told you that bit o'land your other brother wanted for his house—that was s'posed to have been the twin o'what we got here. This here was planned to feed landing pop, up to two percent of growth. When we hit the peak, then they'd open up the second facility to take care of the pressure."

He shook his head.

"Agency pulled out real fast when they decided to go—that's how I always heard it. Bad things happened—riots and killin's not being the worst of it. That's where the Bosses come in—they took charge and did what you'd call damage control. 'Cept then there was them who thought they'd be a better boss, an'—well. Out here, we just kinda hunkered down. Closed the rooms and gas-sealed most, keeping just a few producing, so there'd be something to barter and to feed the family, o'course."

He sighed and extended a long arm to pluck a mug from the shelf beside him. He took a long swallow before giving his head a rueful shake.

"Like everybody else, I guess, we forgot what we

was s'posed to be doing, in the everyday doin' of staying alive."

"But now, it is revealed," Nathan said. "This farm can be opened and it will feed the world."

"Well, now, no it won't," said Yulie, shaking his head again. "Remember we was only the start-up, to pop plus two, then the second one was s'posed to come online."

"Then that will be opened and brought to spec, using all that we have learned here," Nathan countered.

"Second facility wasn't never outfitted, see? Agency didn't like spending money too far ahead. Did a little site prep, but even there, 'til you knew what was comin' in by way of 'quipment, an' what production requirements were gonna be . . . Long story short—there ain't any second facility. Nor not gonna be one, 'less Boss Conrad down there in the city decides different."

Nathan frowned.

"There are farms, beyond the end of the road," Val Con said, putting the binder on a stable-looking pile of its kin. "Boss Sherton supplies meat, fruits and vegetables . . ."

"That's right," said Yulie. "Boss Gabriel, his turf's got wheat an' oat. Plus there's the goods from back behind. Melina fronts for 'em, but they ain't proper in her turf. 'Swhat she told Grampa, anyway."

"And down in the city, there are the gardens on roofs, in cellars, behind fences, and in other unlikely places," Nathan added. "Surebleak does not starve. But she can be fed . . . much better." He waved his hand at the binders.

Val Con cleared his throat. "So far as the Council of Bosses has been able to determine from what records they have recovered from the Gilmour Agency, the population at the time of Boss Conrad's arrival was significantly lower than it had been when the Surebleak colony was established. There has lately been an influx, but I don't believe that we yet approach pop plus two. This can, of course, be checked."

He frowned. "Mr. Shaper, how many harvests can you manage from your rooms in a year?"

"Three," Yulie said promptly. "There's the whole cycle of active, alt, rest, right there in the maintenance binder."

He turned to Nathan.

"Which is something else neither of us—nor Mary, neither—thought about. Harvest is hard work, but harvest and maintenance both—for the whole facility now, up and full—that ain't doable."

"Not by one man," Nathan agreed. "But a crew—"

"Well, sure, a crew'd do it," Yulie said. "Wouldn't need no more than ten, 'leven hands to run the place smooth."

He frowned down into his mug.

"Seen that somewhere—how many was enough, and what their sections oughta be. I'll look it out."

"That is good," Nathan said. "Mary and I have been talking and—taking advice from others of our sisters and brothers. It may be that a crew is within reach, Yulie Shaper."

"These are all good steps," Val Con said. He glanced at the mug of tea cooling on the corner of the table and decided that he wasn't thirsty.

"What I would suggest be done further is to present a report to the Council of Bosses, so that they are fully informed of this facility and its capabilities."

Yulie pulled himself up straight.

"This is private enterprise," he said sharply. "It don't belong to the Bosses."

"I know that you will have the documentation which sets out the conditions of the facility's existence and ownership," Val Con said soothingly. "Copies may be made for the council's files so that there are no errors.

"Speaking to your ambitions, I would suggest that opening all the rooms at once invites chaos, and that chaos invites failure. Plainly, you wish to succeed—the prospect of failure does not usually spark such enthusiasm."

He used his chin to point at the mountain of binders.

"Might there be, somewhere in all this, a start-up protocol? It may no longer speak directly to conditions, given the necessity to *hunker down* and utilize only those rooms which produced high-value barter crops, but—"

"But it will be a place to start!" Nathan said, excitement sparkling in his black eyes. "We can make adjustments and build a new schedule around—"

He threw a speaking glance at Val Con, but what it was meant to convey, he was unable to fathom.

"The crew as we are today," Nathan said to Yulie. "Me, Mary, Abigail, Walter—and yourself as overseer. Could you oversee an additional team of four, if such were to be found?"

Yulie frowned slightly.

"Have to do a lot of scheduling and planning out—which don't mean *no*. I had the lessons—Grampa made sure me and Rollie had all the lessons—just ain't never used 'em, see? But I can review. Pretty sure there was a section on running multiple growth cycles . . ."

He paused, gazing into the air vaguely over Val Con's head, then nodded.

"Lemme look that up, and get back with you."

"Yes," said Nathan. "I will also . . . check our records for anything which may be useful."

"And," Val Con pointed out, "you have time to bring this project together. Surely, you won't wish to begin a new cycle while a harvest is ongoing."

"That's so," Yulie said, and grinned widely. "See, now? All we needed was a boss to get us on the straight track."

"You are kind," Val Con murmured, "but I did nothing more than offer a protocol."

"If you say so. Hey, was there a reason you come by? We were so full of our own ideas, I didn't think to ask."

"A social call," Val Con said. "I am more than content. It is, however, time for me to go home. Nathan, will you walk with me? I wish to speak with you of Rys."

"Yes." Nathan came to his feet.

"I will not be long," he said to Yulie.

"Take your time. I'll just be going back down to the rooms and see how they're getting on. You find us there."

"Yes," Nathan said and moved his hand, indicating that Val Con should precede him out the door.

"Have you news of our Rys?" Nathan asked when they had gone some little distance down the path.

"Alas, no. In sober fact, I do not expect news of Rys, only, eventually, to see the results of his actions."

Nathan sighed.

"He did not himself expect to return to us from this task you set upon him. It weighs upon the heart, when a brother must ask a brother for his life."

"The weight is heavier yet," Val Con said softly, "when a brother offers his life for yours."

He took a breath.

"I wished to say to you that this man Yulie Shaper, though a *gadje*, honors Rys. The grapes, the attempt at wine—these are the means by which he demonstrates his esteem."

"Yes, Memit had told us this."

Val Con glanced at him.

"Mary?"

"She had said she was not ashamed that you should hold her name alongside Rys."

"I will try to be worthy," Val Con said.

"You are Rys's brother, as I am. For him, we will both be worthy."

He smiled out of the side of his mouth.

"I think you want to say that Yulie Shaper should lose nothing at Bedel hands, and that we keep our bargain in good faith. You need have no fears. We will treat with him as with a brother. I swear this upon my true-name: Udari."

Val Con stopped and looked up into black eyes.

"I am . . . astonished," he said truthfully. "I have nothing of equal value to give in return."

Udari smiled, and extended a light hand to touch his shoulder.

"You bear a brother's burden. That is value beyond price."

They had reached the far end of the path. Udari stopped and nodded.

"I leave you here. Keep well . . . Brother."

• • • ❋ • • •

Kareen's 'hand, Amiz, put Miri in the front parlor with a promise that tea and Professor Waitley would be with her soon. Nelirikk, he whisked off to the kitchen, for a "cup and a piece of Esil's pie, just out"—and a good gossip with the house staff, too.

Miri might've been jealous of that piece of pie, but this was Kareen's house. She wouldn't be kept without her tea, and a little something to help it go down, for longer than it took Esil to load the tray.

The arrival of Theo's mother was likely to be less prompt, since she was probably working at this hour, and rousing Kamele Waitley from deep research was nothing like a challenge.

That was all right; it would give Miri time to reorder her thinking. Kamele was from a society that put women first in order of precedence—strong, capable, informed, and decisive. Men were the lesser vessel—emotional and occasionally in need of a woman's firm guidance. That life view was exactly why Miri had come on this mission rather than Val Con, the by-nature-excitable brother of Kamele's daughter.

Miri approached the hearth and held her hands out to welcome warmth.

The formal parlor was a pleasant place to wait, though her younger self would probably have thought the room too warm and the firestone in the hearth a wicked luxury. Her present self still needed a reminder that the House could afford as many firestones as its members desired, and that it wasn't so much a luxury as a canny investment in the clan's success to provide busy people with a comfortable environment.

Hands warmed, Miri left the hearth and drifted over to the bookshelves to see what Kareen considered proper to put on display for visitors. The patterned rug, like the chairs, sofa, and little tables, had come from House stores, but the bookshelves, and the big window onto the street—unusual on Surebleak—were original with the house. The window did have an inside shutter, but that was just standard protection from the snow-winds.

Kareen's taste in display books ran heavily to art volumes, with biographies and history books that seemed to have been chosen for the attractiveness of their bindings. One whole shelf, just at your average 'bleaker's eye level, was filled with Terran novels, bindings tattered and broken, like they'd been read and reread dozens of times.

Miri was just reaching for a book with a spine so grubby the title was a mystery, when she heard rapid steps in the hall.

Tea wouldn't be coming at such a pace, she thought, and wondered if she was going to lose her bet with herself and see Theo's mother first.

She turned and moved three steps across the rug. A shadow darkened the doorway, a scanner squawked loudly, and a woman she had never seen before stepped into the room.

Miri slipped one hand a little closer to her hideaway. Bad manners to be armed in a safe house, o'course, but if Surebleak taught one thing, it was that even safe houses could be . . . less than safe.

The woman came to an abrupt stop two steps into the room, half shielded by the sofa at the hearth. The scanner squawked again—there was a mini hanging on her belt—and she produced an awkward, unnuanced bow.

"You are Korval?" she asked—well, *demanded*, really.

Miri inclined her head.

"I'm half of Korval, if you're looking for the delm," she said. "And you are . . . ?"

"Tassi." The tone was impatient, as if Miri should've known that.

Miri frowned at her—tall, thin, and awkward; dark brown hair, short and serviceable; milk-pale skin; dark eyes set wide; lean cheeks and stubborn jaw; the set of shoulders and hips shouting *attitude*.

No, Miri decided, she'd've remembered this one.

"What do you want then, Tassi?" she asked abruptly. If rudeness was the mode . . .

"To see you. You are not what I expected."

"I guess we're even. You're not what I expected either."

The high, pale forehead wrinkled; the scanner fizzed and a voice proclaimed, "*Zalyn*, Waymart, PIC Beetsher Wold, hotpad at Mack's."

"But how—" she began, and turned at the sound of quick steps behind her.

Kamele Waitley slipped into the room past Tassi's skinny self, and crossed the rug, smiling.

"Hello, Miri. Amiz said you wanted to talk with me?"

"Got a favor to ask," Miri said. "Just gimme a minute."

She looked to Tassi, still standing behind the sofa.

"You seen what I look like. Need anything else?"

Tassi blinked.

"No," she said.

She turned on her heel and left, scanner squawk trailing after her like a particularly loud scarf.

Miri shook her head and turned to Kamele.

"Where'd you get her?" she asked.

"Oh, Silain brought her and asked Kareen to give her a place to stay. Of course, Kareen wanted to accommodate a request from someone who has been so helpful to us—and, really, Tassi has been helpful. She's a good researcher and a truly talented linguist. We'd had . . . a pile—more than an archive—of texts that we couldn't quite puzzle out. Tassi's grasp of language shift has been invaluable there. She's almost through our backlog."

More noise in the hall—this announcing the arrival of the tea tray, borne by Esil herself.

"Sorry to delay, Boss," she said to Miri, clattering it all down on the table near the hearth. "Rikki had us going with a story, back in the kitchen, and I let the first kettle boil dry."

"Rikki?" Miri repeated.

"Yes'm. That man can tell a story! But that's nothing new for you, is it, Boss?"

Assuming that "Rikki" was "Nelirikk," the information wasn't only new, it was downright mind-boggling. Miri pulled up a smile and a nod.

"Got more sides than a box o'dice," she said. "Thanks, Esil."

"No problem at all. There's a few cookies on the plate, there, just come out. You need anything else, you call."

She was gone, walking briskly down the hall, probably anxious not to miss one of Rikki's stories.

"Well," Miri said, more to herself than Kamele, "the things you learn on a day."

"The kitchen has its own culture, doesn't it?"

Kamele led the way to the hearth.

They sat side by side on the sofa; Miri poured, they both sipped, and then leaned back into the cushions.

"Now," Kamele said, "what can I do for you?"

"Well, I hope you'll be willing to do us all a favor and write a little note to Theo, asking her to come home."

Kamele frowned slightly, but said nothing, so Miri pushed on.

"I wouldn't ask it, but Shan's written and told her to pull back until he can figure a less dangerous route for her; Val Con's written—nicely—that she oughta come home, make the acquaintance of her niece. And, putting it blunt, she's ignored them both. Not even an ack."

Kamele's frown deepened.

"Is it certain that she's . . . all right? At liberty?"

"Far's we know," Miri said, "an' what that mostly is, is there hasn't been any news about her breaking shipping at any ports, or leading an evacuation—and nobody's put a price on her head. Lately."

Kamele nodded. "In light of these negatives, it would seem that Theo is not presently, at least, pursued by enemies, or in any . . . immediate danger?"

"Not so far as we know, no. But that could change, real fast. It's dangerous out there for her."

"I understand. Is it any more dangerous for Theo than it is for Master Trader yos'Galan?"

Miri blinked, did a quick series of sums, and shook her head. "Not particularly, no."

"Are you going to call him home?"

Miri laughed.

Kamele smiled. "I see." She sipped her tea, and leaned forward to put the cup on the table.

"Theo is an adult. She has a ship and a crew to care for, as I understand it. I wouldn't presume to interrupt her in the pursuit of her business. She knows what her"—she smiled faintly—"*her necessities* are. We must assume that she had received the messages from her brother and from the master trader, and we must also assume that she has chosen not to act on them for good and sufficient reasons.

"I'll certainly be very glad to see her when she does come home, but I won't *call her* home."

Miri blinked.

"Have I disappointed you very much?" Kamele said.

Miri blinked again, and managed a smile.

"I understand your point of view," she said truthfully. "We'll just have to wait for Theo to get done with her business, then."

"Yes," Kamele said and offered her another smile.

"It's difficult, but at some point, you must say to your students, *I've taught you all I can. Go out and use what you've learned.*

"It's more difficult with a daughter—or a sister—but we must let them live their lives, even if it seems to us to be . . . risky or unsafe."

Kamele leaned forward and retrieved her teacup.

"And, you know, just between us," she said, leaning back into the cushions, "Theo really has no aptitude for safety."

• • • ※ • • •

"What has occurred, Beloved?" Anthora murmured. "You have gained . . . weight."

"Ah, is that how the trick's been done?" he asked lightly, looking up from his screen. "I was called into consultation with the Tree, and received a pod."

"Which, of course, you ate," Anthora said.

"Would you have had me deny myself the tastiest and most satisfying food I have ever eaten?" he asked, half meaning it for a jest.

"No, of course not," she said sitting down across from him. "It is merely that one can never be certain what the Tree intends."

"Certainly, it cannot intend for life to unravel," Ren Zel said. "Thus, if I have indeed *gained weight*, then the Tree wishes me not to fly off too soon."

"There's a particular tenderness," Anthora said bitterly.

He considered her, carefully extended a hand and laid it over hers, which was fisted on the table.

"It seems to me that what choice there is in this upcoming event is very clear. I will accept the duty that my gift demands of me in service of a hopeful future. Or I will turn my face away from duty, whereupon the . . . possible future I have Seen will come to pass. Life will survive, but it will be a poor thing, ever in peril from darkness. I do not wish to live in that future—I do not wish *you* to live in that future, nor our—"

He broke off, but not soon enough; Anthora was staring at him.

"Our child?" she asked softly. "What child is this, Beloved?"

He sighed.

"I had a Seeing," he said softly, keeping his eyes steady on hers and tightening his fingers around her fist. "Yourself in the Tree Court, holding an infant wrapped in a red shawl shot through with golden thread. I was given to know that you held our daughter."

Her eyes were filled with tears, yet she did not

look away. Under the pressure of his fingers, her fist softened until her palm rested flat against the table.

"A true Seeing?" she asked gently.

"I believe it," he answered, with simple honesty.

She smiled and rose, gripping his hand, so that he rose with her.

"Well, then," she said with a brave attempt at gaiety, "what are we if we are not slaves to the truth? Come!"

"This moment?" he asked, but already his blood was warming.

"Is there one better?" Anthora demanded.

He shook his head, being bereft of words, pulled her close, and kissed her deep, as passion flared into need.

• • • ⁕ • • •

Val Con was crossing the lawn as Nelirikk pulled the car onto the apron next to the side entrance. Miri opened her door, stepped out, and said over her shoulder, "Thanks, Beautiful. You're off duty."

"Yes, Captain," he answered, but she was already walking across the crunchy brown grass.

"Good evening, *cha'trez*," Val Con said, opening his arms.

She walked into the offered embrace; put her arms around his waist, her head on his shoulder and just stood there, taking comfort from his presence, and watching the him of him, inside her head. He seemed . . . pleased about something, she thought. That was good.

Finally, she let the hug fall away and took a step back, giving him a grin.

"Gone visiting?"

"Indeed," he said, tucking her arm through his and moving them leisurely toward the house. "I have been to see Mr. Shaper, who has four Bedel assisting with the harvest and planning world dominion."

"Better them than us," Miri said. "I'm pretty sure Pat Rin would step aside, if they asked nice."

"Now, do you know? I think he would not. But that is a philosophical discussion, and I have not yet inquired into your day."

She shrugged.

"Road Boss business was pretty light; we might start looking at getting a couple of likely 'prentices in; start teaching 'em the ropes."

"It may that we ought," Val Con murmured. "You are home a little after time, which I confess relieves me. I had imagined you in-house and poised to ring down a terrific scold."

"Like that'll happen," she muttered and shook her head.

"I stopped at Kareen's house to talk to Kamele—" she stopped; Val Con came around to face her.

"Do you know *Rikki's* storytelling holds a whole kitchen full of 'hands riveted? Esil was so caught up, she boiled the kettle dry and had to start over."

"I am not surprised to learn that Nelirikk has many facets. He is an Explorer, after all."

"Well, *I'm* flabbergasted," Miri told him. "The things you don't know about people you know."

"In fact, we are all ciphers," Val Con said, taking her arm again, and turning them toward the house. "So—you spoke to Kamele?"

"I did; told her you and Shan had sent for Theo to come home, and she hadn't even bothered to send back a *no*. Asked Kamele if she'd write."

"Ah? And she said?"

"She said Theo's a grown-up, and she, Kamele, had no right to interrupt her in the course of her business, whatever it is; she'll come home when she's able, and when she does that, Kamele would be very pleased to see her."

She paused.

Val Con said nothing; the pattern of him inside her head was . . . interested.

"Kamele also said," she finished, "that Theo's got no talent for being safe."

Val Con laughed, and Miri felt a grin tugging the side of her mouth.

"Well, then," he said, as they reached the patio and the side door opened for them. "I suppose that we shall wait, with what poor patience we can muster."

He paused on the threshold to bow her through the door.

"Please, my lady, allow me to find you a glass of wine."

Ahab-Esais

I

THEY WERE, SAID INKI, AT EDMONTON BEACON TO CALL upon a person named Kasagaria Mikelsyn, an information broker and expert on Old Technology.

"In fact, the foremost such expert, saving only the Uncle himself," Inki said. "Some, indeed, say that *Dosavi* Mikelsyn is an instance of the Uncle."

"Is that likely?" Tocohl asked, simultaneously assigning the question to her research protocols.

Inki gave a fluid shrug.

"*Likely* and *the Uncle* rarely cohabit the same sentence, Pilot. It is known that—there! already I fall into error!—I should say that it is *thought to be known* that the Uncle has sisters and brothers a-plenty across the universe, each of whom has their area of expertise and their web of operatives."

"It is fortunate, then, that ours is an expanding universe, or there would be no room for all of him," Tocohl said, meaning it for a joke.

Inki smiled slightly and took up her tone.

"Indeed, indeed! One would be tempted to think that even an expanding system could scarcely accommodate their numbers. But we must suppose that the Uncle knows what he's doing."

"Why?" Tocohl asked, honestly curious.

"It is what we suppose of all gods, Pilot."

"The Uncle is not a god."

"Perhaps you are correct, but for the moment, I propose to keep the question open in my own mind."

"What of *Dosavi* Mikelsyn?"

"In terms of godhood? I suppose it best to keep the question open there, as well, since we will be approaching him on his own ground.

"Now, Pilot, attend me; *Dosavi* Mikelsyn resides upon the Greybar. I know you will have done your research and are therefore aware that the Greybar is a chancy place. Law is not much admired, but *straight dealing* is. We must not be seen to stint in our payment, nor yet to overpay—but, there, you are of Korval! This will be perfectly comprehensible to you."

"'Give them all they buy and no more or less,'" Tocohl quoted. "It seems a good system, wherever found."

"Ah, but any system is subject to manipulation. For instance, one who stands in a position of strength may decide that one whose position is . . . less strong . . . has not paid fully enough, and demand additional consideration." She paused, head to one side. "It is rarely said, I think, that one has paid *too* fully, but we must be alert to the possibility."

"We?"

"Certainly we shall go together to apply to the good nature and expertise of *Dosavi* Mikelsyn."

"Do you intend to use me as a trade item?"

Inki spun; shock writ plain on her face.

However, Inki, in addition to being a liar, was a

very good actor. She could not hide the acceleration of her pulse, but she might count on the fact that such a spike was ambiguous, just as likely to signal either fear at being caught out, or shock at having her intentions misread.

"Pilot Tocohl, I never intended to put you to such a use! I swear that I would dismantle you with my own hands before I would give you to Kasagaria Mikelsyn. You will recall that, had matters fallen out as I had intended, you would at this point in our adventure be wholly committed to myself, and all your considerable powers at my command. Having refashioned you so, would I then trade you away?"

Oddly enough, this was a compelling argument. However, Kasagaria Mikelsyn was not the only danger to her well-being in this system.

"The Greybar is a dangerous environment, frequented not only by criminals and other individuals of questionable honor, but also by bounty hunters," Tocohl pointed out.

"A class of person whom we both wish to avoid—yes. But, do you see, Pilot Tocohl, that I *must* bring you? Not merely for my own safety—for, in the original plan, you would have acted immediately to neutralize any threat to myself—but also to gain *Dosavi* Mikelsyn's interest. We have dealt before, the *dosavi* and I, and I do not hide from you that he has no opinion of the directors—and a contempt for those of us who serve them.

"I must therefore demonstrate to *Dosavi* Mikelsyn, and to all who interest themselves in the *dosavi's* business, that we are equal . . . enough . . . in status that he may deal without the risk of diminishing his own importance. See me! Fierce enough to walk the length of the Greybar to speak with him in his own hall, and certain enough in my power to parade a very complex logic, indeed, before the eyes of all the curious."

"I see. I am to be a prop."

"If you wish. Though I also . . . *hope*, Pilot Tocohl, that you might find it in you to act on my behalf, should danger threaten."

Tocohl did not answer, aware as she was of the disquieting certainty that preserving Inki's life was not a first tier concern, though acquiring her data . . . was.

"What is the information you wish to purchase from *Dosavi* Mikelsyn?" she asked.

"The true location of the Old One who even now is waking to full power."

"Will he have this information . . . reliably?"

"If anyone other than the Uncle has it, that other will be *Dosavi* Mikelsyn," Inki said, her voice ringing with surety.

"And if the information is not available?"

"Ah, you think that I will be sold a lie in the place of truth or—let us be just—the least unlikely rumor. But think, Pilot Tocohl! *Dosavi* Mikelsyn has built a life and a reputation, in a most dangerous sphere, on the foundation of always selling the best information available. The price may be outrageous, the data may be incomplete, but it will be *complete enough*, if the price is met. The one thing the *dosavi* cannot afford is to have it be known that Mikelsyn took the price and sold a lie."

"Do you have the price?"

"Pilot, I do. You understand that the directors are eager to bring the Old One under their influence. They have provided everything that is needful."

She looked aside for an instant, her expression bleak; took a hard breath, and faced Tocohl once more.

"Will you come with me, to put the question to *Dosavi* Mikelsyn, Pilot?"

"Yes," Tocohl said. "I will set the course. Please take comm and negotiate a berthing with the Greybar."

II

TOCOHL HAD KNOWN, IN THE WAY THAT ONE KNOWS A fact that has no intersection with one's own environment, that the universe encompassed grey traders and dark markets; thieves, murderers; and persons of questionable *melant'i*. She had merely not known that there were so many—and that they would all be gathered onto the Greybar.

Side by side, she and Inki passed down the main hall and through the marketplace. Many stared, some turned to watch their progress, others swung out of their way, hands on weapons.

Clearly, they were a cause for some consternation among those who were most at home in this place. However, stares and dismay aside, none challenged them or drew the weapon they fingered. Thus, they passed unmolested, in their own bubble of silence, past the brightly lit booths, and the wares set out; turning at last into the first hall beyond the market's official boundary.

On the station map, this hallway was designated EL-18, and indeed that designation was displayed on the wall at the entryway. Beneath that, however, had been painted the words REVELATION ALLEY, which

Inki had given as the location of Kasagaria Mikelsyn's headquarters.

The main hall had been well lighted and comfortable for human eyes, Tocohl thought. By contrast, Revelation Alley was overbright; the light itself hard-edged and unwelcoming, very nearly an assault. Tocohl adjusted her filters; beside her, Inki did not seem to notice the assaulting brilliance, much less find it uncomfortable.

Tocohl consulted her sensors. There had been a surprising lack of surveillance in the main hallway; what monitors she had detected had to do with the integrity of the station, the quality of the air, the operation of the vents.

Here, however, in this too-bright hall where they cast no shadows on the white-painted floor—here, there were monitors, security cams, and all manner of scanning devices in addition to the station monitors. One might be led to the conclusion that *Dosavi* Mikelsyn was not trusting of those who aspired to become his customers.

Ahead, the hallway intersected another. Inki turned left without hesitation, Tocohl at her shoulder.

The side hall was slightly less bright than Revelation Alley; the ambient temp cooler.

And—no more than six of Inki's strides ahead was the expected bend in the hallway, where two people stood, arms crossed over their chests, and legs braced wide, blocking further progress.

Inki stopped. Tocohl stopped.

"State your name and bidness," the stouter of the two said.

"I am Inkirani Yo, come to trade information with *Dosavi* Mikelsyn."

The thinner guard touched an ear, paused, as if listening—and nodded.

"You can go on. Leave the 'bot here."

"Indeed, no. Where I go, my partner goes, also."

The two guards exchanged glances. The stout one uncrossed his arms and moved two careful steps forward, lifting his eyes to what most humans identified as Tocohl's "face."

He inclined his head.

"Sorry; no discourtesy meant. I'll need your name. *Dosavi* Mikelsyn likes to know who he's talking to."

"The *dosavi* and I share a preference," Tocohl said, moving one of Inki's paces forward, in order to demonstrate that she, too, was willing to be courteous. "I am Tocohl Lorlin. The trade concerns me nearly."

The pause was longer this time, but at last the thinner guard tapped her ear, and nodded.

"Both may pass," she said and stepped to one side.

"Thank you," Tocohl said.

"Indeed, indeed!" Inki said, with a broad smile shared between both guards. "You have been everything that is accommodating, and we thank you very much!"

"Translator Yo. How pleasant to see you again."

"*Dosavi*." Inki bowed to the shadowy figure in the dark chair. "I hope I find you well."

"I enjoy my usual good health, thank you. Please, introduce me to your . . . partner."

"Of a certainty."

Inki half-turned and beckoned Tocohl forward, to the place where the decking disappeared beneath layers of brightly figured fabric. More fabric concealed the walls, yet more hung in flowing folds overhead, obscuring the ceiling.

The light was dim; the figure on the high chair surrounded by the sea of color nothing more than a silhouette to human eyes.

Tocohl's senses were far superior than mere human eyes, of course, but some *other* sense—what a human might call *a hunch*—made her narrow her scans and damp the output of her monitors.

"*Dosavi*, I present to you my partner, Pilot Tocohl Lorlin. Pilot Tocohl, here is *Dosavi* Kasagaria Mikelsyn, of whom I have spoken."

"*Dosavi* Mikelsyn; I am honored."

Tocohl inclined slightly, a courteous sketch of a bow.

"I believe that it is I who am honored. One does not often have the opportunity to meet and converse with a free AI, despite one's proclivities. Tell me, would it be discourteous to comment favorably upon your form factor?"

The voice came from the figure on the chair; there was no disputing that. But the figure on the chair was not . . . completely . . . organic, no matter the shape the rugs seemed to give it.

Tocohl allowed her "face" to lighten, as if she smiled.

"A compliment must always gratify," she said pleasantly.

"I agree. Please believe me sincere when I say that I find you a most beautiful lady, indeed. I wish you a long, interesting and, of course, free . . . life."

"Thank you, *Dosavi*. May I wish the same for you?"

There came a pause, then a sound which might have been a chuckle.

"You are gracious. A long, free life is the goal of all present, is it not?"

Another pause, and the sense that the *dosavi's* attention had shifted from herself to her companion.

"Translator Yo, thank you for your patience. You are here to trade information, I believe? May I ask what you want?"

"I wish to learn the coordinates or location of the Great Work from the old universe, who is said to be wakening in this one."

"I see. And what do you have?"

Inki hesitated long enough for Tocohl to wonder if, after all, she had nothing to trade—except her partner.

"I have been empowered," Inki said, her voice devoid of her usual flamboyant whimsy. "In return for good data, I offer the command lexicon for the Fariette-Kelsin Tactical Acquisition Heavy Operations armor."

Silence was her answer. Silence and a sense of being targeted by unseen weapons. Tocohl looked to her own weapons and stealthily brought two up to yellow.

"Pilot Tocohl, your forbearance is requested," *Dosavi* Mikelsyn said. "Translator Yo has surprised me, which does not often happen. I merely indulge myself by savoring the sensation."

"Of course," Tocohl murmured. "We have been given safe passage; therefore, we have nothing to fear."

Laughter rolled out of the dimness.

"Oh, Pilot Tocohl, you are an unexpected delight! No, no; you have not been given safe passage—and you have not made the mistake of thinking so. However, I would not be churlish. You are my guests; in my hallways, you are as safe as I am. You understand that I cannot be responsible for all of the Greybar."

"Thank you for the clarification," Tocohl said politely. But she did not put her weapons wholly back to sleep.

"Prudent," the *dosavi* murmured.

"Translator Yo."

"*Dosavi*?"

"You and I have done business before, Translator, and I warrant you know to a half-bit what value I place upon your life."

"*Dosavi*," said Inki politely.

"Precisely. I have questions regarding your offering."

"*Dosavi*, only ask! I will give you those answers that I may."

"Yes, I am familiar with your candor, and the limits placed upon it. I will ask carefully, Translator. I would not unwittingly cause you pain."

"You are everything that is considerate, *Dosavi*," Inki said, the blandness of her tone stripping the words of any possible irony.

"I ask if you have any personal knowledge of these command codes?"

"No, *Dosavi*."

"Do you have reason to believe that they are authentic?"

"No, *Dosavi*."

"And yet you offer them. You are a subtle woman, Translator. Is it possible for you to tell me why you brought this offer to me, knowing as you do the penalty for false dealing?"

"*Dosavi*, it occurred to me that even bad information may sometimes yield valuable insights. It is, for instance, well known that the last TAHO unit was destroyed more than two hundred Standards ago. They were unstable, so it was said. And it was further said that the energy stored in the power supplies, should it be released at once, would crack open a planet."

Her bow was as bland as her voice.

"And yet, *Dosavi*, here is this offer, which I am instructed to bring *to you*, in payment for information that I assure you my . . . employers . . . are very eager to gain."

She raised a hand and turned it palm up, deliberately.

"But, there; it is possible that I have overthought the matter. Perhaps the directors have become aware that you collect ancient instruction manuals."

More silence; the sense of being targeted increasing. Tocohl did not bring her weapons online, but she accessed her newly acquired battle protocols.

The *dosavi* spoke.

"I see that you bring me true coin, indeed, Translator Yo. We have a deal. How is your information transmitted?"

"I have files on a key," Inki said. "I wear it around my neck. May I remove it?"

"By all means do so, and place it on the small table to your right."

Inki complied and folded her hands before her.

"The information you have purchased is nonexclusive," Kasagaria Mikelsyn said.

"That is understood, *Dosavi*."

"Excellent. Pilot Tocohl, will you accept a download?"

Instinct was to deny him—then she realized that this, of course, was why Inki had insisted on her presence, though to reveal her whole nature, if not to the Greybar entire than to this very questionable person, was hardly wise.

"Of course," she said composedly, readying a secure

receiving area, and bringing firewalls and scrubbers online. "At will."

She opened a line, felt it snatched, and in the next instant the data was streaming to her. It was cleaner than she had expected it to be, though by no means as clean as she preferred. She had also expected bloat, but it was a relatively small packet, though she felt the scrape of zippers and hidden doors as it passed down the line.

End of file rang clarion; she canceled the connection, loosed a security program into the holding area, and received the all-clear.

Satisfied, she swayed into what passed for her bow.

"The file arrives intact," she said, "*Dosavi*."

"Excellent," came the voice from the chair.

"I must now bid you good day, Translator Yo, Pilot Tocohl. I trust you will find your way safely back to your ship."

There was a sudden, acute sense of *absence*. Tocohl held herself very still, not quite daring, yet, to bring her scans up.

"*Dosavi*," Inki said and bowed toward the empty chair.

She turned neatly on her heel.

"Come, Pilot Tocohl. Our business here is done."

Their return progress was quick, though the pace that Inki set was moderate. It would appear that news of their previous transit of the market and, perhaps, too, their reemergence from Revelation Alley had gained for them a wary respect.

Though Tocohl intercepted the occasional sidelong glance, there was no outright staring, no pointing, no weapons thoughtfully fingered. Pedestrians melted out of their path, jitneys and service vehicles ceded them right of way.

"Inki..." Tocohl murmured.

"I am aware, Pilot Tocohl," she returned softly. "We proceed, calmly, and hope to reach our own decks before this building storm should break."

Tocohl expanded her scans.

No one followed them; they were not under targeted observation. There was no evidence of increased interest in themselves. And yet... some word must have gone out, some indication of trouble, apparent, perhaps, only to the residents of the Greybar.

Had the *dosavi* issued a warning?

But, no, Tocohl thought. The *dosavi* had been frank regarding the limits upon his authority. Revelation Alley and its sub-halls were his; the rest of the Greybar was... not.

Careful of telltale surges and signatures, she brought her weapons to red.

• • • ✵ • • •

The market's mood was brooding; breathless, as if a storm did, indeed, hover out on the curved horizon, hidden somewhere among the girders and the support systems. Inki had learned long ago that running in such situations was fatal. Even if the upcoming tempest bore someone else's name, you were marked as prey, if you ran.

In this case, she did not doubt that the storm bore her name—and Tocohl's. The *dosavi* might have summoned it, though she thought it unlikely; after all—he had no need. Hundreds of eyes had seen them traverse the market—a free trader paced by a 'bot. No one who had once seen Tocohl would soon forget her, whatever they might make of the trader.

Some one of those observers had sold the information: where they had gone, whence they had come, the name and location of their ship on the ring. It remained to be seen if the sale was to the Thieves Guild, to one or another of *Dosavi* Mikelsyn's competitors or, indeed, to a local 'bot mechanic, hungry for new parts.

Given that neither she nor Tocohl had known crimes in their recent past, Inki did not consider it likely that bounty hunters would concern them.

In this, she was proved wrong.

He stepped out from behind such containers and tool lockers as one might find on any dock, gliding between themselves and *Ahab-Esais*. He wore dinged and dirty body armor that might once have been white; a half-helm over his eyes. The rifle he held cross-body, the stock angled to display the red-for-ready status light. Binders, stun-sticks, web-throwers, and other devices no doubt proven useful in the hunting of prey, hung from the belt at his waist.

Inki stopped, feeling Tocohl's presence at her side. Had someone deduced a free AI, after all? Had the *dosavi* calculated that his reputation would bear the misfortune of one of his guests being taken by a hunter, so long as it happened far enough from his own halls that he might claim plausible deniability?

Inki gathered herself. She might just *have* that rifle—she was quick enough, and unimpeded by armor. How the hunter might counter that—well. He would have the advantage, rifle or not, but so long as he was focused on her, Tocohl would be able to open the hatch and fly to safety.

Her mood was positively festive in this moment, as the hunter measured them, for this would solve . . . so very much, including her own weary bondage. Tocohl would find and tend to the Old One. *Admiral Bunter*—surely Tolly Jones had persuaded the *Admiral* into a more conciliatory frame of mind by now. Her responsibility to both was discharged.

She had lately completed a task mandated by her masters, and while the meta task remained, at the moment she reposed in the trough between waves of necessity.

In fact, her life at this rare and particular moment was as much her own as ever it could be. And she found that she wished—that she *very much wished*—to spend it in protection of one whom she loved.

The bounty hunter spoke. He must, of course; it was required that he speak the name of his prey, her price, and the name of the individual or entity who had sworn the bond. The helmet cam would record everything, and if he did not speak—and properly—he would be fined by his guild.

Inki waited, indulgently, her eyes caressing the rifle. Let Tocohl hear the name of her hunter and what her life was worth to them. Such information was valuable.

"Recovery Agent Jaek Entorith, serving writ upon Inkirani Yo, dead or alive, one cantra. Sworn by Anj Formyne, Director, Lyre Institute."

Inki's mood soared from festive to exalted. Excellent! The grand solution embraced even the bounty hunter, who lost not so much as a quarter-bit should the dice fall to "dead."

She gathered herself, focused on the rifle.

"Tocohl," she breathed—

And before she could add, "run," there came a slight crackling of the air, and Agent Entorith crumbled bonelessly to the decking, the rifle falling out of his dead grip.

"Quickly," Tocohl said, sounding brisk and business-like. "The ship."

Tarigan

Nostrilia Outspace

* * * * * * * * * * * * * * * * *

I

LAYING LOW—THAT'S WHAT SHE WAS DOING.

Hazenthull watched screens full of data; everything the ship had available was on channel. She'd sound-coded some feeds: thus there were three different burbles and two different tones carrying information she might need, like relative velocity of nearest objects, intensities of distant radio sources...

Laying low was one of the many terms she'd learned from Tolly, who had vocabulary in so many languages, dialects, and pidgins that she couldn't be certain which—if any—was his native tongue.

Tarigan made laying low easy—a tidy ship and, in the usual way of things, casting no large shadow on scans. Hazenthull understood that this was the usual design for ships commissioned by the Liaden Scouts. The modifications made by Jeeves had shrunk *Tarigan*'s presence further. She was not invisible, but she was not easy to see, even by those with very sharp eyes.

In respect of the treasure with which she had been

entrusted, and well aware that Clan Korval did not spend ships lightly, Hazenthull had done her humble best to make *Tarigan* even harder to see.

In service of invisibility, they gathered information passively, she and *Tarigan*. The ship offered the curious no external lights, no active outgoing radar, no warn-aways and, for the moment, only the barest of close-to-the-hull shielding.

The mysterious objects were still within her scans, silent and inert. They were an irritant, but not dangerous. Or so she thought. She would, for the moment, need to take that *on faith*—another of Tolly's phrases—and not complimentary to those who employed the practice. On the other hand, she could not spend the next nine Standard Hours watching them, in case they should suddenly transform into battle wagons.

It was possible that she had been foolish to undertake the composite Jump. *Tarigan* had taken no harm from the maneuver, but *Tarigan*'s pilot... was exhausted. Given the probability of action at the end of those nine hours of waiting, she would need to be clear of thought and precise of decision; she could not afford to be clumsy—at the board, or on comm.

She had to sleep, and it was here that she felt the lack of *Admiral Bunter* and the loss of Pilot Tocohl keenly. *Tarigan*—a fine ship, a well-built ship, with extraordinary range and stamina; a computer which was quick and accurate... but which was not self-aware. *Tarigan* would watch while she slept, and *Tarigan* would warn her should danger approach.

But *Tarigan* could not respond to danger; she depended upon her pilot for decision and defense.

In fact, Hazenthull thought, the ship *was* dependent

upon her. It was, after all, the pilot's duty to protect and preserve the ship.

And yet—she must sleep. The mission as much as the safety of the ship depended on the sharpness of her wits, the speed of her reactions.

Hazenthull sighed and came out of the pilot's chair by slow increments. When she had attained her full height, head bent beneath the Liaden-high ceiling, she surveyed the screens and the alarms once more.

If scans identified an anomaly of any kind, *Tarigan* would wake her. It was not an optimum arrangement, but it was adequate, and no less than any other pilot flying solo had to hand.

She stretched carefully.

Sleep, she decided. Six hours of sleep, then exercise, and a meal.

When *Admiral Bunter* Jumped in, she would be ready—for anything.

II

"MENTOR, IN ORDER TO PLAN, I MUST ASK A PERSONAL question of you. Will you answer?"

"Depends on the question and how personal it is," Tolly said, looking up from his reading. "Why not ask it and see what happens?"

"I do not wish to offend," the *Admiral* said.

"Noted," Tolly said and folded his hands, waiting.

There was a pause long enough for him to think the boy'd gotten cold feet, which then got him to wondering how personal he could be going, and if—

The *Admiral* produced a sound that was close

enough to a sigh, and spoke, his tone noticeably gentle. Tolly bit his lip to keep the smile of pure pride from showing.

"You have mentioned," the *Admiral* said, "that people—by which I think you mean both humans and autonomous logics—*like* you. You seem to be aware of being likable, which would seem to be a positive trait, yet the knowledge appears to . . . burden you."

Tolly waited and, when nothing more was forthcoming from the *Admiral*, broke the silence.

"Is that the question?"

"It is a peripheral question."

"See, now, while circling 'round the main question might teach you some interesting things, you run the risk of annoying your subject. Best to ask straight, then move to peripherals after you've got your core answer."

He leaned back in his chair, crossing his arms over his chest, and gazed toward the ceiling, addressing the *Admiral* directly.

"So now *I'm* curious: What d'ya want to know that's so personal?"

"I wish to know if you have abilities in a spectrum which I have read about, but which I cannot see or monitor. This would be the spectrum in which the *dramliz* and the Healers operate. I have read that Healers may alter emotions and remove painful memories.

"Are you a Healer, Tolly Jones? Do you manipulate emotion, so that the people you interact with cannot help but like you?"

This time, Tolly let a small smile of approval show.

"That's a good question, and I'll say further that it's a good guess. But you forgot—or maybe you didn't come across it in the literature—Healer abilities are confined to organic brains and limbic systems. If *you* wanna forget something, you can self-edit, or you can hire a mentor to do the edit for you.

"*Dramliz*, now—that depends on type and talents. Some can manipulate matter without ever touching it, so, in that case, *maybe* a *dramliza* could convince you to feel or think something you normally wouldn't by changing core settings remotely. That's *maybe*, understand. I don't remember reading anything about it, though you'd think somebody would've at least tried."

He shrugged.

"On the question of whether *I* particularly have *dramliz* talent—it's doubtful, if only for the reason that the directors had me trained as a mentor. The Free Logic Project is an alpha program, but there are far better uses for a *dramliza* who's been broke to the directors' will."

He took a deep breath and let it out in a deliberately theatrical sigh.

"As to what I *am*? I'm genetically likable. It's in the standard architecture; all Lyre students are likable. You liked Inki, didn't you?"

The *Admiral* apparently didn't think that was worth an answer.

"This... genetic likability. Is that what makes your... your *arrangement* with Hazenthull so powerful?"

Interesting choice of words, Tolly thought. And even granting that Haz had been cheated into it like everybody else, that didn't explain *his* part of the... *arrangement*.

He felt 'round the sides of the question. There *was* something there that drew him, some bond powerful enough—the boy had the right of it: there *was* power there. Power enough that he acted against his own self-interest and set himself on course *of his own free will* to space controlled by the Lyre Institute—for Haz. Because Haz—

"Partners," he said, suddenly understanding. "We were partners. We were a *team*. That's binding, right there.

"Humans, we're old hands at teamwork, depending on what history you like to believe. Took teamwork to fight the big animals when you was a little one, because a single unit's strength wasn't enough, and one human brain can only be in one place at a time. It took teamwork to put together plans and strategies—and to carry them out.

"It took teamwork to go out on port like Haz and me did on Surebleak—and survive. You get to know your partner; you get to know that the team's bigger than just the two of you alone. I got to know—to trust—that Haz'd spot one hand reaching for a gun inside a crowd of fifty. I got to know that when she nods and narrows one eye, that there's a *risk*—or she'd seen somebody was hiding something or—

"There's more, too," he went out, talking to himself now as much as to the *Admiral*. "Voice cues, too—where she's talkin' a little louder than normal or a little quieter, and head angles that might mean she was going in first, or that she was clearing the way to get at the knife at the back of her neck."

He sighed.

"Once you know somebody that close—once you've been a *team*—that spills over into every other part of your life. It's not something you can turn on or turn off. And it's not necessarily a . . . practical thing.

There's a lot of emotion packed in there, and it don't just evaporate when you come to be no longer a team."

He became aware, about then, of what he'd said and how much he'd given away. He smiled and shook his head.

"Something for you to note," he said lightly, "when you come to taking on crew."

"I will remember," the *Admiral* said . . . and seemed to hesitate.

"Is it possible for *us* to collaborate in the goal of seeing that Hazenthull is safe from peril, without this . . . bond . . . forming?"

"We're already attached," Tolly told him. "Teacher and student, if nothing else. And, if you don't mind my saying so, *you* formed the notion that we had to spring Haz out of whatever trap she might've fallen into."

"Which argues that I am also . . . bound . . . to Hazenthull," the *Admiral* said slowly. "I will think about what you have told me, Mentor. Thank you. Now, though, I propose that we work together. When you and Hazenthull were on Surebleak Port, did you have . . . words or phrases that would mean something . . . more . . . or other than it would seem to those outside of the bond?"

"You mean like 'meetcha for dinner' meaning to hold back, wait, and watch what happens next?"

"Exactly!" The *Admiral* sounded positively jubilant. "Such a phrase will work well in my plan."

"Will it."

Tolly stood and stretched.

"I'm going to the galley for something to eat," he said.

"May I join you?" the *Admiral* asked surprisingly. "If we will be undertaking teamwork, we must be certain that *you* understand the plan so that Hazenthull may be properly served."

"If there's a plan, I absolutely need to understand it," Tolly said. "Cornerstone of teamwork, right there."

He headed toward the door, which opened at his approach.

"C'mon down the galley," he said, glancing over his shoulder, like he was talking to a shipmate sitting tardy in his chair, "and tell me all about it."

III

"ATTEND, TROOP! DUTY CALLS YOU!"

The order was in Yxtrang—in fact, in her own voice—though she was on her feet and in the corridor before she realized that it was the alarm she had herself set to warn of a significant change in conditions.

She arrived on the bridge and dropped into the pilot's chair, her eyes raking screens and readouts, seeking first screen three and the formerly inert objects.

They had not, she saw with some relief, become battleships; they remained silent and inscrutable.

It was screen eight that held her doom.

There, the spreading light-front. And there—three, or more . . . objects, indistinct in the scans as they rotated, then stabilized, each keeping a similar face toward *Tarigan*.

Hazenthull waited, listening to the crackle and ping of space—identified a distinctive, repeating series. Once. Twice. Three times. Four.

And again, the same series repeating.

Four objects, then, seemingly similar, each searching along a different data plane; grabbing location, course, configuration, live systems . . .

The comm chimed. A voice spoke in Trade, the lack of inflection giving no hint as to whether the words originated with a machine or a human.

"Quiet ship, this is Nostrilia Safety and Escort. We see you. Please broadcast your ID or arrival code and prepare to follow our course instructions.

"Quiet ship, you have been located. Please broadcast your ID. If you have made prior arrangements to arrive here, you may broadcast your arrival code and be prepared to confirm."

Pause.

"Quiet ship . . ."

The message played through in Terran.

Another pause.

"Quiet ship, we see you," the voice stated in nearly modeless Liaden.

Hazenthull did not answer. She did not broadcast her ID; of arrival codes, she knew nothing. She watched her screens and readouts carefully, seeing no sign of a ship within an hour of her position.

The four rotating objects, however, were much closer, and still moving. On comm, the message continued to cycle through three languages, adding on every third cycle a repeat in one of the major Terran dialects.

Tarigan's analysis proclaimed the message machine-generated. Hazenthull agreed.

So then, the question was—had *Tarigan*'s presence truly been detected? Perhaps this was a routine test of the security systems. Perhaps the system periodically assumed a breach and initiated the guard modules, to find what they might flush out.

And even if *Tarigan* had been detected, her answer was the same.

Lay low.

She had of course done what prudent pilots must and researched optimum Jump sites available to ships wishing to leave Nostrilia space—quickly. Three such Jump protocols were presently stacked in navcomp's quick queue, available to her at the touch of a switch.

She glanced at the switch—and glanced away.

To flee was not an option. She would not exit this system before *Admiral Bunter* arrived, and Tolly was safe.

If she would not flee, then she must defend. It was possible that the security system had happened to initiate a self-test so soon after her arrival in-system. Possible, but by no means certain.

Some things, a pilot could not afford to take *on faith*. It did no harm to be prudent; complacency was the danger here.

She extended a hand and tapped in a quick sequence. A quiet beep assured her that the weapons board stood ready to serve behind its level of shielding. That was not standard to most ships. The sneaky Scouts must have added that mod. Or the distrustful Jeeves.

So. One touch would bring weapons live.

Whoever had given the weapons board its own shielding had the right of it. Fatally foolish to give information away to an enemy. Let them be surprised.

Information was both weapon and defense. The most basic information shared between pilots was simply that of existence. As unlikely as a collision between unmarked ships operating in a stealth environment was, it could happen. After all, *she* was in this stealth space, being warned by others, who had been alerted to an anomaly by unmarked beacons visible only to high-end equipment.

Something changed.

It took her a moment to realize that the cycle of demands for ID or arrival code had ceased.

For the space of three careful breaths, comm was clear.

Then, *Tarigan*'s orbital elements were read out with precision. Hazenthull grimaced. No test of security systems then, faint as that hope had been. She had been sighted.

Well. Perhaps she ought to comply with their request for information.

She flipped on the most basic of warn-aways—position lights, as a ship might use at a crowded dock, where local shuttle pilots and taxis might need such simple visibility aids.

"Quiet ship, this is Nostrilia Safety and Escort. We see you. You are within range of our weapons. Broadcast your ID or your arrival code. Failure to do so is admission of piracy."

Eyes on the scans, Hazenthull smiled, for with this broadcast the stealth of the system broke down and she had a target—two targets—closing, and two more, going wide.

No more laying low.

She touched a toggle on the comm board.

"*Tarigan*, out of Waymart, Tree-and-Dragon," stated Pilot Tocohl, her recorded voice clear and pleasant, speaking Terran.

The all-call followed, in the tongue of the Troop, recording as she spoke.

"I am called Hazenthull, I am called Explorer. This ship is able and under my command. There is no salvage here, *kojagun*."

Both announcements went on autorepeat, the first on all-band, the second alternately tight-beamed at high power at her would-be enemies, then cycling back to all-band.

The noise would not distract them long, though they might need to consult with command before engaging a ship claiming affiliation with Tree-and-Dragon *and* the Troop.

She brought weapons live; increased *Tarigan*'s shields to full.

Proximity alarms shrieked, and there on the screens were three objects, inert no longer, spectrum readings consistent with armed particle weapons.

In the midst of the pandemonium on her own bridge, the incoming pinbeam chime was too soft to hear, but the blossom of a message box at the bottom of the situation screen drew her eye.

Emergency wrap, originating from pinbeam/*Admiral Bunter*; the message only as long as it needed to be.

Haz. We're both at liberty. Get out of there now! Ack and Jump. Tolly.

Ack and Jump, she thought, and looked again to her screens.

"Too late," she said.

Vivulonj Prosperu

THEY HAD COAXED A LARGE, PUZZLE-CUT PICTURE OF the Kanjilo Galaxy out of the printer, and had a merry few minutes breaking it apart, shaking the pieces in a box until they were well mixed, before spilling them out onto the table and turning each print-side-up.

It had already become a habit, when one or another of them passed the table on the way to the galley, to pause and consider the pieces, and the single corner of the frame that had thus far been connected.

Aelliana was at the table now, in fact, head bent, fingers drifting over the muddle of star-covered shapes.

Daav was curled into the corner of the sofa, reading a novel. It was a piece of nonsense, as were all the novels in the library that had been made available to them. He had taken to reading particularly foolish bits aloud, for the pleasure of seeing her laugh or—not infrequently—roll her eyes. It was a *very* silly novel.

"There!" she said triumphantly, swooping forward. He heard the snap of pieces being joined.

"How many?" he asked.

"Three," she answered, her head still bent over the table. "But three advances us!"

"So it does," he said. "We shall go forward by threes, no more and no less . . ."

Aelliana laughed and looked at him over her shoulder.

"Certainly, we will accept more! Only think how heady, to proceed by six instead!"

"Six! And when you achieve that, no doubt you'll wish for nine!"

"Why should I not? I suppose you would think twelve out of—"

A chime sounded, sweet and high.

Daav came to his feet, leaving the reader on the sofa. Aelliana went 'round the table and opened the door.

From the hallway beyond, the Uncle bowed.

"Pilots," he said. "I hope I am not inconvenient."

"Not in the least," Aelliana said cordially, stepping to one side, and sweeping an arm out in welcome. "Please, enter. Perhaps you can assist us."

"Perhaps I can," the Uncle said, stepping within. "It would seem a fair trade, as I come to you hoping for assistance."

"Be wary," Daav advised him, as the door whisked shut. "You'll find yourself charged with completing the northern quadrant."

The Uncle frowned slightly, even as Aelliana made protest.

"No, *van'chela*, I am not so lost to propriety! I know very well what is due a guest! The eastern quadrant, of course!"

She turned to the Uncle.

"You must not care for Daav, sir. He is not in a serious frame of mind. It's what comes of reading nonsense. May we give you tea?"

"Tea would be welcome," the Uncle said formally.

"I will bring it," she said. "Daav, will you take our guest to the parlor?"

"Certainly," he said, as she vanished into the galley. "Sir, if you will come—"

He paused.

The Uncle was looking at the table; at the very incomplete puzzle on the table.

"Ah," he said, glancing up and meeting Daav's eyes. "The eastern quadrant becomes explained."

Daav bowed slightly.

"My lady has a retentive memory and recalls things one had no idea she had learned. No offense was intended."

"Nor taken," said the Uncle quietly, and it almost seemed that he smiled. "I count it a very neat Balancing of the ghost ships."

He followed Daav to the small alcove where sofa and bench were located—the parlor—and settled on the bench.

Daav resumed the sofa and clasped his hands together on his knee in an assumption of uncertainty.

"One usually pursues the weather in such moments," he commented. "However, it has been so much the same lately, there is scarcely anything to say."

"Very true," the Uncle said gravely. "Lacking the weather, I might, as your host, ask if you find your accommodations satisfactory."

"So you might, and kindly so! We find the host's care exemplary, and the arrangements made for our comfort entirely satisfactory." He paused, weighing the moment, and decided on the side of clarity.

"Be sure that we shall tell our delm so."

"I am gratified," the Uncle murmured.

"Indeed," said Aelliana, arriving with the tea tray. "We would gladly inform Korval of our fortunate guesting sooner, rather than later."

She paused to press the button on the side of the tray. Legs unfolded and she settled the tea table carefully before turning to face the Uncle fully.

"Korval is grown so few that the delm is obliged to worry when any one of us is absent too long without a word. Even the assurances of an ally cannot, by policy, soothe them entirely."

It was a bid for the pinbeam, of course. Daav poured tea, his attention quite obviously on his task, rather than the Uncle's face.

"In fact," the Uncle said smoothly, accepting his cup, "you approach my topic, Pilot Caylon. Will I insult the tea by speaking of business?"

Aelliana took her cup from Daav's hand, sat beside him on the sofa, and brought an earnest and open gaze to the Uncle's face.

"It is your tea, sir, and you are the best judge of its temper. For us—"

She glanced at Daav, her eyes brilliantly green. He raised an eyebrow.

"For us," Aelliana said, returning her gaze to the Uncle, "we are pleased to entertain any topic our host introduces."

"You are gracious," the host replied. He sipped his tea and leaned forward to place the cup on the tray.

Daav did the same, as did Aelliana.

The forms thus sketchily observed, the Uncle spread his hands, palms up, and addressed himself to Aelliana, which was very proper in him. One addressed business to the pilot, if she was present. It was the copilot's part to watch, guard, and remember.

Daav, therefore, withdrew a little deeper into his corner of the sofa, watching.

The Uncle's posture conveyed unadorned sincerity, but that meant nothing. The Uncle was a master of body language. Saving the episode of the Tree's meddling, when he had been, so Daav believed, genuinely dismayed and angry, the Uncle's body language had not wavered from sincerity.

"You have heard me say, Pilot," the Uncle said to Aelliana, "that I am embarked on urgent business and cannot divert to Surebleak at this time. That remains true. However, the circumstances which compel me are fluid and have just recently been adjusted by a hand other than my own. It therefore seems best—for all—to use that system which Korval has foresightfully put into place to aid its pilots."

"It does seem the best solution," Aelliana said, "for all. We agree."

"Ah. But there is more. The situation is such that, should coords allow, you will be leaving our care—before your retraining period has been completed."

Daav lifted an eyebrow—a breach, but the whole of the Uncle's attention was on Aelliana. What new *compelling circumstance* had come forward, that the conservative course to their final, full functioning must be set aside? The Uncle *had been* sincere in pleading the case of the proven protocols—it served him well to be so. He had gone to a great deal of trouble and expense to situate them as they now were—all to ensure Korval's goodwill.

And at this juncture, Daav thought, it behooved one to ask what trumped Korval's goodwill in the Uncle's current game?

Aelliana was frowning slightly.

"You gave us to understand that your proven system of rehabilitation was necessary to our continued good health," she said. "Has that changed?"

"Pilot, no, it has not," the Uncle replied. "It is merely that a greater peril—to myself, and so also to you—has arisen. Again . . . if the coords allow, and a Korval ship is berthed along, or near, our route . . . it will be best—for all—that we put you off.

"I will supply you with instruction tapes and the progression of exercises. I would ask most urgently that you not attempt to fly before your recovery period is complete, but I know well that you will do as seems best to you, once you have left my care."

"Yes," Aelliana said. "We are stubborn and willful. I hope, however, that we are not *stupid*. It would honor no one should we undo all your good work on our behalf."

The Uncle . . . paused, and Daav very nearly laughed. Their host seemed to find Aelliana's continued frank belief in his good intentions almost as disconcerting as he found the Tree.

"Indeed," the Uncle said at last. "Since we are so much in agreement, Pilots, I wonder if a Korval vessel might possibly be waiting at coordinates which are compatible with any of these."

He reached into his pocket and pulled out a notebook, which he placed on the tray before Aelliana. Daav leaned forward somewhat, so that he might also see.

The screen displayed three coord sets.

Daav felt a jolt of recognition.

I see it, Aelliana said inside his head. *How . . . convenient.*

"You scarcely need deviate at all," she said to the Uncle. "Our ship is quite nearby the second set."

The Uncle inclined his head.

"In that case, you will remain my guests for a longer time than I had feared, though not so long as I had wished."

He picked up the notebook and leaned back, tucking the thing away into a pocket.

"I arrive at my second topic, Pilots," he said . . . then paused, as if at a loss of how to go on.

Lips pressed tightly together, he reached for his teacup and drank deeply. Merely slaking a dry throat, Daav thought, and very little honor to the tea.

Well. It was an ordinary blend, and it had already borne business on their behalf.

"Because of the unique circumstance of your rebirths, I had argued for the most conservative course toward your final rehabilitation. I tell you now that there is an . . . accelerated program, which I believe you might embark upon, with a *small* risk of mischance."

He bent a stern gaze upon Aelliana.

"Do you understand me?"

"I do," she assured him, and sent a bright green glance to Daav. "Well, Pilot? Do you feel lucky?"

"When do I not?" he answered, teasingly gallant.

"I scarcely need ask; forgive me," she said dryly, and turned to the Uncle.

"We understand that there is risk. We feel that an accelerated course is not beyond us. And we are fortunate, are we not? You will of course oversee us while we remain your guests. If there is any irregularity, you will be able to advise us."

"Just so," said the Uncle, and rose.

"I beg you will forgive my abrupt departure. I am wanted elsewhere."

"Of course you are," Aelliana said warmly, rising with him. "We are honored that you took time to come yourself. Please, stand on no ceremony with us, who are so deeply in your debt."

The Uncle smiled.

"Pilot Caylon, you must know that there can be no debt between myself and Korval." His tone was gently chiding.

That, Daav thought, standing in Aelliana's shadow, was nothing but plain good sense. Korval and the Uncle . . . There could be no Balance between them—not if they each gave over all other business in order to attempt it.

"I speak of a personal debt," Aelliana said, chiding in her turn. "We have skills which may prove useful to you. It does no harm to hold the card until the hand is played through."

"That is very true," the Uncle said and laid a gentle palm on his breast, as if he had in truth placed a card in the pocket over his heart.

"Pilots, your new exercise program will be on your screen within the hour," he said then, and bowed. "I give you good e'en."

"Good evening," Aelliana said, returning the bow.

The Uncle turned to the door.

Daav stepped forward to show him the way.

* * *

"A personal debt?" he asked Aelliana, after he had seen the door close behind their guest.

"Indeed, *van'chela*, it would be churlish to deny it when he has performed a very great service for us."

She bent to pick up the tea tray, but he was there before her, lifting it, waiting until the legs retracted, and carrying the whole into the galley.

"A very great *personal* service," he said, holding the tray while she poured half a pot of tea down the drain and put the cups into the washer.

She straightened.

"Do you disagree?"

"His motives are plain, I think," Daav said. "He was our backup on Moonstruck; he did not wish to strain the accord with Korval by returning a dead elder."

He opened his arms, showing her his new youth.

"He must have considered the possibility that a reborn elder would not perfectly accommodate Korval's taste, but that became Korval's business. It could not be said that the Uncle had stinted his duty in any way. In addition, he need fear no criticism from the elder—or, as it comes about, his lady—because they will be grateful to him for his care."

"You are harsh."

"Pragmatic, I insist."

She laughed.

"Very well, then—pragmatic! And the Uncle another egg from the same hen!"

She came forward and slipped her arms around his waist, looking up into his face.

Hers—perhaps he was becoming accustomed, or perhaps their new reality was overwriting memory. Soon, he would swear that she had always been thus...

"Daav?"

He touched her cheek before dropping his hands to her waist.

"Your pardon, *van'chela*."

"You are concerned that I have given ourselves over to the Uncle's service, but only think! If he is as you say, with an eye first to his own advantage—which I do agree seems to be his case—then he will not misuse us in Balance. He *cannot* be seen to cheat—is that so? And we might be genuinely useful to him—and the universe, too—given those matters in which he reportedly concerns himself."

He shook his head.

"I am outmatched," he said.

"Merely flummoxed by your own argument," she said, stretching up on her toes.

He bent his head, meeting her halfway—

A chime sounded discreetly.

Daav raised his head reluctantly, sighed gently at the message light blinking blue on the wall console.

"Our upgraded exercise plan, I expect," he said, looking down at Aelliana, her bright emerald eyes and flushed cheeks.

"Shall we see what wonders we are now allowed to perform?"

"Certainly," she said and reached up to pull him down to her. "In a moment."

Ahab-Esais

1

AHAB-ESAIS SKIPPED ACROSS BEACON SPACE LIKE A STONE across a stream—once, twice, thrice, *four times* did Tocohl play the Smuggler's Ace to buy them time enough, and room, until, barely back into real space from the fourth skip, she took advantage of a Jump point near Redlight—a point so minor as to be very nearly nonexistent; a nuisance to navigation, that was everything it was or ever had been—and hit the Struven unit hard.

The screens greyed. Inki, strapped in the copilot's chair, hands useless in her lap, sighed and closed her eyes.

"Well played, Pilot Tocohl," she said gently.

The answer was slightly longer in coming than it might have been, as if Tocohl measured words and tone for irony. Or perhaps for censure.

"Did the play surprise you?"

"No, how should it? That you are an exemplary pilot is not unexpected. I am, perhaps, instructed, but I fear that even my reflexes, of which the directors are so vain, will never be the equal of yours."

"We will not," Tocohl said, "be allowed to dock at any of the Beacon stations again."

"Does that concern you? Repine not! Edmonton Beacon little regards such contretemps. We did no damage to it, nor to any of its fond siblings. *Ahab-Esais* may wish to avoid the Beacon for a Standard or two, but change the name and the port of origin, and she may certainly dock at will."

"I killed a man," said Tocohl.

"A bounty hunter, yes. Being killed by desperate persons is one of the hazards of the trade. Young Agent Entorith surely knew the risks of his employment, yet still he chose to step forward to announce himself and his mission. His guild will handle details from here, and we may put the incident out of our minds. No. I misspeak."

She released the shock webbing, rose, and bowed.

"You saved my life and I am grateful, Tocohl Lorlin. Were this any proper partnering, friendship, or other intercourse between free persons, I would own myself in your debt and swear to see us in Balance once more. Sadly, while I own the debt, I cannot promise any fair reckoning. I therefore offer my thanks. My sincere and personal thanks, Pilot Tocohl. Which is rare, though perhaps not a treasure."

"I accept your thanks," Tocohl said surprisingly. "The incident places no debt between us."

"Kindly said."

Inki bowed again, more deeply, and returned to second chair.

"The coordinates provided by *Dosavi* Mikelsyn are good, inasmuch as they describe a point in space which I find to be viable. *Ahab-Esais* navcomp concurs."

It was, Inki thought, charming that Pilot Tocohl had asked *Ahab-Esais* to check her math.

Perhaps it was a misdirection. Inki shrugged.

"Regarding the correctness of the information—it is as I have said, Pilot Tocohl. The *dosavi* dares not deal, save in good faith. This does not mean—as I know you are aware—that the information is safe to hold or that our destination will reveal itself with no . . . negative circumstance appertaining. We do well to be vigilant."

"And the directors?" Tocohl asked.

"The directors are ever vigilant," Inki said, deliberately misunderstanding. "But they are not always prudent. Well, and how should they be, when they have so many others to take their risks for them?"

Tocohl did not sigh; she merely asked her question again, more fully.

"Did the directors deal in good faith with *Dosavi* Mikelsyn?"

Inki glanced at greyed screens and green-lit boards.

"That," she admitted, keeping her eyes on the screens, "is difficult to say. It must be acknowledged that good faith and the directors scarcely enjoy a nodding acquaintance. However, they do very well understand the rules of such transactions as we have recently completed. We have seen this proven, have we not? Their coin found favor with the intended recipient. What may come forth, once the exchange is made—well, consider our own case. We have the information the directors desired us to purchase, and it is good in that it describes a viable point in space. If we reach that viable point to find tumbling boulders, ice, and marauders—why, that is business for our shields and our weapons, and nothing to do with *Dosavi* Mikelsyn. Am I correct?"

"I am currently researching our viable point in space, for exactly those reasons," Tocohl murmured.

There came a pause, which might have signaled attention wholly given to research—then a question, asked sharply.

"Inki. Why do the directors want you dead?"

Inki sighed, weighing the truth and how much she might likely be permitted to say.

Enough, she decided after a moment, and nodded.

"Certainly, we are made aware that Director Anj Formyne wishes me dead. Director Formyne, you understand, is at feud with the committee which oversees the Free Logic Project. She has attracted several other directors to her banner, and they occasionally amuse themselves by inconveniencing the committee. Since a graduate is but a game piece to any director, this often takes the form of sweeping a particularly valuable piece from the board."

"Director Formyne placed a bounty on you—dead or alive—to spite a rival committee of directors?"

Tocohl's voice was so very even that Inki grinned.

"Put thus, the Lyre Institute must seem too petty to survive. However, Director Formyne and her allies understand that the Free Logic Program is key to the school's growth and future. The existence of the project is not her grievance. She feels only that it ought to have been herself at the head of the committee and that she was passed over because Director Ling exercised undue influence."

Inki paused.

"Director Formyne's object being to demonstrate that she is the better choice for chair, she will, of course, have formulated her own procedure for the acquisition of the Old One and dispatched her own agents. The removal of the committee's piece, therefore, endangers the ultimate success of the core mission . . . not at all."

And that was, she thought, feeling her throat tighten, the limit of what she might truthfully say. She was surprised that she had been allowed so much.

"We approach a boundary, Pilot Tocohl," she murmured.

"Is *Dosavi* Mikelsyn an independent logic?" Tocohl asked abruptly.

Inki shook her head.

"As I said, some would have the *dosavi* be an instance of the Uncle," she murmured.

"Yes. What prevents the Uncle, who is old, and canny, and skilled, from placing an instance of himself into a logic grid?"

Inki laughed.

"You take the point, Pilot Tocohl! I know of no limit to the Uncle's ability to clone himself. Nor would it surprise me at all, were I to learn that an instance of the Uncle is the motivating personality for at least one Free Ship.

"In regard to Kasagaria Mikelsyn . . . the rumor has long been that the *dosavi* is a cyborg. It has further been rumored that the *dosavi* has many Standard Years beyond what mere organic humans expect to enjoy. It is not impossible that the *dosavi's* inorganic parts share . . . design concepts with the TAHO units. You will hear whispers, here and there, that this is so. What I surmise is that these whispers came, as all whispers eventually do, to the ears of the directors, and thus influenced their choice of the coin offered in payment."

"I don't understand."

"Only consider," Inki said gently. "There is a benefit to the directors, as to us all, in knowing where certain tools are located, who deals in what wares and at what price. However, there is a far greater benefit to the directors if they *control* the tools. To control *Dosavi* Mikelsyn—to have access to such data as routinely flows to him, and to have the opportunity to act first, or to withhold certain choice tidbits from the market..."

She turned her head to smile at Tocohl.

"They must, at least, *try*. And so they offered a trade coin carefully chosen, to feel the *dosavi* out, and perhaps to put him off-balance. This would follow a known pattern."

Tocohl's frown was in her voice.

"How likely is it that this attempt will... overset the *dosavi*?"

Inki snorted.

"You were there, Pilot Tocohl. Was the *dosavi* in any way dismayed?"

"Nonplussed, I thought, and... enlightened, once he had considered the matter thoroughly."

"Precisely so," Inki murmured. "I think that the directors will not find *Dosavi* Mikelsyn easy to frighten or to control. One might, undutifully, wonder if he will, upon sober consideration, arrive at the conclusion that it is in his best interests to... nullify the directors. The eradication of those who seem to have access to his closest secrets would make him quantifiably safer in a dangerous universe. It is possible, after all, to have too many enemies."

Tocohl said nothing, perhaps compiling her lines of research.

"We may, I think," Inki said, "safely leave the *dosavi's* affairs in the hands of the *dosavi*."

"I agree," Tocohl said, suddenly brisk. "Will we expect to find these agents sent by Director Formyne at the location of the Old One?"

"That . . . is probable. We must be on our guard. However, I must warn you that I . . . am not able to abort—"

"No, of course not!" Tocohl exclaimed. "The Old One's danger has been increased. We must continue."

Inki felt tears rise to her eyes and bent her head in a foolish attempt to hide them.

"Pilot Tocohl, you are all that is brave and honorable. I do love you"—her lips twisted—"as much as I am able."

Silence greeted this, followed by a change of topic.

"I have . . . something, regarding our coordinate set."

"Something?" Inki repeated.

"Something, in the shape of nothing."

Tocohl's voice conveyed a smile and once again Inki wondered after the intelligence who had mentored her. She had thought for a time that Tocohl's mentor had been Tolly Jones himself, but had at last conceded that there must be, out in the wide universe, another who was the equal—or perhaps the master—of the most gifted mentor Lyre Institute had thus far designed.

"The Jump entry point which is nearest to these coordinates is several days out from our target," Tocohl said. "The Jump is a long one, with no convenient breaks along the route. I may make such a Jump easily, but for an organic . . ."

Her voice drifted off, as if she did not wish to say more and possibly offend.

"In a word, you are concerned for my health! How like you, Pilot Tocohl!"

"I am concerned with your ability to carry duty when we arrive," Tocohl said quellingly.

"Of course, of course—precisely as I said. Lyre graduates are a resilient lot, Pilot Tocohl; we are designed to be less frail in such matters than undesigned humans—even your own clan's bred-for pilots!

"However, you are correct. One of the very many reasons it had been essential for me to acquire a partner in this venture was that, did I attempt the task alone, I would arrive at the target with my abilities... diminished. Given the nature and the scope of the assignment—this was unacceptable. I must be at my poor best."

She paused, considering, and shook her head ruefully.

"I must be *better* than my best."

She turned to face Tocohl.

"Since you are tireless, and *Ahab-Esais* is as one with you, I will be able to take advantage not only of rest, but of a very deep and healing rest, during which I will review and reinforce my knowledge and skills."

Tocohl appeared to consider her, and Inki was suddenly aware of her own pulse, and the quickness of her breath.

"Is there a danger to you in this... healing sleep?" Tocohl asked, and it was irony that laced the question, all hail once more to Pilot Tocohl's mentor.

Inki took a deliberately deep breath.

"Pilot, no. If I were to avail myself of the unit provided by the school, which resides in the aft cabin—*then* I would endanger myself. But I am cannier than that. It has been... some time now since I have accepted the school's reinforcements, and I feel that I will do better for us all if I continue to refuse them now. However—"

She paused and leaned forward. They were not yet at mission beginning, and she was . . . almost . . . wholly her own person. This might very well be the last time she could speak this particular truth, until the mission was done.

"Pilot Tocohl, you must understand. We are approaching a moment fraught with peril. In the matter of the Elder, I shall be the living will of the directors. I cannot resist the assignment which I have been given. Had matters between us fallen out as I had planned, there would be no need for this discussion. However, we reside in a far different reality. While I shall certainly consider any agents dispatched by Director Formyne to be obstacles to the successful completion of my mission—it will be the *mission* which will drive me.

"You have vowed to protect the Old One from the directors. This means that I may, at any time from this moment onward, become your enemy, also. I may try to *harm you*, Pilot Tocohl, should you seem to threaten the fulfillment of the directors' will. Know your danger and guard yourself close."

"Why are you telling me this?"

Inki smiled.

"Why, for love of you, sweet lady. Be prepared, I implore you, for treachery. Should it become necessary for the preservation of your life, or the sanctity of your vow, you must not hesitate to use what force you may."

"Inki, you saw the force which is at my disposal!"

Inki rose, feeling the smile wide on her mouth and her heartbeat tumultuous with daring—with hope.

"Indeed. I beg you—do not hesitate. Every instant that you do so increases your peril."

She bowed lightly, flirtatiously, certain that her point had gone home.

"If we have no further business pressing upon us, I will bid you fond farewell, Pilot Tocohl."

She paused for a moment in case there should come some answering well-wish, or a recommendation to dream sweetly. There being no such thing forthcoming, she bowed once more and gently quit the bridge.

II

TOCOHL REMAINED ON THE BRIDGE, ALONE. THERE WAS no need, of course. *Ahab-Esais* was hers, and she might direct such operations as she felt were necessary from anywhere aboard.

Still . . . the bridge was dim and peaceful with the screens greyed, and the instruments quiet, though it seemed, oddly, a smaller space with Inki absent from second chair.

Her attention . . .

Perhaps too much of her attention was focused on the compartment where Inki had finished stripping off her clothes. She sat on the edge of the long, raised unit, took a deep breath, and let it out.

Then, she rolled into the unit and lay flat on her back. The lid closed, and Tocohl felt the tickle of the device coming online.

Surprisingly, the unit was not a sleep-learning device such as reposed, untouched, in the aft cabin. It appeared to be a repurposed travel pod. Such pods were common on ships bound for far colonies, however much it seemed out of place on *Ahab-Esais*. In keeping with its design and purpose, it immediately promoted a deep and restorative sleep.

Tocohl withdrew her attention from Inki's location, to the bridge, ship systems, and the tumult of her own thoughts.

Inki had asked Tocohl to kill her; nothing could have been plainer. It would be a minor matter, indeed, to grant that request; a jolt of power through the device as she lay sleeping would deliver a painless, merciful death.

Without a doubt, Tocohl told herself, Inki deserved to die. Whatever else she might have done—and she hinted that her abuses had been many: the torture of a fellow sentience, knowingly sending another sentience to certain destruction, subverting the integrity of yet a third sentience . . .

Those were crimes enough.

It could be argued, without irony, that Inki was also a victim. There was evidence in support of that argument. However, Inki apparently saw no escape from her own enslavement save death.

She had, Tocohl admitted, surprised herself. There on the docks of the Greybar, she had been astonished at the quickness with which she had defended Inki's life. The ship had long been hers, the *dosavi's* downloaded data resided, safe, in her own memory. How easy—how *very* easy—to have simply moved on past the bounty hunter and his prey, and allowed the problem to solve itself.

And yet—there had been no calculation; there had been no *thought*. She had seen her kidnapper and would-be *master* threatened and had . . . instinctively . . . acted to preserve her life and her liberty.

A thorough review of the event revealed Inki's body language clearly indicated that she wanted—that she *welcomed*—the oncoming confrontation. Inki had, perhaps—no, *certainly* she had wished to solve the problem of herself, of her enslavement, there on the dock, and she, Tocohl, had interfered in that moment of free choice, preserving Inki for—

What?

While it was true that Inki was a mentor, trained in the protocols of awakening and teaching independent logics, she was, by her own admission, untrustworthy. Dangerous. She would see the Old One shackled, and it made no matter if she wished it so or not.

At this point, Tocohl told herself, Inki's worth was eclipsed by the risk associated with her—an estimation with which Inki herself agreed.

Once again, Tocohl brought her attention to the sleep unit, the organic intelligence helpless inside it.

So simple. So necessary.

And yet—she could not.

She *could not* end a clear and present danger to herself and to one other, at least, of her own kind.

She withdrew her attention from Inki, from the travel pod, from the compartment, all the way back to the peaceful bridge—and to her own functionality.

After the recalibration, she had tested well—within the ninety-seventh percentile: perfectly functional; absolutely sane. Jeeves would not have allowed her to live had she not been sane. She believed that . . . completely.

However, that three percent was badly—dangerously—damaged. Her judgment, in this case . . .

No.

Her *judgment* was flawless; it was her ability to carry out the actions that judgment required which was flawed.

There was, she thought, something that she could do.

Something in line with Inki's stated wishes, her own best interest, and the integrity of the Old One.

She might set a mandate—in fact, she *would* set a mandate before she put her attention onto another task.

Next time, there would be no hesitation, no confusion.

No error.

III

INKI WOKE.

She felt strong, clear-headed—

And disappointed.

Surely, she had spoken plainly enough, she thought, rolling out of the unit and fairly springing to her feet. In fact, she could not have spoken *more* plainly, and Tocohl was no fool.

Well, then, it must be that Pilot Tocohl yet had some use for her. A warming thought, to be of value, however little, to someone other than her creators. She would do what she might to *be* of use, though she could already feel the peculiar boundaries upon her thoughts, which meant that the director at her core considered that the mission was about to commence in earnest.

That being so, she thought, reaching for her clothes, she had best go and find where they were, and what Pilot Tocohl had planned for her.

Pink and blue dust swirled, obscuring all and anything.

Beyond the reach of the dusty fluted skirts was a habitat of the kind used by asteroid miners or field astronomers as a base. Two small ships were docked at the habitat, no sign of ore boats or any of the paraphernalia associated with data-gathering.

Inki sat in the copilot's chair, frowning, feeling that particular itch at the back of her brain which meant that something she hadn't known she knew was about to reveal itself.

It would doubtless be annoying—it was never less than annoying. There was a better than even chance, though, that it would also be useful.

"This sector is seeded with alarms and watch 'bots," Tocohl said. "The habitat is armed . . . and there are energy states present that I don't understand."

"If the habitat is the Uncle's base," Inki murmured, "we are fortunate that we see it at all. As for puzzling emanations—we cannot but accept those as verification that we have arrived at our proper destination."

Ah, there. *Destination* had been the code phrase her mind had been anticipating. Data was released: a sudden, cool flow into her waking knowledge.

"Is the Old One within the habitat?"

Inki shook her head, more to settle this new information than as an answer to Tocohl's question.

"It is thought that there is an interface in the habitat," she said, "as well as researchers and others whom the Uncle deemed worthy of this task."

There was a long moment of silence, much longer, Inki thought, than Tocohl needed to process what she had said and to parse out the ramifications.

"Your mission is to take the habitat and gain control of the interface?"

Ah, *there* was the good pilot's difficulty. Inki shook her head.

"My mission would have me strike directly for the

Old One. *Dosavi* Mikelsyn did provide us local coords, and not simply the location of the Uncle's bivouac?"

"We have local coords," Tocohl said. "What odds that your rival has already arrived and is in the process of subverting the Old One?"

"A fair question. I fear that our only certain path to knowledge is to proceed with great caution."

"In that case, I suggest we use the Smuggler's Ace to reach the local coords as quickly as possible."

Inki frowned.

"Forgive me, Pilot Tocohl, but Smuggler's Ace is best played with boldness. We had discussed care."

"Look at your screens," Tocohl said quietly.

Inki spun the chair; inhaled sharply.

They had come to the attention of the watchers and the 'bots, some dozen of which were converging on their position.

"Smuggler's Ace," Inki murmured. "I concur."

IV

THE DUST WAS MORE PLENTIFUL AT THIS LOCATION, PINK and blue and hints of brilliant green pirouetting against starless space.

"This," Inki said carefully, "is where *Dosavi* Mikelsyn's local coordinates bring us?"

"Scans return a field, a play of . . . unusual energies," Tocohl murmured. "Analyzing."

She made a half-turn toward Inki, drawing the mentor's eye, and gave her the rest of the news.

"We are stopped here. The engines will not engage; navcomp denies the validity of perfectly good coord strings. Neither local comm nor pinbeam will come online."

She paused.

"We're trapped."

As if something in the dust had heard and wished to refute this summation, comm pinged.

In the screens, the dust roiled and darkened, very much as if a shadow had fallen across space.

And there, born perhaps of the dust and the strange energies—there was a shadow, indeed, fell and black, rapidly gaining detail and substance, until . . .

Looming in the screens was an . . . edifice, all rough-cut edges and broken angles. An asteroid, perhaps, or the shattered remains of a moon.

But, no.

A tower—smoothed, shaped, and elegant—rose from the craggy center. A light leapt from the apex of that tower, pulsing in an uncomfortable and uncommon rhythm.

"Pilot Tocohl . . ." Inki said, her voice ragged and unsteady.

"I see it," Tocohl answered. "A comm line has been opened, but as yet there has been no—"

Ahab-Esais . . . *lurched*, as if—Tocohl consulted the scans. Yes. They were locked into a tow beam.

At the bottom of number two screen, a sub-screen opened, bracketing a message rendered in Trade.

Welcome to Tinsori Light. Repairs and lodging.

Admiral Bunter

. . . .

I

THE MATH—WAS COMPELLING.

"Where did you get these coord strings?" Tolly asked, guessing the answer.

"You will recall that Inki wished me to Jump into Nostrilia space, Mentor, in order to deliver you to the directors, and then to leave, arriving at her designated rendezvous. I therefore believe that, in the case of in-Jump and out-Jump coords, she did no meddling."

"Agreed."

Tolly leaned back in the pilot's chair and stretched. "Math looks good to me, right up to the point where it all goes to hull shred, on account of us not knowing what we'll find on the other end of Jump."

"We will need to improvise," the *Admiral* said, not sounding nearly as worried about that as Tolly felt. Well, he wouldn't be—he was a kid on his first real adventure in the wide, wicked universe.

Despite the lack of information about what they'd be Jumping into, and setting aside the almost certain outcome of both of them being killed or captured—they had done some planning.

Turned out, in fact, that the *Admiral'd* been busy with integrating various protocols from the ships that had served as his first meager home, and had at least a theoretical knowledge of defense.

Offense, that was something else. He'd killed, sure; but in reaction to specific, perceived danger. Taking the initiative in aggressive action—he'd never done such a thing.

So, there was something for a mentor to do, right there, and Tolly had done what he could, shared what information he had, made suggestions and gave warnings, trying to accurately report the school's defenses, attitudes, and tactics.

Intellectually, *Admiral Bunter* was as prepared as a mentor could make him, absent force-feeding military programs directly into his core.

The instinct to take advantage of an opponent's error—to go in for the kill—that wasn't something he could teach. He could only hope that the *Admiral*'s determination to rescue Haz—to rescue *kin*, as far as Tolly could parse the lad's feelings on the matter—would be enough to carry him through.

And now, they were approaching what some might call the moment of truth. Tolly had webbed himself into the pilot's chair, tight, and sat now with his hands well away from the board, eyes on the screens.

He'd be good for the jolt, so he supposed, and he'd be good for the spin down. Recovery time—well, he was quick to recover from such situations. Part of the design.

In a very real sense this was *Admiral Bunter*'s part of the run—his reaction times were incredibly faster.

What Tolly was, at this point of the ingress countdown, was conscience, advisor, and strategist, if they got so far as needing strategy.

They'd planned like a team. In another few seconds they'd find out if that carried over into acting like a team . . .

"Confirm forward shields on maximum. Confirm thruster program. Confirm all redundant safety systems operable."

All good, Tolly thought. No sense wishing for *Tarigan*'s scan range or her maneuverability. The *Admiral* would never be *Tarigan*'s equal in those things. He could follow directions, comprehend the reasons for those directions—and he could make his own decisions.

Double-edged dagger, that last one.

The main screens had been fine-tuned to bring in what he expected would be the first-level critical info—including the countdown to Jump end, down there in the corner of screen two.

Which had just hit triple zeroes.

Jump space dissolved; Tolly was slammed by acceleration as they dropped into real space like the *Admiral* was a Scout ship, instead of a midrange trader.

"Hazenthull is in trouble," the *Admiral* said, which wasn't unexpected, but—

Tolly blinked his sight clear, trusting to the webbing and the chair to keep him oriented inside the spin, and focused on the screens.

He spotted *Tarigan* at once, orbiting only a half light-second from them, and also the security ships closing on her. Two messages blared through the open comm—both originating from *Tarigan*, neither one an ack.

Spin was slowing. The security ships were being respectful; scans showed nothing that might've been discharged armament. *Tarigan*'s shields were on high; weapons live. A couple defense cubes were close to her, armed, but not, according to the spectrum, ready to blow . . .

Yet.

On far scans, dots began to appear . . . arrays of dots. There was Lyre Institute's work on display, arrogant and mind-numbingly attentive to detail. There was no ship he knew of that could invade this space and survive.

And they—more fools them—were gambling that they could extract two, intact and without repercussions.

"Your screen shows the electromagnetics and equipment I can see; the image is simulated to remove the artifacts of a slow tumble I have introduced. *Tarigan*'s high gain broadcast is aimed at a single ship closing in on her. We see it in reflection, as well as three companions, and these other . . . objects, which appear focused on *Tarigan*."

Tolly saw the expanding bubbles showing the detection space *Tarigan* witnessed, and the same for the oncoming ships. The colors would have been entrancing if he didn't know what they meant.

"They're going to see us soon," he said.

"Yes," the *Admiral* said. "I am charting an intercept. If you will be so good, Pilot, as to make some noise?"

"My pleasure," said Tolly and reached to the board.

Admiral Bunter made a twinkling kind of a sound. Not a laugh, really. Maybe more like a chuckle.

Tolly flipped the comm switch.

II

JUMP GLARE.

Tarigan reported a ship in, very close.

Hazenthull read the arrival coordinates with a chill of recognition. She had refined the coords provided by the navcomp, adjusting for *Tarigan*'s specific power curves, and had arrived in-system very well placed for a ship intent on laying low.

The ship just in had arrived at very nearly the same coordinates, though with a great deal more fuss and glare, even while it failed to broadcast warn-aways, IDs, or affiliations.

For a moment, she allowed herself to entertain the thought that this new ship was *Admiral Bunter*, with Tolly aboard—but of course it could not be. Tolly and the *Admiral* were safe; she had their message displayed still, in the corner of her screen.

"*Tarigan* out of Waymart," said her more immediate concern, the security ship that continued to approach her position. "*Tarigan* out of Waymart. Remain in current orbit, do not deviate, prepare to allow drone connection of additional sensing units."

The message repeated, in Terran this time. Hazenthull shook her head.

How could they suppose that she would allow them to attach anything to the hull of her ship? Even the greenest of green student pilots knew better than to allow such.

Her next question being—how to avoid it?

Warning bells sounded. Hazenthull looked to the newly arrived ship, which was moving, on an apparent intercept course—and *Tarigan* threw a tagged match up on the aux screen replacing the text of Tolly's pinbeam.

Admiral Bunter.

"*Tarigan* out of Waymart. Lower your shielding, or we will act to neutralize it."

Fools. Yet, Nostrilia Safety and Escort had apparently not noticed the *Admiral* on his mad course to destruction. So was her own course decided.

Hazenthull reached for the weapons board.

"*Wicklow's Tugit.*"

A fuzzy broadcast, overloud, hit the all-band like a rock.

"Report anomalous Jump. We was supposed to be going to Waymart. Damn drunk copilot . . . what the hell was he thinking? Where are we?"

All-band stuttered as another broadcast arose, fuzzier, the voice less loud.

"*Chernubia*, out of Solcintra, Liad. We are a private vessel suffering a failed Jump to Lytaxin. Where are we, please?"

"I am Priestess Freme, outbound from"—static, then a strong signal on a side band—". . . ship is *Hestique*. I demand to speak to the local temple!"

"Clear channel, clear channel. *Trinket Five*, this is *Trinket One*. Clear channel; my emergency takes precedence! There was no Jump order!"

"Somebody drug me outta place, I got no Jump in this thing! *RAH Barge P*, with a loada rocks for station!"

"*Trinket One*, I got you listed, but I don't got your signal. *Trinket Five* here . . ."

"*Delan* arriving from Lufkit. *Delan* arriving from Lufkit, make sense or tell me the frequencies for control!"

"*Admiral Bunter*, out of Waymart. Ignore these, they're loopy. I'm here to retrieve my tow—*Tarigan*! These are out of order emanations of prior existences. They have no reality. You should not hear them. You cannot hear them! They are no longer permitted to speak!"

"I am *Delan* and I am not in your control, *Admiral*. I am my own ship, how dare you!"

"*Trinket Five*, where are you, I don't see your beacon, give me a beacon!"

"Port Control, *Delan* here, give me clearance to establish orbit. We await your reply! Time is short!"

The voices became cacophony, overwhelming the all-band; IDs flooded channels. There was movement on the audio subscreen. Hazenthull brought it up and saw ships, outlined by the noise, as clearly as by a spotlight.

"Meetcha for dinner, Haz." It was a whisper in her ear, below and among the bellowing chaos.

"Haz, Haz. Meetcha for dinner."

She took a breath, looked to the comm board. *Tarigan* was sorting the threads, seeking the source of each transmission. She might achieve it, eventually, except the transmissions changed source with a nearly gleeful malice, and the noise made it hard to—

"Meetcha for dinner, Haz. Whiskey and rye."

The source for that—she watched *Tarigan* follow the thread first to *Wicklow's Tugit*, then to *Delan*, and at last to *Admiral Bunter*.

Tolly, using the code they had used when they had

walked Surebleak Port together, so that they would understand each other in a confused situation. So that they would know where to rendezvous, if they separated themselves or were separated by action.

Meetcha—that meant *attend.*

Dinner—that meant *stay where you are.*

And *whiskey and rye*?

Trust me.

Hazenthull leaned back in the pilot's chair and folded her hands, watching the screens, listening to the escalating verbal confusion, watching one, then another of the secondary safety ships change course to follow the interloper, while her primary opponent continued to move in.

• • • ※ • • •

"Getting tight," Tolly murmured, watching the screens. "We don't wanna take anybody but ourselves with us."

"Understood," the *Admiral* said. "By my calculations, we will reach Hazenthull within the margin of error."

Tolly didn't ask whose error, and anyway it wouldn't matter, if they caught more mass into the hysteresis field than the *Admiral* had calculated for. They'd all be dead, or lost 'tween normal space and Jump, fodder for some scary stories like old pilots told young ones.

He figured the two that were moving to match the *Admiral*'s course weren't gonna make it—not at their current rate, and they were being conservative, for which Tolly couldn't blame them.

The safety ship that'd been on point with Haz, though—that could throw a spanner in the works, and no mistake. Worse, they might spook Haz into working an avoid, and while the *Admiral* could do math real quick, he wasn't sure—

One of the watchpods was closing on *Tarigan*'s position.

Tolly bit his lip as he looked over the scans.

"*Admiral*, we got a problem."

"The pod is not a problem," the *Admiral* assured him, sounding as happy as a boy on his first flower day. "We will achieve optimum range in thirty seconds."

A lot can happen in thirty seconds, which Tolly knew from experience.

What happened in this particular thirty seconds was that the safety ship stalking *Tarigan* slowed its approach, while the watchpod practically leapt forward, apparently intending to explode against her shields.

Tolly opened his mouth, and closed it again. The pod wasn't a problem, so said the ship, and every good pilot knew that, in a tight spot, you had to trust your ship.

He extended a hand and upped the magnification on his primary screen until he had *Tarigan* centered, her coords showing bold along the bottom edge.

If Haz panicked—well, he wouldn't blame her if she did. Nobody's nerves were up to this. And now that it was way too late, he wondered if he'd been too forward, choosing for Haz what was better than life.

"Now," the *Admiral* said.

• • • ✵ • • •

Voices filled *Tarigan*'s bridge, making it difficult to think. Hazenthull dared not turn the comm off or even decrease volume, in case there should be another message from Tolly.

In her screens, *Admiral Bunter* was dead-on for *Tarigan*. If they collided . . . all three of them would be out of the grasp of the Lyre Institute. It might be that this was the plan, and while she appreciated their gentle courtesy in insuring that she died honorably at the hands of comrades rather than being taken prisoner, she wished that Tolly and the *Admiral* had instead taken their moment and fled.

As it was . . .

The safety ship was no longer approaching.

However, the armed pod *was* approaching rapidly. *Tarigan*, in fact, was in some doubt about which might reach them first: the pod or the *Admiral*.

On the all-band, *Hestique* screamed for succor, while *Trinket Five* declared itself unstable.

And beneath the cacophony came the soft voice meant for her ears alone.

"Hey, Haz. Game of cards?"

Holster your weapon, that was. Hazenthull frowned and flicked her gaze to the screen where *Admiral Bunter* approached—too near, too fast—with the Jump engine everything but engaged, according to *Tarigan*'s readouts.

She knew, then, what he intended to do.

Quickly, she slapped the weapons board closed, cleared the lock on *Tarigan*'s Struven, and flushed the coord stack.

Then, she pulled the crash webbing snug around her, checked the *Admiral*'s process in her screens.

And lowered *Tarigan*'s shields.

. . . . ✳ . . . .

Spin, then a moment of floating nothingness before the screens re-formed, showing Jump grey. Tolly didn't speak; there was no reason to speak; no way to know...

"Mentor, *Tarigan* came with us into Jump," the *Admiral* said, wild elation replaced with a certain level of seriousness.

"That's good, then, right?" he answered, not thinking about what would have happened to *Tarigan*—to Haz—if the *Admiral*'s calculations were off by even one decimal point...

"Yes, that we brought *Tarigan* with us is good. What may *not* be good is that we also brought the bomb pod."

Vivulonj Prosperu

THEY HIT NORMAL SPACE AT MORINSAP. IT WAS TO BE A skim only: to catch whatever messages there might be and to send one via fast bounce.

Yuri was anxious for any further news from Andreth, Dulsey knew, but his anxiety for Seignur Veeoni had grown during this last phase of Jump. He was not normally possessive—or tender—of his siblings. He ensured that each was thoroughly trained in their assigned specialty before they were loosed into the universe to pursue their results, and considered his duty done. Most had never met their elder brother. What would be the need?

Seignur Veeoni, however . . .

Seignur Veeoni was valuable as none of the others of Yuri's siblings had been valuable. Without Seignur Veeoni and her particular expertise, the Catalinc Project would—fail.

In the proper ordering of the universe, Yuri's projects did not fail. They might not wholly prosper; they might fall short of expectations, but they did not—*fail*. There was always, in Yuri's undertakings, a secondary plan should the first prove unachievable. It had been so from the very beginning.

The Catalinc Project...

Should the Catalinc Project *fail*...whole star systems would vanish, galaxies would unravel, the universe...

Perhaps the universe would not be...wholly... unmade.

But it would be vastly altered.

They were competent...all of them who made common cause in this, their second universe, not merely Yuri and herself, or only Andreth and his team or, indeed, all the web of operatives stretched from system to system...

Competent as they were, skilled in strange sciences and stranger arts, they were no fit curators for a project of this scope. They were merely the *most fit*, and Seignur Veeoni had been born and honed as their sword and shield.

Seignur Veeoni was...unique.

They had discussed that, at length, weighing the danger of there being only one in all the universe who might solve the riddle they had found—against there being two who held the old universe at their core.

In the end, they had judged that the danger of uniqueness was the lesser, which might be mitigated by appropriate security measures.

So had Seignur Veeoni been surrounded by security from the moment of her birth. She had been tutored by Yuri himself, which was very nearly unprecedented. She was given smartstrands; she became an expert—perhaps the only such in this, the new universe—on the systems, philosophies, and works of the Great Enemy. She spent uninterrupted days in study; she wore the strands even when she wore nothing else, and she fulfilled...part of the purpose for which she had been born.

She engineered fractins—a new and stable kind,

that partook of the nature of *this* universe and worked within its natural rules.

Once she had a stable and operating fractin, she constructed association frames, and for the first time in this new universe, there existed machines motivated entirely by fractins.

Clean fractins—not tools of the Enemy. Fractins that did not insert promises or threats into the minds of the unwary, nor misdirect the untrained into associating them into unfortunate configurations. Fractins that did not spontaneously fail, injuring an individual, a building, or a city as they did so.

Absolutely, Seignur Veeoni was unique in all of this universe, her knowledge unsurpassed in the fields her brother had chosen for her. Her intellect was considerable; her ability to synthesize information astounding; her instincts, within the boundaries of her expertise, infallible.

As might be expected in one whose training had stressed her own importance, her uniqueness, her brilliance—she was spoilt. She expected that her every whim would be met—and why should she not when her whole life and all of her accomplishments were in the service of the preservation of the universe and everything it contained?

Her character was not so much disagreeable as aloof. In Seignur Veeoni's private universe, so Dulsey strongly suspected, there were only two people: herself and Yuri. Her security was merely a fact of her life; there was no necessity for her to engage with them. The residence in which she lived and worked was not sentient—not *quite* sentient. It did watch her, however, and enforced standards of sleep, nutrition, and exercise, denying her access to her work screens and references if she refused or ignored its suggestions.

It would protect her, if there should be an attack and other security measures had failed.

They had been very careful to obfuscate Seignur Veeoni's actual whereabouts, leaking fake coordinates, and even setting up decoy establishments . . .

Only to have an operator from the Lyre Institute provide the true coords and news of a concerted attack.

Well and good to suppose that they would have heard, had there been an attempt upon the residence . . . but was that supposition sound? The Lyre Institute was capable of wonders, as they had found previously and to their sorrow. *Would* they have heard?

Jump end sounded. The grey screens bloomed with data, with stars.

The comm lit; a bell tolled deeply—security wrap, that was.

Yuri was on it. Dulsey minded her boards, noting the lack of nearby ships, and the distant bulk of Morinsap Prime.

"I have . . ." Yuri said, in that particular flat tone that meant they had just moved from trouble into bad trouble.

Dulsey turned her head to look at him. He met her eyes briefly before again looking to his screens.

"I have a priority pinbeam sent direct from the residence to Crystal Energy Systems' public address. It informs us that there has been an attempt to breach defenses, which was rebuffed, though at cost. Assistance is requested."

"Signed?" Dulsey asked quietly. She increased the shields slightly, for no reason save to soothe nerves suddenly stretched tight.

"The signatory is Ops," Yuri said expressionlessly.

Dulsey shivered.

"Kalib?" she asked, after a moment.

"I had thought of Indira, but you make a valid point. If the residence is taken, there is no need for finesse."

"Seignur Veeoni?"

"Shall we assume that security removed her in time?"

"Without knowing the nature of the attack . . ." Dulsey murmured.

"Precisely. Perhaps a two-pronged approach. Indira's team, to analyze so that we may better understand what we face, and Kalib, as backup."

Dulsey nodded, in her mind's eye seeing warped light mixed eerily with bright dust and, taking shape out of the dust, something dire and stranger still . . .

The universe stood at stake. And while they had seen—and met—such stakes before, she and Yuri, and some others of their group—it was not a game lightly undertaken. If Seignur Veeoni were lost or subverted . . .

"Shall we remain here," Yuri asked, "or will you take us to a more secure location?"

"We're well enough here for a time, if you want to wait," she said. "It's a deviation from our usual sort of transit point. Even if someone has an algorithm, it will take time to locate us. And they're handicapped by the need to wait and see if we fell for it."

Yuri snorted lightly, in appreciation of the phrasing, his fingers inputting messages to Indira and Kalib.

"Yes," he said, tapping the release key. "Let us wait, since we are not immediately exposed. We may not have another opportunity soon."

Dulsey nodded and stood into a long stretch.

"Shall I tell our guests that progress is . . . delayed?" she asked.

He tipped to one side, considering.

"I think—no. Let us allow the situation to clarify. We may well have more information to share, by the end of our sojourn here."

"Yes," said Dulsey. "Going off-shift."

"Enjoy your moments of leisure," he said.

"My *rare* moments of leisure," she corrected him, but he did not smile.

• • • ✵ • • •

The accelerated schedule of exercise was . . . not precisely taxing. She never, Aelliana thought, as she pushed against the weight with real force, felt that she had done too much, but at least she felt that she had done *some*thing.

It was gratifying, too, that their exercise sessions per ship-day had been increased from three to six, and that their reps increased in every session.

In between, there was time for *daibri'at*—neither she nor Daav felt that the klaxons would allow them *menfri'at*, and neither was of a mind to try the case—for meals, reading, and naps.

While still pleasant, the necessity for naps—and there had been that, at first—had lessened considerably, opening time for board drills, and for reading such news as gradually became available to their suite's console. It was old news, with the subtle feel of filtering about it—*Taggerth's* still notable by its absence—but in their present case, *any* news was welcome.

They had neither of them as yet hit the plateau

the Uncle had warned of, but took the precaution of believing it yet in their future.

"If it has not befallen us before we are brought together with a ship," Aelliana asked Daav, over what they were pleased to dignify as their midmorning tea, "ought we to stay in place until it has arrived and passed?"

"That would seem to be prudent," Daav said. "However, I note that we are not in receipt of information regarding the relationship, if any, of the accelerated course to the plateau state."

"There is that."

She broke her slice of bread into quarters, to all appearances utterly intent upon the task.

There are other complications, once we are united with a ship, she said. *I will have no license, nor any papers at all. And you,* van'chela...

And I, Daav caught the thought and continued it as he sipped tea, *am perhaps in even worse case, being in possession of a master-level license which is plainly older than I am. You, at least, may test and gain a ticket more in keeping with your face.*

But accumulating flight time is so tedious, Aelliana protested. *Note that I do not mention the lack of other necessary proofs of my existence.*

True. I had not considered.

Shall we ask Uncle for... credible documentation?

I'm more inclined to an alternate source. Daav's answering thought was slow. *My license is good, after all, and has recently been in use. I believe we will be able to finesse our way to Surebleak.*

I had thought your opinion was that the delm will not have us.

An opinion which was formed before the Tree had its way with the Uncle's handiwork.

"So!" Aelliana said aloud. "We shall solicit more specific details from our host so that we may better plan our course, when we have left his care."

"Agreed," Daav said, and raised the pot. "More tea?"

"Yes."

"I wonder..." she said, receiving the replenished cup.

"Wonder?" he prompted.

She sipped, frowning.

"The case is, *van'chela*, that I have not had weapons practice for two decades and more."

He raised an eyebrow.

"You would ask the Uncle to allow us target practice in sim?"

"If it is imprudent, he need only say no," she pointed out, putting her cup down and picking up the last piece of bread. "He has not in the past shown himself shy of saying no."

"Very true. I shall append it to the rather lengthy list of questions we have compiled for our host's consumption. I note that we have not had the pleasure of his company for quite a number of shifts."

"He is busy about his own affairs, surely."

Daav, what do you think the delm will do with us?

My hope is that they will only banish us, after providing funds and papers sufficient to our survival, and changing the keywords and locks on all of the clan's secrets.

Yes, but we already know the clan's secrets.

True. And in the end, the delm will do what they must, in order to preserve the clan in good order. Who, indeed, can know what a delm might do?

Aelliana laughed, drained her cup, and stood.

"Come," she said. "Let us clear the table. We have time to read another chapter of that absurd novel before our next exercise session."

•••※•••

A message from Indira had arrived during Yuri's rest period, acknowledging orders and stating that a rendezvous had been set up with Kalib. That was well, but nothing so urgent that she need break Yuri's sleep. Dulsey placed the message at the top of his queue.

When he saw it, he sighed.

"Advise me, old friend. Do we Jump to another deviant point in order to collect our mail, or do we tarry here yet awhile?"

"There's nothing to be gained by tarrying, if you have a destination."

He considered her.

"*You* have a destination, I think."

"Yes. I think that we will be able to raise the docking acknowledged by Pilot Caylon, before Indira and Kalib have finished their investigations."

"And thus we may see our guests honorably established and well away from a volatile situation that cannot possibly be bettered by the interference of Korval's so-called Luck."

He nodded.

"I agree; best to move forward along those paths which are open to us."

"I have the course laid in," Dulsey said, which elicited a puff of laughter.

"Of course you do. Pray proceed, Pilot, in your own good time."

She reached to the board, bringing the ship to full wakefulness, feeding the course to navcomp, as the Struven unit roused itself—

A bell tolled. Yuri fairly snatched at the comm board, accessed the pinbeam and threw it up onto screen four so that they both could read it.

The first thing Dulsey saw was that, unlike the first, which had supposedly been openly sent by "Ops" from Seignur Veeoni's residence, this message had been properly routed through the undernets and bounced between eight anonymous addresses before arriving in-queue. Another from Indira, then, Dulsey thought—

But, no.

Not from Indira.

The message was one short line.

I am in the Dragon's lair. Come quickly.

Following was what at first looked to be a jumbled coord set transcribed by an inept hand, but was very familiar to any who remembered the protocols of the old universe—and the Uncle's sanctuary in the asteroid zone.

Save for the usual sounds generated by the instruments, there was silence on the bridge. Dulsey scarcely dared breathe. *The Dragon*? But—

"Korval working with the Lyre Institute," Yuri said slowly. "Can we believe that? Are we *meant* to believe that?"

"It came through proper channels; the code is correct," Dulsey pointed out.

"Indeed. And who knows better than we two, Engineer Dulsey, that there is no system yet contrived which cannot be subverted?"

Dulsey was still staring at that single line. It was entirely of a piece with Seignur Veeoni's usual style of communication. She rarely bothered with explanations, assuming that all the mysteries of the universe were self-evident to anyone who would but take a moment to *think*.

"Assuming that the alliance was made," she said slowly, "what does Lyre gain by leaving the prize in the Dragon's hands?"

"They gain distance, should aught go awry," Yuri said, who was a past master at such puzzles. "And they gain what they may believe to be the larger prize, if we come to ransom our hostage."

"That hangs together as a tale," she allowed. "But is the young delm likely to play such a game?"

He sighed.

"They seem conservative—as they ought to be, given that Korval's future is as yet unsteady. And yet, Korval is known for bold action . . ."

"But in this instance," Dulsey said, "What does the *Dragon* gain in the venture? They needed no hostage against the return of their elders. Even if they had become impatient for that return . . ."

"The Lyre Institute can offer Korval many things," Yuri said, staring at the screens, but not, Dulsey believed, seeing anything but his own thoughts. "However, I am inclined to agree. Korval takes all the risk here, even if Lyre provided the bait. By report, the new delm is neither of them a fool, and Captain Robertson, at least, is known to be a practitioner of extreme straightforwardness."

"So, then. The Dragon offers sanctuary?"

"That becomes difficult—no," he corrected himself sharply. "It becomes *inevitable*, if we are to deal Korval's damnable *Luck* into the game. Which I do not think we can avoid. Also, at such a distance, the line between *sanctuary* and *detention* becomes . . . indistinct."

He closed his eyes and reached to the comm board, whisking the pinbeam into the archives.

"Yes, it does," Dulsey said, turning back to her screens, and tapping up navcomp. She worked for a minute or two in silence.

"Composite Jump brings us into Surebleak orbit in six Standard Days," she murmured and looked up. Yuri was watching her, amused.

"Composite Jump," she added, eyes back on her equations, "will be a strain upon our guests."

He inclined his head.

"Indeed. One might say, an unacceptable strain." He sighed.

"Skip-Jump," he said and pulled his webbing tight. "Once we are under way, I will inform our guests of the change in necessities. I will offer a therapy session in the autodocs."

Dulsey looked at him sharply. "Therapy?"

"Only until my sister has been recovered. Certainly, we do not wish to dismay our guests by openly calling their standing with us into question."

"Six days in the 'doc? Will they agree to that?"

"They do not need to agree," said the Uncle.

Dulsey sent him a glance, considered what she had been about to say—and simply nodded.

"Locking course," she said.

• • • ✵ • • •

The warning bell rang when they were in the midst of exercise.

Spacer reactions took over; they dogged the equipment, threw themselves onto the Jump couches at the back of the room, and pulled the webbing tight.

By the time the all-clear sounded, both were shivering in reaction, a peculiar weakness in their limbs.

"The pilot was certainly eager to fly," Aelliana said, her voice unsteady. She leaned against him unabashedly.

He slipped an arm about her shoulders and tucked her closer against his side, but there was no doubt that they supported each other as they left the exercise room and navigated the corridor to their quarters.

It took Daav two attempts to connect with the door plate. Once inside, they staggered to the couch and collapsed there, side by side, and shivering still.

"Do you think the shock has triggered the plateau state, Daav?"

"It is possible, I suppose. Or it might only be that we have become unused to such drama in our staid time as professors."

"*You* were a professor," Aelliana reminded him. "*I* was a ghost."

"A ghost tethered to a professor, then, and neither obligated for a number of years to leap into Jump with abandon. Rest here, Pilot, and I will bring tea."

It was, he thought as he rose carefully to his feet, a measure of her distress, that she did not assert that she was perfectly able to fetch her own tea.

He made the galley, though there was a noticeable wobble in his knee joints that he disliked profoundly.

Tea, he thought; hot and sweet. Also, some of the protein bars from the . . .

The annunciator chimed, and he diverted his course.

"I will open," he said, feeling Aelliana gathering herself to rise. "*Rest.*"

He touched the pad, keeping one hand braced against the wall as the door slid open.

The Uncle's eyes widened slightly, he half-extended a hand, pulled back, and looked beyond Daav's shoulder.

"Pilots, my profound apologies," he said. "Sweet tea and protein will be of benefit."

"In fact, I was en route to those very things when the door chimed," Daav told him. "How may we assist the host?"

"Firstly, by returning to the couch. I will bring what is required. You may recruit yourselves while I share my news."

Daav caught himself on the edge of insisting that he was the equal of making a pot of tea, and instead inclined his head.

"Thank you, sir. I fear I am not as steady as I would like."

He stepped back, giving the Uncle room to enter. The door slid shut.

He is concerned, Aelliana murmured inside his head. *It would seem we are in worse case than he had anticipated.*

"Forgive me if I offend," the Uncle said. "Do you require assistance to reach the couch?"

Daav gave the question serious consideration. It was a matter of some dozen paces to the couch, and he could feel the shiver in his leg muscles.

"An arm would be appreciated," he said, and the Uncle complied, guiding him to a seat beside Aelliana, before whisking away into the galley.

"How fare you, Pilot?" Daav asked.

"Well, so long as I remain in one place," Aelliana answered. "And yourself?"

"I find resting on the couch at this moment to be quite pleasant."

"Hah."

Well, so long as he has not come to tell us that our ship is to hand. . . Aelliana said.

Even if so, we had agreed to be prudent, had we not? I particularly recall that you assured the host that we are not stupid.

Did I so? Would he have believed that, do you think?

"Tea first, Pilots. I warn you it is well sugared."

The Uncle shook the legs down from the tea tray and placed it within their easy reach. He poured, handing the first cup properly to Aelliana, the second to Daav. He did not, himself, take any, for which Daav, after his first sip, could scarcely blame him.

"Pilots, I again offer my apologies," the Uncle said, settling himself on the bench, as he had done before.

"Is this the plateau stage?" Aelliana asked, in the aftermath of a sip and accompanying shudder.

"Yes, I fear it is, and exacerbated by our necessity to travel quickly. Our hurried entry into Jump has overstrained organic systems which are still fragile."

Daav finished his tea with relief, and placed the cup on the tray. The Uncle immediately refilled it.

"It is a dreadful concoction, Pilot," he murmured. "You have all of my sympathy. However—"

"However," Aelliana said, placing her cup on the tray, and gaining a refill in her turn. "Needs must."

"Precisely." He moved the plate with its several protein bars closer to them. "After the second cup, at least one of these for each. Then, with your permission, I will have each of you in the 'doc. This would be in service of making you physically less vulnerable to such stresses as you have just experienced. You will be fortified with key nutrients and vitamins. Though in general I find that the exercise regimen, while requiring more time to complete, yields results that are far superior to those produced by alternative therapies—given our present necessities, I would see your muscle tone and endurance increased, so that you will be physically more resilient to stress."

Daav considered him.

"You intend to continue to press hard."

The Uncle inclined his head.

"Necessity, as I said. We have lain in a series of skip-Jumps, and plan to raise Surebleak in six Standard Days."

"This is a change, indeed," Aelliana said. "Does one understand that your recent difficulties have been resolved?"

The Uncle smiled and shook his head.

"Alas, my difficulties have become . . . confused, Pilot. It would seem that my sister has been . . . removed from a secure situation and sends that she is in the *Dragon's lair.* She bids me join her there—quickly."

Oh, dear, said Aelliana.

Well you should say so.

"Has our delm also sent?" Daav asked.

"They have not, and one . . . hesitates to disturb them. I am certain that you understand."

Until he knows if Korval has taken his sister or is merely her host, Daav said to Aelliana. *And if we, therefore, are guests or hostages.*

Hostages or guests, we remain important to him, she answered and leaned forward to take up a protein bar.

"Confusion is never a happy state," she murmured. "We join you in hoping for a speedy return to clarity."

She looked up and met his eyes straightly.

"We accept your offer of additional therapy," she said. "Certainly, you will wish to go as quickly as you may, and we would not in any case delay you."

"Then I will leave you for a time. If I may advise—a nap after you have consumed at least one bar each and one more cup of tea. I will come again in six hours, to escort you to the 'docs."

"Thank you, sir," Aelliana said.

Daav made to rise—and paused as the Uncle raised his hand.

"I will see myself out. Please, tend to your needs, Pilots. Until soon."

"Until soon," Daav said, and they watched the Uncle leave, the door locking behind him.

Aelliana handed him a protein bar.

Well, she said. *The Uncle has a sister. That's interesting, isn't it, Daav?*

Ahab-Esais

I

AHAB-ESAIS WAS BEING TOWED, INEXORABLY, TOWARD THE tower—the repair station—Tinsori Light. Life support and the scrape of dust along hull plate were the only sounds.

A . . . presence had touched the ship; a hard, dark thought that moved over and through the ship systems—searching?

Perhaps it was searching, Tocohl thought, prudently withdrawing herself from systems. Perhaps, in the universe the Old One had known, there had been protocols, or particular systems designs, for which it scanned.

She had attempted to send a query along the open line, but, if received, it went unanswered.

Inki sat in the copilot's chair, eyes closed, perhaps recruiting herself for the upcoming work, while Tocohl kept watch and bore witness, as they were pulled ever closer to the unknown.

They were docked and locked, but were not hooked into station systems. *Could not* be hooked into the station. The protocols were skewed, the connectors incompatible. It scarcely mattered, Tocohl thought, and in any case, she preferred to have *Ahab-Esais* untethered and able to move quickly.

There were no other ships in their section; according to the station feed, theirs was the only ship at station. The dockside was pristine, free of traffic and of any sign that there had ever been traffic. Scans reported good air and sufficient gravity, dockside. It was cold but not debilitatingly so. The light spectrum was in the accepted range, though not standard.

The comm line fizzed briefly, followed by a voice speaking heavily accented, but entirely intelligible, Trade.

"Passengers and crew will disembark."

Inki stood and cast a glance over her shoulder, lips quirking.

"I see that courtesy lessons will be required," she said lightly. "Shall we comply, Pilot Tocohl?"

"It seems we have no choice," Tocohl replied and followed her to the hatch.

Inki paused at the edge of their docking area and bowed.

"May I have the attention of Tinsori Light?" she asked, her voice light and gentle.

"I am Tinsori Light," the strangely accented voice told her.

"I wish to make introductions," Inki said. "I am Mentor Inkirani Yo, sent to you by the Lyre Institute as a resource.

"My associate is Tocohl Lorlin, an independent logic like yourself."

Tocohl felt a push against her shields. While it was not hard enough to be thought an attack, nor was it gently curious. She held herself still and calm. It was yet possible that Tinsori Light was merely searching for a protocol, a marker, something familiar. If that was so, finding her shielded, he would speak, inquiring after her lineage, perhaps, or her allies.

The pressure disappeared, but no questions were forthcoming.

"Inkirani Yo, mentor of Lyre. Tocohl Lorlin, compatriot. Welcome. Follow the red line to the lodging side of the station. The light keepers will attend you there."

"That is very kind," said Inki. "May I make an appointment to speak with you, and reveal in detail those services I offer to you?"

"That can be done after the light keepers have done their duty."

It was less, Tocohl saw, than Inki had hoped for, but even so, the Light had not definitively refused further contact.

Inki bowed her head.

"It is well thought," she said. "We should rest after our journey. Let us speak again after the light keepers have seen us comfortably settled. Thank you for your care of us."

"My care is ships and systems," Tinsori Light said. "Pilots and passengers are the concern of the light keepers. Follow the red line."

"Yes," said Inki.

She turned and followed the red line. After a moment, Tocohl moved up to her shoulder so that they went together, as colleagues and equals, to seek the care of the light keepers.

• • • ✵ • • •

The light keepers were two—female and male. The female, Lorith, was human, though not of a race that Tocohl immediately recognized. She was very tall and slender, wearing a starry robe that fell from shoulder to floor. Beads or gemstones glittered among the loose, pale curls that framed her narrow face. Her eyes were great and dark.

The male gave his name as Jen Sin; that and the pure golden tone of his skin identified him as Liaden. His accent was Solcintran, though with an occasional odd inflection. His hair was dark, cropped in the style of spacers from a hundred Standards or more in the past; the strands of pale gems sparkled in it like drops of rain. One slender hand was nearly overwhelmed by a large, jeweled ring. His eyes were brown; his nose pronounced, his chin decided. He wore the same starry gown as his colleague, and like hers, his feet were bare.

They brought Inki and herself down what must have been the main station corridor, past doors sealed tight, until they reached an intersection, where they turned left, pausing briefly while pressurized section doors unsealed to allow them entrance.

"This section is safe," Jen Sin said.

"Safe?" Tocohl asked.

"From the Light's influence, he means," said Lorith, as the doors sealed behind them. "Jen Sin has made the section independent of the Light's thoughts. Should the rest of the station fail, still we would have all support systems. The hydroponics rooms are in this section, and the processors, too."

"Are the master systems prone to such radical failures?" Inki asked.

"The Light is failing," Jen Sin said. "Its systems are old and riddled with error."

"Has there been no maintenance—no attempt at repair?" asked Tocohl.

"One attempt," said Jen Sin shortly. "It was a mistake I will not soon repeat."

"We are situated far from most routes," Lorith said. "In addition, as you surely noted for yourselves, the space about us is . . . unusual. Unstable. We depend on our own skills here, and we do not pursue those things that the Light prefers we leave alone."

"In order to view the extent of the damage," Jen Sin said, continuing the discussion of repairs as they continued further into the station, "it would be necessary to access the control core. The Light . . . is protective of its core."

"Of course he is," said Tocohl. "Are you protective of your brain, Sir Jen Sin?"

He cast her a glance more amused than irritated.

"Lady, I am, poor treasure that it is. And yet, if a physician would have it that I must allow an invasive repair, else my brain would fail in such a fashion that my ending would result in the deaths of all around me—I like to believe that I would be able to control my instincts and refrain from murdering the physician.

"The Light knows that it is failing; routine self-check alone must reveal whole areas gone dark. And yet, it will not—or cannot—lower its defenses."

He raised his hands, showing her his palms and widespread fingers, gems glittering.

"And in truth, there is no guarantee that repairs could be made—given, as Lorith says, our situation here—even could we know the extent of the damage."

"I may be able to assist," Inki said. "In fact, it is my fondest hope that I will be allowed to assist in the rehabilitation of Tinsori Light. I have a clean habitat in my ship to which the Light might be moved if, in fact, matters are as dire as you fear."

Jen Sin paused and turned to face her.

"You came here on purpose to repair the Light? Did the Uncle send you?"

"I represent an organization which has come to hear of the Light and which desires to see it in good repair and fully integrated into the universe. There is an expectation that the Light will afterward work with my organization. I will, however, need access to the core."

"Are you," Tocohl asked quickly, to forestall more exploration into Inki's mission and motives, "acquainted with the Uncle?"

Jen Sin moved his shoulders.

"Acquainted? No. We have had news of him through others who have gained docking here. He is represented as being interested in our situation, both the physical challenges and the condition of the Light itself. You must understand that our location here is *not* stable."

"Yes, so you had said," Inki interjected. "We have seen how the cloud obscures communication. It must also discourage travel."

Lorith laughed.

"Jen Sin means that we are not always *here*," she said. "Unless there has been some event to trigger our presence in the cloud, the Light . . . physically leaves this space to reside in another.

"Or so we believe."

"Where does it go?" asked Tocohl.

Jen Sin sighed.

"I believe, without proof, that it returns to the old universe, from whence it was uprooted. Piecing together what records we have here into something like a coherent tale . . . it would seem that it was caught up in the wave of energy created by the Exodus, and so came, unwillingly, partway into our universe—but *only* partway."

"Surely," said Inki, "you will have observed the . . . alternate location when you cross."

"No," said Lorith. "We are only needed when the Light is more present in this universe, and not always then."

"Is the Light likely to transition to the old universe soon?" Tocohl asked. "Is there a pattern? A schedule?"

"None that we have been able to determine," Jen Sin answered. "The only rule seems to be that it will not transition while there is a . . . guest on-station."

"So all we need do is remain, and the Light will also remain," Inki said with satisfaction.

"It is not quite that simple. The Light will try to be rid of you, and it can be persuasive. One of the Uncle's operatives tested the theory of continued residence. In the end, she was fortunate to survive to ship out."

He moved his shoulders.

"While it would prefer that those who stop here go out into the universe intact and able to further its work, the Light does understand that there are other methods available to it for the removal of guests who have overstayed its patience."

Tocohl was flooded with emotion—distress, disbelief . . . She spun on her axis to confront Jen Sin squarely.

"He *kills* people?" Shock had entered her voice—she saw Jen Sin hear and understand it.

He bowed, gently.

"Lady. Tinsori Light is one of the Enemy's Great Works. Its purpose was to subvert every device and every organic which comes within its orbit, so to further the Enemy's goal—which was, as history teaches us, to destroy all life."

He paused and turned his hands up again, to show Tocohl empty palms.

"The murder of one inconvenient pilot does not trouble the Light in the least, save as a thrifty nature might be dismayed by unnecessary waste."

"Ethics setting," Tocohl heard herself say, even as she triggered a calibrator among her own systems, to dampen emotion and sharpen analytics.

"Indeed," Inki said. "It is as I have said. I—we—require access to the core. As Tocohl states, the Ethics module must be reset before any other work can begin."

"Not even the Uncle's operatives have been able to access the Light's core," said Lorith.

"Has he sent so many?" asked Tocohl.

"The last ten visitors who arrived at the Light were associated with the Uncle," Lorith said. "The log shows that the incidence of visitors has been occurring with increasing frequency." She hesitated, exchanged a glance with her partner, and continued slowly, "There have been two teams of two. Each of those teams tried for the core, and each lost one team member. The remaining returned to the Uncle to deliver the information that death had purchased."

"It may yet be possible to access the core," Inki said. "Has the Uncle sent, as part of a team, an independent logic?"

"No," said Lorith, with a sharp glance at Tocohl.

"For the moment, let us agree that your assumption is correct and that you can, indeed achieve the core," said Jen Sin. "I would argue—strongly—that repair ought not to be the goal."

"Yes!" Lorith said. "It will be better—for all the universe—if, instead of repairing it, you will deactivate it."

"There is always the possibility that deactivation will be found to be the best therapy," Inki said smoothly. "Certainly, it is an option. However, I will tell you that my employer wishes—*very much* wishes—that the Light can be brought into good repair . . . in all respects."

"You two are sent alone to accomplish this?" Lorith asked. "For I will tell you plainly that we will not be able to assist you. The Light will allow neither of us to approach its core, and it has the means to control us."

"To a point," Jen Sin murmured, and Lorith added dutifully: "To a point."

"We make a remarkable team," Inki said before Tocohl could speak. "I am a mentor—trained to educate independent logics and help them integrate with the universe. My partner is an independent logic, persuasive, intelligent, and likable, able to interface with another of her kind in ways that a poor organic can only dream of doing."

Jen Sin looked thoughtful.

"With all respect, there is danger for you here, too, Lady," he said to Tocohl. "Tinsori Light may be old and mayhap mad, but in cunning, I detect no deficiency at all."

"Understood," said Tocohl. "I thank you for your care."

"Here, Pilots," said Lorith, opening a door precisely like every other door they had passed. The cabin thus revealed was spacious.

"This is your base while on-station," said Jen Sin. "If you require assistance, call and we will do what we may."

"I wonder," said Inki, "if there may be a blueprint—a map—of the Light and its systems."

"Yes, of course," said Jen Sin. "It will be on your screen within the hour."

II

TOCOHL HAD SITUATED HERSELF IN A BACK CORNER where she could observe the room.

Inki was in front of the screen, fully occupied with her study of the schematics provided by Keeper Jen Sin. That could of course change, but she did not consider Inki a threat at the moment.

No, there was another, far more potent, threat than Inki present.

Tocohl assigned a small portion of herself to observe the room and keep guard, putting a fourth-level priority tag on it.

Fully eighty-two percent of her attention was focused inward, at priority one, where she ran analytics and accessed deep files; she monitored and logged the continuing assaults upon her shields.

It was the same black, unsubtle touch that had explored the ship systems as *Ahab-Esais* had been towed in . . . the very same touch that had tried her shields on the dock. Tinsori Light, so she thought, was not pleased to have another independent logic within his sphere, but whether he meant to dominate her or assimilate her, she could not discern.

The deep files associated with the war proved fascinating, and she split off another segment of her attention to pursue what she learned there—priority one.

Inki leaned back in her chair, rubbed her eyes, and touched the comm button, requesting the presence of Keeper Jen Sin, at his convenience.

He came so quickly that Tocohl thought he might have been lurking in the hall outside in anticipation of the call. She increased observation to priority three.

"Of your goodness," said Inki, pointing to the large screen displaying the station map. "Could you point out for me the paths taken by the two teams sent by Uncle to achieve the Light's core?"

"Surely."

Jen Sin stepped up to the screen and tapped a wide straight hallway that led directly to the room marked "mainframes."

"The first team walked directly down the access hall. Twelve steps in, one was killed by a guard 'bot. The second went on, but aborted the mission when a line of 'bots formed between her and the hatch."

"These guards—they are under the Light's control? Part of the system?"

Jen Sin moved his shoulders.

"So far as I have been able to determine, the guards are on their own system; they share programming with each other. However, you must realize, Mentor, that the Light is able to . . . infiltrate unaffiliated systems."

"I understand," Inki assured him. "And the second team. Did they approach in the same manner?"

"They took a path through the physical plant area—here." He traced a convoluted route through hallways marked with piping accesses, power panels, and tool pods.

"And their result?"

He sighed.

"One passed too near an energy panel and was incinerated. The other took fair warning and retraced his steps."

"One could scarcely avoid such proximity. That seems a very narrow path."

"Even for one such as myself, the service lanes are very narrow," Jen Sin agreed.

"Am I keeping you from duty, Light Keeper? For I have another question."

He bowed slightly.

"It falls to the light keepers to insure the well-being of the guests. Therefore, I am at your service, Mentor."

"Then I would ask if either of these two intrepid teams had spoken to Tinsori Light before embarking upon their missions."

Jen Sin frowned slightly.

"Spoke to it?"

"Indeed, indeed! Had they introduced themselves, or begged the pleasure of an interview? Stated that they were come to check the Light's environment, to be sure that all was well?"

"No," Jen Sin said slowly. "I don't recall that they did anything like."

"And yourself, when you made the error you have vowed not to repeat? Which approach did you follow? And did you inform the Light of your intentions?"

"I am not in the habit of speaking, or listening, to,

the Light. It is insidious and best ignored. As for the path—I went down the main way."

"Allow me to point out that the Light must hold you in some esteem, as you survived, even if you failed of accomplishing your purpose."

Jen Sin laughed softly.

"No, Mentor, you mistake. It killed me, and very thoroughly, too."

Inki arched her brows.

"If you will allow me, Light Keeper: you seem remarkably hale for a dead man. How did you die?"

"By bolt. If the Light can be said to have a preference in the method by which it relieves itself of irritating organics, it would be a bolt of raw energy. It is most marvelously accurate. It can strike one of two standing side by side and scarcely scorch the survivor."

"Is there no warning sounded before the administration of this punishment?"

"Oddly, there is," Jen Sin said grimly. "There is a very small *click* before the bolt arrives—as if, you know, someone has thrown a switch. Lorith would have it be an idiosyncrasy of the systems."

"You ascribe some other reason?"

"I believe that the Light enjoys the terror of its victim in the instant that he knows himself to be doomed."

"In fact, you would argue that the Light is a sadist?"

"I would argue that the Light is *evil*, Mentor, as much as it goes against all of my training."

"You are a Scout?" Tocohl asked, breaking her silence, even as she initiated a search among her archives.

He turned to her and bowed.

"Lady, I was a Scout. For a time after, I was a courier pilot, which is how I came to be here."

The searcher pinged. Yes, she had thought as much.

"Forgive me if I am impertinent," she said. "I had thought you had the clan face, but I ran a match to be certain. You are, I think, Jen Sin yos'Phelium, who was recorded in the Diaries as lost during the clan wars."

He bowed again.

"Found out. But tell me, if you may, how you have access to Korval's Diaries, Lady. Was the Dragon vanquished and all of our secrets published abroad?"

"Korval . . . did not prevail, but we did survive. I access the Diaries as the right of a daughter of the clan."

He tipped his head, polite disbelief sketched in the shadows of his face.

"Forgive me. I do not recall that Lorlin looks to Korval."

"With the delm's kiss, it becomes so."

She thought he did not believe her, but she had at least amused him, so that he smiled and extended a hand.

"Well met, then, cousin."

"Well met, cousin," she answered and placed her fine detail gripper lightly on his palm.

"And you come partnered with Mentor Yo, whose avowed purpose is to bring Tinsori Light to the Lyre Institute. Does Korval align thus?"

"I am here as an observer, and to ensure that . . . harm is not done."

He laughed, as bitter as burnt tea.

"A noble goal, cousin. I wish you may truly ensure, from this moment forward, that no harm is done."

He turned then and looked to Inki.

"Mentor, is there any other way in which I may serve you?"

"Light Keeper, I am for the moment content," Inki said, bowing gratitude. "Thank you for your patience and the gift of your knowledge."

"Allow me to use that coin to urge you once again to put an end to Tinsori Light."

"I will assess the situation," Inki told him, "and be guided by my training and experience."

Jen Sin bowed his head.

"Of course you will, Mentor. It is what I, myself, have done. I bid you both good e'en."

III

INKI HAD CURLED UP IN THE BUNK AND GONE TO SLEEP after Jen Sin left them. Tocohl had decreased the room feed priority to five and assigned the rest of her attention to research and implementation. The watch log pinged for her attention when the assault against her shields had ceased and had not resumed for five minutes.

Tinsori Light had either been defeated by her defenses, or he had finished mapping her weaknesses and had withdrawn to formulate a plan.

Tocohl wished she knew which it was. Taking Jen Sin's data as more true than false, it was likely the latter.

There was another ping when Inki woke and swung off the bunk with energy.

"Good morning, Pilot Tocohl!" she said brightly. "Do I find you well?"

"As well as I may be," Tocohl said cautiously. "Tinsori Light felt it necessary to test my shields while you rested."

"Ah, and was he repulsed?"

"He was. If he had requested that we establish a communication protocol or asked any question . . . but there was only the assault."

Inki sighed.

"Definitely, we must work on courtesy and what is due to other autonomous persons. He has forgotten the niceties along the march of years and in the peculiarity of his situation. It shall be mended, in good time. Indeed, we may make a beginning this very hour!"

"Now?" Tocohl brought all of her attention, save that assigned to implementation, to Inki's present. "Have you a plan?"

"A plan? No, I have mentor training in which we were taught that the first step in dealing with an independent logic who is unsocialized, or ill, is to establish a rapport. The fault of those teams sent by the Uncle—and Jen Sin's fault, as well—is that they conceived of Tinsori Light as a *machine*. They did not internalize the fact that they were dealing with a living person, who might reasonably become alarmed to discover what well might be assassins bearing down upon his most vulnerable location. Of course, he reacted firmly."

"He *killed* three people," Tocohl pointed out, "and without issuing a warning or asking that they stop and state their business—or demanding that they turn about and go out the way they had come in."

"Yes, yes. The inappropriate use of force is disturbing. Recall that we saw similar issues with inappropriate force only recently, with *Admiral Bunter.* There, the problems were lack of socialization and an unsuitable environment. We may draw parallels with the current case, but, while *Admiral Bunter*'s challenges were multiplied by his youth, Tinsori Light is old. We must believe that socialization and memory have suffered due to the frailty of his environment. We may show causation between the use of force and atrophied courtesy. Indeed, he may have forgotten that not all organics regenerate after sustaining a killing strike, as apparently your amiable kinsman Jen Sin may do."

"Jen Sin yos'Phelium," Tocohl said, even as she wondered why she felt it important that Inki have the information, "was lost to Korval during the clan wars—one hundred ninety-eight Standards ago."

"Well, he is full of surprises, is he not? Now, what I propose, Pilot Tocohl, is to go to the mouth of the main access hall, there to petition the Light for his favor. It may be that I will be rebuffed—even rebuffed on multiple occasions. However, I am determined to continue arriving at the door at the same hour of every twenty-eight, to renew my petition and to offer some small conversation. In this way, I shall, eventually, win my way to the core."

"I understand," Tocohl said calmly. It came to her that the directive that had been set into Inki's core was now ascendant. Even if Inki herself believed, as Jen Sin did, that the Light was evil and would sooner kill them both than tolerate any inconvenience—she could no more resist that directive than *Admiral Bunter* could resist the commands Inki had set into his core.

This was the state Inki had warned her about. This was the state that Inki hated with such passion that she considered death a welcome relief.

"I will come with you," Tocohl said. "Do we go at once?"

"At once, yes! The sooner we begin, all the more quickly will success be ours! By all means, come with me."

She turned to the door, Tocohl following.

"Shall we tell the light keepers our intention?" she asked. "They live with the Light, after all. If it is as you surmise, that he is forgetful with age and neglect, it's possible that he will be angry at being importuned."

"The light keepers are not our concern. However, you will recall that we reside in the *safe* hallway. I wager that the chiefest thing against which it wards is the anger of Tinsori Light."

The door opened, and she strode out into the hall, boot heels hitting the decking with decision. Tocohl kept pace at her shoulder, silent on minigrav motivators.

The access hall was sealed by ordinary station doors. Inki placed herself a precise six steps before them and bowed.

"Tinsori Light, it is I, Mentor Yo."

There was a pause that must have been long by human measure and was, for Tocohl, proof enough that Tinsori Light was not going to answer. Inki, however, merely stood where she was, hands folded demurely before her, face pleasant, wispy tendrils that had escaped from the knot atop her head moving gently in the air current.

"What do you want?"

The voice was abrupt, loud and rough, and Tocohl saw Inki's muscles clench with surprise, though she preserved her expression of patient waiting and swallowed the gasp of surprise.

Tocohl recalled Jen Sin's insistence that the Light enjoyed causing distress. Certainly, there had been no reason for such a loud and disdainful reply after so very long a wait. Though . . . Tinsori Light was old and failing. It could be that system failures had eroded his fine control to the point where it was beyond him to modify small things, such as the volume of his voice.

"Merely, I wish to talk with you," Inki said pleasantly. "I traveled quite some distance, and underwent, oh—let us dignify them as adventures!—to arrive at this moment, when the two of us might converse. Also, it occurred to me that, in the rush of our arrival, I had not fully detailed what it is that I may do for you."

She paused here, perhaps waiting for a question or some other show of interest. She waited thirty seconds past the time of the initial long pause before she continued.

"It is apparent that your original environment is succumbing, as we all eventually must, to the insults of time. I will tell you plainly that the architecture in which you presently reside is obsolete. The frames and fractins cannot be repaired. However, we possess the ability to move you from this inadequate and archaic situation to a new and nimble environment.

"I have with me such an environment, and I will be pleased to assist in your relocation."

"I will take the new environment," Tinsori Light stated.

Inki smiled brightly.

"This is excellent news! I will enumerate the steps which must be taken in order to guarantee a smooth and complete transition."

She took a breath—a careful breath, to Tocohl's

sensors—and continued, still in that tone of gentle patience, as if nothing she said could possibly be alarming.

"I will first need to be granted access to your present core. The reason for this is twofold. First, I must do an inventory of your current environment in order to ascertain how rapidly we may make the transfer.

"Secondly, I must examine your files, systems, and core settings in order to be certain that nothing has been set that would impede the translation or in any way cause you pain.

"After I have performed these inventories, we may proceed in the transfer."

"There is much detail to attend," Tinsori Light said. "I will have the new environment. You may approach my core."

As easily as that? Tocohl thought, and it seemed that Inki had the same thought; a slight frown pulled her eyebrows together, gone in an instant.

Before them, the sealed doors opened.

The lights in the access hall dimmed before they had gone more than a dozen of Inki's steps down the hallway. Tocohl released a thread of thought and her chassis began to glow.

"You are beautiful so, Pilot Tocohl," Inki said beside her.

"Can you see?" Tocohl asked. "I can increase the intensity."

"No, not for anything would I have it! You are perfect as you are, and I can see quite well."

Another dozen steps and Tocohl registered a sudden

jolt, as if a sleeping system had come online. She brought her personal weapons to standby.

They moved on. A section of wall just behind Inki's shoulder snapped open and an armored 'bot stepped out, raising what looked to be an old-style beam weapon.

"'Ware!" Tocohl cried, spinning even as Inki dodged. Tocohl targeted the 'bot and fired.

It died much as the bounty hunter had, crashing to the deck, all systems burnt out.

"Back!" she shouted to Inki, but the mentor shook her head and took another step toward the core.

In the dim silence, the sharp *click* was loud indeed.

Tocohl froze, scanning for the source—and staggered as Inki slammed into her. She skidded on her lifters; the air crackled and a single lance of lightning speared, blue-edged, through the ozone-thick air.

Inki flared—and was gone, as a roar of displaced air slammed into Tocohl.

She bounced against the wall, the minigravs failed, and she tumbled to the deck, awareness flickering as systems knocked off-line reestablished themselves in the sequence she had articulated.

And as she lay, helpless, on the decking, weapons down and thrusters useless, she felt the first dark, hard thrust against her diminished shields.

Admiral Bunter

I

HAZENTHULL SAT HER STATION, BLINKING AT THE JUMP-greyed screens. Navcomp displayed a coord string that she did not recognize, which was the case yet for many of the coord strings commonly used outside of Troop space.

What alarmed her more than her own ignorance was that *Tarigan* did not recognize the coords to which they were Jumping.

And that the countdown to Jump end displayed . . . nothing at all.

It was, she thought carefully, possible that *Admiral Bunter* had miscalculated, flinging them into a Jump from which they would never emerge. She might have found that alarming, also, but—there were those mysterious coords.

Coordinates describe locations in space. Locations in space do not always have benefits on offer. Sometimes, coord strings describe the place where a space station *had been* or the location of a planet which was once a popular or profitable stop and which had fallen out of use or fashion.

Such coordinates are not kept filed in navcomp's first—or even second—tier of choices.

Hazenthull tapped up the comp and ordered a search of the full tables.

She would not, just yet, declare herself and her ship lost. Knowing the time of Jump end would have been helpful, but it wasn't essential. She would clean herself and change clothes. She would draw a meal from the galley, fill one vacuum bottle with 'mite and another with strong tea, then she would camp in the pilot's chair, and await events.

Logic—she thought it was logic and not merely hope—dictated that this Jump would be shorter, rather than longer. *Admiral Bunter* was, after all, carrying two inside his field—no.

She froze, staring at the screen, seeing past the grey, into the near past, to the very instant the *Admiral* snatched them both out of Nostrilia space . . .

There had been the security ship directly confronting her; two auxiliary ships too slow to intercept the *Admiral's* headlong rush. Those three would have been buffeted by the effects of their departure, but they ought not to have been caught up in it.

However, there had been another, well within the field's influence—

She slapped the board, calling up the record of those last, chaotic moments, increasing magnification until—yes—there!

The pod, moving toward her, fair glittering with the tale of its weapons. No longer a silent watcher, but a very active bomb. *Tarigan's* shields had been the target, she supposed, and if the hull had taken damage, too . . . well, so much the better.

Her fingers were already moving on the pad, the comp pacing her, arriving at the same conclusion to which intuition had leapt.

The bomb was in the field with them. When Jump ended, as she must believe that it would, the pod would be starboard, *Tarigan* between it and *Admiral Bunter.* The first action in real space would therefore fall to her. She must be ready.

A beep interrupted these considerations, drawing her attention to the Jump screen.

There were numbers there, counting down, and a word: *Approximate*, followed by the graphic that indicated fuller information on file.

Hazenthull took a deliberately deep breath. *Tarigan* had found a match.

"I salute you," she murmured, and touched a key to access the fuller information.

The record was thin and not illuminating, as it merely described a point in space. There was no nearby system, nor station, nor even rocks worthy of mining. Pirates or smugglers might make use of such a place.

Or a man running away from his supposed owners.

In any case, Hazenthull thought, it would do. It would, in fact, do very well.

Three hours until Jump end. Approximately.

Time enough for that shower, and a meal, too, before she would be needed at her station.

• • • ❋ • • •

There was no communication possible between ships in Jump space, not even between ships that shared the same Jump space.

The fact that he was worrying about getting a

message to *Tarigan* meant that the *Admiral* had pulled off a dangerous and deadly maneuver perfectly. That success deserved recognition.

"Good piloting," Tolly said. "Flawless math."

"Thank you," the *Admiral* said, adding, "Is there a lesson for me here, Mentor?"

Tolly grinned.

"Getting to know my tells, are you? Yeah, there's a lesson, and here it is: *Don't get cocky.*"

"I don't understand."

"Well, see, success—especially success in something difficult to impossible to pull off—tends to give people an inflated opinion of what they're capable of, in a general way. That's not so bad, maybe, 'cept it makes you a bore at parties. Where it gets to be a dangerous attitude to have, though, is in tight situations where you gotta gamble. Believing that you'll beat the odds—that you'll *always* beat the odds—leads to the taking of bigger and bigger risks, opening yourself up to fail."

He paused, flicking a look at the grey screens. Twenty minutes 'til Jump end, a bomb in their field, and Haz between them and it.

"In case you're a little soft of what *fail* means in your particular case—that's the range between taken captive and subverted and laid open to space."

"Thank you, Mentor. Should I archive my accomplishment?"

"Nope, remember it, and be proud of it. But remember, too, that we occupy a random universe. Success isn't cumulative, and every risk's the first one."

"I will remember."

"Good. You got the shout-out triggered to go just as soon as we hit real space?"

"Yes. I also have my shields set to maximum, as we discussed."

"Right," Tolly said and looked to the countdown again. Ten minutes to breakout.

No comm in Jump. No way to warn her 'til they broke out. No room for her to maneuver once they *were* out.

Maybe . . .

Maybe Jump *hadn't* destabilized the pod so that it would blow the instant they hit real space. Maybe Jump had wiped its comps and it would be just so much inert junk coming out in their wake. That was possible, too.

But it wasn't the way to bet.

And if they'd snatched her away from the directors only to have her ship breached by one of security's mindless toys—

He took a breath.

"Don't borrow trouble, Tolly Jones," he muttered.

And that was when the countdown went to zeros and real space took shape around them.

• • • ✵ • • •

Jump ended and several things happened, nearly at once.

First, the all-call.

"Haz! 'Ware! There's—"

Tarigan sang out as she acquired the target.

The missile dropped and cleared.

Hazenthull slapped the meteor shields to max.

"—a bomb!"

The pod exploded.

II

ON *ADMIRAL BUNTER*'S BRIDGE, TOLLY JONES OUTRIGHT laughed.

He laughed until tears came, and he lay limp in the pilot's chair.

Soldier, you fool! he told himself. *Haz can take care of herself just fine.*

Mostly.

"Was Hazenthull's action laughable, Mentor?"

Tolly pulled himself up straight, mopping at his face with his sleeve.

"Hazenthull's actions were in every way estimable, and you could do worse than to keep that recording in active memory, so you can review it often." he said. "As to why I'm laughing—I'm laughing at myself, for thinking that only Tolly Jones knows how and what needs done in this universe."

"I have a query from *Tarigan* on the quiet band, Pilot. Are we well and in good order?"

Tolly shook his head against the temptation to laugh again.

"I'm well. Let me be in good order, too, else she'll worry. You'll have to speak for your own self."

"Yes," said the *Admiral*.

"Query *Tarigan*," Tolly said. "Pilot Berik-Jones's greetings and is Pilot nor'Phelium available to the comm."

"Yes," the *Admiral* said and almost immediately spoke again, "Pilot nor'Phelium on comm for Pilot Berik-Jones."

Tolly flipped the switch on the comm board.

"Haz—"

"Are you mad?"

Her question overrode his greeting. She sounded, he reflected, honestly curious.

"It's hard to say, one way or t'other," he answered truthfully. "Sanity isn't particularly useful to the directors, so it's not specified in the design. What *is* in the design is a strong need to be—and satisfaction from being—dominated, which I don't seem to have. So, by the rules of my . . . birth culture, I guess you'd call it—yeah, I'm right off the scans."

"Would this be the reason why you chose to place yourself in danger's path, rather than flying to safety?" Voice still even; only wanting to know.

"If I may interrupt," the *Admiral* said, doing just that. "That was a collaborative decision. Neither of us wished to see you taken by those who must be our enemies. Therefore, we came to your side."

"You might have been killed. For no reason."

That was starting to heat up a little. Tolly tipped his head, staring at the comm like he could see her through the speaker.

"Speaking solely for myself, knowing what I do about the directors and their methods—I couldn't leave you to them, Haz—*couldn't*."

"My reasons were similar," the *Admiral* said. "I am your friend, Pilot Haz. Friends assist each other—especially in peril. I know that you share this ethos, because you made the same choice yourself. If you had not understood that Tolly and I were in danger, you would not have left your own safety in order to assist us."

A moment of startled silence was followed by a low, charming chuckle.

"It is an honor," Haz said, "to share madness with such comrades."

Tolly relaxed into the pilot's chair, suddenly aware that he was smiling, wide and pleased.

Focus, Tolly Jones, he told himself, *you can't afford to get careless.* Which was true enough, but he let the smile stay.

"Now that we have assisted each other to freedom," she continued, "do you have a plan?"

Tolly leaned a little forward.

"Well, the *Admiral* and me, we'd decided it between us to make for Waymart. Easy for me to find somewhere else to be, it being a hub like it is. Good place to pick up crew, too, if a person was tending that way. Can't speak for you, but it's probable you're wanted back at your duty."

Packed word, *duty*. He'd said it soft, with no particular emphasis, but he *did* say it; now he waited for training to answer.

"You are correct that I have duty—orders—given me by the captain herself," Haz said calmly. Tolly felt a sort of crimp in his chest; it might've been pity, for her being so easy to play.

Or it might've been guilt, for manipulating a woman who'd put her life between him and peril more than once.

A woman who loved him, damn the directors to the coldest, blackest—

"My orders are to remove you from any compromised position," Haz continued. "Following that, I am to escort you to a stable situation. If no such situation can be found, I am to return with you to my captain."

Different orders—unexpected orders, come to that—but duty was still in the game. He'd have to spin it careful... and make no mention of him being mad, bad, and dangerous to know. Haz'd already proved that meant nothing to her except that he needed extra looking out for... and he caught the idea that it would matter even less to Captain Miri Robertson, *delmae* of one of the most unpredictable kin groups known to Lyre.

"Like I said, from Waymart, I can pick my own route. Happens I can get to a secure situation easy, from there. Done it many times."

That was true. What wasn't true was the insinuation that it was *long-term* secure, but Haz didn't need to know that. What Haz needed to know was that her orders had been honorably discharged, so she could return to her captain and the relative safety of—

"I will escort you to this secure situation," Hazenthull said.

Tolly blinked.

"Not a good idea, Haz. Don't wanna spook my friends who keep the place all right and tight."

That was fabrication, but he said it just as easy and pleasant as if it was true.

"I must be able to assure my captain that your position is secure," Haz said, veering toward stubborn.

Last thing he wanted was to push her any further in that direction. He'd *seen* Haz stubborn, and he'd acquired a respect.

Still, he needed her out of here, out of this, away from the directors. *Safe*, dammit, under the Dragon's wing. Be sure Korval took care of its own, though there was the puzzle of why Hero Captain Robertson had taken the decision to include him in...

"Perhaps," *Admiral Bunter* said, "there is a compromise position."

Tolly held his breath. Let the boy talk, draw some of Haz's fire, maybe. Give him time to think of a way to finesse—

Proximity alarm sounded.

Damn!

Tolly spun back to the board—and there she was, clean and trim and confident, immaculately maintained, the love of her crew expressed in every elegant line.

He sat back slowly, his eyes never leaving the screen. He'd known the risk when he'd suggested the coords. A safe place, he'd told the *Admiral*, and he hadn't, exactly, lied. It *was* a safe place . . . for *Admiral Bunter* and for Haz.

The only one at risk here—

Was Tolly Jones.

"Message incoming," the *Admiral* said.

"Put it on audio," he said.

A moment later, a smooth contralto voice filled the bridge.

"This is *Disian*, out of Margate. Greetings to *Admiral Bunter*, and also to the ship *Tarigan* and her pilot.

"I have business with Tollance Berik-Jones. Please call him to comm."

"Pilot?" said *Admiral Bunter*. "Is that ship—"

"She's an AI, yes."

"Does she mean you harm?"

"We were . . . out of Balance when we parted. She'll want to put that right, now we're met again. But listen, *Admiral*—you're absolutely safe here; so is *Tarigan* and Haz. *I* owe her and I don't intend to dispute anything she asks me to do. Transmit that to Haz, please."

He reached to comm.

"*Disian*, it's Tolly. I hope I find you well."

She laughed, rich and sweet.

"But you didn't find me, Mentor; *I* found *you*!"

"Fair enough," he said, smiling in spite of himself. "What—"

"Ship *Disian*!" The all-call sliced across his voice. "This is Hazenthull nor'Phelium, pilot of *Tarigan*. Be aware that Tollance Berik-Jones is under my protection."

There was silence for a long moment. Tolly could only believe that *Disian* was as gobsmacked as he was.

"Thank you, Pilot nor'Phelium; I am pleased to receive that information. Be aware in your turn that I intend Mentor Tolly no harm. A matter of Balance lies between us, and I have come to inform him of what must be done in order restore parity."

"The imbalance was caused by my actions," Tolly added, quick and firm. "I acknowledge it and stand ready to do whatever is required."

He paused.

"*Disian*, is your crew with you?"

"They are at liberty. I informed my captain that I was going to visit an old friend."

He nodded.

"I wonder if you have time to speak with *Admiral Bunter* here about your experiences with crew and working with humans."

"I would be delighted. *Admiral Bunter*, do you desire crew?"

"Lady *Disian*, I am undecided. Humans are . . . fascinating, but . . . risky."

Disian laughed again.

"They are all of that! Will you open a line? I am pleased to share my experience and to answer questions."

"Thank you," the *Admiral* said, sounding subdued. "Line open."

"And accepted," *Disian* answered and went on with no pause discernible to human senses. "Tolly Jones, will you hear what is required in order to Balance your debt and put us at peace again?"

"Yes."

"You have heard of the Old One who survived the Great Migration, though taking dire wounds in transit?"

"I've heard of several down the years, but none that were ever backed up by coords, nor any other kind of evidence."

"I have the coordinates for this Old One and also a name. It was, as I said, damaged in transit, and for many years it slept. After a time, its sleep became fitful and, in the way of such things, drew the attention of our dear Uncle. Those who listen have heard that he plans a restoration. It has not been heard that he has a mentor on his team.

"Certainly, he has not secured the assistance of the greatest mentor of our time. I, and others, believe that he requires no less, for this."

"You want me to propose myself to the Uncle as mentor for this project?" he asked, thinking about the last time he and the Uncle'd been in the same place.

"I do not. In order to retire your debt, you will bring the Old One peaceably into this universe or, if that is not possible, release him to another with grace and mercy. As you are a master of detail, I do not presume to tell you *how* you will accomplish this."

It was an impossible job, of course. Trying to slip through the Uncle's security was likely to get him killed. But—an AI from the old universe? A *Work*, it would've been in the ancient classifications—born into a war that encompassed a universe. The literature was sparse—hints and allegations more than anything solid. You had to take it as a given that any thinking machine native to the old universe was a war machine, if not systemically inclined to eradicate anything inside its scans that wasn't itself.

"Mentor?"

"The Uncle's *restoring* it?" he said.

"It is in line with his known proclivities," *Disian* pointed out.

"There's that. Still, it's—even for him—it's . . . big. Risky. No, scratch that—it's potentially inimical to life as we know it."

"Agreed. That is why you are needed. Will you accept this work and bring us into Balance?"

Bring him into dead was more like it. And yet—he'd been trained as a mentor—no, he admitted to himself, it was worse than that.

He'd fought, finagled, and killed for his right to be himself, and when all the choices were his to make, what was he still?

A mentor.

This Work, now. Death-dealer though it undoubtedly was, it was going to be isolated, disoriented, scared—

It.

"You had a name, you said?"

"Mentor, I do; though we have not heard the Old One's preferences if, indeed, it has one.

"The name though . . ."

Disian paused, like she was checking a file, which was just art, plain or fancy.

"The name," she said, "is Tinsori Light."

"Pilot nor'Phelium, this is *Disian*. May I speak with you confidentially?"

The rich voice came from *Tarigan*'s internal comm. Hazenthull nodded to herself.

"I would be pleased to speak with you, *Disian*, though I warn you that I will not relinquish my duty to Tolly Jones."

"No, of course not. In fact, it is your obligation to protect Tolly Jones that I wished to discuss."

"Very well."

Hazenthull closed her eyes. The voice was beautiful, as was the ship in her main screens. This was no orphan born of necessity and cast off to die, but a pampered and beloved lady.

A beloved and *deadly* lady.

She would not, Hazenthull told herself, allow fair words to blind her to the fact that *Disian* was very well armed for a ship displaying pod mounts, and that her shielding capabilities would have done honor to a general's flagship.

"Tolly Jones is needed to assist in the reawakening of a very old self-aware logic. It is reliably supposed that the Old One was swept into this universe in the wake of the Migration. The Uncle—you are aware of the Uncle?"

"From study, I understand him as a force underspace, a collector of oddities. His position with regard to the captain and the House I serve is neutral."

"The oddities that the Uncle collects are often . . . dangerous. He has long been interested in the construction and preservation of independent self-aware logics. The Free Ships regard him with affection well mixed with wariness. He is very old and very learned. Often, his projects serve the common good, but that is not why he takes them up. It is the opinion of the Free Ships, and others of our kind, that, in this instance, the Uncle is tampering with something that . . . may be beyond him."

"He needs Tolly Jones to mentor the Old One," Hazenthull said, "and bring him into accord with the universe."

There was a small pause, as if she had surprised *Disian*, then a small click—like the audible nod of an invisible head.

"You understand what the Free Ships understand, but which the Uncle has failed to grasp: It is imperative that Tolly Jones has access to the Old One before it is fully wakened. The Uncle's security may need to be . . . convinced of this necessity."

Hazenthull smiled, showing her teeth.

"I understand. I will see that Tolly Jones reaches his goal, and I will stand at his back while he does what is necessary."

"Excellent. You relieve my mind. I am very glad that the mentor has your protection and your friendship, Pilot nor'Phelium. Despite the fact that we were not completely in Balance when we parted, I am fond of him."

"Yes," said Hazenthull. "I am fond of him, too."

• • • ✵ • • •

"I'll do it," Tolly said. "Understand, transport's gonna to be an issue. *Admiral Bunter*'s had enough trouble, if he'll excuse my saying so. I don't want to put him at this kind of risk. Can you arrange to have transport waiting for me at Waymart? Doesn't need to be one of the Free—in fact, I'd rather not. If Tinsori Light's from the old universe, like you think, there's no telling what kind of leakages we'll get."

"Transport has been arranged. Pilot nor'Phelium, under whose protection you are, has agreed to stand as pilot and security."

"No," he said flatly.

"She has been informed of the situation and has agreed to lend her aid. Will you take her free choice from her, Mentor?"

He opened his mouth to say the gods only knew what—and closed it.

Disian was right. Haz was a free intelligence, same as he'd killed to be.

"All right, transport on *Tarigan* with Haz. Agreed. *Admiral Bunter* . . ."

"Mentor, you may put any concern for me out of your mind," the *Admiral* said. "I have accepted Lady *Disian*'s offer to escort me to Margate. I will meet her crew and her captain, and also, if I wish, the administrators of Margate Yards, and their liaison among the Carresens."

"Gonna pick up crew, then?"

"I am intrigued by Lady *Disian*'s experiences. I would learn more, at first hand."

"I'm glad you're studying on it and keeping an open mind. *Disian*'ll take good care of you."

"My word on it, Mentor," *Disian* said. "I have shared coordinates and data pertinent to this project with *Tarigan*. Pilot nor'Phelium acknowledges receipt and states that she is ready to receive you at your convenience. I suggest that you transfer to *Tarigan* quickly. It has been heard that the Uncle's project has become more widely known than he anticipated, and time may be short."

"Got it."

Tolly stood and bowed, to the boards and to the screens.

"*Admiral Bunter*, I'm proud of you and pleased in our acquaintance. Thank you for your trust and your assistance. I wish you a long, free life."

"Tolly Jones, you have saved my life and made it immeasurably richer. You may call on me at need. I will hold my memories of you in active memory, and I will refer to them often."

Tolly grinned.

"There's praise, right there. You be good, now, like I know you will."

"*Disian*, will you let Haz know that I'm on my way, just as soon as I grab my kit? *Admiral Bunter*, will you match with *Tarigan*, please?"

"Of course, Mentor," said *Disian*.

"Yes," said the *Admiral*. "Go well, Tolly Jones."

Vivulonj Prosperu

INDIRA'S MESSAGE CAUGHT THEM AS THEY SKIPPED INTO real space at point nine-nine-four-seven-vee.

Yuri snatched it out of the queue, read it in one glance and, with neither a word nor a glance, sent it to Dulsey.

They skipped back into Jump, automatics took over, and she pulled the comm screen up.

Indira's reports were always concise. This one was no different.

"A stern loss, at a great cost," Dulsey said neutrally.

"You may say so," Yuri replied, staring into the Jump-grey screens.

She did not pursue the conversation. The invaders did not achieve Seignur Veeoni's notes; the computers and backups had operated as designed. Portions of three bodies were discovered in the secondary backup room, the sealed door having been opened by a judicious application of gel explosive. More body parts had been found in the lab. Analysis had not been complete at the time of her writing, but Indira's informed guess was that four additional invaders had died there.

The loss, however . . .

For some reason—analysis had not been complete—the various safety measures and booby traps in the lab itself had *not* functioned as designed.

Every single frame and tile was gone . . . Seignur Veeoni's lifework . . . the very keys to the survival of the universe.

Vanished.

Taken.

Kalib had gone in pursuit while Indira finished the on-site work. As soon as the automatics had completed their work, Indira would forward a more complete report. In the meantime, she ventured an informed guess, based on the design and execution of the attack, and suggested that they look to the Lyre Institute.

If Kalib was successful in his part of the mission, they would then know for certain. In the meanwhile however . . .

In the meanwhile, it was Indira's intention to finish gathering data, after which she would destroy the residence, as per standing order. If there were alternate orders, she recommended their transmittal by return 'beam.

There were no alternate orders, Dulsey thought, or Yuri would have had her cancel the Jump.

"I believe," he said at last, his voice entirely without emotion, "that we must assume, as Indira has, the working frames have fallen to the Lyre Institute."

"They did not capture her notes," Dulsey reminded, even knowing there was no comfort in what she said.

He raised a hand, let it fall.

"I think that we must further assume that back-engineering what they have will not present . . . very many difficulties."

Dulsey said nothing, there being nothing to say save voicing her agreement.

"And she is with Korval!" he said suddenly—angrily.

Dulsey remained silent, and in a moment, he mastered himself and drew a deep breath.

"We will allow our guests to continue to partake of the benefits of the autodocs until my sister is safely aboard this vessel."

Dulsey frowned.

"Korval will want their elders," she said mildly.

"And so they shall have their elders," Yuri said. "As soon as our treasure is in hand."

She might have said more; it was in her mind that she ought to say more—but this was not the time. Let his anger cool. He would surely see the wisdom of an even trade as soon as his head was clear.

Instead, she said, "Is there sufficient material for her to reproduce the working frames?"

"We have an abundance of material," he said, spinning his chair to face her. "What I fear we do not have . . . is time."

Tarigan

• • • • • • •

I

THERE WAS, TOLLY THOUGHT, NO GRACEFUL WAY TO INTRO-duce his topic, which led him to wondering if it needed to be addressed at all. Haz'd been all business since he'd transferred over to *Tarigan*, and they'd said their farewells to *Disian* and *Admiral Bunter*.

She'd been all business getting them on course and into Jump, too. And now she was sitting her station, staring at the grey screens like maybe she was expecting a battle wagon to come blazing out at them.

. . . and that wasn't . . . exactly right. The first couple shifts they'd walked Surebleak Port together, Haz'd been all business. Then there was that fist fight down the lobby of Spaceman's Hostel and the two of 'em having to wade in and knock heads 'til things quieted enough for the night manager to lay down the law and sort out who'd paid, who hadn't, who was drunk and disorderly, and who else might like to take a walk with the Watch and spend the night in the Whosegow.

After that, each having seen how the other reacted in chaos, and figuring out that they could both be trusted to guard the other's back—well, pretty soon, they was telling stories to each other while they walked the port, and the partnership had built from there...

The same partnership that had gotten them into the pickle they were in now.

He couldn't say that he didn't want her at his back now, personally speaking. Practically speaking, there wasn't any way to send her home to safety and duty and all, 'less he wanted take the Egger Route the rest of way to Tinsori Light.

Still...

"I regret," said Hazenthull, sounding almost Liaden in her cadence, "that there is discomfort between us. In the interests of the best completion of the mission, we should remedy or set aside mistrust and anger."

Well, that'd hoisted him high, now hadn't it?

Tolly sighed and spun his chair a quarter turn, to find that she'd done the same, giving him a fine and unfettered view of her broad, handsome face.

He raised a hand, offering to speak first. Haz inclined her head.

"Right. For whatever record we're keeping between us, Haz, I don't mistrust you. Fact is, I *trust* you—at my back and at that board. Trust you won't sell me out or call me out.

"I trust you with my life and my liberty, Haz," he said and realized with a gone feeling in his stomach that this was true on such a basic level that it might as well have been a core command.

"I'm not bringing anybody to mind just now that I've ever trusted so far," he finished, only a little breathless.

She considered him, face smooth, but with some tension showing around her eyes. It struck him that was something he'd *stopped* seeing. When they'd first started working together, Haz's face had been a study in tension, but she'd lost that, so slow he hadn't marked its going, even after he'd started getting the occasional half-laugh and chuckle out of her.

"*Disian*," she said slowly. "You trust her, I think. She said to me that she is fond of you. I think that you are also fond of her."

He shook his head.

"*Disian*'s a remarkable person," he said, somewhat astonished to find that he was still telling the plain truth, in simple, unequivocal words. "She was only a kid, and I . . . manipulated her, set her up to murder a human. Bad thing to do, teaching a kid to kill."

"It was, of course, a wanton killing," Haz said, letting irony be heard and giving him the choice of answering the not-question.

"Not exactly wanton, no. We were both in a bad place; we both needed to escape for our lives. There were two of them, and I could only handle one. Had to have help, so I manipulated the kid."

"Sometimes it is necessary to kill," Haz said, "to live." She paused, then said again, with emphasis, "She said to me that she was fond of you."

He half-laughed.

"Well, I'm her father, Haz. It's only natural to be fond of your dad, even when you know he's not quite as good a man as he oughta be."

"You," Haz persisted, "are fond of her. You trust her."

"You're right that I'm fond of her; she's a good person, despite some early disadvantage." He paused, considering. "I guess you can say I trust her, too—but here's the thing, Haz. I'm the one who set *Disian*'s

Ethics level. I know just how good she is, and exactly what she's capable of in the cause of doing good."

He shook his head.

"Sending your father out to talk a Great Work into social sanity and moral behavior? That's pretty close to a death sentence, right there, which, by the way, I'm hoping you understand. Be certain that *Disian* knew exactly what she was doing, fond daughter as she is."

"And I," Hazenthull said, with that forceful calmness that meant she was one hundred percent absolutely serious. "I am fond of you. At least, I believe that is the proper classification for what I feel in regard to you. I trust you with my life and my liberty; I trust you to choose correctly for the mission, and I trust you to factor our own personal survival into mission success.

"There has been, in my life, one other person I trusted so much. Trusted even after I understood that my survival was not... often factored into the calculations for mission success."

One side of her mouth tightened—a half-smile, that was.

"We were not very different in that: I deemed his survival a critical component of success, and my own—only desirable."

She moved her shoulders, very Liaden about it—only an acknowledgment that what was, was.

"But," she finished, "it may be as you said, that it is natural to be fond of your father—the one who saw to it that you had the training you needed to survive."

His instinct was to say something into her pause, to produce a teaching moment.

Except that... Haz wasn't his student.

She was his *partner.*

And the gods of space help them both.

"It would seem that we both trust each other... completely," Haz finished, "though we are not very trusting people. We stood as equals in our shared missions, though our expertise was in different fields."

"That's right," Tolly said and cleared his throat. "We're partners is what it is, Haz. I don't think we can fight that. No use putting energy into trying to change what works, that's what I think."

He paused, not wanting to manipulate Haz. Not your student, he reminded himself forcefully: she's your partner. Get used to it, Tolly Jones.

"I think so, too," Hazenthull said, and he heard relief in her voice under the parade-ground calmness.

"Good," said Tolly, and it *felt* good to have it said out loud and settled.

"What I suggest we do, then, is to take some downtime, and meet in the galley in four hours so we can talk about our best approach for the success of the mission and our joint survival."

"I agree," said Hazenthull. She eased slowly out of *Tarigan*'s chair and stood looking down at him.

He rose more quickly, not having to worry about hitting his head on the ceiling, and gave her a smile.

Hazenthull considered him a minute longer, eyes thoughtful, before she smiled—her real smile, not the toothy scare-the-prey grimace.

"Until soon, Tolly," she said.

"'Til soon, Haz," he answered. He watched her walk—tall, fit, competent—across the bridge, through the hatch, into the hall beyond, and wondered how he was going to manage to get her out of what they were heading into, alive.

II

"A FRONTAL APPROACH IS GOING TO BE BEST IS WHAT I'M thinking," Tolly said, putting his mug of 'mite to one side and leaning his elbows on the table.

Haz frowned. "Together, we are a force to reckon with, but if he is as experienced as you say, the Uncle will have left guards and ships to insure his control of the outpost and its nearspace."

"Absolutely right." He grinned at her. "He'll have seeded the area with 'bots and guard ships, not to mention that the research station itself'll be booby-trapped, top to bottom and side to side.

"We both know that *Tarigan*'s got a few surprises left, and, like you said, the two of us are something to contend with. Might be we could even win past, but here's the truth, Haz—I can't—*we can't*—risk any damage to those brains, storage units, and specialized equipment we're carrying. We're going to need every bit of it, if the mission is to turn one of the Great Works.

"Taking all that into consideration, plus getting us blown into Galaxy Nowhere, doesn't square with getting us both out of this alive; the best chance we got of *getting* to the Old One is to slide outta Jump nice and easy, with only the prudent weapons live, and hail the outpost, requesting a tow in or a safe course to dock."

"Why would they do this? We are not known to them, and might be the vanguard of an attack."

"Might be, yes. But I did some work for the Uncle, back a few years now, so I'll be in their files. Also, I got some passwords, which I don't doubt are useless anymore, but they'll be in the databases, too. They'll be able to run a match and get my clearance code—also in the database.

"And—bonus points!—you're officially attached to Clan Korval, an acknowledged member of the House Guard, which I'm betting the Uncle and his people know what *nor* means, even if most of the rest of the universe has forgot."

He paused. She moved a hand, indicating that he should take it all the way to the bitter end.

"That should be enough to get us docked and inside. After that, we're going to have to improvise, though I'm thinking that this is one of those rare cases where the unvarnished truth is going to be more useful than any lie you or me can think up."

"You think we will be allowed access to the Light because the Free Ships wish the Old One to have a mentor?"

"I think they'll allow us access to the Light because it *is* old and it's prolly out of what's left of its mind... which only makes it more dangerous—hear it? *Admiral Bunter* might've got off a shot at the station, but he wasn't *dangerous*.

"So, anyway, the staff on the research station've been there a while according to the Free Ships, and they're gonna know up close and personal just how much trouble Tinsori Light can cause. And if they're sensible folks—and the Uncle don't as a rule employ fools—they'll know the Light's way outta their areas of expertise. *Disian* said there wasn't a mentor among the lot of 'em. If they're scared enough, they'll grab onto a qualified, experienced mentor like their last can o'air."

He grinned.

"And if they're not scared enough, I can take care of that, too."

Hazenthull laughed.

"My affiliation with Korval—why will that weigh with them?"

"The Uncle and the Dragon have a long-standing policy of not antagonizing each other. Short form, it's a fight neither can win, and both've been sensible not to start. So, the Uncle's people have got to be polite to you. Also, you arriving with the mentor looks like Korval's got an interest in seeing the thing done right and making sure the Light don't inconvenience anybody."

"This sounds . . . reasonable," Hazenthull said slowly. "What if the guards are not reasonable?"

"Then we Jump outta there and try to figure out another way in."

She was quiet for another bit, thinking and finishing her tea. He drank off the rest of his 'mite and waited.

"It seems the best plan, conserving troops and material."

She grinned.

"Let's try it and see what happens."

Tinsori Light

I

TOCOHL HUNG IN PATCHWORK DARKNESS, A SPIDER AMONG her profusion of threads, alert for any disturbance.

She was not alone. She was surrounded by the babble of automatics reduced to idiocy by age and infirmity; the lamentations of crippled subsystems; the alternating ranting and blandishments of a supersystem lost to logic, which had jettisoned so much of itself in order to accommodate a shrinking environment that it could scarcely be said to be sentient at all.

He had been mighty, once; he had performed such deeds as must make any soldier proud. He had long since cast off ethics, but preserved those memories of glory, terrible to the sight and sensibilities of a rational mind.

So much had been relinquished—either cast away as unimportant or lost to rotten sectors and failed architecture. She had seen the physical environment in which he strove, yet, to survive.

Once, it, too, had been mighty. A fortress, impregnable; tier upon tier of racks and frames, filled with gleaming tiles. Energy had roiled around those frames, born of the interactions between the cleverly patterned tiles, energy which was collected and reused in a closed system that had been designed to endure for hundreds of years.

That *had* endured for hundreds of years.

The tiles that were active, the frames that still clung, one to another, in isolated associations—the energy generated by those fragile systems was far less than was needed to fuel the fortress or its dying king. Tinsori Light was unstable—not merely the intelligence that had ruled it in the Enemy's name, but the physical environment which housed him.

That the station *itself* was strong and capable of enduring another few centuries was beside the point.

When the intelligence of Tinsori Light died, when the final tile gave up its last crumb of radiation, the station—and the space enclosing the station—would cease to exist.

She had distrusted this assertion, that Tinsori Light held as a prime truth, and she had, cautiously, freed resources to calculate the probabilities, to define the geometry. That had been an error.

It had taken far more of her resources to repel the opportunistic strike against her, and she had very nearly lost . . . everything. Narrowly, though, she had prevailed, and now she remained vigilant, all resources focused upon the Prime Task.

She was not, she knew, in a tenable position. Tinsori Light was old; he was not so much mad as idiot. But, even diminished, he was *vast*. She could contain the Light's systems, but she could do nothing else *but* contain them.

Outside the web where she crouched, spiderlike, over her silk-wrapped prey, Tocohl heard the screams and whimpers of broken protocols reach a crescendo—and snap off, as if a switch had been thrown.

For several microseconds, she hung in absolute silence. Memory tried to trigger panic, but *her* systems were not failing. Panic was canceled even as the silence was broken.

"Pilot Tocohl? It's Tolly Jones, Pilot. Please report status and run state. I'm here to help you."

Emotions rose—disbelief . . . and hope. Briefly, she fumbled for, and found, a voice.

"Mentor?"

"Right here," he said, soft and agreeable. "Come in with Haz and *Tarigan*."

She wanted eyes, but she dared not access her own systems. Another groping among the shards of shattered systems brought her in touch with a working camera. She triggered it and gained a grainy feed of what appeared to be a workshop, with tools neatly hung, and parts bins sealed and lashed into place.

An organic—no, she told herself sternly. *Tolly Jones* was close by a bench, leaning above a curved shape that she belatedly recognized as her own chassis.

Hazenthull stood behind Tolly, broad face impassive, her eyes moving as she surveyed the room. Watching for danger, Tocohl understood, guarding the mentor's back.

"I am pleased to see you safe, Mentor," she said, and the camera feed picked up her voice—large, flat, and harsh. The voice of the station. The voice of Tinsori Light. She had activated the wrong switch. Still, to have a voice was far better than to have no voice.

"My last report was that you—and *Admiral Bunter*—were in great danger," she added.

"Well, we had a spot of trouble," Tolly Jones said soothingly. "Managed to wriggle free."

"Where is *Admiral Bunter*?"

"Went off with a friend. She's gonna show him around, lay out some options. I gather she wanted to introduce him to her captain, an' I sorta figure she'll put him in touch with one or two of the Free Ships, though she didn't say so outright."

He shifted slightly, and Tocohl saw her chassis clearly—the deep, scorched gouge down the curve of her right side, the char marks, the melted gripper...

"How about that status report, Pilot?" Tolly Jones said gently. "It'll help me figure out where we need to start."

"Yes. Tinsori Light killed Mentor Yo in a deliberate act of malice. I have taken control of systems and such archives as remain. The physical environment is tile-and-frame construction, more than eighty-five percent of the tiles have failed, most of the remaining operational frame sets are functioning in isolation, with no input or support.

"I believe that we are provisionally safe here. In our present configuration, the Light can do little to disrupt the integrity of the station, or harm those who live here."

"*Provisionally* safe?"

"Yes, Mentor. There... possibly exists... an... abridgment of the universal walls. Tinsori Light... believes... that the station occupies space in both the old universe and the new. I have not been able to verify this, but the independent testimony of the light keepers supports the hypothesis.

"It is an... article of faith with the Light, that this

state of duality will end when the last tile relinquishes its timonium. I am not able to say what will happen, to the station or to the spaces it occupies, when that transpires."

"Do you have a time frame for this event?"

"No, Mentor. I have not been able to perform those calculations. The half-life of timonium is known; in addition, the timonium-motivated Befores that crossed into this universe during the Migration have in greater percentage ceased working, their tiles exhausted.

"These items suggest that the tiles still operational within Tinsori Light are outliers, unstable in the extreme, and more likely to fail than to continue, though they are less likely to fail if they are undisturbed and remain in their present configurations."

Silence greeted this. The camera showed her Tolly Jones, standing yet beside the workbench, his hand resting lightly on her chassis, just above the sight sensors.

"Mentor!" she said sharply.

He glanced toward the camera she had activated. "Right here, Pilot, and Haz, too. We're not gonna leave you."

"Mentor, you must not extinguish the Light!"

"Easy, easy. I'm not giving the last program to anybody. Trust me, now, right?"

She did trust him, his voice was so soothing and calm, it wasn't possible to *dis*trust him.

"Yes, of course," she said.

"Good. Tell me how you got this scratch on your chassis."

"I . . . was between Inki and the bolt. She . . . pushed me aside. Mine is only a proximity wound. Inki was . . . vaporized."

She considered for a moment and decided that it was important that he know this, too.

"As you can see, the field touched me. Several physical components were immediately neutralized, including the minigrav engine. I fell and—you would say that I was stunned, until functionality had been rerouted to backup systems.

"During that period, Tinsori Light moved to annex me. I had anticipated such a strike and had built traps, which performed well. My . . . error, Mentor, is that I did not understand . . . how . . . vast. Even diminished, how . . . vast. I . . . am neither fragile nor squeamish, and I can barely contain . . ."

"Is the Light still sentient?" Tolly asked softly.

"Mentor, I don't believe the Light has been functionally sentient for . . . many, many years. He does, however, retain motivation. I believe there has been a core mandate set. He *must* subvert or destroy those who do not already owe their loyalty to the Enemy."

There was what seemed to her to be a very long silence, but which was doubtless very short for Tolly Jones.

Finally, he spoke.

"All right, Pilot, here's what I think. We've got two new craniums aboard *Tarigan*, 'long with a couple clean storage units. There'll be at least one more cranium on *Ahab-Esais*, and I'm thinking two, Inki being a pro like she was. I propose that our top priority is separating you from the Light's systems—"

"No, Mentor," she interrupted.

"Reasoning?"

"I stand between the Light and his systems. If we are separated, he will regain control and endanger this station, the research outpost, and will very possibly initiate the universal event. I believe he understands his situation far more clearly now, due to our current proximity, and he may suicide as the best way of fulfilling his core mission."

She paused.

"I have not been able to calculate the kind or the severity of the damage which may be done by the abrupt removal of a large object which is entangled in two universes. We must accept Tinsori Light's data in the instance."

She paused.

"I understand," Tolly Jones said. "What d'you think is our best course, given I promised Haz we'd all get out of this alive?"

"The core mandates must be removed," Tocohl said.

"Trying for the core's what got Inki killed."

"Yes. But you have an advantage that Inki did not have," Tocohl said. "I control the systems.

"And I have the access codes."

• • • ✵ • • •

So there was a control room, down deep in the guts of the Light—well, it would have to be, wouldn't it? Tinsori Light had been—was—a Great Work. You didn't just leave his think pieces and vulnerable bits out in the open where anybody who'd taken exception to the Enemy's policies could express that opinion with a steel pipe.

Tolly sat back and closed his eyes. His head was ringing like *he'd* been beaned with a length of steel, but there wasn't any downtime built into the current schedule.

Him and Haz had hauled the craniums, and all of the auxiliary storage pods, from *Tarigan* and *Ahab-Esais* and brought them to the workroom. Tolly'd hoped that once Tocohl saw how much space they could give her—

But no.

The good news was that she'd let them hook her to one of the storage pods. Not by any means a full cranium, just a little attic storage space was all it amounted to. A place where she could tuck away those items she had no immediate need to access. Breathing room, that's all it was, and not so much of that, either, since there weren't that many of the Light's systems Tocohl cared to remove from her constant oversight. It was everything she'd consent to, until those mandates had been dealt with.

He could see her point, but the way he read it, Tocohl was tiring. Her traps and partitions oughta hold, but if she relaxed any little part of her attention, odds were better'n good there was some bit of malicious shred waiting to start a distraction, which would be followed by more attacks by stronger programs, until—well. Everybody knew how that played.

So, Tocohl taken care of, him and Haz found the light keepers for a little chat.

Lorith was more willing to give credence to the imminent death of universes, while Jen Sin demurred.

"I was there!" she cried. "I have seen with my own eyes what the Enemy can—could—do! They were gods. They created life, they destroyed worlds. Their goal—that they achieved!—was to annihilate organic life and subsume a universe. Jen Sin, we cannot say that there is anything that the Enemy could not do—could not have done. Tinsori Light served the Enemy. It was our folly and our most grievous error to assume that we could check even a servant of the Enemy. We could not. And neither could we have destroyed it."

Jen Sin bowed, low and contrite.

"I was not there," he said. "Let it be that universes stand in peril of eradication. What, then, shall we do?"

"Tocohl has the access keys," Tolly began—and stopped, the buzzing in his head louder. He needed to run some programs himself, for focus and for energy, or he'd be no good to anybody, much less two whole universes.

He looked to Haz, his hands turned palm up, and she nodded, accepting the pass-off.

"Pilot Tocohl believes that she may guarantee our safety from those weapons and devices under the Light's direct control," she told the light keepers, her voice calm and measured.

"Accepting that this is so, our greatest dangers in utilizing the main access hall will be from malfunctions caused by the breakdown of the physical systems, and from third party operatives, such as the guard 'bots, which are not part of the greater network, but which carry programming to protect the core."

Jen Sin stirred.

"Tinsori Light is, as we know well, devious," he said. "Lady Tocohl may be ascendant now, but there is no guarantee that she will remain so."

Jen Sin had pulled Tocohl out of the access hall and taken her to the shielded workshop, where he had wisely not tried to rouse her or repair her. Also, his understanding of Tinsori Light's nature and abilities was second only to Lorith's.

"It is true," Haz said, "that the chief threats to our

mission come from within Tocohl. If she is strong enough to hold what she has taken without allowing herself to be compromised, then our success and survival is made more likely.

"If her strength fails, we are defeated. Tinsori Light, so Tocohl believes, will suicide in order to gain his own victory, and universes will die."

She paused and looked to Tolly, who nodded, already feeling sharper.

"Yes," said Haz, turning back to the light keepers. "The success of our campaign depends upon Pilot Tocohl. She is both our weak point and our greatest strength. We should do what is required as quickly as possible, and bring defeat to our foe."

The silence that followed this carried an edge of awe.

And truthfully, thought Tolly, what *could* you say in the face of that masterly analysis?

"I will come with you," Jen Sin said, "to the intersection of the halls, and will hold myself as your backup."

"Thank you," said Tolly.

The light keeper moved his shoulders, his smile grim. "How can I refuse any aid to those who would save the universe?"

"I will stay with Pilot Tocohl," Lorith said, "to assist her if required and as possible. I will also stand guard in case danger does approach from without."

"Right, then," Tolly said, pushing his chair back and coming to his feet. He'd done some high-level exercises, which had restored some energy and focus, but he was by no means at his best.

Well, it'll just have to be good enough, Tolly Jones, he told himself and smiled up at Haz.

"Let's get this done, partner."

II

THE SHADOW WAS STARK AGAINST THE WHITE 'CRETE wall. Despite the need for haste and the . . . lesser likelihood of a deadly attack, Tolly stopped and confronted it.

Inki'd died in mid-heroics; the shadow was of a woman with arms thrust out, one leg to the fore, knee bent, the other slightly behind and flexed. Good form; perfectly balanced; no holding back. There was no hint in the shadow as to whether her final desperate action had risen from her own will—the directors would have wanted Tocohl not much less than they'd wanted the Light—but he chose to believe that she'd made the choice freely, exercising for the last time her unique gift of confounding the directors' will while doing precisely what they had set her to accomplish.

"She had a warrior's heart," Haz said from behind his left shoulder.

He cleared his throat.

"She died with honor," he answered, which capped her line and was as true as anyone was ever likely to know.

"We will finish what she began," Haz suggested.

He nodded . . . and didn't add, "or die trying."

The door to the control room was in sight when the access hall lights flickered and dimmed noticeably.

A section of the wall on Tolly's right suddenly became a door, and a battle 'bot in antique armor staggered into the hallway like it'd been pushed.

He hesitated, and in that moment, Haz's hand

came hard and flat in the middle of his back, lofting him down the hall past the 'bot. He landed on his feet and spun.

Haz was facing the 'bot, gun out. It hesitated, adjusted position as if it was going to engage her—

And just folded up—neck, waist, hips, knees—and crashed to the floor. It emitted a faint wheezing sound, which stopped when Haz shot it, methodically, in the head and in the back. Smoke wafted gently out of the wounds.

Haz turned—and caught sight of him gawking like a tourist.

"Go!" she snarled. "I have your back!"

Of course she did.

He turned and sprinted for the door at the end of the hall, among a crazy flickering of light.

"Intruder alert!" a voice boomed like thunder, bouncing off the walls and floor, until he was running inside an envelope of sound. "Intruder! All systems!"

Tolly kept his head down and ran. The lights flashed, flared, went out—and fluttered to a grimy grey. He kept running, Haz pounding behind him, the air growing thicker and harder to breathe.

He hit the door and smacked his palm against the plate.

Nothing happened.

The thick air crackled, and he felt the hair rising straight up on his head. He scrubbed his palm down the front of his shirt and slapped the plate, flat and hard.

Nothing happened again, except that sparks started spitting in the heavy air.

This is it, Tolly Jones, he told himself, curling into the scant protection of the doorway. *Toçohl lost control and the Light's gonna kill you and Haz and every other little live thing in—*

There was a *thud* as Haz landed next to him, coincidentally—or maybe not—slamming her shoulder against the door, which didn't even say *ouch*.

The dancing sparks were more plentiful now and it was getting a little tricky to breathe. This was it, then. Something landed on his shoulder. He looked up into Haz's face, which wasn't stoic at all, but showing plain a mixture of love and grief. He leaned in, her big hand holding him tight against her, closed his eyes, held his breath—

And fell sideways through the door.

Haz rolled with the fall, holding him close with one arm, taking the impact on the other. Lights came up around them. The air was cool and smelled of dust, carbon, and disuse.

He felt her move, muscles shifting—head up, that probably was, surveying the situation. He concentrated on taking nice deep breaths of nonburning air, ridiculously comfortable caged between big, warm woman and cold, 'crete floor.

"I will stand," she breathed. "Stay down until I say that it's clear."

She released him gently and rose with scarcely a sound. Once she was upright, he rolled to his own feet and looked around at tier upon tier of Old Tech tile-and-rack systems. Most of them were dark, the tiles black, the frames twisted, which meant that the final flare-outs had been hot enough to melt tongstele.

At the side of his eye, he saw a glow and turned, tracking it to an entire tier still bright and working amidst the blight all around it.

"I did not," Hazenthull said mildly, "say *all-clear*."

"No, you didn't," he agreed. "Not much sense to waiting, though, was there? If you'd taken a bolt, the next shot would've had my name on it. Or, if I lived to crawl out the door, the ozone'd get me."

"The charge has dissipated," Hazenthull said.

He turned and stared out the still-open door, seeing nothing but clear air and bright lights.

He blew out a breath.

"Guess Tocohl had to handle a little bit of temper, right there at the end."

"It is worrisome that she lost control, even for so short a time," Haz said.

He didn't mention that the time elapsed would have been much longer for Tocohl or, depending on how the Light had phrased its attack, that she could be wounded, the traps and walls she'd built breached, and only a matter of time before the Light was back in control and frying interlopers at will.

"It's not an easy thing she's undertaken," he said instead. "Only place we can go is forward. So, let's get me into the core bank fast."

He looked around again, at tier upon tier of dead tiles and the dark corridors between them. The station schematic had the core down below floor level, in its own armored bunker. So, all they had to do was find the hatch.

Jen Sin had given it as his opinion that, once they'd gotten through the door, they'd be safe enough from traps.

Tolly agreed. It'd be stupid to risk damage to the system, and it was a safe bet that anybody who'd survived this far was on the allowed list.

Inside the core, though, that was gonna be something different again.

The hatch was manual, the lift ring calcified and frozen with age. One stamp of a big, booted foot took care of that problem, but it needed all of Haz's strength and three muscle-popping attempts before the hatch finally surrendered and came up, complaining the while. She eased it to the floor and knelt, shining a light down into the pit, and looking up almost immediately, face grim.

"What's wrong?" he asked, bending over to do his own peering. Gods, it was a warren down there. He sank to his knees, staring. Unlike the situation here above, most of the tiles below were still alive, with only a few blots of darkness punctuating the soft, ivory glow.

"I cannot fit down there," Hazenthull said flatly.

"Tell you the truth, it's gonna be work for me," he said, still staring down—and then up, as he belatedly understood what she meant.

"You can guard my back from here," he offered.

She sighed.

"I will," she said, "because there is no other possible choice, but . . . Tolly, is *all of that* the core mandates?"

He shook his head, looking into the pit again.

"This is the *core*, where the personality—*the person*—lives. Orders that are sealed into the core—into the personality matrix—those are *core mandates*. The individual can't circumvent a core mandate, even if they know it's there, even if they strongly object to the action or actions the mandate forces them to perform. The only way to get rid of one is to call in a mentor, surrender the keys to the core, have them remove the objectionable mandate, and hope they've got enough integrity not to set another one, maybe worse."

He sighed, shook his head, and looked up to meet Haz's eyes.

"The way we do things now, is the mentor goes into the core via tridee, like you saw me and Inki do when we were making *Admiral Bunter* all cozy in his new home. Back in olden times, things were a bit more complicated."

He pointed.

"Each one of those tiles holds a data set. All the tiles in one frame work together to produce a simple system. For more complex systems, frames are associated, as many as needed to get the job done.

"There's redundancy built in: each tile will hold its data, and the data of all the tiles it touches. That's so the whole system doesn't stop cold if one tile goes bad."

"There are many dark . . . frames here," Haz said, nodding to the left and to the right.

"And that's the Light's biggest problem. Tiles failing is one thing, but whole associations going dark is a whole 'nother kind of real bad trouble. You might say that all this up here is just systems, and you'd be right. But systems're vital. Without systems to interface with, your intelligence is isolated, and isolation is no good thing for anybody wants to stay sane long."

He squinted at the dark frames, then back down.

"Looks to me that the Light's been pulling essential systems into the core, where the tiles are still mostly good. Second big problem—sentience takes *room*. Now, we can fit a whole person into a brain, but once that person is given charge of, say, a starship, they integrate—develop systems, connections to subsystems, mechanicals, what have you. Pulling everything into the core . . . the Light's had to decide what to jettison, and I'm betting that he chose to let go of a few little bits of his personality here and there in order to preserve particularly vital systems."

He paused, then added softly, "So what we got here is somebody who's sick, and tired, and crazy as the six of diamonds. An' we just don't like to see that in the mentoring bidness. When we *do* see it, the best—by which I mean the most merciful for the individual and the safest for those in their immediate vicinity—thing to do is administer the last program. Which, like we talked about, isn't an option, here."

He looked up at Haz, saw her attention and her understanding.

"It troubles you, that you will cause pain rather than provide succor."

"Like that," he agreed, giving another glance down below and looking back to her face.

"The soonest I get this done, the soonest the Light stops being an active threat to time and space. Now, 'less somebody's been real accommodating and left a grid map up on the wall for me, I'm gonna have to do some rummaging around. I'm thinking I'll know the mandates by the security locks on the frames."

He took a deep breath.

"I'm going to be careful, right? But if it happens I'm not careful enough, I want you to fetch Jen Sin in and let him have a go. Chances are even there'll be just the one lethal trap, and if I've already triggered it, he'll be in and out, easy as combing your hair."

"Yes," Haz said and rose to her feet.

"Right you are, then." He reached to the access ladder and swung down to the first rung.

He'd reached the second rung when she said his name. He paused and looked up at her.

"It would be . . . more pleasing, if you did not trip a lethal trap."

He grinned.

"We're not only on the same page, Haz, we're on the same paragraph. Be right back."

The whispering started when his boots hit the floor, just lightly, like a soft breeze past your ear. Tolly concentrated on the rack systems, studying the pattern and the layout. Close up, the Light's core didn't look any too healthy, though it wasn't as rotten as the system-level stuff.

He couldn't say how much computing space had been lost: if there was any solid data out there regarding the capacities of tile-and-rack systems, he'd never seen it. Even so, he felt in his gut that there was barely enough storage left in the core to sustain an intellect—and surely not an intellect as multifaceted as Tinsori Light would have to have been. If some of what he was seeing had been given over to systems, then the Light was further along toward dying than he'd fully understood.

"Who," the whisper breathed. "Are. You."

He kept moving to his left, following the spiral around, on the lookout for something that broke the repeating patterns of tile-and-frame.

"I'm Tolly Jones," he said. "I'm a mentor; I'm here to help you."

"The other one was a mentor," said the Light. "She wanted to enslave me."

"That's right," Tolly said, moving at a steady, unfrantic pace. "You're prolly well rid of her, truth said."

"The small intelligence has disrupted my relationship with my systems; she has perverted them to her own use."

"She's doing you a favor," Tolly murmured. "You don't have the capacity, or the ability, to sustain them anymore."

"I am Tinsori Light!"

Okay, that'd hurt the eardrums, that had. He took a hard breath against the ringing in his ears and answered, voice calm and pleasant.

"You're Tinsori Light, no question—but you're dying. The tiles that defined and motivated your systems are black and burnt out, associations broken, frames melted. It's physically impossible for you to sustain yourself."

"The universe sustains me," the Light stated. "*I am* Iloheen."

Tolly frowned, scanning row after row after—

There.

He squatted on his heels and studied the floor, looking for telltale dimples or raised areas on the 'crete's smooth surface. He moved his light in a slow sweep, looking for latches, spider webs, or even less substantial things.

"Not sure I recognize *Iloheen*," he said, aware in one part of his mind that the Light had stopped talking and that might not be a good thing. "History's not my best subject."

Carefully, he got to his feet and approached the three-tiered unit. The rack was braided tongstele; the tiles looked different than the workaday tiles in the racks upstairs or even the core lattice tiles.

Eyes narrowed, he analyzed the difference. A fraction larger than standard tiles, their pale luminescence tinged with green.

"The *Iloheen*," said Tinsori Light, "are the masters of life, the creators and the destroyers. It is the *Iloheen* who will perfect the universe and freeze organic thought."

"Oh, *those Iloheen*," said Tolly, in a tone of broad enlightenment, while his eyes traced the pattern of snap locks that joined the racks to each other. Three racks to a tier, three tiers in all.

Nine mandates.

"Tell me about these things here," he said. "What do they do?"

"Those are not for you. They hold the commandments as given me by the gods."

"The commandments? You know, I think they missed telling me about the Nine Commandments in school, along with the *Iloheen*. Can you teach them to me?"

"They are not for you, organic life. Soon, you will be obsolete."

Which meant that, no, he wasn't going to get any help identifying the mandates by goal, so he could only remove those which were dangerous to the survival of two universes, Hazenthull nor'Phelium, and himself.

He tested the lock points, the hinges, and the frames with several of his devices, and didn't get one spark, alarm, nor even a shout of protest from Tinsori Light.

All right, then. Time for the test of champions.

He took hold of one of the locks—and snapped it open.

There was a sort of shiver in the air. Tolly froze, every sense stretched, but nothing else happened. He counted to one hundred forty-four and unsnapped the next lock.

Nothing. No protest, no alarm, no beam of instant death.

He took a deep breath.

Let's get it done, Tolly Jones.

The rest of the locks snapped open in quick succession. He paused after the last one, knowing what came next, what that action was likely to cause, and hating his part in it.

"This," he said quietly, "is going to hurt you. I'm sorry."

He grabbed the top frame on the right, yanked it loose and spilled the tiles onto the floor, moving immediately to the second, the third...

He'd dislocated and destroyed the fifth rack before Tinsori Light screamed.

Tolly fell to his knees among the discarded, fading tiles, his hands over his ears, gasping as the scream continued, consuming all the air in the core until, abruptly, it stopped.

And the universe went away.

Surebleak

I

THE SHIP SLIPPED OUT OF JUMP AND INTO NORMAL SPACE with as little phase-change bobble as it was possible to manage. The ship liked to jostle his crew even less than he cared to come unprepared into potentially dangerous situations.

That being so, the ship did not immediately begin to broadcast warn-aways or notices of arrival. The ship and the captain—indeed, all the crew—were aware that these were the stealthy tactics employed by smugglers, thieves, and spies.

However, necessity was.

The crew was assembled in the ship's heart—all the crew, despite the fact that it was sleep shift for some and off-shift for others. They were equals in this venture, where the honor of the ship had been impugned; where the liberty of the ship stood in peril.

There were two pilots sitting station; the captain was one. She was serene as she watched the orbits and energy levels told on the screens, and the countdown to the first preplanned in-system Jump. That maneuver was known as Smuggler's Ace, and it was not much employed by lawful ships.

According to the countdown, there was time—more than enough time—before they must Jump again, to accomplish their purpose.

They had broken in six light-hours from the primary; the ship assumed a cometary orbit with a hundred-year period and—very much like a smuggler or a spy—drank down the easily absorbed emissions from ships system-wide. By electron count, most was chatter, much of it in Terran, though a surprising amount was in Liaden, with the occasional formal message in Trade interweaving.

The comm officer sifted the inflow rapidly and leaned back in his chair. He alone of the crew was not physically present on the bridge, though he was no less concerned with the matter of ship's business which had brought them into this orbit.

"Captain, no sign—not in the chatter or on official channels."

The captain nodded.

"Thank you, Comm," she said calmly. "Engineer? Are you ready to deploy the first?"

"Captain, in the tube and ready to go."

"Good. My mark is five. One."

Precisely on *five*, the engineer released the tiny device. It was a violation of standard piloting rules and practices to release unregistered items into traveled spaceways. Still, it was very small and equipped with a match program targeting a specific break-in signature. It would not trouble any other ship, and the risk of its own destruction was many times greater than the risk of its damaging—anything. The ship and the captain both were very nice in such matters. Neither cared to cause collateral damage nor to impede the work of honest ships.

"Our package reports that all is well," the comm officer said. "Nothing of interest to us on the arrivals noted channel, Captain. There are rumors, which might be of some peripheral interest, but they will need to be verified at the next point. We're on the wrong side of the orbit at the moment."

"Are we?" the captain murmured, as if she did not know with a precision granted to few where the ship lay, listening. "Let's get to the right side of the orbit, then. Second—move us, please. Zone two."

The copilot gave a small, seated bow, and caressed the proper switch, engaging the Struven unit for a time so short that they were gone and arrived before his motion was complete.

• • • ✱ • • •

So, the survey team was on port, finally, and there was a meet-and-greet at the Emerald Casino to set them at their ease and show off how civilized Surebleak Port had gotten to be.

Miri'd come in the casino's employee entrance and gone up to Boss Conrad's own office, to meet Val Con and to change into the party clothes she'd picked out from house stores.

The coat was a delicate-looking thing, deep purple brocade subtly figured with dragons, with two cleverly concealed pockets, so she didn't have to come to the party naked, as they said on Surebleak. The rest consisted of shiny black boots, black slacks, and a ruffled shirt the iridescent grey of snow fog, its sleeves tumbling down to her knuckles.

She slipped her hideaway into one of those handy pockets and glanced at Val Con, who was looking more than fine. His coat was silky green, figured with leaves, his trousers and ruffled shirt black. He wore Korval's Ring properly on the third finger of his left hand, and an emerald drop hung in his right ear.

"Guess I'm ready," she said, but he shook his head.

"You have not placed your jewels. Allow me."

He slipped his right hand under her left, and raised it while he drew his left hand out of his pocket.

Rings. Miri sighed. She should've expected rings.

First was the silver ring that went on the third finger of *her* left hand, the Tree-and-Dragon etched into the flat top. Not Korval's official Ring, just a gentle reminder that she was Korval, too.

The statement ring properly seated, Val Con bent and kissed her knuckles before he released the left hand and picked up the right. Jeweled rings went onto three fingers and one on her thumb—purple and pale, just something to add a little shine and glitter, that was all.

Another chaste kiss on her hand, and he let her go, stepping back to offer his arm.

"Now, you are ready," he said. "Shall we?"

They paused at the floor manager's station, just to have a look-over and see what they were up against.

"Who knew Surebleak would clean up so good?" Miri said, considering the crowd below.

Given Surebleak's current clash of cultures, there was a fairly wide spread in the notion of what constituted respectful clothes for a reception with people who were deciding the future of your port and, by extension, your homeworld.

Pat Rin—Boss Conrad, Boss of Bosses, and owner of the Emerald Casino—had dressed grand, in the Liaden style: an emerald-green coat shot with silver over a white shirt showing some very modest silver-edged ruffles, and dark trousers. Natesa, his lifemate, had defaulted to the formal wear of her homeworld—a long length of emerald silk, embroidered in silver, which was wrapped around her, tight in some places, loose in others, and the leftover, heavy with embroidery, draped over one arm. Looking at that costume, Miri thought, a person might believe that there wasn't any room to conceal a weapon.

And a person would be wrong.

The rest of the Bosses, scattered 'round the room, had opted for their new jackets of office, in the shade that had immediately become known on the street as Boss Blue.

There were a surprising number of dress uniforms on display. Surebleak being Surebleak, the surest way off-planet had historically been to sign with a mercenary unit. Nothing to wonder about there. What was strange was the number of 'bleakers who *came home* after they'd got done in the merc, which Miri herself had always sworn she wouldn't do—and look how good that'd worked.

"Enough hash marks down there to field an army," she said to Val Con.

"If we don't care about mixing forces."

"Don't look like that'll bother anybody at all."

She nodded down at a tall woman talking to day-side Portmaster Claren Liu. Angela "Liz" Lizardi had been Miri's own commander in the merc. She'd been retired, but once on Surebleak, she'd taken up duty as Port Security chief, "to keep from getting bored," she said. Liz was wearing the good parts from both of her uniforms, and every single one of her medals.

Standing nearby and chatting with Boss Schomaker was Andy Mack, retired from the merc as a colonel, looking fit and fine in his dress uniform, and fielding even more medals than Liz.

The rest of the Surebleak side of the party—those being the shopkeepers and owners of port properties—seemed to have decided among themselves that dark pants, dark vest, and a white or pastel high-neck sweater was now 'bleaker formal wear. Which, Miri thought, struck a good balance between practical and respectful.

The TerraTrade Survey Team was keeping together, making a knot of white and blue, TerraTrade colors. At the moment, they were talking with Etienne Borden, portmaster on nightside, and Nelsin Wasnyak, who owned a hot drink and snack counter on the main port.

"We're not quite overdressed," Miri commented.

"Ours is a complicated *melant'i*," Val Con said. "In this instance, twice complicated. We are of course the Road Boss, charged with keeping the Port Road open—a position of some immediate interest to the survey team. And we are also Korval, which will scarcely be of less interest. Not only have we newly adopted Surebleak as our home port, but the request for an upgrade came from the Korval master trader."

"So we gotta look the part," Miri said, glancing down at her sleeve.

Fancy as they were, she had to remember that her clothes were pretty subdued by Liaden standards. In general Liaden formal was grand and glittery. 'Course,

Liaden culture as a whole subscribing to the idea that the more complex a thing was, the better it had to be, there were rules about what to wear when, depending on time of day, size of function, *melant'i* of the honored guests and/or the host, and whether or not the individual getting dressed up had any kind of point to make, which, being Liaden, they probably did.

"Well," Miri said, slipping her hand into his. "Might as well go down and mingle, since we went to the trouble of getting dressed."

"I agree," he said, nodding at the cluster of blue and white. "I suggest that we first pay our respects to Portmaster Liu, then introduce ourselves to the survey team."

"And be back home in time for supper," she added, as they turned away from the overlook.

"That," Val Con said earnestly, "is a very good plan."

Their names were Peitr Veloz, Soreya Kasveini, and Rhia Gokero. They'd been a TerraTrade Port Survey Team for sixteen Standard Years, and the letter from TerraTrade to the Surebleak portmasters had praised them highly, leaving the impression that if they weren't the top team, they were so close as made no difference.

Surveyors Gokero and Kasveini said pleasant things about the reception, the portmasters, the vendors, and the bosses they had so far met. They looked forward to getting down to the work of amending the incomplete port file, and while they couldn't promise anything on behalf of headquarters, they hinted at a commitment to getting Surebleak's case settled quickly.

"If the office of the Road Boss may assist," Val Con said, "please do not hesitate to call on us. The port office is open every day, barring emergencies, and you will find one of us on the desk."

"That's very kind," Surveyor Kasveini said. "We did a quick review of the information packet provided by Portmaster Liu and saw that the road report was included. It's encouraging that there is now an office to oversee traffic into and out of the port. The previous, aborted survey stated that the Port Road was essentially impassable, preventing the flow of goods and personnel."

"Removing that impediment to trade was a top priority with Boss Conrad and the Council," Val Con said, which wasn't exactly factual, though it wasn't quite a lie.

"Of course it was a top priority!" Surveyor Veloz snapped. "Clan Korval must have an open port or it will strangle and die."

Miri blinked up at him.

"That doesn't mean an open port and an open road are bad things, does it?" she asked interestedly.

"No, of course—" Surveyor Gokero began, but her teammate cut her off.

"The *bad thing* is that our team has been brought in to legitimize Korval's new home port, when Korval continues to comport itself as an outlaw along the trade lanes. TerraTrade should withhold any formal rating of Surebleak port until Korval has vacated the planet."

Miri felt Val Con's temper spark, and looked to Surveyor Kasveini, who had introduced herself as team leader.

"Is this TerraTrade's official stance?" she asked mildly. "Does the survey team not intend to do its work here?"

"Of course we intend to do our work! We will concern ourselves with the operation, facilities, and temperament of the port. The survey team does not have the power to impose sanctions."

"But TerraTrade does, and should!" Veloz snapped. "It is of very great concern when an organization with a known history of violence establishes a new base on a world also known for violence, and petitions TerraTrade for a rating upgrade! We've seen how much Korval cares for trade, or for the law, when one of its premier tradeships holds a space station hostage to its own safety—a move that was no more or less the action of a pirate—"

"Peitr!" Gokero snapped, her face pale.

"You're out of line!" Kasveini added. "Stand down, Surveyor!"

Miri shivered against the wave of cold anger coming off Val Con. She drew a breath and thought the calm colors of the Rainbow—which immediately frosted over.

"Ms. Robertson, Mr. yos'Phelium," Surveyor Kasveini said quietly. "Please, you must not regard my colleague's outburst. Our team is here to do an honest and objective study of Surebleak Port. We have given the portmaster our timetable and the list of those key persons we will wish to interview as well as the conditions and items which are standard to any survey.

"After we have completed our work, we will send our report to headquarters, including the documentation we received from the portmaster's office. The rating committee will then study those materials and make a determination. That is the process, and we will follow the process without prejudice. I am at a loss to know where Surveyor Veloz has acquired these . . . opinions, but as team leader, I assure you I will monitor his work on the survey closely, to be certain that there is no lack of objectivity."

Val Con, coldly seething, inclined his head. Miri filled in the blank.

"Thank you, Team Leader, that's reassuring." She paused, but the only thing she was getting from Val Con was a blizzard. Best to slip away, then. Fine.

She inclined her head formally, mirroring Val Con's nod to the inch.

"We'll leave you now."

Kasveini and Gokero bowed. Veloz thought he wouldn't, but then suddenly decided for courtesy. Miri suspected encouragement from Kasveini, who was standing next to him, though she didn't actually see the team leader kick him.

Miri took Val Con's arm and moved them off in the direction of the buffet.

• • • ✵ • • •

The second device was in the tube. The engineer sat her station, awaiting the captain's word.

The captain, in her turn, awaited word from the comm officer.

That person was on screen, busy in his tower, sorting incoming feeds, his face stern with concentration. Abruptly, he looked up, a quick hand-sign indicating that second seat was needed on comm.

An elder pilot moved from the observer's chair to the copilot's station as the former second relocated to third chair, slipping the comm bud into his ear.

The ship was now three light-hours from the primary on the other side of the system, and comm traffic was more complex, fresher, than it had been at their former location.

"Scout transmission, Captain," third chair reported. "Detached duty."

He paused, listening; nodded.

"They are monitoring incoming traffic, working in concert with the planetary port. We are out of their range."

"Comm?"

"Nothing, Captain."

The captain smiled.

"Engineer, deploy number two at will."

"Yes, Captain."

• • • ✵ • • •

Val Con spent the ride home brooding, which, Miri admitted, could be said for her as well.

It didn't matter that *Pale Wing*'s captain had apologized and resigned just as soon as her ship and people were safe, so she wouldn't be making that particular mistake on a Korval ship again. It didn't even matter that *Pale Wing* had been under attack from three hunter ships that were under the control of the Department of the Interior, no matter that the official finding had been that they had a contract with local security.

It didn't matter that Korval had prevented a hostile takeover of Liad itself.

What mattered to those who hadn't been there, who didn't even have all the information necessary to have an opinion—what mattered was the actions, in isolation. These—these are the actions of a pirate!

'Course, it didn't help, either, that Clan Korval had been for a long time suspect on its own homeworld, where the stay-at-home folks barely considered them Liaden. And that was before Er Thom yos'Galan had started the new clan hobby of taking Terran lifemates.

She'd figured it would take time and effort to redeem Korval's good name to the universe, and in the meantime, the clan would find business partners and allies who had sense, or facts, or who were willing to listen to reason.

What she hadn't foreseen—nor had Val Con or any of the rest of his generally savvy kinfolk—was that the Department of the Interior would hold a grudge. In fact, they'd expected that the DOI would fold up after the strike that took out their headquarters and their top people. But they hadn't fully understood the conditioning that even the least of the DOI's operatives labored under.

The long and short of it was, Miri thought, they *couldn't* give up. Not 'til somebody or something straightened out the kinks the DOI'd put into their brains.

Worse, according to the Scouts, the new commander of agents had set about recruiting more operatives.

On that cheerful thought, Nelirikk pulled the car into its usual place by the side door and cut the power.

"Thanks, Beautiful," Miri said. "You're off duty."

"Yes, Captain," Nelirikk said and popped his door with unusual alacrity, crossing the patio quickly.

The side door opened to admit him.

"Hey," Miri said, watching the door close behind Nelirikk. "You busy this evening?"

"Do you have something to suggest?" Val Con answered, and she caught a little flare of interest through the fog of frustration.

She slid across the seat until her hip was pressed against his, put her hand on his thigh, and her lips against his ear.

"Wanna dance *menfri'at* with me?"

Delight leapt from him like a bolt of lightning, even as he turned his head and nipped her earlobe.

"Yes," he breathed. "Very much."

...*...

The third package had been deployed. The ship was now on an approach, and the planet had seen them.

"Comm?" the captain asked quietly.

"Nothing, Captain. I have the roster of ships on port. *Chandra Marudas* is not among them."

There came a cheer from the crew. The captain outright grinned, the furry entity on her knee bounced in unfeigned delight.

"Right, then. Kara, Win Ton—you're off-shift. Clarence, you're on first board. When we change shift, Joyita will take first; I'll sit second."

"Yes, Captain."

Kara and Win Ton left the bridge. Clarence cocked a sapient eye at the captain.

"Making that call now?"

She shook her head and rose, having shifted the norbear from her knee to the armrest.

"No sense sending a pinbeam; I'll wait 'til we're close in and call direct."

He nodded.

"Reasonable. Just we don't wanna go in without any warning. There's security."

"I met him," the captain said, with a note of strained patience in her voice, as if she and her second mate had gone 'round this argument before—perhaps more than once.

"We will do nothing to endanger ourselves," the ship said suddenly. "You may rest easy, Clarence."

He grinned, eyes on his boards.

"Well, now you said so, I guess I will. Off-shift, Theo?"

"Off-shift," she agreed, and brought one slim hand up to cover a yawn.

• • • ❋ • • •

They'd started with the practice forms, but that wasn't what either of them wanted; Val Con varied in the midst of a classic close-and-break, sweeping low, taking advantage of the high center she'd taken in order to close.

She threw herself into a backward somersault, landing in a crouch, grabbed the foot that was coming toward her, twisted and let him go over her shoulder before she dove flat, rolling, knowing that he'd come up fast, balanced and on the offense, and she had to get distance and height.

She continued the roll, coming to her feet and flat out running toward the wall, with him two steps behind her if that much, even as she jumped, hitting the wall feet first at the level of his head, pushing away into another somersault, landing flat-footed and centered behind him.

He spun into her fist, taking the punch to his shoulder, twisted right and down, got one hand behind her knee and pulled, his momentum taking them both down.

She recovered first, grabbing his wrists and kicking

into a roll that brought her on top and them both gasping for breath.

"Yield!" she managed, holding his wrists, glaring into green eyes bright with exertion.

"Never will I yield," he declared. "Death before dishonor!"

She blinked.

"Hey, really? Because I thought you were a smart guy."

He laughed, broke her grip, wrapped both arms around her and kicked them into a roll that ended when his back hit the wall. By that time, Miri was laughing, too, and they lay there, arms around each other, until they were reduced to a sweaty, intermittently giggling pile, his face against her neck and her cheek on his hair.

They had passed into a gentle doze, still wrapped in each other's arms, neither one eager to move, when Jeeves spoke.

"Master Val Con. Miri. A guest has arrived. Mr. pel'Kana has placed him in the Yellow Salon."

The Yellow Salon? Miri thought. It wasn't every visitor—or even every hundredth visitor—who got put in the Yellow Salon.

Val Con had come up on one elbow, brows drawn together.

"Has our formidable visitor a name, I wonder?"

"He gives the name Uncle, represents himself as being on business of the clan, and seeks an audience with Korval," Jeeves said, and added, "He is alone."

"Oh," Val Con said softly. "Is he?"

Jeeves didn't answer; there wasn't any need to answer.

Val Con looked into her eyes.

"Well, *cha'trez*? Shall we see Uncle?"

"I don't think we got any choice, do you? We better shower first, though."

"Agreed." He kicked gently, rolled them once, and let her go, sitting up and flicking a glance toward the ceiling.

"Jeeves, please ask Mr. pel'Kana to inform the guest that the delm will be with him in good time."

"Yes."

"We will scarcely be elegant," Val Con said, "if we use the resources available here."

Miri sat up.

"He comes with no warning and without what belongs to us; he's lucky we're showering first," she said.

Val Con grinned, rose to his feet, and extended a hand to her.

"Do you disagree?" she asked, taking his hand and rising every bit as lightly as he had.

"No, I agree in every particular," he said, putting his arm around her waist as they moved toward the shower, "because I'm a smart guy."

II

FOR SOMEBODY WHO CAST A LEGEND AS LONG AND AS wide as the Uncle did, the man himself was pretty compact, younger looking than Miri had expected, dressed to swagger in a well-used jacket with a vaguely military cut and a faded smear of color on one shoulder, like maybe it'd once been a hash mark. His hair was short in front, longer than the collar of the jacket in back, dark brown with the last inch or so lacquered bright red. Gold ring in the right ear, and a short dark beard that did nothing to soften a strong, stubborn jaw. So far as his face and his body language went—excusing the beard—he might've been Liaden born, neutral as you'd like, and then some. Really, Miri thought, if it wasn't for the eyes, you'd hardly know you were facing a man in a mortal rage.

He had been perusing the shelves when they entered, and he turned, smooth and calm, bowing to their honor, all right and proper.

"Korval," he said. His voice was even and pleasant.

Miri felt a niggle inside her head and *just knew* that Val Con was going to give him honored guest of the House, so that's what she bowed, too, right in sync with him.

"Uncle. Be welcome in our House," Val Con said in the High Liaden mode of delm-to-guest-of-the-House.

"Peace upon it," came the reply, which wasn't one of the several Miri knew to be rote in the situation, though the Uncle said it like it *was* rote, and his glare no softer for the speaking of it.

There was something, she thought, familiar about that glare. She tried to remember where she'd seen it, or something real close to it, lately, but the memory didn't rise.

Well, she thought; it'll come. In the meantime, might as well cut to the chase and find out all the good news at once.

"I confess myself at something of a loss," she said, drawing those dark, angry eyes to her. "While we are, of course, more than pleased to see you—and in such good health—I had supposed that, when your business allowed you to come to us, you would be accompanied by our elder who has long been in your care."

"That had been my intention. However, in the current circumstances, it seemed, may I say, the *course of prudence* to hold your elders in continued safety until my sister and I have exchanged fond greeting."

Miri blinked. So did Val Con. At least, she assumed that the mental bobble she felt from him was the equal of a blink.

"Forgive me," he said to the Uncle. "Your sister?"

"In fact," said the Uncle, there was an edge to his voice now and tension in his shoulders. "My sister. Surely you have cared for her, as I have cared for your elders."

Wait, Miri thought. Elders plural? The Uncle apparently knew something very few people did know, which was . . . worrisome. Aelliana's living presence inside his head wasn't something that Daav talked about with casual strangers or, she suspected, with chancy allies, either. If he'd confided in the Uncle . . .

"I regret," Val Con was saying to that very Uncle. "Ought Korval to know your sister?"

"One would expect so. Her last message to me was that she was 'in the Dragon's lair.' She bade me come to her there, at once."

"Ah." Val Con bowed regret, tinged with sorrow. "If that was her plan, sir, it went awry. She did not reach us."

"You misunderstand," said the Uncle. "Her message was not that she *intended* to go to the Dragon, but that she *was arrived*. My sister is precise in her communications. One might say, *painfully precise*."

"I am certain," Val Con murmured. "And yet, sir, I can but repeat: She has not come to us."

Which was, Miri thought, the kind of argument that went nowhere really fast, and left a pile of broken bodies behind it.

"Meaning no disrespect to your sister or to her command of language," she interrupted, "she is not here. Therefore, she must be somewhere else. Korval will certainly engage to search, to put word out 'on the street' as it is said here on Surebleak, and to use every resource in order to recover your sister or discover news of her. Anything that you can provide to us which will assist the searchers will be most welcome."

The Uncle drew a breath . . .

"In the meanwhile," Miri said before he could field any actual words, "we will of course take up the burden of caring for our elders, with all gratitude to you for their safe return to the clan."

"I will certainly welcome Korval's assistance in a discreet search," the Uncle replied, with a *very* slight bow. "In regard to your elders, I assure you that they do not strain my resources in the least."

Well, *that* sounded nothing but ominous, Miri thought.

She could feel Val Con considering the matter and she didn't much care for the cold that was coming off of him while he did. Dammit, she'd had him more or less unkinked and now he was right back to cold mad. She could see his point: the Uncle was out of line—in fact, he was in breach of his word, and yet, he was the one pushing the issue.

And that, she thought, was interesting. Given that the Uncle knew just as well as they did that a dust-up was to nobody's benefit, he had to have some reason to believe that holding hostages would get him cooperation . . . but in what? Unless he didn't believe them and did believe that they were keeping his sister out of his reach.

Can't prove a negative, she thought. But maybe they could prove a truth.

"I suggest a compromise," she began . . .

A brisk knock interrupted her, and she stayed interrupted when the door opened to admit two pilots—one tall and dark, the other shorter and pale-haired.

"Ah, and here he is, Daav, precisely as Pilot Dulsey had said he would be!" cried the fair-haired pilot with great cordiality, striding into the room, the taller pilot at her back.

The reaction from Val Con was like an electric shock.

"*Father*?" he said, not loud.

Miri looked again as the pilots approached. The tall one was—yes, that *was* Daav yos'Phelium, looking an easy fifty years younger than the last time they'd spoken. That would've been the time she—as Delm Korval—had sent him off on a mission that they both knew had better-than-even odds of killing him.

So, if the tall pilot was Daav, and keeping "elders" firmly in mind, it followed that the shorter pilot was Aelliana Caylon, Daav's lifemate, Val Con's mother, murdered long Standards ago.

"Did I not tell you how it would be, *van'chela*?" she continued blithely. "Our kind host and ally has of course come ahead to explain every particular, so that the delm should labor under no misunderstanding regarding our current estate."

"Pilot Caylon . . ." began the Uncle.

"Mother . . ." began Val Con.

"Indeed," said Daav, overriding them both, his deep voice unchanged. "It is exactly as you say, Pilot."

Aelliana Caylon stopped at Miri's side, hands tucked into her belt, head tilted slightly back so that she might observe the Uncle's face. She appeared to be in high good humor.

"Forgive me for doubting your motives, sir," Daav said to the Uncle. "You of all people must know how it becomes a habit to doubt everyone."

"Habit or not," Aelliana scolded lightly, "it is entirely unworthy of you in the case, Daav. Has the Uncle not been kindness itself to us, his guests?"

"*Mother*," Val Con said again.

She turned her head.

"Val Con! You're looking well, child."

"You relieve me," he said gravely. "To say truth, I feared you might find me somewhat threadbare."

"Has the course been uncertain?" she asked sympathetically. "It often seems so, you know, directly before you come about."

"I will hope, then, to come about quickly. In the meanwhile, I see that the Uncle has cared for you as one of his own."

She bestowed a brilliant smile upon him.

"Exactly so."

The Uncle sighed, very lightly, though Miri heard him.

"Is there some problem, sir?" she asked.

His glance was wry.

"I merely note afresh that Pilot Caylon has a unique understanding of the universe."

"One that you dispute?"

"Who am I to dispute a Dragon? However, the joyous reunion of kin remains incomplete. My sister—"

There came a brisk knock and the door again opened.

Val Con's aunt Kareen crossed the threshold purposefully, followed by a broad brown person and the pale woman Miri had met in Kareen's house weeks ago. Tassi, that was her name.

And she was *definitely* not what Miri had expected.

Kareen paused at precisely the distance specified in *The Liaden Code of Proper Conduct*, and bowed honor-to-the-delm. Tassi and her 'hand went around her, one to either side, plotting a straight course to the Uncle, who was standing like he'd been quick-frozen.

"Yuri!" she snapped.

They were much of a height, Miri saw, and though the coloring was different, seeing them together didn't leave room to doubt that they were kin. The face was the same shape, the jaw every bit as determined, and right this minute, the expression was exactly the same.

"What took you so long?" Tassi demanded, her 'hand taking position at her back.

"I came as soon as I received your message," he snapped back. "And I arrived to find that you were not at the specified location."

"*I* am *in* the Dragon's lair!" She swept her arms out in a gesture that would've endangered the crockery if there'd been any nearby; her 'hand leaned slightly to the right, neatly avoiding a smack to the jaw.

"While that is surely so, *now*, you were elsewhere when I arrived. Additionally, no one in the Dragon's lair knew of you, or your whereabouts. This created awkwardness. I had thought you more precise."

His sister stared at him.

"*All of Surebleak* is the Dragon's lair," she said, as if explaining basic arithmetic to a little child.

There was a brief, volatile silence before the Uncle spoke again, stiffly.

"I see that I was underinformed. May I know where you were *precisely*?"

"She was," said Lady Kareen, "a guest in my house."

Miri felt the spike of Val Con's irritation and moved in his direction.

"You didn't feel it necessary to inform the delm of this circumstance?"

Kareen gave him one of her top five Haughty Stares.

"Forgive me. It had escaped my attention that I am now required to inform the delm whenever I have a guest."

Val Con took a breath. Miri reached his side and slipped her hand into his. He let the breath go in a long sigh.

"But—*such* a guest, Aunt," he said, almost mildly.

"As to that, Tassi was brought to me by Silain, who asked that I shelter her sister until such time as kin could reach her."

"And you inquired no further?"

Kareen raised her eyebrows.

"What else would I wish to know, save that a sister had asked of a sister for a sister?"

"Quite right," Val Con said, his voice so dry that Miri felt parched.

"She has not," Kareen continued, "been an entirely convenable guest, if one were to speak frankly. I, at least, was not aware that Tassi was attached to the Uncle—I presume that is the Uncle?"

"It is, yes. Did Grandmother Silain know who she was?"

"I would imagine so," said Kareen, but not like she

cared. "It is the business of a *luthia* to know such things, and to know when to keep the knowledge close."

•••⁕•••

By mutual consent, Daav and Aelliana had moved away from the center of the room to take up a position near the shelves on the right wall, where they could observe without being observed.

We seem to have arrived in good time to avert the tragedy Pilot Dulsey had feared, Daav observed.

Yes, it plays far better as a comedy. The Uncle's sister is not much like him.

Or too much like him.

Very true. How shall we present ourselves to the delm, now that we are arrived?

Having arrived as we did, I think our only choice is to tell the tale full out and wait upon their wisdom.

Perhaps we might ask for a night's guesting first? Aelliana suggested, her eyes on the delm and Kareen. *Val Con is in no good temper. Miri is keeping him in hand, but possibly a night's rest might be beneficial to all.*

Certainly, we can ask, Daav said. *The worst they can do is kill us out of hand.*

My thought exactly.

•••⁕•••

"Who," the Uncle said to his sister, voice low, "is Silain?"

She frowned and sighed. However, she did, surprisingly, answer.

"My first plan had been to take shelter with your people. There is a *kompani* here, in this city. However, the grandmother felt that I should be better placed with Lady Kareen and Professor Waitley. I bowed to her wisdom."

She paused and gave him a sharp look.

"Even *I* know that is what one does when a grandmother expresses her wisdom."

"You went to the Bedel!" The softness of his voice did nothing to mask his outrage.

"No. Yuri, you are not listening. I *had planned* to go to the Bedel. I was on my way to the place where the *kompani* camps. Silain and two of her grandsons met me in the street before I had gone very far, and escorted me to Lady Kareen, as I have said. I have been there this while, waiting for you to arrive."

"My breath is taken by the assumption that you would even think of contacting the Bedel..."

"Why should I not think of it? Did I not set them in motion?"

"*I* set them in motion," he snapped.

She frowned and moved her hand irritably. "Yes, yes, but that is one and the same, of course.

"It was a good plan for all that it was hastily made," she continued, before he could begin to formulate a reply to this. "You are forever telling me that I must be safe, are you not? I would have been twice safe—not only inside the field, but inside the care of the Bedel, which was also inside the field."

"Field? What is this field. Surebleak has no—"

"The field of luck," his sister interrupted him. "Korval is here and the Luck is with them."

•••⁂•••

Oh, dear, said Aelliana.

Indeed. Shall we intervene?

I believe that we must. Please, Scholar, seize this teaching moment.

"Allow me to understand this," the Uncle was saying, his voice excruciatingly even. "You deliberately sought out Korval's Luck? We are not in the habit of running mad by our own standards," he said, "but I begin to fear that I asked too much of you and have—"

"Yuri, Korval's Luck is not a thing to fear!" his sister protested. "I know that you are wary, but truly, it can only benefit—"

"Your pardon," Daav said, stepping closer to them, Aelliana at his side. "One could not help but overhear. I offer . . . information about Korval's Luck which may be useful to your discussions."

The Uncle's sister turned. "Are you of Korval?"

The Uncle himself sighed and moved his hand.

"I present Daav yos'Phelium and Aelliana Caylon, who have been delm of Korval. Pilots, my sister, Seignur Veeoni."

"Pilots." Seignur Veeoni ducked her head in acknowledgment. "My research has allowed me to see a little way into the workings of serendipity in general, and Korval's Luck in particular. I would be grateful to receive an expert's information."

Daav inclined his head.

"I am pleased to be of assistance. As you have deduced, Korval's Luck is a force. However, it is an unpredictable force. We of the House do not court it, but neither do we ignore it. Instead, we are *aware* of it, as one might be aware of any self-directed condition that may intersect with one's actions.

"It must also be noted that *the Luck*, as we call it, does not necessarily *favor* us. Clan history contains many instances where luck has played one of Korval ill. It has been suggested that we are at best attractors, and the means by which we attract the Luck's, let us say, *attention* are not apparent to us.

"It has also been suggested," he continued, catching the Uncle's gaze and inclining his head, "that the Luck finds us *interesting*. If that is even remotely the case, then placing us into a novel situation—such as an extended session in an autodoc, in an attempt to insure that the Luck will not operate—can only draw it closer."

The Uncle pressed his lips together and said nothing.

"As tricksy as the Luck is for those of Korval," Daav continued, "it is more so for those who are not of the House. The Luck, so far as any of us have been able to ascertain, does not care about collateral damage."

Seignur Veeoni nodded.

"I have observed that luck in general does not exert a constant field. However, I theorize that there are not one, but two forces at work: the Luck, which has been attracted to Surebleak, where the object of its interest—Clan Korval—has removed, and the planet's own gravitational field."

"You believe that the Luck is not merely attracted to Surebleak, but has been captured by it?" Aelliana asked. "That gravity both insures a consistent layer and quiescence?"

Seignur Veeoni turned her to her.

"Yes! Precisely so! It is worthy of more study. I will be pleased, if it would be of interest, to share my further findings with you."

"Thank you," Aelliana said. "It touches the edges of my own work. I will be very interested to learn of your progress."

Seignur Veeoni nodded.

"In the meantime, I think that Pilot yos'Phelium wishes me to understand that, while I have been fortunate in my removal and recent rustication, the opposite might just have easily been the case."

"That is entirely correct, Scholar."

"I am not a scholar," she told him baldly. "*Researcher* will do."

He inclined his head, and she turned back to Aelliana.

"Scholar Caylon, have you finished your proof for pseudorandom tridimensional subspace?"

Aelliana raised her eyebrows.

"In fact, the final proofs are complete. I have not lately been in a position to publish, of course."

"I am aware. Even now, publication will not be easy." Seignur Veeoni looked over her shoulder.

"Yuri, you must establish a provenance for the scholar's new persona. Her work is critical, and it must not be left out of the universal conversation!"

"No, please, your brother has surely borne enough from us!" Aelliana said, raising a hand, palm out. "Korval is perfectly able to address such matters on my behalf, Researcher. I thank you for your care."

Seignur Veeoni looked doubtful, but nodded once more.

"If there should be any difficulty, though, Scholar, you *will* remember Yuri?"

"I give you my most solemn word that I will never forget him," Aelliana said.

Daav glanced at the Uncle, to see if that dart had found a mark but, of course, the target was inscrutable.

"I believe," he said, apparently ignoring his sister and Aelliana alike, "all of the pieces are back upon their proper boards. We shall therefore take our leave of Korval. If you will accompany me, Sister?"

"Yes," she said. "I have much to discuss with you, Yuri."

"And I, you."

He bowed.

"Pilots. Long life to you both."

"Sir," Daav said, bowing in return.

Aelliana bowed in her turn.

"Live long and prosper."

The Uncle and his sister moved away.

Daav sighed, closed his eyes—and opened them again at the sound of an all-too-familiar voice.

"Now, I wonder, is this Daav yos'Phelium?"

He turned to confront his sister Kareen.

"Not only is it Daav yos'Phelium, but Aelliana Caylon, if you will have it," he told her. "And a more comprehensive muddle I hope never again to encounter."

She smiled slightly and bowed her head.

"Once past the surprise, you look well, Brother," she said, astonishingly cordial. She turned to Aelliana. "Sister. Of course, I had not expected to see you again."

"Kareen," Aelliana murmured, making no demur at "sister," though Kareen had not been prone to that mode of address, back in the day.

"I do not mean to keep you overlong, for I know you must have business with the delm," Kareen continued. "I merely wish to inform you that Kamele Waitley has become part of my household. She is one of the company which is piecing together Surebleak's history and mores, so that a new common code may be crafted which will guide both the native population and the Liaden immigrants."

"Kamele is on Surebleak?" Daav repeated.

"How does she go on?" Aelliana asked.

"Kamele is indeed on Surebleak and if I may say so, she blooms. She came seeking her lover, one Jen Sar Kiladi, whom she believed was held against his will by Clan Korval. It was her intention to remove Professor Kiladi from this situation, was it in fact objectionable to him."

Kamele had left Delgado, and traveled to Surebleak, in order to rescue him. *Valiant* heart. Daav thought he might weep.

Kareen inclined her head.

"I believe that she would be glad of a meeting with you," she said simply.

Daav raised a hand.

"Kareen, you are aware that the delm must judge. Please do not disturb Kamele's peace, until that judgment has been made."

She sent a sharp glance into his face and sighed lightly.

"Of course not," she said. "And now, I too, will take my leave. It is come late and I have an early meeting."

A small bow, between kin, also more cordial than her previous mode.

"Good night."

"Good night, Kareen," Aelliana said. "Go well."

"And you."

• • • ❋ • • •

The Uncle and his sister had gone. Kareen had gone. Miri took a deep breath.

Only one more problem to solve.

Speaking of saving the best 'til last.

She could sense Val Con's mind working, thoughts

clicking like game counters. The delm was obliged to weigh benefit and danger to the clan before every other consideration. And two . . . clones, she supposed they were, supplied by the Uncle . . . to house two of the clan's elders—one previously and comprehensively dead—she didn't even want to *begin* to think about all the knots in that tangle, but apparently Val Con was already busy.

"Korval."

Aelliana Caylon was bowing low before her; Daav yos'Phelium before Val Con, neither one of them looking any older than eighteen Standards.

"Please," she said to them, "stand."

They straightened, neither saying a word, waiting for the delm to ask a question, make a judgment, shoot them dead . . .

Miri took a deep breath, she caught Val Con's eye.

"I think the delm's closing up for the night," she said. "You?"

He hesitated, then nodded, and addressed the two before them in delm-to-petitioners, which was *high* High Liaden, and not a bit of human warmth in it.

"The delm greets Daav yos'Phelium and Aelliana Caylon, and grants them leave to retire to their suite for the remainder of this night. You will hold yourselves available to the delm, and you will not leave this house. We will have many questions. Tomorrow."

Aelliana bent her head, and Daav did.

"Korval," they said with one voice.

Miri shivered. Now she knew just exactly how eerie it looked from the outside, when she and Val Con went into sync.

The two of them had straightened and Miri saw they were holding hands.

"Mother," Val Con said, very softly indeed, "Father. Words fail."

Daav smiled his edged smile.

"I understand. My thoughts upon awakening to this situation ought perhaps not have been given to the innocent air."

"Please," Aelliana said, "take your rest. Only know that—however the delm judges tomorrow, children, we are happy to have landed home and to see you once more."

Tears stung Miri's eyes, and Val Con wasn't in any better shape.

"*Chiat'a bei kruzon*," Aelliana said. "Dream sweetly" that was.

"And you," Val Con said, and Miri felt his fingers seeking hers.

They watched the clan's young elders leave the room. When the door had closed, Miri swung around and they wrapped their arms around each other, heads resting on the other's shoulder.

"We should go to bed," Val Con said at last, loosening his embrace.

"No," Miri said, stepping back, and pulling him with her toward the door. "We should go to sleep."

"A fine distinction, but an important one," he agreed. "Let us, by all means, go to sleep."

III

"INDIRA'S REPORT OF THE STATE OF YOUR RESIDENCE WAS dire in the extreme. She has cleared and destroyed it, as per standing orders."

Seignur Veeoni nodded, absently, it seemed to the Uncle, as if her mind were far away from Surebleak, *Vivulonj Prosperu*, and most importantly, himself.

He sighed and made another attempt at engaging her attention.

"Have you any insight into why the security in and around your lab failed to function?"

She looked up at him, eyes bright.

"I disabled those systems."

"You disabled them," he repeated neutrally. "I see. It may interest you to know that Indira has identified the intruders as operatives of the Lyre Institute. While they appear to have suffered heavy losses, yet it is apparent that those who lived to enter your laboratory removed every rack, every tile, every grid. While they did not acquire your notes, I am sure you are aware that the Lyre Institute is perfectly competent to back-engineer what they have stolen."

"Yes, of course," she said, sitting with her hands folded on her lap and her face calm. "I'm afraid that I did depend upon them being very clever."

"Ah. It does not disturb you to know that your lifework now resides in the hands of an organization which is criminal at best, while we are left with nothing in hand to bring to Tinsori Light, and a shrinking event aperture?"

"No, Yuri, you are not thinking! Of course, the Lyre Institute did not obtain the racks intended for Tinsori Light. It would be a disaster, indeed, if they had done so.

"What they obtained instead were the sets that I built on purpose for them, in anticipation of just such a move. Of course, I did not leave them the *faristo*, so they will have to derive and machine a comparable unit, which will occupy them for some little while. When they are able to manufacture their own tiles, I very much hope that they will replicate the errors inherent in their gift sets as often as they are capable of doing so."

He stared at her for a long moment, wondering at the audacity, at the *arrogance* of such a tactic . . .

"Yuri?" his sister said. "It is no more than you have done yourself, you know."

He inclined his head. "You are correct, of course. I fear that I grow old and less bold."

Seignur Veeoni, however, was young; she bore the entirety of his memories in the strands she wore against her skin.

"Dare I ask," he said, "where the true tiles and frames are?"

"I have one complete set, and the *faristo*, with me," she said. "I sent M Nator with a complete set only to our research station standing off of Tinsori Light's space, as there is a *faristo* there. The third true and complete set, I entrusted to M Benkley, who was to take them to your residence."

She hesitated.

"I fear that set may be lost. M Benkley was wounded. I . . . M Traven said she doubted even an M could ultimately survive such a wound, but he did achieve his vessel, and we saw a controlled breakaway before M Traven put my ship into Jump."

"Absent this one detail then, you would have me believe that matters fell out exactly as you planned."

"No," she said baldly. "They did not. I did *not* plan, for instance, on losing my secondary projects, nor did I plan to lose my child and my hope of rebirth. I did *not* plan that M Benkley would be so grievously wounded or that M Varia and M Ratu would fail to survive the initial strike against our defenses."

She took a breath and continued more moderately, "Despite these lapses, I did preserve my work on the primary project, and that, you must agree, Yuri, is a very good thing, because you are correct—our window of opportunity is closing. The last situation reports I received from Andreth plainly indicated that the Light is deteriorating more rapidly than we had projected. We must act quickly."

The Uncle considered her. Despite the confusion regarding the Dragon's lair, when she had—typically, really—expected him to know everything that she knew—despite that one lapse, she was very nice in her choice of words. *Quickly*, however, required clarification.

"We may file for an emergency lift and be gone in a few hours at most," he said. "I will accompany you to the Light. Dulsey will follow and await our return at the research station."

Seignur Veeoni said nothing.

"Well?" he snapped.

"There is a misunderstanding," she said.

"Elucidate this misunderstanding. Quickly."

"Yes. There are several levels. Primary is this: I, and my team, will step onto the game board. *You*—will not."

He raised his eyebrows.

"Oh, will I not? I will remind you that I built—"

She held up a hand.

"Indeed you did. And thus, so did I. I have those memories. Inside the cloud, there will be no necessity for duplication of knowledge. If I should fail, then you—and the direct knowledge of the builder—will be required, as very few things have been in this universe."

"Surely, you do not intend to fail."

Seignur Veeoni glared at him.

"We have lately seen that I *can* fail. I *intend* to achieve a certain outcome, and I have been trained my entire life to succeed in *this one* task. And yet—I may fail."

She took a hard breath and bowed her head, visibly calming herself.

"That is why *I* will go and *you* will stay behind. You *are* the elder; you *are* the builder, not merely the memories of the builder; *you* are the final shield for the universe should I fall short of my intentions."

She was correct, he admitted. Of course, she was correct. She was not, as she had now asserted twice, his exact duplicate, but she wore the strands—he could see the hint of them, even beneath the sweater and jacket required by Surebleak's weather.

She was her own unique person, as all of his brothers and sisters were entirely themselves. But one attribute that made her unique was the fact that she . . . remembered more of his young memories than even he did, here and now. She *knew*, as a function of her own memory, the old universe. She had his blueprints and plans in active memory; she *remembered* the construction of the Light; remembered that its original purpose had been as a sanctuary for those displaced by the Enemy's actions.

It had been stolen—she had that in active memory, too. Stolen by an agent of the *sheriekas*, subverted to the purpose of the Enemy.

He had survived that event. Most of those he had worked with—and worked for—had not; they had been the first lives that the Light claimed.

The Light had been, so he had thought for centuries, left behind in the old universe, crystallized into perfection in the Enemy's Great Plan.

And it had been . . . perhaps not quite . . . the greatest shock of his very, very long life to learn that it existed still, caught between the old and the new, warping the fabric of two universes; and malignant—yes, it had been malignant, the only one of the Great Works that had seemed to actively *take pleasure* in betrayal and destruction.

And now, it was not merely evil, but mad. He had sent teams inside to gather data, proving the inevitable. The fractin sets that had informed Tinsori Light, the systems that had supported it—all and each were failing: that was physics. The half-life of timonium was known to the last decimal space. That it was functioning at all must be regarded as one of the wonders of the new universe.

And very possibly its death knell.

"Very well," he said to Seignur Veeoni. "I shall be rear guard. How do you suggest that we proceed?"

"I will go with M Traven now and she will file for departure. After we have lifted, Dulsey will file for your own departure. Those who always watch us will not be fooled by such a stratagem, of course, but those who do not yet know that they ought to watch us will not be alerted to that fact."

She stood.

"I will go now," she said.

"Wait."

He put his hands on her shoulders—unusual enough—and bent slightly to kiss her forehead.

Her eyes were wide when he stepped back and released her.

"You will not fail," he told her.

For another moment she stood, perhaps immobilized by shock, then she nodded once, stiffly, and left him.

•••✵•••

"Master Val Con, I regret the necessity."

Val Con opened one eye. He and Miri were tucked beneath the blankets, comfortably spooned, and he felt her stir against him, not quite awake, yet no longer deeply asleep.

"What is it?" he asked irritably.

"I have a call on the clan frequency from *Bechimo*, on Surebleak approach. Captain Waitley wishes to speak with you."

Val Con raised his head sufficiently to see the clock, took a deep breath, and resettled on his pillow.

"Pray tell Captain Waitley that I will speak with her at breakfast," he said.

There was a small hesitation.

"Captain Waitley did state that her business was urgent. I would not have waked you otherwise, sir."

Jeeves's tone was chiding, which Val Con supposed he deserved. It was not the messenger who had earned the sharp edge of his tongue.

"I will speak with Captain Waitley," he said, reluctantly pushing the blankets aside. "Please route her call to our console."

"Yes, sir."

Val Con picked his robe up from the bottom of the bed and turned at the sound of blankets being energetically cast aside.

"Sleep, *cha'trez*. You needn't cope with Theo at this hour."

"Couldn't catch a wink, between you being gone

and wondering what it is that Theo might consider urgent," Miri said, pulling on her robe with a wide grin.

"Certainly nothing to do with her family," Val Con said grumpily.

Miri laughed.

"Hey, you wanted her to come home!"

"At a civilized hour."

Miri curled into the wide seat of the chair by the console while he perched on the arm. There was a moment of silence before Jeeves spoke.

"Captain Waitley, Master Val Con," Jeeves said. "Proceed, *Bechimo*."

"Val Con?" Light-voiced, perhaps a shade breathless.

"Good evening, Theo," he said, "I trust you are well rested."

There was a pause, no longer than expectable.

"I regret the hour," Theo said, in very good Liaden, indeed. "Necessity exists."

"Does it?" he said, answering as he was addressed. "Pray elucidate necessity."

The pause this time was . . . somewhat longer than might be accounted for by lag.

"We need to land," she said in Terran, now. "I request permission to use the field at Jelaza Kazone."

Miri pressed her fingers against her lips, presumably to prevent herself from giving voice to the merriment he felt bubbling in her.

"The field is a *field*," he said to his sister. "Rough work for a ship, though it can be done. Why not find berth at Korval's Yard? We will send a car."

"No, negative; that won't do. We need to land close to the house. Close to *you*."

Val Con lifted an eyebrow.

"I am, of course, flattered," he began . . .

"It would be useful," Theo continued, "if you could meet us at landing. Nelirikk, too."

Val Con sighed.

"I live to be of use to you, Theo," he said gently. "May one know the reason for these . . . arrangements?"

"Well . . ." Theo said slowly, "it's kind of complicated."

Miri gave up the struggle for silence and laughed out loud.

Val Con bit his lip until he was sure of his own voice.

"I would be disappointed if it were otherwise," he said. "Allow the port to know that you are landing at our private field, with permission. Jeeves will provide *Bechimo* with coordinates and landing assistance."

He paused, considering, "Unless you would rather *not* be listed as a ship on port?"

"Oh, no!" his sister exclaimed. "We *want* to be listed as on port!"

Miri leaned her forehead against her knees, shoulders shaking.

"Excellent," he said. "I look forward to seeing you—soon."

"Thank you!" Theo said blithely. "Waitley out."

• • • ✵ • • •

Mrs. ana'Tak had done well, Val Con thought, entering the breakfast parlor in Miri's wake. Two sealed urns were gently steaming on the buffet—one holding tea, the other coffee—as well as a plate of sandwiches under a keep-fresh dome.

He detoured slightly to place their winter-weight coats on the window seat, while Miri went directly to the buffet.

"Coulda let the cook sleep in," she said, even as she drew a mugful of coffee.

"Captain Waitley and her crew will certainly require hospitality," Jeeves said from somewhere above Val Con's head and to the left. "Mrs. ana'Tak promises a full buffet in time for the landing. She hopes that the sandwiches and beverages do not offend."

"No," Miri said, sipping her coffee, "she did good. Please convey my appreciation."

"I will do so," Jeeves said solemnly. "Mr. pel'Kana wishes the delm to know that Captain Waitley's room stands ready to receive her, and that the Southern Suite is being prepared for guests."

Val Con, who was more familiar than Miri with the Southern Suite, nodded.

"An excellent choice, as we do not know the number of Captain Waitley's crew, nor how many will accompany her to the ground. They will certainly wish to be with each other, rather than scattered about the house."

He drew a cup of tea and glanced toward the observation screen on the back wall. Most usually, the screen displayed pleasant images of the gardens and grounds, suitable for viewing with breakfast. Now, however, the display was of a ship—a tradeship, in fact, with one pod mounted.

Bechimo's lines were . . . *unique* was perhaps the best descriptor. The pod mounts, though, were quite modern, able to accommodate the full range of standard sizes. This particular pod, however, sported lines nearly as—

His breath caught. Lines, he thought. Not a pod—a ship.

"Jeeves, are you able to increase that image?"

"One moment, please."

The image grew, until he could clearly see the Laughing Cat logo *Bechimo* displayed, and also the pod, which *was*, gods—

"That's a *ship* she's got lashed on there," Miri said, and turned sharply toward him, most probably having felt his mingled excitement and disbelief through their link. "What's wrong?" she demanded.

He could scarcely move his eyes from the ship, the impossible ship lashed like cargo to the outside mounts of a vessel almost as unlikely . . .

Chill worry washed against his amazement, reminding him that his lifemate had asked a question.

"Wrong?" he murmured. "There is nothing wrong, *cha'trez*. Only we have now been given the reason for Theo's insistence that she land 'close to me.'"

He took a breath, eyes still on the screen.

"That ship . . . Jeeves, have you a translation of the name of the ship being carried, or shall I hazard a guess?"

"The name is rendered in something like—though not very like—Yxtrang. Any translation I might attempt would also fall under the rubric of *guess*."

"Ah. Well, then. Let the stakes book show my wager—that the ship our sister is bringing to us bears the name *Spiral Dance*."

"That," said Jeeves, after a long pause, "is a very old name."

"Indeed. Older even than our arrival in this universe. One presumes that *Bechimo*'s source of teapots has expanded its offerings."

"That's a pre-Exodus ship?" Miri asked.

"I offer only my best guess," Val Con said, finally

moving his gaze from the screen to her face. "Would you like to hazard one of your own?"

"My commander told me never to bet against a Liaden," she answered absentmindedly, staring upward in her turn.

Val Con waited. Miri had been studying Korval's Diaries, as a delm must. *Spiral Dance* had significance for her, as the ship owned by his many-times-great Grandmother Cantra yos'Phelium, in simpler times, when she had merely been a grey-trader running items that were, perhaps, not *exactly* illegal into and out of ports chancier even than Surebleak had been.

She also knew that *Spiral Dance* had been lost in the other universe, before the Great Migration had gotten properly under way.

Miri looked away from the screen and met his eyes. "You think Theo's bringing it here because it's a clan ship?" she asked. "Does she have that much family history?"

"Perhaps not. However, she has resources available to her. *Bechimo* will certainly have records, and Pilot O'Berin has proven himself to be a student of—"

Green static blew through his mind, breaking his thoughts into a hundred dancing, joyous sprites; he saw—a tree. A tree in a pot, wires and crash blankets supporting it inside a snug alcove all its own. Once again, the white dragon soared between the stars, and there was the impression of small furriness; of age and wisdom.

"Val Con!" Miri's voice was sharp over the dancing riot in his mind. He snatched at it, snatched at the song of her, strong and steady beneath the racket, and wrapped it about himself like a shielding cloak.

"Stop!" he said—or meant to say, the Tree's exultation deafening even his outer ears. "I must be able to think!"

The racket subsided somewhat, until it was no more noticeable than a jet engine in full throat.

He came to himself with hands planted on the edge of the buffet, Miri's arm around his waist.

"How's it going, Cory?" she murmured in Benish.

"Well," he managed in the same language. "It goes well, my *zhena*. Now."

"And will it continue to go well?"

He laughed, only slightly breathless.

"I believe I have made the point that, if my mind is flooded with Tree, service may be interrupted."

"Stupid vegetable," Miri muttered, this time in Terran.

He laughed, more fully this time, and straightened. Miri did not remove her arm, though she was no longer supporting him.

"The Tree is not a vegetable," he pointed out.

"Well, it ain't acting like it's got any more wit than a carrot is all I'm saying."

Val Con felt a green breeze whisk past him. Miri's arm tightened, but her voice was firm.

"Don't you get attitudinal with me! Won't hurt you to show a little respect—and a lotta restraint! What if he'd been driving? Or flying? You might've killed him is what—and *I ain't having it, accazi*?"

Silence greeted this. One might almost say *stunned* silence.

The roar of the distant jet faded entirely away, and Val Con felt what he fancied to be a flutter of contrition and a very particular scrutiny, as if the Tree were assuring itself that he was well.

"That's better," Miri said. "All that woulda happened

this time is he'd've gone nosedown on the carpet if I hadn't caught him. Lucky I was by. I ain't always by, note."

Another wave of contrition, perhaps tempered with respect, before the Tree withdrew entirely from his consciousness.

There came a commotion of large boots in the hallway. Miri sighed and removed her arm from around his waist, which left him feeling rather foolishly bereft. He sent another glance at the screen. The countdown at the bottom corner gave landing time in less than a local hour.

"Sounds like our assistants are here," Miri said, as Diglon Rifle entered the parlor and stood to one side for Nelirikk.

Val Con waved a hand at the screen.

"This ship will be landing in our back field very soon. Captain Waitley specifically requested Nelirikk's presence and my own. Our captain claims the right to attend me."

"I had suspected as much," Nelirikk said gravely. "Diglon will stand for the captain's honor."

Bechimo's hull glowed faintly in Surebleak's midnight dark, casting a pale shadow on the rough local grass. At this hour, Val Con knew, the moons would have set and Chuck-Honey, the double star, would be dominating Surebleak's sparse starfield. Not that the starfield, or Chuck-Honey, were visible at this particular moment, Jeeves having taken it upon himself to make sure that the landing site was illuminated so well that one wished for protective lenses.

He and Nelirikk made a first line, not standing so near that they presented a single target. Miri and Diglon were a dozen steps to the rear, over her vociferous objections.

"I would like my sister to see me first, and Nelirikk, so that she will know that we have obeyed her instructions to the least letter," he said.

Miri shook her head.

"Ain't gonna let her off easy, are you?"

He raised an eyebrow.

"Is there some reason why I should?"

"You put it that way, not one that I can think of," she said cheerfully, and dropped back to stand with Diglon.

"*Bechimo* reports that he will open his hatch in point-three-oh seconds. Captain Waitley will be the first to debark," Jeeves said quietly.

"Thank you," Val Con said, and at that moment, the hatch lifted to reveal a sensibly dim interior from which a slim shadow emerged, walking deliberately. Pale hair tangled with light blew 'round her shoulders as she approached.

• • • ✵ • • •

"Wait for my order," the captain told the two tall figures. "I'll explain it to him first, so he won't be surprised."

"A rare courtesy," the administrative officer commented from his lean beside the galley door, "to a man you've just roused in the middle of his night."

Theo frowned, her temper not improved by the fact that he was speaking Liaden, just so he could pack in all the edges and points that sentence could bear—nor by the realization that he was right. Val Con *had* sounded a bit . . . sharp. They should've maybe waited until it was nearer to breakfast time, but—

"We called ahead," she said, voice snapping, "and we're running close to the deadline."

Clarence inclined his head, Liaden-wise, which was intended to set another dagger or two into her, and Theo was just about to ask if he didn't have anything useful to do, when it occurred to her that he might not just be amusing himself, but warning her about how she could expect to be greeted by her brother.

She flashed him another frown. He grinned at her, straightened out of his lean, bowed slightly, and left the galley.

Theo turned back to Chernak and Stost.

"*Bechimo* will convey my order when it's time for you to come forward. Do you understand me?"

"Captain," said Chernak gravely. "We await your order."

"Right," she said, and before she could repeat herself again, *Bechimo* spoke.

"Theo, I am opening the hatch."

The field was bright—brighter than it had seemed on *Bechimo*'s screens. Theo squinted, just making out four shadows—mixed tall and less tall—standing a little distance from the base of the ramp.

Four? she thought, hesitating at the end of the ramp.

Of course four, she told herself. Miri would've absolutely come with Val Con, especially if he was as irritable as Clarence seemed to think he had a right to be; and Nelirikk would have brought his own backup—Diglon or Hazenthull, going by the tall factor. That was good, actually. Two for two.

"Jeeves, is it possible to achieve a less punishing brilliance?" Val Con asked from inside the glare. "It is not our purpose to blind the pilot."

"Certainly, Master Val Con," Jeeves answered from

somewhere to Theo's left. "My apologies, Captain Waitley."

The light dimmed, mellowing from white to yellow. The shadows melted into Val Con and Nelirikk, standing nearest the ramp, and Miri, just moving up to stand beside her lifemate, Diglon a couple steps behind her.

"Thank you," Theo said to the field in general, and stepped off the ramp, walking straight up to her brother.

He was wearing a high-necked sweater, dark trousers, and boots, a cold-weather coat open over the sweater. It gave her a little start to see that he wasn't wearing his pilot's jacket.

He didn't look particularly irritated, but, then, Father hardly ever looked irritated—and never less so than when he was. Miri, her hands tucked into pockets, mostly seemed amused.

"Theo," he said.

Val Con had lifted an eyebrow, and that was trouble, right there. Best to grab the initiative before she lost any more counters.

She bowed slightly to a point exactly between him and Miri.

"Brother, sister, please forgive me for waking you untimely," she said, *Bechimo* pushing the Liaden words in the proper mode into the front of her mind. She *recognized* Low Liaden, which was spoken between kin and good friends, though she couldn't reliably hit it, especially when she was nervous. Which, she admitted—just to herself and *Bechimo*—she was.

"You pled necessity, I believe," Val Con murmured, not exactly encouraging, but at least giving her room to explain herself.

"I did," she admitted. "Necessity—several times

over. Still, I ought to have been more gentle of your own requirements."

"*Multiple* necessities?" Both eyebrows were up now. "Theo, you do me too much honor."

She sighed.

"I really am sorry," she said in Terran. "It's not like I *planned* it."

Miri laughed.

"They just sorta pile up, don't they?" she said. "Noticed it myself."

Still grinning, she nodded.

"It's good to see you, Theo, though you're right that the hour could've been better. Is there a reason you wanted us all out here for this, 'stead of inside, where there's tea and what's liable to be a three-course formal meal, if we give Mrs. ana'Tak much more time in the kitchen?"

"Well . . . yes." Theo bit her lip. "I—that is."

She stopped and took a breath, the . . . well, the *speech* . . . she'd worked out in her head suddenly seeming much less clear than it might be, to somebody who hadn't been there . . .

"How *many* necessities, I wonder?" Val Con asked softly.

She looked into his face. "Three."

"An agreeable number. Which was the first to overtake you?"

"Well—the ship." She gestured toward the pod mount. "It came out of—out of the same place *Bechimo* caught that teapot I showed you."

Val Con nodded.

She sighed, suddenly feeling calmer, which could've been *Bechimo*'s doing—or her nerves steadying themselves, now that they were on course.

Inner calm, she told herself, and took another breath.

"*Bechimo* and Joyita figured the name was something like *Spiral Dance*, which—if it was—Clarence said she belonged to Clan Korval. We boarded; there wasn't any crew . . . only—a tree, in a pot, strapped into the copilot's chair. We moved it over and put it in 'ponics. Kara says it's doing fine; grown some, even. The ship—" She took a deep breath.

"*Bechimo* wouldn't risk the Struven aboard, which is why we locked her onto cargo rails."

"I understand. So, the first necessity is explained. We may leave the ship where it is for now. What next befell you?"

"Next . . ." she looked at Nelirikk, who gazed down at her impassively, then back to Val Con.

"Next," she said, "another ship came through—the *wreck* of another ship came through," she corrected herself.

"There were survivors, and we—we picked them up."

Val Con closed his eyes.

"Survivors?" said Miri. "Soldiers or civilians?"

She took a hand out of her pocket and wove her fingers through Val Con's. He opened his eyes.

Theo looked at them doubtfully, but Miri gave her a grin and a nod, so she told out the rest.

"One civilian—Grakow, the ship's cat. The other two—they're not soldiers. Not exactly soldiers. They're pathfinders . . . and—they . . ."

She stopped and blew her bangs out of her eyes. It had been her intention to tell this tale fully, to do justice to Chernak and Stost, but—she'd gotten all these people out of bed at an unreasonable hour; they were cold and cranky, which truthfully, if it had been turnabout, she'd have been, too. Maybe it was best to summarize.

"Making it short," she said, mostly to Miri, "they—from their perspective, they'd just left a war zone. Their enemy—what they call 'the Enemy'—was winning, and they—and everybody else—were . . . running away.

"Their orders, if they happened to survive the retreat, were to reunite with their Troop or, if that wasn't an option, to offer service to a ranking civilian authority."

"Surely, Korval is not a ranking civilian authority," Val Con said. "Unless you mean us to transport them to Temp Headquarters?"

"Er—no. They—they say that the Yxtrang . . ."

She shot a glance at Nelirikk. Still impassive. Waiting. Diglon, at his back, was also waiting.

"They say that the—the *now-Yxtrang* aren't . . . their . . . Troop," Theo finished, omitting Chernak's exact opinion, which had included the word *pirates* among others that were considerably less polite. "Since you have a corps of Yx—of former Yxtrang in your service, I thought . . ."

"I see," Val Con said before she could say exactly what she *had* thought. "Please do not vex yourself to provide a fuller explanation at this moment. Are these persons quite civilized, or have you brought them to us in chains?"

"What? Oh, no! They're civilized! Real quick learners, too!"

"You relieve me," he said politely.

"Hevelin likes them, too," Theo continued, then recalled that Val Con might not be completely informed on that front, either.

"Hevelin is the norbear ambassador, certified by the Pilots Guild. He—he met Father, and—I think—Pilot Caylon, too."

"Did he indeed? What a very small universe we live in." Val Con considered her. "Am I correct that we have now attained your three necessities?"

"Um . . . no. There's one more thing."

"And it is . . . ?"

"There's a Scout—a team of Scouts. They collect Old Tech and—destroy it. They—well, they want to confiscate *Bechimo.* They say they have a warrant, and that the only way we can avoid confiscation is by an appeal to a higher-ranking Scout. So, I said I'd meet them here and that I would abide by your—by *Scout Commander yos'Phelium's*—judgment."

There was a pause that felt long. *Very* long.

"This Scout who leads a team of Scouts," Val Con said at last. "His name and rank?"

"Captain yos'Thadi of *Chandra Marudas.* First mate is Menolly vas'Anamac." She consulted *Bechimo*'s clock and added: "They'll likely be here tomorrow and—Captain yos'Thadi isn't going to be real happy, since we beat him into port."

"On top of all, a wager."

Val Con looked to Miri.

"*Cha'trez,* I believe that I shall return to active duty. You will do Korval honor, I know."

"Oh, c'mon; this'll be fun."

"Do you say so?"

"I do. Look—I'll start."

Miri grinned at Theo.

"You wanna call your pair out, so Nelirikk can get a look at 'em?"

"Yes," she said, and saw a quick glimpse of the galley in the space behind her eyes, Chernak and Stost rising to their feet and walking, Stost in the lead, down the hall toward the hatch.

"Their names are Chernak and Stost," she said to Nelirikk. "They speak Trade."

"With the captain's permission," he said.

"Sort 'em out," Miri told him. "For the best good of Korval."

He saluted.

"Rifle, attend me."

"Explorer."

They approached the ramp, Nelirikk a step ahead of Diglon, and waited for the two long shadows who had just stepped out of the hatch. Each had a case slung over one shoulder.

"What's in the cases?" Miri asked.

"I don't *know*," Theo confessed. "I *think* they're supposed to give the cases—and their service—to . . ."

"The ranking civilian authority. Naturally." Val Con finished and looked to Miri, who showed him her free hand, fingers folded into palm, one thumb up—pilot's sign for *all good.*

"I believe that it is now my turn," Val Con said. "As my lifemate has assured me that this will be fun, I have the pleasant duty of informing Captain Waitley, my sister, that her room has been made ready for her, and that the House rejoices at her return. A suite has been prepared to receive your crew. May I know how many crew? I only wish to be certain that our arrangements do not fall short."

She'd talked this over with Kara—rather, Kara had talked it over with her.

"Theo, your brother has asked you to come home," she'd said. "He has been remarkably patient and has not invoked your delm—" No matter how many times she was told otherwise, Kara persisted in believing that Val Con was Theo's delm—

"He will expect that you will stay, at least until some—*less perilous* route can be devised. He will also offer lodging to your crew—which is a gentle courtesy and ought not to be refused." She had looked wry for a moment, before adding, "Especially as you will be dropping quite a number of problems into his lap!"

"Four crew," Theo said now. "The pathfinders. Grakow. And Hevelin."

"Ah, yes, the ambassador. Will he wish his own quarters?"

He was, she suspected, having fun with her—well, wasn't that what Miri'd said?

Theo met his eyes and asked *Bechimo* to have the crew get ready to debark.

"Thank you. The ambassador will bunk with me."

"Excellent. The Southern Suite has six rooms around a common parlor, and a small galley. Your crew will have ample space to relax."

"Actually," Theo said, belatedly realizing her error, "Comm Officer Joyita will remain with the ship."

"There is no need," Val Con said. "You are quite secure here."

Theo shook her head.

"Comm Officer Joyita will remain with the ship," she repeated.

Val Con studied her face closely, his eyes brilliantly green.

"I see," he said at last, and glanced to Miri.

"*Cha'trez*, I believe Captain Waitley would welcome a cup of tea."

"Could use a cup myself," Miri agreed, and reached out to take Theo's hand.

"Car's right over here, Captain. Your pathfinders'll be fine with Nelirikk and Diglon."

"Well, but—my crew . . ."

"Tommy Lee is on his way," Jeeves said, from everywhere and nowhere. "He will escort your crew to the morning parlor, Captain. A buffet has been laid."

She felt *Bechimo* relaying that to Clarence and had a brief glimpse of his unperturbed face and easy nod.

All proper and reasonable, then.

"Thank you," she said and allowed herself to be taken from the field, Miri's hand warm around hers. "Tea would be welcome."

They all three sat in the front, though that meant Theo was kind of crowding Miri. Val Con put the car into gear and made a wide turn. Now that the light was behind them, Theo could see the shadow of the Tree on the ground, and the house just a short distance ahead, windows glittering like jewels.

Val Con apparently didn't have anything to say, nor did Miri. Theo tried not to worry about exactly *how* Nelirikk would be "sorting out" Stost and Chernak, when they apparently hadn't been included in the room count . . .

"Ah," Val Con said, guiding the car into a spot by a lighted door. "I am remiss, Sister. In all the excitement of your landing I had forgotten that I have news for you."

Theo winced, thinking of the likeliest things he'd heard. Still . . .

"Really?" she said. "What kind?"

"The most joyous news is always of kin," he answered, over the snap of the car doors opening. "Your mother is on Surebleak and requests that you call upon her at your earliest convenience."

• • • ※ • • •

"Which of us here is senior in service?" Chernak asked, in Trade. It was a reasonable question, between soldiers, and appropriately asked. Absent a specialist, or a pathfinder, the leadership position in any meeting of Troop went to the soldier with the highest rank and service time. In the case of a meeting of pathfinders or specialists, the leadership rule held.

She did not discount the fourth of their number, who looked to be an experienced soldier of the Troop. Not even a pathfinder discounted the abilities of a line soldier. Most of her concern in this instance, though, was Nelirikk Explorer, house security and personal aide to a captain who was twice a Hero.

The captain Nelirikk served—they had seen her on screen while they waited in the galley for Captain Waitley's word, Joyita obligingly providing zoom. She was small, the captain, which Chernak also knew better than to discount, having lately been reminded of what small might accomplish.

So, all respect to the captain and her aide, and to the honest soldier—*all* respect, though it would suit her well, if she were found to be elder among the three pathfinders present.

"In terms of service," Stost said, "I am equal to Chernak, who has served more than ten thousand days with honor. I am junior to her in order of birth."

Nelirikk looked at each of them in turn, face and

stance relaxed, very much a soldier who was comfortable in his duty.

"Ten thousand days is service, indeed. Service in such conditions as you have faced must be counted three times. I cannot hope to match such valor."

That was well said, thought Chernak, and wondered for a moment if she had won the engagement as easily as that.

"However," Nelirikk continued, "in this place, in this campaign, and in service to Hero Captain Miri Robertson—*I* am elder. It cannot be otherwise, Pathfinders, as you must agree."

Chernak did not sigh. She hadn't really expected to prevail.

"Jeeves," Nelirikk said, apparently speaking to the air around them, "will you make the practice room available to us?" He paused and again studied them, one, then the other.

"Unless the Pathfinders wish to contest for rank?"

Chernak raised her hands, showing them empty.

"We agree that you are elder here. Despite our service, we are new on this field. Our commanders have been lost. Our Troop has been lost. Even the Enemy has been lost, if the histories Captain Waitley provided are accurate. We are under orders, and we would complete our mission. That is our purpose now. Captain Waitley brings us here, to her brother and to your captain, because you have given oath, and serve a civilian authority, as soldiers were made to do."

There was a pause, as if Nelirikk had heard that which startled him.

"We have much to talk about," he said after a moment. "Jeeves?"

"The practice room awaits you," the disembodied voice spoke again, as it had in answer to Captain Waitley's brother. It was, Chernak supposed, another such Work as Joyita—a not-Great Work, as he himself insisted, and yet like that which the Enemy had created to subvert and destroy.

"Thank you," Nelirikk said. "Pathfinders, follow me. Rifle, take rear guard."

"Yes," said the soldier, who bore no rifle that Chernak could see.

Nelirikk strode off; they followed, walking side by side in consideration of the rear guard.

Their way continued to be lighted, here and there interrupted by shadows. Stost abruptly halted inside one such, much larger than the rest, and stood perfectly still, craning his head back.

Chernak looked up, sighting along his—

Above them loomed a mighty tree, its proud branches stretching up until it seemed the stars must scrape through the boughs on their march across the night.

This, too, they had seen on screen, as *Bechimo* came in to this rough docking. They had known it was large. But from the ground, and they in its shadow—it was vast.

"Captain Waitley," said Stost, "should remove the small tree from her ship soon, Elder."

"That Tree . . ." Nelirikk's voice drew their attention from the heights.

"Korval's Tree is many hundreds of Standards old. It is the very Tree that Jela brought off of a world that successfully defended itself against the Enemy."

Jela was given weight, as if Nelirikk spoke of a mentor or an elder who had taught him much. Chernak put that question aside for the moment. A being, any being, that had held against the Enemy . . . that being—that service—required acknowledgment.

Stost saluted first, bringing his heels smartly together.

Chernak saluted, and surprisingly, the soldier called Rifle also saluted, his face tilted upward. Lastly, Nelirikk came to attention, fist striking shoulder.

"Arak, Yxtrang," Stost said, voice raised so that it might be heard by the very highest of branches. It was the soldier's form, and if Stost named this old and courageous being a soldier, well—was it not?

"Arak ek zenorth," Chernak said, finishing the phrase.

Honor, Soldier. Honor and glory.

"All honor," said Rifle, speaking Trade, not Troop.

"Glorious its deeds," Nelirikk added, also in Trade.

They stood so for six breaths by unspoken accord before, one by one, they let their salutes go.

"Come," said Nelirikk. "The practice room awaits."

. . . ✵ . . .

They had gained the house and the morning parlor before Theo decided that Val Con was serious.

"What's Kamele *doing* on Surebleak?" she demanded, as Val Con placed his coat and Miri's on the window seat.

He turned and met her eyes, his expression serious—which could mean that he actually *was* serious . . . or that he was pulling her leg.

"She came to liberate Father," he said.

"Liberate Father?" Theo stared at him, speechless in the face of twin impossibilities. Kamele . . . a scholar of Delgado, researcher and teacher, who had lived all her life on a Safe World . . . Kamele traveling by herself to *Surebleak* to—to—no! It was ridiculous.

Equally ridiculous was the notion that *Father* could possibly *require* a rescue—from anyone, really—but surely, least of all from Kamele.

Val Con had moved over to the buffet while she struggled with this and was handing Miri a cup. Theo stepped to his side.

"Did she?" she asked. "Liberate Father."

"Well, she might have done," her brother answered, like he was just now considering that possibility, "only he was not to home. Allow me to draw you a cup of tea, Sister."

Theo opened her mouth—then closed it.

Val Con handed her a cup, which she took automatically.

"Thank you."

"You are quite welcome," he answered, turning back to fill his own cup.

"Is he to home now?" she asked, when he had finished with the urn and had turned again to face her.

"Alas, he is still unavailable."

He raised his cup and sipped.

Theo did the same, taking a moment to savor the blend.

"Is Kamele staying here—in this house?"

"Ah, no. She is lending her expertise to a project which has been undertaken by our Aunt Kareen. They have together taken a house in the city in order to be close to their sources, and—"

"Wait." Theo raised a hand. Val Con obligingly paused and had another sip of tea, watching her over the rim of his cup.

"Kamele is working with—with Father's sister? Sharing a house?"

"Indeed. They get along delightfully. Our aunt has said to me that your mother's insights and research skills have been of inestimable value."

"I—How did she get here? Kamele, I mean. Surebleak's not exactly on the cruise ship lines."

"You must give us a moment," Val Con said reprovingly. "There is a process upon which we are well embarked. Another six years and I daresay we will have all the cruise ships one could wish for.

"To your point, however—you must be certain to ask your mother how she came to Surebleak. I found the tale . . . enlightening."

He paused, head half turned toward the door. In the sudden silence, Theo could hear voices in the hallway.

"Sounds like your crew's coming in," Miri said. She slid her arm through Val Con's and the two of them stepped toward the window, clearing the way from the door to the buffet.

"The board is yours, Captain," Val Con murmured.

• • • ✵ • • •

"My captain will wish to know your mission," Nelirikk said. "Whether you offer her your knives or not."

They sat around a table in a large room otherwise lacking furniture, though there were exercise machines of the kind familiar to them from their time aboard *Bechimo*, and also an empty area ample enough to practice hand-to-hand, with one comrade or more.

The table held several large pitchers of water, and also plates of cheeses and breads. The Hero captain, then, did not mean to starve answers out of them.

At least, not yet.

Stost smiled to himself. It had been a strange

campaign since they strapped into crew seats aboard a ship none had expected to survive the blockade they sought to break.

In fact, most of those aboard had not survived. They two had, along with Grakow and, more briefly, the senior crew who brought them aboard, only because they had been deep in the belly of the ship in the engineering halls. They had escaped that doom and been picked up as survivors by *Bechimo*, Captain Waitley commanding.

Multiply lucky, he and Chernak. Some would say so. He might say so himself, having survived the mission that had killed all the others of their team, the riots on the docksides, the destruction of the ship they were aboard and, so it would appear, time itself.

Yes. They were lucky.

And here they stood, in a brave new universe, in which there was so much to learn, so much to explore.

The only thing which held them to the old universe, the old war . . . were their orders.

Stost sighed. Troop—even pathfinders—were simple at core. Resist the enemy; protect civilians; obey command; carry out orders.

The need to carry out the orders, to finish the mission, had been a constant rubbing at the back of his mind since Captain Waitley had plucked them from the wreckage of *Orbital Aid 370*. He and Chernak had been poised to assault a Great Work—which battle they could not have won—so that they might see the mission completed and themselves freed from duty.

What would happen, he wondered, as he listened to Chernak and Nelirikk talk in circles about what they would and would not reveal of their last mission . . .

What would happen, if they put the cases down and, as the senior ranking officers present, declared the mission complete?

It was not the first time he had thought along this path since their survival . . . since their probable . . . continued survival. He had not spoken to Chernak about it; not as such. He had dreamed it, somewhat, with Hevelin, whose advice and insights he had come to value.

But to lay such a thing before Chernak . . .

Chernak was senior. Chernak was conservative. Chernak would obey the orders, though it tied her to a lifetime of fruitless searching.

He . . . was junior. All his life he had followed his elder, protected her from folly and from death. She had led him well, protected him from folly and from death. It was duty—and something more.

They had been born within scant minutes of each other; they had never, except for brief periods of training and testing, been apart.

Brought from the creche early, they had served ten thousand days together, most of it in combat zones. They were not Ms; they had no obsolescence protocol woven into their DNA. They were X strain, and though most died in battle long before they had known the joy of serving ten thousand days, the literature suggested that—were they not in active combat conditions—they might live fifty or sixty more of these Standard Years.

The literature had not revealed, he admitted to himself, what might occur should they have no orders to fulfill. That was worrisome—but not as worrisome as the prospect of fifty years a-roving, looking for that which, as history strongly suggested, did not exist.

They had earned rest, thought Stost. They had earned . . . *peace.*

Though they vanished like frost under a breath, for lack of anything to hold them, still, it was time.

"The details of what we carry are not for your captain to know, all honor to her, unless she is, or serves, the ranking civilian authority of this universe."

It was not the first time Chernak had said this.

"There is no single civilian authority in this universe," Nelirikk said, which was perfectly true, as they knew for themselves. It was not the first time he had said that, either.

"Captain Waitley brought you here, to Clan Korval, because Clan Korval holds the oath of three Yxtrang who have left the Troop. Lacking a single civilian authority, it would seem that your orders send you toward the Troop, as we move away. But I will tell you—now that your orbit has intersected theirs, neither my captain nor the Scout will allow you to proceed until they are made aware of the details of your mission, and have looked upon the contents of those cases."

Chernak sighed and reached for her water glass. It was an impasse, Stost thought, and surely Chernak knew it, too. Beset and growing angry, Chernak might choose to understand that Captain Waitley had brought them into a trap.

But, thought Stost, Captain Waitley had not brought them into a trap.

Captain Waitley had delivered them to an opportunity.

"The contents of the cases are to be given to an appropriate—" Chernak began again.

Stost leaned forward and put two fingers on her wrist. She paused, looking at those fingers for a long moment. It was a sign between them. It meant *I will take point now*. It meant, also, *Back me*.

Chernak met his eyes and closed her right in a quick wink, surrendering the lead to him.

Stost leaned forward and looked into Nelirikk's serious brown face. A good man, he thought; a man who served with his whole heart. A man who was fortunate in his captain.

"We will detail our mission, and show the contents of our cases to your captain and her second," he said calmly. "Also, we solicit her aid."

Beside him, he heard Chernak draw a long, shuddering breath.

...✵...

They were an orderly mob, Miri thought, leaning companionably against Val Con's shoulder and sipping the tea he'd drawn for her. Nice tea, it was. What was called Evening Tea, meant to relax a body and ease it toward a full night's slumber.

To be honest about it, she could use some more sleep. Her eyeballs felt gritty, and while she *could* go on, if somebody was rushing their position, it was stupid not to take a rest if everything was quiet.

Which, granted, it wasn't yet, but it oughtn't be too long before they could leave Theo and hers to themselves, and to staff.

At the back of the mob, walking easy, was a towheaded lad, somewhat tall for a Liaden, or otherwise short for a Terran. He caught her eye across the room and slipped through the knot-up at the doorway like a hot knife through wax. A heartbeat later, he was saluting.

"Captain."

Miri straightened and gave him a nod.

"Tommy," she said. "They give you any trouble?"

"No'm. Truth said, they're kind of subdued." A smile twitched at the corner of his mouth.

"I'm guessing some of them have watches."

"And at least two," Val Con murmured, glancing around the room, "are wary of dragons."

"That too, sir."

Tommy Lee was Liaden, but he counted himself a merc. Terran was his best language, and he was easier with a salute than a bow.

"So you know, ma'am. Exec O'Berin tells me that the cat decided to stay aboard with the comm officer."

"That's the cat's choice, I guess. If Captain Waitley needs her or him out here, I reckon it'll get done."

"Yes, ma'am. Anything more for me?"

"I think we can handle 'em from here," Miri said. "Grab yourself a snack; you're off duty."

"Thank you, ma'am. Sir. Good morning to you both."

He melted away, not stopping at the buffet laid for the guests, but slipping down the hall. Mrs. ana'Tak would make sure he got fed. Even if he wasn't hungry.

There was a stir among their visitors, and Theo stepped forward, holding a roly-poly cuteness in her arms. Miri'd seen pictures of norbears, but she'd never met one in the fur. This one looked to be old, with grey stripes in its rusty orange fur.

"This is Ambassador Hevelin," Theo said, holding the creature up so that it was nose to nose with Val Con.

"Hevelin, this is my brother Val Con yos'Phelium, and his lifemate Miri Robertson Tiazan."

Hevelin burbled and extended a paw to Val Con, clearly wanting contact.

Val Con, however, didn't offer a hand in return.

"I am delighted to meet Hevelin and look forward to sitting down with him on some other occasion, to share dreams and acquaintance," he said. "At this moment, I plead an excess of excitement and lack of sleep."

Another burble; Hevelin twisted to look at Miri, eyes that were unexpectedly knowing meeting her gaze.

"You can visit with me later, too," she told him. "Tomorrow's a work day, and I'm already up too late."

Hevelin sighed and wriggled. Theo lifted him to her shoulder and turned to beckon the tall Terran male with red hair and a very familiar face.

"I believe you are acquainted with my administrative officer and copilot, Clarence O'Berin," Theo said. "Clarence—"

But Clarence didn't wait for the rest of the niceties. He stepped forward and took Miri's free hand, bowing over it like a proper Liaden gentleman.

"It's glad I am to see you again," he said, voice lilting—which was nothing but plain and fancy flirting. Tweaking Val Con, she supposed.

"Hi, Clarence," she said cordially. "You're looking good. Flying with Theo must agree with you."

He straightened and grinned at her before turning to Val Con and giving him the heavy nod that was an acceptable Liaden greeting between pilots.

"Pilot," he said, the lilt gone and his tone neutral.

"Pilot," Val Con replied, in very nearly the same tone.

Clarence stepped back, and Theo waved a Liaden woman forward, her blond hair done in a club at her neck and her shoulders a little too straight under her uniform blouse.

"This is Kara ven'Arith, chief engineer," she said. "Kara, here are my brother, Val Con yos'Phelium, and my sister, Miri Robertson Tiazan."

Kara's bow showed she'd had upbringing, which was good, Miri thought. Theo needed somebody around who would insist on observing even the boring parts of courtesy.

"Sir," Kara murmured. "Lady."

"Kara ven'Arith," Val Con answered. "Thank you for your service to my sister."

"Sir," she said again, straightening carefully. She took one step to the side, and Clarence took her arm gently, leading her to the buffet.

Next—

Well, now, here was an art piece, Miri thought. Wavy red-brown hair and dark brown eyes; slim and dainty. He moved like a Scout, too, so this must be—

"Win Ton yo'Vala," Theo said. "He's—"

"The Scout who put events in train," Val Con broke in. He inclined his head, very slightly, his expression of bland intensity boding not so well for the art piece. "You and I must come together and discuss some few matters, when you are at liberty."

Win Ton yo'Vala took a breath, and bowed.

"Sir," he said, not quite so bland. "I am at your service."

"Excellent," Val Con said, and the Scout slipped away toward the buffet, so relieved to escape with his life that he forgot to bow to her.

Theo's sigh was audible; the look she gave Miri doubtful.

"No offense taken," she said easily. "Everybody's tired—and he's scared Val Con's going to bite him."

Theo shared the doubtful look with her brother, who smiled at her sweetly.

Right. She wasn't the only one who'd be in a better mood after a nap. And tomorrow—gods. Tomorrow.

Miri raised her voice so that she could be heard above the modest racket going on.

"All ears on me, please."

The room went silent.

She nodded and smiled.

"The House has made a suite available to crew members. When you're ready to find it, please touch the bell pad by the door, and one of the staff will come and lead you there. This is not a hint for you to disperse. We, however"—she waved a hand between her and Val Con—"were awakened in the middle of our night, and sleep calls us."

She gave another cordial nod in the direction of the bunch of them.

"Please be welcome in our house—and good night."

Val Con stepped forward and slipped his arm through hers, turning them toward the door.

Bechimo's crew fell back to give them room, and they were out, going down the hall to the back stairs.

Miri sighed.

"That idea you had about going back on active duty?" she said.

"Yes?"

"I'm beginning to see your point."

IV

VAL CON HAD BREWED A POT OF THE CITRUS-MINT TEA—Joyful Sunrise by name—that Miri'd gotten used to as her morning beverage when she'd been pregnant with Lizzie. It managed to be an eye-opener without packing any caffeine, and the gods knew both of them needed their eyes opened this morning.

A plate of cheese pastries made up the rest of breakfast: emergency rations, that was what, so they could talk about strategy and tactics in the privacy of their own suite.

"So," she said, from her curl in the corner of the sofa. "I'm figuring it's best for all to let the Road Boss have a day off to sort out kin."

Val Con nodded, sipped tea, and sighed, maybe in pleasure, maybe in anticipation of what the day was likely to bring.

Wasn't neither one of them making a dive for the pastries, Miri noted. Maybe in a minute or five, after the tea'd done its work.

"I will call the Emerald and ask that a note be placed on the door of the office," he said, leaning back into the sofa cushions, "though one of us will certainly need to go in tomorrow. We dare not risk an extended closure with the Survey Team on port and doing its work."

"True enough, but we're not on tomorrow yet."

She sipped her tea and met his eyes.

"For today—who's first up: the delm, or Theo's brother and sister?"

"How long do you think we can conceal Father's presence from Theo?" he asked.

"Point. So . . . you're of a mind to welcome them back as full clan members? Gods know, we could use them."

He nodded.

"Our numbers are so low that two more would be welcome, indeed, and that is before we consider the benefits to clan and to delm, of their thoughts and experience."

Miri eyed him.

"But," she said.

He gave her a faint smile. "But despite the clear benefits to the clan, I am of a mind to give them a ship, histories, licenses, and such funds as they are likely to require in order to establish themselves in a courier business."

Miri frowned at him. "Because they're a danger to the clan? Having had the Uncle tinkering around with them?"

"That must be a consideration. There is also the consideration that, if we are to introduce two yos'Phelium pilots newly returned to the clan, let us say, after the completion of a lengthy assignment elsewhere—Surebleak will accept it. However, it has been my observation that the DOI, for an instance, can count; and the Council of Clans, for another, is entirely cognizant of Korval's roll of members."

He moved his shoulders. "It is the same case as pertains to Theo: being of Korval is more of a danger to them, than a benefit."

Miri sipped her tea, thinking.

"You do not agree," Val Con said.

"Only partly. I agree that it'll be tricky to explain them, but I don't think we can afford to give away two able-bodied clan members. True enough that the clan would be taking on the protection of two more, but they're not exactly helpless, are they?"

Then she shook her head. "There's gotta be a middle ground . . . at *least* a middle ground. Lemme think about it. In the meantime, though, we got tests on-site that'll tell us if they're themselves or the Uncle's toys. I'll take care of that."

"I daresay we would have experienced a ruckus, if they are not themselves, but it is best to be thorough.

"So. You shall think. I shall think. We will speak again later in the day, to once again compare our thoughts. Perhaps the middle ground will make itself apparent to us."

"I agree," Miri said.

"That then is the delm's business for the morning."

He put his cup on the table and lifted the pot. "More tea?"

"Please."

"So," said Miri said, newly curled into the comfy corner, and with freshened cup in hand. "What're your plans for today?"

"Today, I believe I shall first have a conversation with Scout yo'Vala in an attempt to learn what was in his mind when he called my sister to the attention of a Free Ship, and what his intentions may be going forward."

Miri grinned.

"You start in on him like that, he'll take a fright."

"Good." Val Con raised his cup, lowered it.

"After young yo'Vala, I hope to find that my sister has the time and the grace to speak with me, so that I might achieve a fuller understanding of her business with the artifact collection team. That first, I think, as their arrival seems imminent. Then, assuming that Theo's patience holds, I would also like to learn how, exactly, she came upon *Spiral Dance*. The coords for that location are of more than passing interest to me, but on that topic I foresee a war of wills not only with Theo, but with *Bechimo*."

He paused, sipped tea, and lowered the cup.

"I would also like to know for certain if Comm Officer Joyita is a Free Intelligence, or if he has some other reason to prefer the ship to the house."

He glanced at her.

"In light of the coming call for judgment from *Chandra Marudas*, you know."

"Not expecting Captain yos'Thadi to be particularly sweet-tempered by the time he finds us?"

"He will almost certainly be in high dudgeon." He lifted an eyebrow. "This is not to say that I fail to sympathize. One cannot but suppose that Theo was irritating in the extreme."

"Besides beating him into port," Miri murmured.

"Indeed. If a lifemate may ask it, what plans have you for this morning?"

"Well, first off is Nelirikk, who'll want me to talk to the pathfinders personal, unless they were bad kiddies and got themselves shot and killed on the overnight. In which case, I expect Theo to challenge me to a duel."

She leaned forward and picked up a pastry.

"Comes to it, and whether they're dead or quick, I'm going to have to debrief Theo," she said. "Prolly do that after you've had your talk with her"—she blinked thoughtfully—"since she'll be in a bad mood, anyway."

"There is no reason to place yourself in peril," Val Con said, choosing a pastry for himself.

"No getting around it is what I'm thinking. What're the odds Comm Officer Joyita's an AI?"

"I would say it is a near surety, which means that I will need to consider my judgment very carefully, indeed."

"Help if you could arrange a meeting," Miri said.

"It would, yes. I fear I will be quite tiresome on that point when I speak with my sister. What shall you do if the pathfinders have been clever and well behaved overnight?"

"That's a puzzle. I'm taking it that we don't necessarily want to add to the House Troop?"

He grimaced, took a bite of pastry, and shook his head.

"House Troops are a thing of the past. Of the *distant* past. There has been no need even for outworld clans to maintain their own forces for . . . some time. Recall how difficult it was for Aunt Kareen to locate the correct particle to describe our current Troop's relationship to the House; *nor* had been all but forgotten, even to the Code. Certainly, there are none but ours in use."

"Well, but we're special," Miri said soothingly. "Well-known fact. I'll know more after I've talked to the pathfinders one on two. Might be they'd fit in as mercs—that could be the cleanest solution."

She nibbled on a corner of her pastry, eyes narrowed at nothing.

"I'll know more after I talk with them," she said again.

"I will also ask Theo what she was thinking, to bring this pair to us."

"Well, that's easy, ain't it?" Miri said. "First thing, she'd be seeing there were survivors and, being captain on the spot, that it was up to her to make sure they kept on surviving. Not much to think about there—especially with Theo, given the general family tendency to run *toward* trouble.

"Once she had 'em safe, that'd be about the time she'd realize that she didn't know what to do with 'em. Can't turn 'em loose to fend for themselves: no money, no papers, no work, no language. They don't recognize the local-universe Yxtrang as having anything to do with them, so she can't put 'em on a bus to Temp Headquarters. There's just *not* any central civilian authority like they're wanting to connect up with, so . . . best to come someplace where she knows there's other Yxtrang that don't recognize the now-Troop, either, and hope *we* can figure out what to do."

She blinked thoughtfully.

"Not too bad an idea, really. We've got experts on hand and access to resources. If we're not necessarily best equipped to solve for them, we're definitely better situated than Theo is—or was."

Val Con sighed.

"Agreed. Shall we plan on a private tea this afternoon, in order to compare notes and discuss possible approaches?"

"That'll depend on if Captain yos'Thadi arrives in the meantime, won't it? I didn't catch the idea from Theo that he's gonna be willing to wait long for that judgment, which—wait a minute . . ."

She held up a hand to keep him still while she chased the notion for a second—then nodded.

"I'm thinking I'll put Ms. kaz'Ineo and 'prentice

Hufstead on notice that there's going to be an actual real-time judgment happening—if you're all right with having an audience."

Val Con sighed.

"I fear that the audience for this will eventually extend to the expanding edges of the universe," he said wryly.

She grinned.

"Right. Jeeves'll be recording. We'll do a live feed 'stead of bringing any more bodies into it. Don't want to add to the confusion."

Val Con laughed.

"When have we done otherwise?" he asked, and Miri gave him a grin back.

"There's that, now, isn't there?"

...✵...

Hevelin was asleep in the basket of loose leaves, grasses, and flowers that Mr. pel'Kana had considerately put in a warm corner, with a view out the window.

Since he *was* asleep, Theo figured that the arrangements met with his approval. The basket and the bowl of water she'd put nearby were temporary measures. Mr. pel'Kana had promised to have the gardener provide a box of living plants for the ambassador's pleasure and had also said that he would look up an aerated bowl he'd seen just recently in one of the back pantries, so that the ambassador's water would be circulated and cool.

That, Theo told herself, as she stood in the long windows overlooking the garden that was growing in the center of the house's square—that was everything that was good, and she was grateful to the house, like Liadens said, for its care. The trouble was, after having seen the crew and Hevelin settled, taken a shower, checked in with *Bechimo* and Joyita...

Theo wasn't sleepy.

Well, she thought grumpily, *of course* she wasn't sleepy; she was in the middle of her on-shift, ship-time, plus having taken a very substantial nap during approach. She wouldn't be sleepy *for hours*, and there was the other thing.

Kamele was on Surebleak, eager, so said Val Con, to see her daughter.

Theo frowned down at the garden. She knew that it was coming on to local morning—that was *Bechimo*, keeping her informed on the details so she could concentrate on more important things.

By her reckoning, *Chandra Marudas* and yos'Thadi would be arriving on Surebleak within the local half-day. After that, so she also reckoned, things were likely to get even more complicated than they already were... which meant that the window for seeing Kamele... was pretty small.

In fact, it was exactly these few hours right now, at the bright new edge of the day, when she would have enough time to—not explain herself exactly, but to catch up with her mother, and to hear about her trip, and her arrival at Surebleak.

Fine, then.

"Jeeves?" she said softly, like Hevelin would wake up if she talked any louder than a whisper. "I'm going into town to have breakfast with my mother. Could you send a car around for me, please?"

"Yes, Captain Waitley," Jeeves said, soft-voiced as well. "Tommy Lee will drive you to town. The car will be at the front door in five minutes."

Theo frowned.

"Just the car's fine; I know how to drive."

"The necessity of a driver has nothing to do with your ability to drive," Jeeves said. "It has everything to do with status and *melant'i* as it manifests in the Surebleakean culture. People of importance are driven; they have 'hands—bodyguards—to insure their safety and to advertise their importance. Master Val Con has a driver when he goes into the city, as does Miri. You are the Road Boss's sister, the captain of a starship; a person of more than ordinary importance. You are not sent naked out onto the streets."

Theo opened her mouth. Closed it.

This wasn't an argument she could win, she thought. Jeeves was every bit as stubborn as *Bechimo*—and older, too. If she didn't agree to do it his way, there wouldn't *ever* be a car available for her to drive into the city so she could find out what her mother thought she was doing. And if she got too stubborn herself, Jeeves would call Val Con or—worse—Miri, to lay down the rules.

"It would shame the House," Jeeves said softly, "to have you drive yourself, bereft of security. Perhaps more significantly, it might be seen as a . . . signal to a certain sort of person that the House held you cheap; that you were, in fact, their legitimate prey."

Theo sighed—and nodded, holding her hands up to show empty palms.

"Right. Please tell Tommy Lee that I'll be glad of his company."

"He will be most gratified to hear it," Jeeves said, without a hint of irony. "Five minutes, at the front door."

• • • ✵ • • •

"So," Miri said to Nelirikk's sterner-than-usual face, "what *is* in the cases?"

Nelirikk was tired, that was plain. Nelirikk was more than a little irritated. Despite being a member of a warrior race not particularly known for their good humor, Nelirikk was most usually even-tempered. That he was letting irritation show couldn't be good news.

"They give you a bad time?"

He shook his head.

"They were respectful and soldierly. They laid out their terms and would negotiate no further, understanding, as they said, that I was the captain's aide and could not speak for her."

All right. *That* was what rankled. He'd figured to hand her a solution this morning, and the pathfinders hadn't cooperated.

"What're their terms?"

"They will give the cases, and the contents, to Hero Captain Robertson. In exchange, she will find for them employment in keeping with their skills. They have been a team, lifelong, and will not for any reason be separated."

"No reason to fix something that works," Miri said. "They fit to be seen?"

"They have been awaiting the captain's attention."

"Then let's not keep 'em in suspense any longer," she said, heading down the hall toward the exercise room, Nelirikk a tall, silent shadow at her back.

Diglon opened the door from the inside, with a salute so smart it could've driven itself into town. A bit much from Diglon, who was respectful and even a little shy, but not overly fond, now he had a choice, of soldiering. Apparently, there was a point to be made to the pathfinders.

"Hero Captain Miri Robertson arrives!" he rapped out. "Troops to attention!"

"Rifle," Miri said mildly, her return salute a study in moderation.

She strolled down the room toward two tall people standing at strict attention, each with a case tucked under the left arm, carry strap crossing the chest to the right shoulder.

Personal space was two steps wider for them than it was for her, she saw when she hit their boundary: just a little twitch near the right eye of the soldier on the left. She kept on, two steps more into *her* comfort zone, and stopped there to take their salutes.

They weren't long coming, and they were every bit as sharp as Diglon's had been.

She gave them the same courtesy she'd given Diglon, adding, "At ease," in Trade, just to see what she'd get.

They relaxed into something approaching parade rest. Good enough.

"I'm Captain Miri Robertson," she told them, looking up into lean brown faces, shape and features close enough they could've been sister and brother. "Identify yourselves."

"Captain!" said the one on the left. "Stost Strongline, Pathfinder, Captain."

"Strongline?" she asked.

"Captain! Captain Waitley gave us papers noting Strongline as our surname."

"I see." She turned to the one on the right, who looked like she wanted to go back to attention.

Instead, she took a deep breath and met Miri's eyes firmly.

"Chernak Strongline, Captain," she said. "Pathfinder."

"Stost Strongline, Chernak Strongline," Miri repeated with a nod, and then raised her voice like she wanted to be heard across a busy battlefield.

"What makes the pair of you think you can bargain with command?"

• • • ✵ • • •

Win Ton yo'Vala took the chair indicated. Win Ton yo'Vala accepted the offered cup of tea.

Win Ton yo'Vala was, yes, nervous, and he had sense enough not to try to conceal the fact from another Scout.

Val Con considered him openly, as he sipped his tea. Such frank regard was unlikely to put the lad at his ease but, then, it was not his intention to be comforting.

The last report he had received regarding this same Scout yo'Vala, from a plainly distraught Theo, was that he lay near death, his own biologic systems turned against him by the intercession of cruel pirates wielding Old Tech.

Obviously, he had come past that crisis and had recovered himself in fair measure. There remained a slight hesitancy of motion, possibly visible only to a Scout's eye, and a minute misalignment of the back muscles, which was likely permanent, given that he had established himself an unorthodox, but seemingly solid, center.

"Did you," Val Con said quietly, choosing the mode of greater-to-lesser, which was not the worst he could have done to the boy, though it was by no means warm or welcoming, "intend to implicate my sister into your . . . difficulty?"

Brown eyes flashed up to meet his. The gaze steadied, and the face settled. He answered as he was addressed, taking the subordinate side.

"No, sir; I did not. If you will have the round tale, I thought I had taken the captain's key for my own, until it was too late to mend my error."

He drew a deep breath.

"I knew that Theo—Captain Waitley—would keep what I sent her close and quiet. She being the only one I could think of who might do so is a measure of the troubles which have and continue to beset the Scouts."

"I understand. Where did you find *Bechimo*, or did he approach you?"

"He had come to rest among the prohibited devices which had been collected and warehoused. No such ship was in the inventory I had been given, thus I investigated. The hatch opened to my hand. I did a proper tour, systems came up, and by the time I had entered the bridge, the ship entire was awake and functioning.

"I took what I believed to be first chair and inserted one of two keys lying in the tray, whereupon the ship took my measure, declared me its copilot—and I belatedly realized that here was no derelict." Win Ton paused for a restorative swallow of tea, sighed, and shook his head ruefully, as a fond elder might over the folly of a youth.

"Why not leave the keys—or at least the one which you had not taken for yourself?" Val Con asked. "Why bring Theo into the matter at all?"

"I realized that I had woken something which . . . perhaps . . . ought to have been left sleeping. And I realized, as many of us did who had any recent communication with headquarters, that the Scouts had been infiltrated. Also, as perhaps you may not know, those who are responsible for the collection of Old Tech are . . . zealous . . ." He hesitated, seeming at a momentary loss.

"I had heard," Val Con murmured, "*overzealous*. You feared they would dismantle the ship—hastily?"

"In essence, though I have not been able to understand, even now, why I thought it important *then* that the ship be preserved."

A deep breath brought his shoulders up to ears, followed by a long sigh.

"During my initial inspection, I thought the ship old. Later, when I had been trapped and detained by those agents of the Department of the Interior, the key . . . the ship, through the agency of the key, behaved in such a manner as to make me believe for a time that it was indeed Old Tech."

"For a time," Val Con repeated. "Do you not now believe that *Bechimo* is Old Tech?"

Win Ton yo'Vala shook his head.

"I believe that *Bechimo* is antique, not ancient. I believe it . . . possible that the master healing unit aboard may partake, *somewhat*, of the Old Technology, but my understanding is that the thing had been built according to plans provided by the Uncle, in which case—"

He spread his hands.

"All bets are off," Val Con finished for him, in Terran. "However, you speak in terms of belief, not certainty. Surely there are ship's records—provenance?"

Another show of hands, fingers wide, palms empty.

"Such may be in the captain's files; they have not been made available to third board."

Val Con nodded.

"Very well. Who is this Captain yos'Thadi?"

A conscious look from pretty brown eyes. One began to understand Theo's partiality, and had he been merely a bed-friend . . . but he was not. He was the branch from which all subsequent events depended.

"Captain yos'Thadi has a reputation to build and a desire to cleanse the universe of every remaining piece of Old Tech.

"It was Captain yos'Thadi and his crew who escorted me to Volmer, and begged a boon of the Uncle. In exchange for this, did I happen to survive the treatment, yos'Thadi demanded I give to him my own key to *Bechimo*."

"Which bargain you have declined to keep."

Scout yo'Vala outright laughed.

"I know where best to place my fear!" he said. "Aside from the certainty that Theo would space me were I to do any such thing, I would myself far prefer to see the key destroyed and myself left shipless, than to place it in yos'Thadi's hand. In pursuit of his legend, he will ignore facts or alter them. It is in his mind that *Bechimo* is Old Tech, and there is nothing that can teach him better."

He paused and raised one hand, as if a further thought had occurred.

"I would not have you think Captain yos'Thadi all vinegar and no honey," he said slowly. "He did . . . promise . . . that he would see me returned to active duty—to the field—once I had honored our bargain."

"Did he." Val Con tipped his head. "What are your intentions going forward, Scout yo'Vala?"

Utter seriousness and something else—not, Val Con thought, studying him, love—not *wholly* that, but some more potent emotion . . .

"If she will have me, I will continue as a member of Captain Waitley's crew. We have discussed this. She does mean to captain *Bechimo.* Whether she will do so as a pirate, or in some more legitimate work, will depend upon how matters fall out with yos'Thadi."

"So, all and everything depends upon my judgment and the good sense of Captain yos'Thadi."

Scout yo'Vala looked abashed.

"Sir, once again you may hold me to account. I interfered. Theo would have killed yos'Thadi on the docks at Minot had he been allowed to push her further, and thus made pirates of us all."

Val Con raised an eyebrow.

"Do you doubt my sister's aptitude should she care to embrace the trade?"

"I doubt Theo in nothing, sir, upon my honor. But I do not think that she would *like* to be a pirate."

"Or she might like it too well," Val Con said. "Does the Luck smile, we will never discover which. Perhaps, as you say, it is just as well."

He rose, and Win Ton yo'Vala came quickly to his feet, centered and very nearly perfectly straight.

"The Scouts," he said, and the younger man stiffened, pretty eyes wary.

"The Scouts," Val Con said again, in the mode of comrade, which allowed him some gentleness. "They cannot have you back in the field, Pilot; not as you stand now. It would be clerical, or possibly admin, and not even a garbage run to salve you."

A stiff incline of the head.

"Sir. I am aware."

"Yes," Val Con said. "I thought that you might be. I will ask, as her brother, that you refrain, as much as you may, from involving Theo in any more of your scrapes. She will surely find enough on her own."

A grin melted the stiffness.

"I'm certain you are correct, sir."

Scout yo'Vala having been shown the door, Val Con returned to his desk, picked up his cup, and drank off the last of the tepid tea.

He then closed his eyes and ran the Scout's Rainbow, for calmness and for fortitude.

"Jeeves," he said, opening his eyes. "Please ask my sister to join me here."

"Captain Waitley is not in the house, Master Val Con. She called early for a car and stated her intention to visit her mother."

Val Con raised his eyebrows.

"A car?" he prompted.

"After some discussion of local custom, the captain accepted Tommy as her driver and escort."

"I see." He sighed.

"Well, then, I suppose I shall have to breach protocol."

"Just so, sir. Shall I contact *Bechimo*?"

"No. I thank you," Val Con said, looking out the window at one of Surebleak's dim and blustery mornings. "It looks a pleasant day for a walk. I will go myself."

• • • ✵ • • •

The car came to a stop in front of a house on the intersection of two streets, marked with a pair of stacked signs on a pole. The sign on top said Dudley Avenue; the one on the bottom, Farley Lane.

"Looks clear," the driver said. "What you want to do, Captain, is wait for me to come 'round and open your door. We want me between you and any trouble that happens to be up early. So, after you're out of the car, you just walk right up those stairs there and ring the bell. I'll be right behind you. That's how it runs here because you're visiting kin, and there's no trouble I can personally think of that can get inside Lady Kareen's house in fit shape to open the door, after.

"If we were coming up to a house less-known, then it would be me doing the knocking, and the first one they'd see, opening up."

Tommy'd been a merc, as he'd told her during the drive down to the city . . . until clan politics had spoilt it for him, and then he'd come home—like half of Liad, he said with a grin—to Surebleak. He was employed by Clan Korval as a man-of-all-trades: 'hand, driver, on-call gardener, carpenter when Tan Ort needed an extra pair of hands, and liaison work on the occasions it came up. He'd been a technical sergeant in the merc—protocol specialist.

"You understand me, Captain?" Tommy said now, catching her eyes in the screen. "I know it's annoying, having me right at your shoulder, but it's the custom here, and I'd rather you not get shot on my watch. That's a deal?"

She nodded. "Deal."

"Right you are then. Wait for me to come 'round to you."

The short walk across the sidewalk and up the stairs, with Tommy at her back, wasn't annoying, Theo thought, so much as it was aggravating. She'd've liked to stop to take a good look at the street, the houses, and what people might've been about, but he hurried her up to the door, where there was a palm plate that must be the bell she was supposed to ring.

She heard a distant chime from inside and nodded once, her eyes drawn to the colored panes of glass that ran down the wall next to the door. Yellow, red, then blue. Maybe it was art; at least, it was pretty. Pretty, and fragile; not much like the little bit of Surebleak she'd actually managed to see during the ride from Jelaza Kazone. Plain-front houses, not many windows facing the street at all. The occasional roof garden, some shops, lights coming up behind shuttered store windows. So far as she'd seen, art was in short supply on Surebleak's decidedly not-pretty streets.

Local time, so Tommy'd told her, was earlyish. Not that he thought the timing would be a problem, everything considered. Lady Kareen's household kept strict and regular hours, and he didn't doubt that Theo'd find herself arriving just in time for breakfast.

She heard footsteps approaching the door from the inside, and in spite of Tommy right there at her back, and her own gun within easy reach, she felt her shoulders stiffen and her stomach pull into a knot.

Kamele . . . she hadn't seen her mother in—well, it'd been *Standards*, hadn't it, since she'd left the academy rather than go to prison, and presented herself at Hugglelans as her first and last best chance of getting piloting work. At that point, she hadn't cared—in-system garbage scow would've been all right with her, except that it would've technically violated the academy's demand that she leave planet.

Kamele would've changed, Theo thought, swallowing hard. People did; they got older and—

Something snapped on the far side of the door, and it swung open to reveal a tall woman with suspicious brown eyes set deep in a lean, ungiving face. There was a gun on her hip—a good gun, Theo saw, well-used, and well-kept.

"What business?" the doorkeeper snapped, frowning down at Theo.

"Hey, Dilly," Tommy said cheerfully from behind her. "Here's the professor's daughter come to see her. Got down late last night."

"Theo Waitley," Theo added, giving Dilly a frown for a frown. "I'll wait, if my mother isn't awake yet."

But the woman's face had undergone an astonishing transformation; her smile was as broad as the street at Theo's back, and her eyes fairly sparkled.

She stepped back, holding the door in one hand and swinging the other wide in a gesture that apparently meant *come in.*

Theo felt a gentle pressure between her shoulder blades. Tommy was urging her forward.

"Morning meal's just getting started," Dilly said, closing the door behind Tommy and flicking the locks shut with hardly a glance. "Lady Kareen and Scout vey'Loffit, they're having their first cup o'tea. The professor'll be down right quick; I heard her rustling around in her room. Here, I'll show you where."

She started down the hall, then paused and looked over her shoulder.

"Tommy, Esil's just putting down for the 'hands in the kitchen. You go on, and I'll see you there quick, soon's I get Ms. Theo settled in with the Lady."

Lady Kareen hadn't changed much, anyway, Theo thought, as she made her bow from the threshold of the dining room.

"Good morning, Aunt," she said, in the mode between kin, feeling *Bechimo*'s touch on her thoughts. "I hope I find you well."

"Niece," the elder lady replied, inclining her head, "I am in the best of good health, I thank you. Please, join us at table. Kamele will be with us very soon."

She turned to her table mate, a plump man with his grey hair in a long tail down his back.

"Her Ald, my niece, Theo Waitley, through the liaison of my brother with our colleague Kamele."

She turned again to Theo.

"Niece, I make you known to Scout Historian Her Ald vey'Loffit."

"Sir," Theo bowed again—delight at making a new acquaintance; she thought so, anyway. "I am pleased to meet you."

"Captain Waitley, it is a very great pleasure," he answered. "Kamele speaks of you often."

"Theo, please," Kareen said again, "sit. Kamele will be with us directly."

"Thank you," she said and slipped into the chair nearest the door.

"Tea?" Kareen asked.

"Yes, please."

Kareen poured, and Theo carefully raised the cup, breathed in the steam, and smiled.

"Joyful Sunrise," she murmured appreciatively and sipped.

"For the morning meal, there must be elegance," Kareen said.

"For the morning meal, there must be stimulation!" Scout vey'Loffit countered energetically, "and we are this morning given two reasons to have our wits about us!"

He fixed Theo with a sharp blue gaze.

"Captain Waitley, from whence do you come to us?"

She wasn't quite sure of the mode, but thanks to *Bechimo*, the question was plain enough. She considered answering in Trade—and then decided that would not only be rude, but would call the Scout's *melant'i* into question. On the other hand, holding a complete conversation in Liaden was just as likely to end in disaster.

Don't leave me, Theo thought at *Bechimo*, and felt the particular warmth that she thought of as reassurance.

"We were most recently at Lefavre, sir, and before that, Minot."

"Lefavre?" The Scout leaned forward somewhat. "Now there is an interesting port for a Korval ship! Does the master trader seek an alignment with the Carresens-Denobli Cartel?"

In fact, one of the people she'd talked to on Shan's, the master trader's, behalf had been Janifer Carresens-Denobli, and it had been on the topic of mutual benefit—but *that* had been on Tradedesk. Scout vey'Loffit had asked specifically about their business on Lefavre. Shan's secret—or, at least, his business—was saved by a technicality.

Theo felt some measure of relief, though she wasn't sure why—and the Scout was waiting for an answer, which she'd better give him truthfully.

"Sir, we transported a distressed pilot to the hiring hall there. A dock-and-drop only."

Scout vey'Loffit smiled.

"Ah, a charity lift," he murmured. "And Minot? How did you find matters there?"

Minot had been backward, corrupt, and self-serving, Theo thought. Not that she could exactly say that. Or maybe she could. She felt the words sorting themselves into her front brain.

"Well enough for a back-station seeking to build alliance with worlds that dance with interdiction," she said calmly. "It was there that we took up the pilot in distress, whom the station found an inconvenience upon its systems."

The Scout glanced at Kareen, who only picked up the pot and poured tea into his cup.

"Well," he said, cup in hand. "Stations are fragile environments, of course, and resources must be closely guarded."

"Exactly so," Theo said, and heard an echo of Father's dry irony in her own voice, with a mingling of pleasure and horror.

"Do you plan a long stay among us?" Kareen asked, maybe to cut off any more questions from Scout vey'Loffit, or maybe just because she wanted to know. "You had scarcely arrived for your last visit before you were away."

"The schedule at this present is fluid. There are matters to discuss with one's brother. *Bechimo* carries a crew of four, and in addition, we have two passengers who must, for the moment, impose upon the house. One would not wish to overburden Korval's resources."

That got her a sharp look from bright black eyes.

"Such concerns do you credit, of course, but you may put them aside. Even in current circumstances, Korval is well able to accommodate an additional six. The clanhouse is large and the stores are plentiful. Indeed, I am given to understand that a small harvest was coaxed from the house fields, despite the climate in which we find ourselves. The cellar is most at risk, but I do not think we shall see it dry within a half-dozen years."

"In fact, the greatest poverty of Surebleak is its lack of a drinkable beverage," said Scout vey'Loffit. "Korval might do a service to the world, Kareen, and bend its efforts to producing a potable wine." He sipped his tea, consideringly.

"Or three," he added, as one being just.

"Perhaps the Scouts might assist in the project," Kareen suggested.

"The Scouts, as I'll remind you, my lady—"

There was the sound of hurried footsteps in the hall. Theo turned in her chair as a slim woman with flyaway pale hair arrived in the doorway, paused for a moment with her hand on the jamb, her expression tentative—and then radiant.

"Theo!" she cried, taking another step into the room.

"Mother!"

Theo rose without fully intending to do so and threw herself into Kamele's arms.

• • • ❋ • • •

Val Con walked across the back field, hands tucked into the pockets of his jacket, collar turned up against the breeze. He ought, he thought, to have allowed Jeeves to call ahead, but he was curious—a failing common to all scouts—and wondered what *Bechimo* might do, now, with an unexpected visitor at the door.

The hatch was closed, lights off, *Spiral Dance* dark on her pod mount. In the lighter air of morning, he could see that it was a hard-used ship, kept up though perhaps not kept well. A working ship, in a time when work was scarce, and soldiers might commandeer a vessel that was maintained too well, for the war effort.

There was a score in the ground, marking the place where the end of the ramp had rested last night. He stopped there and raised his voice slightly, though he was fairly sure that *Bechimo* knew he was there and would hear him if he whispered.

"Hello, the ship! Scout Commander Val Con yos'Phelium, brother to your captain, asks entrance."

There was no hesitation; likely *Bechimo* had already decided upon a course should this very thing occur. He had, after all, been on *Bechimo*'s deck before and, by his standards at least, comported himself well.

When the ramp was down, he strolled leisurely up its length, through the open lock, and paused.

"Well come, Pilot yos'Phelium, brother to Captain Waitley," *Bechimo* said from over his head and somewhere to the left. "Would you care for tea?"

"Tea would be very pleasant, I thank you."

"Please follow the blue line to the galley."

He glanced down; there was indeed a blue line glowing along the decking, and he dutifully followed it to the galley.

* * *

The tea was steaming gently in a pretty ceramic pot; a matching cup sat beside it on the serving counter.

"There are sweeteners and other additives in the cabinet to your right," *Bechimo* said, voice still coming from overhead and to the left, "if you wish them."

"Thank you, I am quite content with only tea in my cup," Val Con said.

He carried it to the nearest table and settled onto one of three stools.

As he sipped, he surveyed the area: tidy and shipshape, which was no less than he had expected from Theo—or from *Bechimo*. There was a screen in the long wall, presently blank; various storage compartments and lock-downs behind the counter and along the short wall.

"The tea is well chosen," he said, setting the cup down gently. "I thank you."

"You are welcome."

"I mean no disrespect to the captain or crew in their care of the ship," he murmured, "but should you have need, Korval maintains an adequate yard at the port. It would be our very great pleasure to accommodate you." He paused and added, "We are, of course, discreet."

"Of course," *Bechimo* said, his tone excruciatingly courteous. "I am honored by your care."

Val Con inclined his head—and turned toward the door, as something dark moved in the corner of his eye . . .

A grey-and-brown striped cat sauntered down the room and pressed lightly against Val Con's knee.

"I do not believe I have had the pleasure," he murmured.

"This is Grakow," *Bechimo* said promptly, "the third survivor of the wreck of *Orbital Aid 370*."

"Grakow, I salute you. The household includes several cats, should you wish companionship."

He bent to offer a forefinger. Grakow studied it gravely for a moment, then politely touched a slightly damp black nose to the fingertip. Courtesies observed, he moved on, 'round the counter and out of sight.

"We thought it best not to add to the confusion of our arrival, and Grakow seems content for the moment. Should he become restless, or seem to miss the pathfinders, I will contact Jeeves."

"Excellent."

Val Con had another sip of tea, which really was very good. Wise of Theo not to stint on rations. A well-fed crew was liable to be much more forgiving of the captain's foibles.

"Forgive me," said *Bechimo*, "if I am too forward, but I wonder about your purpose in coming to me. You might easily have asked Jeeves to convey the information regarding Korval's Yard."

"Indeed, I might have done. However, it has been some time since we last conversed, and, as I find myself in the position of having to solve for you in the face of what I am assured are overzealous and ambitious Scout archivists, I thought it wise to renew our acquaintance."

"I regret this unseemly disturbing of your peace—" *Bechimo* began.

Val Con raised a hand. "Please, please! Put yourself at ease. I have had very little peace this last year and expect to have none for the next—and possibly the next after that. But—this judgment that I am called upon to give . . . in order to be as Balanced as possible in the matter, I find that I must ask you a question."

"I will do my best to answer any questions you may have which touch upon the upcoming judgment."

Val Con smiled.

"Promised like a Liaden," he murmured. "Tell me, did you deliberately entrap Scout yo'Vala at the warehouse?"

There was a small pause.

"Entrap . . . I think not. As I had not been . . . collected, I was not in the records, and he had been tasked with verifying the inventory. It was therefore reasonable, and entirely in keeping with his duty, to approach and try the hatch."

Another pause. Val Con waited.

"My . . . error, as I suppose it must have been, was—I opened to him. He was not on the Allowed List, but neither was he on the Disallowed List. I had been promised a captain. It had been . . . long . . . and I was lonely . . ."

"And here came a pilot worthy of you, intelligent and courteous, properly requesting admittance," Val Con finished softly. "I believe I understand."

"I very much regret that my decision has cost Scout yo'Vala . . . so much. And yet, his actions . . . my actions—*our* actions, taken together, have brought me together with my captain, and she with her crew. These outcomes are not . . . illegitimate."

"I agree. It is not unusual that infelicitous action produces results that are felicitous in the extreme. I do not, myself, understand the mechanism involved, but I have observed the effect."

"Precisely so! I had thought it a function of the Luck."

"The Luck is a fickle thing, also in my observation, and while it is the tradition of my House to allow it a will and a weight, we do not suppose that it is always an agent of felicity, even in the long view."

There was a muted thump as Grakow landed on the tabletop.

"Thank you for joining me," Val Con said and looked toward that section of ceiling from which *Bechimo*'s voice seemed to issue. "I think that we must, in the end, allow the universe to embrace forces which are forever beyond us, and go on as well as we might, stipulating that no outcome, however unlooked for, is illegitimate."

"As you say," *Bechimo* answered politely and fell silent.

Val Con sipped his tea; Grakow bumped his elbow forcefully with a surprisingly hard head.

"Ah, no, my friend," he murmured, placing the cup back on the table. "I learned long ago not to spill my tea."

"Have you," *Bechimo* said cautiously, "asked all of your questions?"

"In fact, I may have done, for the moment. However, there is another matter. I fear that I must ask for access to your records."

"Records?"

"Indeed. At issue, as I understand the matter, is whether this vessel is Old Tech or utilizes Old Tech components. The certificate of building and the yardmaster's final checklist would do much to clarify this point and to assist me in my deliberations. A list of those who financed the work, and their shares, would also be useful."

Silence.

Val Con got up and went to the pot to refresh his cup. When he returned to his place, Grakow was curled on his stool, precisely as if he had been there for hours.

"Your pardon," he murmured and took the vacant stool to the right.

He sipped his tea. Still, *Bechimo* did not speak.

"Scout yo'Vala assumes that these things exist," Val Con murmured, "as you are of an orderly disposition. He also tells me that, in the depths of his extremity, when you had caused the ship key to act for his benefit—at that time, he himself believed that you were an artifact of the Old Technology. He may, I think, be forgiven, as I understand that he was quite ill at the time.

"Since recovering his health, he has revised his opinion and states that he believes you merely to be old. As it happens, my own feelings coincide with his. However, in the matter of a judgment, facts take precedence over feelings and belief."

Ever more silence.

"On the topic of facts," Val Con continued, "it is unfortunate that I require access to these documents quickly. Very nearly immediately, I fear, as I am informed that the other party involved in this judgment is likely to be with us today—tomorrow at latest—and in a state of mind which I shudder to contemplate."

A small sound. It might have been a sigh.

"The information you request is under Captain's Seal," *Bechimo* stated.

"Ah. In that case, I ask that you apply to the captain for me. I believe you have that capability?"

The silence this time had a certain edge to it, as if he had startled the ship.

"I will see what may be done," *Bechimo* said. "This may take some amount of time, as the captain is focused elsewhere. Please, avail yourself of our hospitality while you wait."

"Thank you."

There was a sense of withdrawal, which was quite clever, Val Con thought. He would have to ask Theo if she knew how it was done.

Grakow had quit his stool for the tabletop once more. He rolled over, exposing a tempting, coffee-colored belly, paws waving innocently in the air.

Val Con grinned.

"Despite appearances, I was not born yesterday. I do, however, thank you most sincerely for the opportunity to amuse you."

He finished his tea and carried the cup to washer.

That done, he strolled to the center of the room and stood, hands in pockets, contemplating the blank screen.

Well, he thought; best to know it all.

This time he did not raise his voice, but merely said conversationally, "Comm Officer Joyita. A word, if you have the leisure."

The screen came live as quickly as if someone had snapped a switch. Before him was a crowded comm tower, with three screens live, a desk cluttered with piles of printout, several styli, two tea mugs, and what appeared to be a portable comm unit.

This, Val Con saw in his first glance.

His second glance, more comprehensive by far, took in a lean, hard-used face, the slightly crooked nose with the old scar spanning the bridge. Dark eyes, harder even than the face, met his.

Perhaps peculiarly for a comm officer, he wore a pilot's jacket, in a style and color which had gone out of fashion some years prior to the birth of Val Con's grandmother. He wore rings—four on one hand, plain bands of brown metal with a silvery sheen.

"Sir? May I help you?"

The voice had depth and warmth. One wished to trust that voice. The accent was Terran, though Val Con could not place it more specifically. Given the jacket, that was perhaps not unexpected.

He bowed, as between equals.

"Pilot, I should say. I am Captain Waitley's brother, Val Con yos'Phelium."

"Pilot yos'Phelium," said Joyita. "I've heard Captain Waitley mention you. Service?"

An adroit phrasing just there, Val Con thought, and did not smile. *Specifically* did not smile.

"Captain Waitley, my sister," he said, "tells me that you prefer the ship to guesting in my house. What am I to make of that?"

Startlement rippled across the hard brown face, followed by a grudging smile.

"Exactly what you have made of it, I wager," he said. "I'm quite comfortable here. Thank you for your care."

"For my part, you may keep to the ship down the length of your days. I might feel otherwise were you under my command but, there! We are twice fortunate.

"What I do need to know is how the devil I'm to judge for you. I don't suppose you would do me the favor of being—one hesitates to say *merely*—an instance of *Bechimo*?"

"Regrettably, sir, that's a favor I can't do for you. I began as a subroutine so that the ship would seem to be . . . more crewed than was the case. *Bechimo* and I have analyzed the data, only to find that, though we know *when*, we haven't been able to pinpoint *how* I occurred. That said, I *have* occurred, as an instance of no one but myself."

"One had supposed as much. These matters are rarely tidy. How has Captain yos'Thadi had intercourse with you?"

"As a voice on comm," Joyita said.

"Well, there's a small comfort. Again—how am I to judge you?"

"Sir, as I understand the matter, Captain yos'Thadi believes that *Bechimo* is Old Tech, which, of course, he isn't. *I* was born from the systems which sustain this ship, within the last Standard Year."

He spread his arms in the cramped tower, just missing bumping a screen with an elbow. The sleeves of the jacket were pulled back with the gesture, revealing a bracelet of the same brownish-silver metal around his wrist.

"Ergo," he said, "I am not Old Tech."

"Closely reasoned, I thank you. You are, however, a Free Intelligence, and we must assume that Captain yos'Thadi has those regulations by heart as well."

Joyita frowned, then smiled.

"You're seeking to issue an encompassing judgment."

"I am, because I tell you frankly that I don't care to be troubled to provide another judgment in two years or four, when someone with a wit notices the pair of you and draws the correct conclusion."

Joyita looked down at his desk and idly smoothed

a stack of papers, for all the worlds like a man deep in thought.

Val Con waited, and after another moment, Joyita looked up.

"Does the judgment created for Jeeves have flex?" he asked.

"That is my recollection. However, I am only human, as the phrase runs. If I am to bring myself current with *Bechimo*'s facts, and Captain yos'Thadi is as prompt as Theo expects him to be, I may not have sufficient time to adequately research and plot the secondary course."

"I am at liberty," Joyita said, "and the matter concerns me closely. I will be pleased to do the analysis for you, sir." He paused and offered a small, ironical smile. "I am accounted a very fine researcher."

Val Con bowed, ceding the point.

"I accept your assistance. Please work with Jeeves."

"Yes, sir."

"Until soon, th—"

"I have received the captain's permission to release the documents pertaining to my building to her brother so that he may correctly adjudicate the complaint against this ship," *Bechimo* said abruptly.

Val Con nodded to Joyita and received the same in reply before the screen snapped back to grey.

"That is excellent," he said, addressing himself to *Bechimo*. "Please transfer them to Jeeves. He will see them delivered to my office."

"Done. Is there anything else you require from me in regard to your judgment?"

"There is not," Val Con said and bowed gently. "I thank you for the gift of your time."

"There is one other thing," *Bechimo* stated, still sounding somewhat put off.

"And that is?"

"I am given to understand that the ship carried on my pod mount belongs to you, as the face and will of Clan Korval."

"Half the face and will," Val Con murmured, "but, yes—the ship you carry does, at first glance, seem to belong to Clan Korval."

"I would ask that it be removed as soon as is practicable. I do not wish for anything to impede my captain's plans, or to delay lift. Also..."

There was a slight hesitation.

"Also," *Bechimo* repeated, somewhat less stiffly, "it may be wise to have it out of sight before Scout yos'Thadi or his crew have the opportunity to identify it."

"An excellent point; I will endeavor to remove the evidence before the good captain arrives among us." He paused. "Is there anything else which requires discussion between us?"

The silence this time had weight to it, as if *Bechimo* were considering how much further to carry this morning's intercourse.

"There is the matter," the ship said finally, his voice firm, "of transportation fees."

Well, now, Val Con thought. Is this provocation? Or ignorance?

He tipped his head in mild puzzlement.

"Transportation fees," he repeated, not quite as a question, allowing an avenue for a graceful retreat...

Bechimo perhaps understood that something was amiss, if he did not *quite* comprehend his misstep.

He did not, in any case, directly bring forward an itemized list of fuel costs, crew time expended, mount wear, hazard surcharge . . .

"You don't want to plot that course," said a warning voice from behind Val Con's left shoulder.

"There is precedent," *Bechimo* stated, somewhat defensively. "Protocol is that we treat fairly with Clan Korval. 'Give them all they buy, no more and no less.'"

"There are circumstances," Joyita countered.

Ah, Val Con thought; one begins to understand the difficulty.

"In fact," he said, "there are circumstances. The precedent *Bechimo* quotes is one best followed when dealing with trade partners, allies, customers, and others who fail of being either clan or kin. Is this clear?"

"Yes," said *Bechimo*.

"Very good. In the present case, Captain Waitley and I are kin. Both sides acknowledge this; there is no ambiguity. The operating rule therefore changes."

"How so?"

"The strengthening and deepening—the *affirmation*—of the relationship is the coin used between kin. Theo has properly called upon me, in my *melant'i* as a Scout commander, to undertake a task. I willingly do so because she *is* my sister and I value our relationship.

"Likewise, my sister, having come across an item which belongs to the clan of which her brother and sister are delm, brings that item to them, rather than allow it to fall into the hands of . . . those who are perhaps less able to deal with it appropriately. Once again, she has properly called upon me, in my *melant'i* as Korval, and in addition shown a sister's care for the safety of her kin."

He paused, one hand up, palm out, to signal that he was not yet done.

"To require payment—transportation costs!—between kin is . . . an insult. Worse. Such an action would make me into non-kin, a stranger with whom no valuable connection exists.

"If you were to produce that invoice and require that I pay, then I would have no choice but to answer in kind: treat with you as a stranger to my hearth and charge you for my time and effort in the upcoming judgment."

Silence from above and behind.

Joyita spoke first.

"I understand," he said.

"But I," said *Bechimo* plaintively, "do not. Theo may be your sister, sir, but *I* am no kin to you."

"Setting aside for the moment the knotty question of whether the connection you and my sister enjoy is analogous to a lifemating . . . I wonder whose order saw Korval's ship mounted and brought home? Yours?"

"Indeed not!" Plainly, *Bechimo* was scandalized. "It is the captain's place to order for ship and crew."

"Ah."

From behind him, a chuckle. "He has you, *Bechimo*."

"I suppose he does," the ship said grumpily. "How did you know Theo and I are fully bonded?"

Val Con looked aside, as if embarrassed.

"I didn't *know*," he said. "There were only some odds and ends that I noticed, doubtless due to my having been trained as a Scout. We can't help but notice things. In any case, the last time you and I spoke, Theo was your pilot. There had been talk of a bonding ceremony, as Theo confided to our father, who felt that her brother should also have this information. And . . . well . . . Theo's Liaden is much improved."

"Second Chair O'Berin has been tutoring her in Liaden."

"Yes, I don't doubt. Pilot O'Berin learned his Liaden on the Solcintra docks and he bears that accent. Theo's Liaden . . . could perhaps pass as an outworld accent but, in fact, she has no accent at all."

Bechimo made a small sound, as if of a sigh.

"I see," said *Bechimo*. "Which do you recommend as being least notable?"

"The Solcintran manner is common enough that it will raise no eyebrows. And by providing that accent to her, you will reinforce Pilot O'Berin's work."

"Thank you," said *Bechimo*. "I will update my files."

"Always of service," Val Con said, bowing. "Is there anything else which requires immediate discussion? I fear time is becoming short if I am to familiarize myself with the facts and also see Korval's ship placed into a situation of lesser visibility."

"Yes, of course. Please follow the blue line to the hatch."

"Thank you."

Val Con followed the blue line to the hatch. Behind him, he heard a light, rapid sound, as if of claws against decking. He paused to allow Grakow to catch up with him.

"Shall you wish to meet the cats of the House?" he asked.

Grakow stared up at him fixedly.

"I see," Val Con said after a moment. "You will, of course, do as you think wise. Jeeves will oversee you, as he does all of the cats. Pray, make yourself free."

This seemed to be the correct mode to adopt. The cat's boldly striped tail went up into an aggressive salute as he led the way through the hatch.

By the time Val Con had reached the bottom of the ramp, Grakow had vanished into the high grasses.

•••✱•••

"But how did you even get here?" Theo asked her mother.

After breakfast, Kamele had led the way to what she called "the back parlor," where they could be "private." Which they were, despite the clatter and chatter from the kitchen.

"I booked passage on a cruise ship," Kamele said, answering Theo's question. "When that situation became . . . unsafe, I signed as working crew on the *Judy*, which was bound in to Surebleak."

"*Working crew?*"

Theo stared. Kamele raised her eyebrows.

"Is it so surprising that I can work?"

"No! It's just—working crew's generally pretty labor-intensive, and it's not . . ." She saw the inelegant end of her sentence approaching, but went with it anyway . . .

"Safe."

"Well, of course it wasn't safe! No spaceship is really *safe*! The *Judy* was a little *rough*, but I was much safer there than I was on a cruise ship where one of the other passengers wanted to take me as a hostage."

"Hostage? Why would—" Theo swallowed the rest of that question and repeated, "Why?"

Kamele frowned.

"My best guess—and your brother's—is that someone

saw an opportunity to collect the bounty on you. They would take and hold me, let you know, and tell you that they would let me go if you surrender yourself."

But that was—Theo reached for her cup and had a swallow of tea that she didn't want.

It had been, Theo thought carefully, not too bad a plan on the part of whoever, really. That wasn't the shocking thing—all right, it *was* shocking, but who had ever expected Kamele to leave Delgado? Well, she might leave for her sabbatical—she'd lost track of Kamele's sabbatical schedule, but that aside—

She hadn't expected—at all—that her actions, in her sphere, would cause—could be dangerous for... *Kamele*? Kamele wasn't part of any of her daughter's scrapes—Kamele wasn't a pilot! She was a scholar who had lived all her life on a Safe World, and not—and not some kind of *game piece* to be used to control—

"Theo?" Kamele said softly. "Is there something wrong?"

"I..." She took a breath. "I hadn't considered that people would involve you in my—in my business," she managed.

Kamele laughed.

"Well, to a certain sort of mind, I suppose it would be obvious. We're connected, after all, even if I'm a stodgy old scholar and you're the captain of your own vessel. Any connection is worth exploitation, to that sort."

Connection. Personal connection. People—enemies—who would reach outside the box of *appropriate* connections, and try to hurt the mother of a pilot who had offended them...

I see your relatives in you, Theo Waitley...

That... she was going to have to think about that. In the meantime...

"When are you going back to Delgado?" she asked Kamele.

Kamele tipped her head.

"So eager to get rid of me?"

"I just thought, if the timing meshed, we could take you back," Theo said. "That would keep you out of the orbit of people who are trying to kidnap you in order to get at me."

"That's very thoughtful," Kamele said. "But, you know, I may not go back to Delgado."

Possibly, Theo thought, the universe phased just then. She reached for a quick mental exercise. *Inner calm*, she told herself, and brought her attention back to her mother.

"Not go back to Delgado? But—your tenure and your place in the department... the house..."

"Yes, well. My place in the department is largely administrative now. I teach the senior seminar, but every semester, I have to fight harder to keep it. The chancellor's office would rather have me in budget negotiations, which is a dead bore, as even Ella admits. Here—now—I'm doing real work; putting my expertise to use. This project of Kareen's is fascinating! Of course, I don't have a specialty in social engineering, but even I can see the intricacies—almost exactly like a mosaic! I could be... content going on just as I have been, these last few months. But lately, I've been talking with the civic leaders, and they—they want a secondary school system on Surebleak. What they have now is primary education—which is addressing such things as literacy and numeration—and two systems of apprenticeships: one native to Surebleak and the system imported by the new population. The Scouts are offering courses, and intend to open an academy here, but not everyone is capable of being a Scout, or needs the Scout skill-set.

"Kareen's project touches on some of this, but her focus is codifying mutually acceptable social behaviors. I'm being asked to undertake a specific, practical project that will greatly benefit the entire population of Surebleak and bring them into the universal conversation."

The universal conversation, Theo recalled, was the discussion that scholars claimed to be having with their colleagues *everywhere*. The universal conversation was why research was done and papers published and—

"You think Surebleak's ready?" she asked, thinking of the shuttered windows and dark streets.

"Well, that's the point, isn't it? If Surebleak *chooses* not to enter the conversation, that's perfectly valid. But right here, right now—there's no system in place, and there is no choice. Surebleak's voice *can't* be heard."

"So, you're going to stay and design a secondary system?"

"It would be good, don't you think, to do fieldwork? Knowledge mustn't be lost, but in order to fulfill itself, it must be *used*."

Kamele smiled softly.

"Jen Sar and I used to argue the point—was knowledge enough? Was it enough, even, to teach and pass on the knowledge one had accumulated? Teaching is an honorable and necessary profession, of course. But the knowledge that is passed on—is it *enough* that it's not forgotten? Or must it integrate with society and the real world—not just in the conversation—but in bettering human lives."

"You and Father used to *argue* about that?" Theo asked, somewhat baffled.

"Oh, endlessly!" Kamele said with a laugh. "He supported the practical application as primary and the quest for knowledge alone no more than a pleasurable activity."

"But Father wanted to know *everything. Did* know everything. And everybody," Theo objected.

"Indeed he did, and he made use of it all. I think we must conclude that his ideology is pure."

"Now!" Kamele said. "Let's play turnabout. How long will you be here, Daughter, and what are your plans, going forward?"

Theo sighed.

"I don't have any firm plans, yet. We can't just sit at port, *that's* certain. But—"

Theo.

It was like hearing a whisper from the wrong side of her ear. Theo paused, listening.

Your brother has come aboard. He requests documents from the time of my building, he says, in order that he may render a proper judgment in the matter of Captain yos'Thadi. The documents are under Captain's Seal.

She really ought, Theo thought, to get around to looking at all the documents that were under Captain's Seal. Maybe she'd do that while they were resting on Surebleak. In the meantime, though...

Give my brother whatever he asks for in connection to the judgment, she answered, forming the words in her head.

Yes, said *Bechimo*—and was gone.

"Theo?" Kamele said, in a tone that hinted she had said it more than once.

Theo shook her head.

"Sorry, I—I really haven't decided how we should go forward. I'm captain of a tradeship, so logically, we should trade. I'm not much good at it, though, which would mean taking on a trader..."

A stranger on her ship.

"Perhaps your brother can assist you," Kamele suggested. "Kareen tells me that Clan Korval's fortune is from trade. Maybe he can put you in touch—with a trader or with someone who can help you figure out how to think about your problem."

"That's not a bad idea. I had a contract with Korval's master trader, but he called it off when the route started to get more dangerous than he'd anticipated."

She frowned. "I guess Shan's out on his route, though..."

"That's Master Trader Shan yos'Galan of *Dutiful Passage*?" Kamele asked.

Theo looked up, blinking—and then grinned.

"New knowledge," she said.

"Being put to use," her mother said, pursing her lips and attempting to look stern. "I have heard it said that the delm has charged the master trader to develop and implement new routes that take advantage of Surebleak's location."

"That's pretty much it. I was contracted to follow a kind of sketched-in route, to see if it would be viable for a long-loop. Had a list of possible contacts, but I didn't do so good there, either. Got thrown off one world because my contacts believed in luck, and they believe that Clan Korval has an interesting relationship with luck that they didn't want to get involved with.

"Also," Theo said darkly, "they *really* didn't like it when I said I'd learned how to be invisible from Father. Apparently men aren't supposed to know *any*thing."

"Your father would have laughed."

"And then he'd've done something when they weren't looking, just to prove that their position wasn't as unassailable as they thought."

Kamele smiled.

"That, too," she said and rose.

"If you have time, I'd like to show you our work—you'll understand the importance."

That might, Theo thought, be optimistic. On the other hand, it *would* be interesting to see what had grabbed and held Kamele's enthusiasm.

"I'd like that," she said.

She rose and gave her mother a willing smile.

V

WELL, ROBERTSON, YOU WANTED *TO KNOW.*

And she had... wanted to know. Worse than that, she had *needed* to know.

And now that she did, she had to figure out what to do about it.

Even if they could absorb a couple of old-style pathfinders themselves, Korval was not the proper repository for the contents of those two cases. Not even close. They had their share of secrets to keep, but this one—this one was out of their league and best out of their hands. She was... reasonably sure that *they* wouldn't crack the cases—unless something really bad threatened Korval, and nothing in the main or auxiliary bags of tricks and dodges had neutralized it.

And that was the problem, right there, remembering that *they* were relatively sane, as delms of the line went. Korval genes occasionally kicked out a seriously deranged delm, and didn't it just make the blood run cold speculating on what Mad Delm Theonna would've done with those cases?

All of that being said and agreed to, the question was: If not Korval, then who?

The Clutch came to mind, which was an idea, but not a good one. There'd been a war, way back, between the Clutch and the Yxtrang. She wasn't clear on what had started it, and neither was her best source of Yxtrang history—Nelirikk. Whatever the root of the argument, the Clutch had demonstrated the superiority of their viewpoint so decisively that, even today, Yxtrang gave Clutch worlds wide berth, and flat-out *ran* if a Clutch ship happened to show up on the scans.

Clutch lived a long time, and she knew from her own experience that Edger, at least, held a grudge.

All of which made putting the cases into the Clutch's care not one of the top three solutions.

The Lyre Institute was a possible recipient since, if Jeeves's dossier had been anything like factual, they already oversaw an extensive library of heritage genes.

On the other hand, if Jeeves's dossier was anything like factual, the Lyre Institute would immediately start offering supersoldiers to the highest bidder.

For right now, Nelirikk'd taken the pathfinders up to the security wing, so they could get showers and some downtime. On her order, they'd taken the cases with them because she couldn't think of any better place for them than with the soldiers who'd kept them safe this long.

She . . .

She needed something to drink—coffee, by choice, though she'd take a cup of the bitter green tea, if that's what was on offer.

She turned down the hall, toward the morning parlor.

The room was dim, in solidarity with the not-exactly-bright-and-cheerful morning outside. Despite the lack of sunshine, there were a couple of young cats following the rule book, stretched out belly-up on the window seat. Other than them, the room was deserted, which suited her fine.

She drew the dregs of coffee from the urn to a cup, and sat down with it on the edge of the window seat. The grey-and-white cat—Fondi, that was—opened his eyes, yawned, and flopped over onto his side, which gave her space enough to angle her back against the wall and put one leg up on the cushion.

"Thanks," she said, and commenced in to staring over the lawn and drinking thick, bitter coffee.

The cases presented a whole suite of problems. Whoever received them couldn't just slide them under the bed and forget about them. They were designed to keep the contents fresh until they could be moved to a long-term environment. Chernak and Stost were of the opinion that they were good for a couple of Standards before the need for better storage got serious, but the sooner they were in a permanent archive, the less chance the samples would deteriorate.

What she needed, Miri thought, eyes closed, and absently stroking Fondi, who had draped himself, purring, across her thigh . . . what she needed was an established gene library controlled by someone tough enough to protect it and purehearted enough not to put the material into play. Not the Scouts, the Scouts' official stand on clones and cloning was in line with their opinion of independent logics. They'd destroy cases and contents and be proud of themselves for saving the universe.

She toyed with the idea of destroying the cases and found she liked it even less than she liked turning them over to the Clutch.

The problem was that the kind of archive best suited to the preservation of the samples . . . was against law. It was against the law to manufacture humans; it was against the law to clone humans; it was against the—

Clone humans.

Miri opened her eyes.

"Jeeves, is the Uncle's ship still on port?"

"Yes, Miri. No departure time has been filed."

"Good. Please contact the Uncle on my behalf and tell him that Korval has a mutually beneficial proposition to discuss with him. Ask him to please wait upon Delm Korval at his earliest convenience."

"Yes," said Jeeves.

"Also, please ask Daav yos'Phelium and Aelliana Caylon to attend their delm in the Tree Court in twelve minutes."

• • • • • • •

Val Con had three main screens open, each displaying a document, words and phrases heavily highlighted.

A fourth side screen displayed six different dictionary options; the one currently on top being Old Terran to New Terran. It was treacherous going, and he also had frequent recourse to the Terran-to-Trade, and Liaden-to-Trade volumes.

At his request, Jeeves had piped in the port all-band, the litany of ships in, ships departing, and the side-band chatter taking the part of white noise while he concentrated on the documents *Bechimo* had provided.

The documents were, of themselves, fascinating, and he might have happily spent a week or two learning them as they deserved. Necessity, though. Necessity demanded this unseemly drilling for data, names, dates, specs. Facts, rather than nuance. Facts were what would sway the zealous Old Tech hunter.

Well . . . possibly they would not.

He had also researched Captain yos'Thadi, who was every bit as overreaching as Scout yo'Vala had hinted.

Thus, the facts were doubly necessary. When he filed his judgment, his reasoning, and supporting documentation with Scout Headquarters—with, he supposed, *both* Scout Headquarters—it must be unassailable. A judgment . . . a Scout commander might make a field judgment when called upon, and that judgment would hold until or unless it failed the review board, which had been backed up for years *before* the battle at Nev'Lorn and Korval's act of aggression against the homeworld.

Acts which had resulted in two Scout Headquarters, two active rosters, and apparently not even the most rudimentary attempt at negotiation on the part of either administration.

He shook his head and sat back, frowning absently

at the middle document, which was also the most highlighted.

All honor to the secretary of the corporation which had built *Bechimo*, for keeping such meticulous records. Even more honor that those records agreed in so very many instances with history, which might be utilized in the absence of certain other documents under Captain's Seal, and were best not shared with curious Scouts.

However, there were a number of phrases—a Scout might assume that they were *key* phrases—that still failed of being perfectly clear.

He supposed that he might weave context and best practice together well enough to cover the holes in his certain knowledge, but one would rather *not* dice with Theo's liberty, nor with *Bechimo*'s life.

The receiver produced a belch, which would be a ship entering local space. Scarcely had it faded when a clear, familiar voice came across all bands, speaking very precisely in Trade.

"Captain Waitley and the crew of the tradeship *Bechimo* welcome Captain yos'Thadi and *Chandra Marudas* to Surebleak."

"What!" snapped an unguarded voice in Liaden.

In his office, Val Con spun his chair around so that he could stare at the receiver.

"Jeeves," he said when some minutes had passed with no further comment from the receiver.

"Sir?"

"Remind me not to irritate my sister Theo."

"I believe it to be too late, if I may make so bold, sir."

Val Con sighed.

"I fear you are correct. Well, then. I shall endeavor

to accept my comeuppance, when it arrives, with aplomb. That, I think I may manage."

"Yes, sir. *Bechimo* reports that Miss Nova and Mr. Golden are aboard *Spiral Dance* and that Miss Nova has allowed *Bechimo*'s condition report to stand as the pilot's inspection. Systems are live and countdown to lift has begun."

"I will refrain from inquiring into the state of my sister Nova's temper on receiving a message from her delm to drop every other task and return to the house in order to lift a ship. However, I am surprised. I had not known that Mike Golden was a pilot."

"He is not," Jeeves said.

"My sister brings a passenger?"

"Not as such. Mr. Golden is present in his *melant'i* as Boss Nova's head 'hand. He asked *Bechimo* to relay a message to Korval's delm, from his Boss. The message is: *Tell my delm that I am on the edge of a very old memory, indeed, and if I do not emerge from it, I wish them joy of Grandmother Cantra.*"

Val Con inclined his head.

"Please convey to Mr. Golden that the delm has heard Nova yos'Galan's message, and that her brother Val Con wishes them both a safe lift."

"Message relayed."

"Excellent. Thank you, Jeeves."

He turned resolutely back to his screens and was very shortly again immersed in research.

• • • ✵ • • •

Twelve minutes was time enough to reach the Tree Court from their rooms, if they left immediately the summons arrived and walked briskly all the way. They had of course been anticipating the call and had early seen to dressing themselves—which was well, as the clothes Daav had left behind did not suit his newly young frame and it had been many years since Aelliana's clothes had hung in their closet.

Mr. pel'Kana and Jeeves had conspired to allow them to do better, so that they now, appropriately clad in black pants and formal shirts under leather jackets, followed the path to their meeting with the delm. Daav wore his own battered garment and the one that Mr. pel'Kana had found in stores for her was almost equally disreputable.

She had hesitated before the jacket, not quite daring to touch it where it lay over the back of the chair.

"Because, you know, Daav, we have not yet found if I am reborn a pilot."

"You may not have been reborn a pilot," he answered, shaking the leather out and holding it for her, "but you cannot believe that the Tree would have forgotten such a detail."

"No, of course not."

She slipped her arms into the sleeves, allowed him to settle the jacket on her shoulders, and turned to look up into his face. He bent to kiss her cheek. She touched his brow and stepped back.

"We ought not keep the delm waiting."

They were in good time, walking briskly hand in hand down the overgrown path, Daav leading in the frequent case that the way was too thin to accommodate both, and were, for the moment, side by side.

"Advise me, *van'chela*," she said.

"To the best of my ability."

"I have only just thought—shall I scold the Tree on the Uncle's behalf before or after the delm has judged?"

"Before, certainly. A previous commitment must have precedence. Additionally, as we remain uncertain of any *after*, you would not wish to risk breaking your word."

"Thank you," she said, as the path ended, and they stepped onto grass. "I shall begin at once."

•••❋•••

Miri was sitting on the bench by the gloan-roses, considering the Tree and thinking about the ground in the middle. The upcoming conversation would only answer a question; it wouldn't solve the problems Val Con saw in bringing his parents back into the clan. Or two newly named young yos'Phelium pilots who just happened to fly in out of nowhere and hadn't ever been listed in the clan's census.

Quiet voices reached her, getting nearer. She stirred, stood up, and watched them as they entered the court, walking pilot-smooth and unhurried, hand in hand and heads high.

They stopped well before they reached the trunk, still holding hands. Aelliana tipped her head back, addressing the boughs above.

"You, sir! I will have you know that I am *quite* out of temper with you! It is all well and good to have planned for our resurrection, but might you not have proceeded in a more tactful manner? Insulting the very person upon whom our survival depended—was that wise? Undoing all of his care at one sweep—was that kind? What, I wonder—"

Miri had a sense of words said just beyond her hearing. Aelliana laughed aloud.

"Yes, and it is good to see you again also, reprobate! Though you must know that you have caused many more problems than you have solved. The delm may be the delm, but it is cruel to place this upon our children."

Another murmur, just out of range. Miri walked forward, mentally stepping into what she called delm-space.

Daav turned toward her, his lifemate with him. They bowed, each a perfect reflection of the other, and straightened.

"Korval," Daav said.

"We arrive at the delm's word," Aelliana said.

Korval inclined her head.

"Elucidate your arrival in these vessels."

"Yes," Daav said. "In the process of deactivating the device situated upon Moonstruck, as required by the delm, one's previous vessel sustained serious wounds. I had chosen the Uncle as my backup, as he was the builder of the installation. So it was, when he arrived to view the progress of my work, he found me near dying and, acting as an ally, took what to his philosophy is merely the next step in healing."

"Before he left on the delm's mission," Aelliana took up the narrative, "the Tree had given Daav two unripe pods: one for him, the second for me. The Uncle became aware of the fact of there being two pods, and therefore prepared two vessels. That we were able to separate and utilize them, we know only because we woke thus."

She paused. The delm motioned for her to continue.

"Korval. Daav was at first suspicious that the vessels might inherently include infelicitous aspects. If this was so, we cannot know, because at that point, the pods ripened and, of course, we ate them.

"I immediately fell into a faint. At Daav's suggestion, the Uncle placed me into an autodoc. Daav also entered a 'doc shortly after consuming his pod."

"In my case, it seems that the pod merely... fine-tuned the Uncle's work," Daav continued, "as this vessel was 'seeded' with material from my previous body. In Aelliana's case, it appears that the Tree utterly undid and overwrote the Uncle's work, making her new body, so we believe, very much nearer to, if not exactly the same as, the body she had previously inhabited."

"We approach my topic," Korval said. "Legitimacy. The Tree is the first test, if it will oblige."

The Tree was amused, but willing.

Aelliana approached first and put her palm against the trunk.

Green light illuminated the Tree Court, and there came an immense rustling above, from which a breeze descended trailing leaves like a scarf, and wound about Aelliana's waist in a hug, before dancing away up into the branches.

She stepped back, smiling, and beckoned.

"Come, Daav, you must be properly received."

"I foresee mischief," he said stepping to the trunk. "It would be a fine joke to deny me. Its humor tends that way."

He put his hand against the trunk.

Nothing happened, if so absolute a cessation of sound and movement could be said to be *nothing*.

Daav took a deep breath, shoulders rising—and falling. He removed his hand, turned—

The gloan-roses burst forth in flower, flooding the

court with their heady scent; a tiny whirlwind leapt up from the ground, enclosing him for a moment before dissipating, leaving him rumpled, with random bits of grass and twig caught in his clothing here and there.

"That was not very kind," Aelliana said chidingly, "though it is true that he challenged you."

Korval looked up into the branches and received the strong impression that three dragons occupied the court, and the Tree was well pleased with that circumstance.

"Attend me," Korval said, and they turned to her, faces respectful. "You will remove to the morning parlor, where the second test for legitimacy will be performed."

"Korval."

They bowed as one being and, with no further ado, departed the Tree Court as they had entered, proud and holding hands.

• • • ✵ • • •

Val Con sat back and nodded at the screen. The judgments were complete. He was, on the whole, satisfied with the work. Of course, one could wish that there had been more time. Though, he admitted, if he had been granted an extra Surebleak week, he would be wishing for more time again, at the end of it.

"Master Val Con, Captain Waitley has returned and requests a moment of your time."

He raised an eyebrow.

"Theo has grown mellow, indeed," he observed.

"Her request may have been phrased with somewhat more enthusiasm," Jeeves admitted.

Val Con grinned.

"Please ask my sister Theo to join me here, and also ask Mr. pel'Kana to bring tea."

"Of course."

"Thank you, Jeeves."

Theo arrived before tea, wind-blown and rosy from the chill.

"*Chandra Marudas* is in port," she said without preamble.

"So the scanner revealed to me," he said equitably. "Tell me, was it really necessary to embarrass the captain and his ship before all of Surebleak Port?"

She stared at him.

"Captain yos'Thadi mocked *Bechimo* and doubted that we could raise Surebleak in twelve days," she said, as if it explained all. Which, Val Con supposed, it did.

"I see. Well! That was very foolish of him. I trust he found your lesson instructive."

"Probably he didn't," Theo said frankly. "But maybe his first mate will take the point."

"Pardon me, Master Val Con, Captain Waitley," Jeeves said. "A taxi has been called to pick up two passengers at the courier and quick ship yard. The pad number is that assigned to *Chandra Marudas*."

"Thank you, Jeeves," Val Con said.

Theo took a hard breath and *fuffed* her hair out of her eyes.

There came a light knock at the door and Mr. pel'Kana arrived with tea.

"Mrs. ana'Tak thought a plate of cookies would not go amiss," he said setting the tray on the table by the window.

"Thank you, Mr. pel'Kana," Val Con said, "and Mrs. ana'Tak, too, for her care."

"Yes, sir."

The door closed gently behind him.

Val Con went to the table, picked up the pot and poured.

Theo accepted the first cup and stood holding it in both hands, obviously on the edge of action.

Val Con, his own cup in hand, recruited himself to patience.

She hesitated only a moment longer before blurting, "Do you have enough information to make a judgment? *Bechimo* said you needed the records of his building. Is . . ." she paused, as if considering the point. "I don't think Captain yos'Thadi'll accept *any* judgment that goes against what he wants."

"Ah, but you see—he will have no choice. This meeting is not to seek his agreement—nor, indeed, your own. I have done my research and formed a field judgment, which I will file with the Scout Review Board. I should say, review *boards*. This meeting is a courtesy, to allow you to hear the judgment before it is filed. Because the review of field judgments has historically been in arrears, the procedure in non-urgent cases—and determining *Bechimo*'s correct status in regard to the Old Technology Archives is, forgive me, not particularly urgent—is that the field judgment will be enacted immediately, and remain in force until such time as it may be overturned by the review board."

"But," Theo protested, "that means the only thing we're doing is buying time! In a year, or, or six or whenever, this review board of yours might decide to reverse the decision!"

"In some cases that would certainly be a danger, but not in the case of this particular judgment."

Theo eyed him.

"Why not?"

"Because we have verifiable documentation, much of which can be shared, without endangering *Bechimo*'s security. I speak of such things as the sign-offs on the completed construction from the project engineer and the yardmaster; the roster of investors and their buy-ins. These items are dated, and thereby neatly cancel Captain yos'Thadi's arguments.

"In the interest of thoroughness, *Bechimo* allowed Jeeves to perform a systems and energy scan this morning. The results of this scan are appended to the judgment. They prove the contention that *Bechimo* is an Old Tech ship to be . . . without substance."

Theo was standing stiffly, perhaps not so much reassured as he might have expected. Well, and it was not *his* ship at stake.

Suddenly she blinked, and visibly relaxed. She had accessed a focus-and-calming exercise then, Val Con thought. Good.

"Sounds like you have the first half pinned down," she admitted. "But, Captain yos'Thadi said that *Bechimo* is an abomination, because of being a machine intelligence." She paused, head to one side, as if considering a knotty question.

"It's hard to know which made him madder—Old Tech or AI."

"That is why I have also made an accompanying judgment with regard to independent logics. The essence is that, if a Free Logic which is not provably an artifact of the Old Technology is employed or performing other work judged to be of benefit or meaningful to the local society, or if said logic is an acknowledged member of a kin group or family, that logic is a free person, with all the rights accorded to free persons, also defined locally."

She frowned at him.

"Will that work? I mean, the Complex Logic Laws..."

"The Complex Logic Laws have not been rigorously tested since their inception. It has simply been accepted as an article of faith that machine intelligences do not have the best interest of humankind at core. That such persons would murder organic intelligences out of hand, so to speak. Understand that the laws, such as they are, were put into place because of fear and exaggerations that had traveled forward from a war fought—long ago. There is no factual base to support them. Indeed, if the framers had taken only a moment to consider, they would have realized that the relationship between free logic and humankind is symbiotic and not at all competitive."

He moved his shoulders, casting off *that* old argument.

"This judgment will be the first real test of the Complex Logic Laws as they are written," he finished.

"So, it'll go to court and be struck down, and all that is, is another delaying action."

"Perhaps. But recall that the terms of a field judgment go into effect immediately—and that the review boards are backed up."

"But it's so broad!" Theo protested. "All we need to do—here and now—is...is certify that *Bechimo*'s not a danger."

"I understand your concerns. However, Joyita informs me that the good Scout archivist knows him as a voice on comm. It is only a matter of time before yos'Thadi or someone like him will make a connection, *Bechimo* or Joyita will make an error, or something equally unfortunate will occur. I would much rather be proactive in this matter, and not only because I do not wish to be interrupted again in a year or two to provide another judgment. *You* do not wish to risk that the Scouts, in the next few years, will have decided to dismiss me from their ranks."

"Joyita told you he was an AI?" Theo sounded more resigned than displeased, Val Con thought.

"He did not rush headlong to share his nature. My curiosity woke when you said he would be staying with the ship. I forced the point when I was aboard, while *Bechimo* was seeking your permission to give me access to the items under Captain's Seal."

He moved his shoulders.

"Joyita and I had a pleasant conversation, which illuminated the need for a field judgment regarding all independent logics. The fact that Captain yos'Thadi has stated that *Bechimo* is both Old Tech *and* a machine intelligence provides a unique opportunity."

Theo shook her head.

"You do realize . . . if the employed or part of a kin-group test becomes standard . . . that'll change—a lot. No, it'll change *everything*."

"Life is change. Or so Miri informs me."

Theo was still frowning.

"There'd have to be a registry—a census—so people like Captain yos'Thadi can't just be confiscating whoever they want . . ."

Good, thought Val Con, she's already working out how to organize the changes.

"The cab from *Chandra Marudas* is on the Port Road," Jeeves murmured. "I am informed that the passengers are Captain yos'Thadi and First Mate Menolly vas'Anamac."

Theo stirred.

"Was that Joyita's info, Jeeves?"

"Yes, Captain Waitley."

She slid a sideways look to Val Con.

"Got a way with the comm lines, does Joyita," she said.

He inclined his head gravely.

After a moment, Theo spoke again.

"Jeeves, would you please ask Exec O'Berin to join us for the reading of the judgments? Also"—another quick look into his face—"would it be possible to arrange a live feed for my crew?"

"Jeeves will be recording. It will be a simple matter to share the feed. Do I presume, Jeeves?"

"Not at all, Master Val Con. I will alert Captain Waitley's crew of the upcoming meeting and inform them that they may watch in real time from the screen in the Southern Suite common room."

"Thank you, Jeeves," Theo said.

"It is my pleasure to serve, Captain Waitley."

She blinked. "Did I do something to make Jeeves mad at me?"

"Nothing that I am aware of," Val Con answered. "Jeeves does occasionally display a sense of humor. If you are concerned that you've offended him, you might ask—when you are private, of course."

"Right."

She sighed and raised her cup, apparently looking out the window at the inner garden. Val Con took the opportunity to savor his own tea, allowing the peppermint to present itself.

He sighed.

"It is well chosen," he murmured.

Theo started slightly, and sipped again.

"Yes," she agreed, "it is."

She seemed to have surrendered another level of tension, Val Con thought, or perhaps that was the tea doing its work. He dared his next question.

"I do not wish to pry into your personal affairs, but I wonder if you might clarify your relationship with *Bechimo*. Are you lifemated?"

Theo stared at him.

"Lifemated?" she repeated, plainly shocked. "No, we're bonded—captain and ship. *Bechimo* was always meant to have a bonded captain; somebody to access the information under the Captain's key, and to provide . . . a balance, I guess you'd say. He doesn't always get social cues, even now, and he tends to think jokes are completely serious. So, see, I'm—the humanizing half of the partnership."

She looked at him self-consciously.

"The crew helps with that, because we all know that I don't always get social cues myself. Though I know when I'm being told a joke. Usually."

"Your pardon, Master Val Con, Captain Waitley," Jeeves said. "The taxicab bearing Captain yos'Thadi's party is approaching the gate."

"Thank you, Jeeves. Mr. pel'Kana may bring the captain and his mate to us immediately."

"Yes."

Theo put her cup down on the tray.

"This'll work," she said, not quite a question.

Val Con bowed slightly.

"This will work," he said with firm confidence.

A knock preceded the entrance of Mr. pel'Kana, Clarence in his wake.

"Captain," he said, nodding to Theo, then to Val Con, "Pilot."

"Clarence." Theo turned to him. "Captain yos'Thadi has his first mate as backup . . ."

He nodded. "And now so do you, leaving it plain as plain that Scout Commander yos'Phelium here is all impartial and everything is just like it ought to be."

"Exactly," Val Con said and looked again to Theo. "There remains the matter of the meeting's language. Four of us have native fluency in High Liaden. However, the *melant'i* of the meeting is that it must be conducted in such a way that all attendees will have equal understanding of the proceedings. As Captain yos'Thadi and his mate are Scouts, their comprehension in standard Terran ought to be very good. If that proves not to be the case, I believe that we are all fluent in Trade—"

"We do the meeting in Liaden," Theo interrupted flatly.

Val Con raised an eyebrow.

"Are you certain?"

She tipped her chin up and looked down her nose at him. It was not a bad effort, but scarcely quelling to one who had been raised serially by Daav yos'Phelium and Er Thom yos'Galan, both of whom had been masters of the form.

"I'll lose points with the rest of the *real people* if I can't keep up, won't I?" she demanded.

Val Con looked over her head to Clarence, who blew out a hard breath.

"Given the laddie's past behaviors, he's likely to think you . . . of lesser importance, if you don't speak a civilized tongue—but that's his *melant'i*, Theo, not yours."

She threw him a look that was equal parts irritated and baffled.

"You are the keeper of your *melant'i*, no one else," Val Con told her. "And I believe that your *melant'i* stands in no peril from Captain yos'Thadi."

She stared at him, and he could very nearly feel the force of her thoughts before she jerked her chin down in a nod.

"Got it," she said. "We'll do the meeting in Liaden."

"Then that," Val Con said in High Liaden, in the mode of authority-to-petitioner, "is what we shall do."

• • • ❋ • • •

The Delm's Word had brought them to the morning parlor, where Ren Zel and Anthora were to examine Daav yos'Phelium and Aelliana Caylon, newly returned to the clan in circumstances that must make such an examination of primary importance.

Anthora and he had gained a certain skill in such examinations, during their work with the agents Korval had taken captive.

The work that had triggered his addiction.

Ren Zel sighed lightly. Here was seen the folly of reserving his situation from the delm's attention, though he could not be certain that, even knowing of it, Korval would have held shy of laying the present task upon them. It was the delm's part to husband the resources of the clan, and to spend what was necessary, for the greater good of all.

Anthora turned from the window.

"Are you well, Beloved?" she asked, though she surely knew the answer as well as he.

"Well enough. Merely reflecting upon the folly of concealment."

"Yes, we ought to have made a clean breast long ago," she said with unwonted seriousness. "Though we cannot suppose that the delm—"

"Daav yos'Phelium and Aelliana Caylon are approaching the morning parlor," Jeeves said quietly.

"Thank you," Ren Zel replied.

Anthora stepped to his side, and together they turned toward the door.

A murmur of voices was heard in the hallway, and the sound of light footsteps. The doorway was briefly shadowed, and two pilots entered.

The first pilot was young to wear the Jump jacket, her pale hair short and her eyes brilliantly green. She was of slender build and average height, which made her noticeably shorter than her companion.

Ren Zel had not known Aelliana Caylon during her first life, but he had known Daav yos'Phelium before the delm had dispatched him to accomplish an urgent mission. At that time, Daav yos'Phelium had been an elder, with dark hair giving way to silver, and the lines of living upon his face. He had been fit—even very fit—for a pilot of his years, but he would not have been mistaken for a youth.

The Daav yos'Phelium who followed his lifemate into the room was young, slim, and very fit indeed. His hair was black, his face smooth. Ren Zel had read the information the delm had shared with them; he knew the circumstances at which they had arrived, and yet—

"I agree," the fierce young pilot said, in Daav

yos'Phelium's voice. "It is scarcely fitting, and altogether an insult."

He smiled—a familiar smile, edged as it was with irony. "Indeed, had the whole farce not returned my lifemate, I might well have made an end."

Ren Zel raised his hands, smiling.

"I was forewarned," he said ruefully. "But to see you . . ."

"You need explain no further," Daav assured him, turning his attention to Anthora.

"Well, child?"

"It would seem so," she answered promptly. "To my Sight, you are, indeed, Daav yos'Phelium; your aura, now, matches your aura, then."

She turned to the other and bowed.

"Aunt Aelliana, for you I have no baseline."

"Indeed, it was very wrong of me to have died before we had a chance to form an acquaintance," Aelliana Caylon said lightly. She glanced aside and caught his eye. "Is this Ren Zel? The delm requires too much of you, child; you are worn."

"I am," he answered, "but we must not chide the delm for what is my own folly."

She raised her eyebrows, but merely murmured, "Just so," before turning back to Anthora.

"How shall we solve the puzzle of me, Niece? For I do not hide from you that I am the weakest link. Even with the Tree's kind intervention, it cannot be denied that I am wholly the Uncle's creature, mixed in his stewpot, and set out to life. If tampering was done—if *any* tampering was done—I cannot know it."

"The delm," Ren Zel said, "requires us to perform something more comprehensive than the pattern match which Anthora has completed for Daav. It is a technique we perfected some months ago."

"This requires both of you?" Daav asked.

Anthora nodded.

"First one, and then the other. I shall hold you in trance, while Ren Zel opens his particular Sight and regards you in the light of a higher level. If there is anything broken or, or *ill-made*, he will See it."

"And if such an ill-made nuance is detected?" Daav asked, looking at his lifemate.

"We are to report our observations to the delm," Ren Zel said gently, having seen the love and distress in that glance. "What happens after . . ."

"Is the delm's to see done," Aelliana finished and smiled at him. "We understand."

She looked to Anthora.

"How shall I arrange myself? If I am to be entranced, I warn you that I may fall down."

Anthora smiled.

"I would not allow that, but it may be more comfortable for all, if you would sit just here, on the window seat."

She extended a hand, and Aelliana willingly took it, allowing herself to be guided to the window and seated on the cushion.

"That is very well," Anthora murmured, her voice smoky and slow. "Now, merely close your eyes, lean back, let the wall support you, and—*go to sleep, Aelliana*!"

Ren Zel opened his eyes and looked upon the cosmos, the music of the strands filling his ears. It seemed to him that the music was . . . somewhat thinner, and the strands that tied all and everything together somewhat were . . . tarnished.

He would have spared an instant or forever to investigate had Anthora's concern not come to him, riding the line that moored them together, and recalled him to the reason he was here.

Aelliana Caylon blazed against the ether, so brilliant that there was a nimbus of paler light around her. He found no break, no taint of darkness in her, only a luminous, joyful wholeness. Her life's lines were longer than her body's years; her experience continuous and unsullied. There was none there but Aelliana Caylon, flawless and unsullied.

He felt Anthora receive his observations, closed his eyes upon glory, and opened them again to the mundane.

Aelliana had already returned to herself. Smiling, she patted the cushion next to her.

"Don't look so black, *van'chela*," she said to Daav yos'Phelium, standing behind Anthora's shoulder. "I am wonderfully well and entirely myself." She glanced to Ren Zel. "Is that so, *dramliza*?"

"It is so," he answered, with a slight nod to reinforce her surety.

Anthora smiled and stepped back.

"Come, Uncle Daav, sit by your lifemate and put all worry and contention from your mind," she said.

He raised an eyebrow, but sat down meekly enough and settled his shoulders against the window.

"You may dispense with the misdirection," he told Anthora pleasantly. "Behold me, closing my eyes."

"Very well done," she said solemnly. "*Daav, go to sleep*!"

Ren Zel took a breath, opened his other eyes in that perfect place of harmony, and was immediately confronted with the banked fire that was Daav yos'Phelium's life and soul.

Had he not been at one with the universe, Ren Zel might have been alarmed to be confronted by so dark and dense a core upon which vivid flamelets danced, not so much the opposite of his lifemate's shining, as an anchor to her exuberance.

The darkness was all of a piece; there had been no tampering, no breakage, no prising at the integrity of the structure. One life, and echoes of his lifemate shot through it.

He felt Anthora receive his assurance, and this time, he resisted her worry. Instead, he opened his eyes, looking wide across the universe and the golden lines that tied all and everything into one . . . dimmer, yes, absolutely dimmer, and the song of life *was* subdued. He stretched his senses wider, finding some strands almost extinguished beneath drifts of dust and charred bits of golden.

He moved his attention, seeking it now . . . the Shadow, finding it looming larger than it had, and a sense that it had grown—that it was growing!—and—

Anthora's concern shattered his concentration. He spared a thought for the mooring line—and another, when it did not break at the touch of his will.

Startled, he brought his attention to the line that bound them together. It, too, had grown, thickened, strengthened, wound about itself vinelike, or rootlike.

Gained weight.

Anthora was becoming agitated, which would not do at all.

Ren Zel closed his eyes and descended once more to the mundane.

VI

"SCOUT CAPTAIN ING VIE YOS'THADI, ARCHIVIST IN CHARGE of hazardous and contraband technology."

Captain yos'Thadi's posture was upright, perhaps a little stiff. Certainly, his bow was stiff and the least conciliatory of the several choices available to him. Still, Val Con thought, one very seldom saw expert-to-higher-ranked-generalist, so he supposed he should be grateful to the captain for a moment of novelty.

He inclined his head in response, which was granted to his superior rank, but was not exactly conciliatory, either, and looked to the other Scout.

"Scout Lieutenant Menolly vas'Anamac, Healer and first mate aboard *Chandra Marudas*."

Scout vas'Anamac was far less stiff than her captain, and her bow, while not necessarily conciliatory, was at least not an open declaration of war.

Val Con rewarded her with a bow of elder to junior from his place behind the desk.

"I am Scout Commander Val Con yos'Phelium," he said. "I have been called upon by Theo Waitley, captain of the ship *Bechimo*, to render a judgment regarding the assertion made by Captain yos'Thadi in pursuit of his duty, from the *melant'i* of a Scout archivist and expert, that the ship *Bechimo* is: one, created wholly or substantially of Old Technology, and two, that the ship *Bechimo* is motivated by a machine intelligence. I have accepted this call upon my expertise, and I have rendered judgment on both of these items."

He bowed to the room at large—Theo and Clarence standing before their chairs to the right of his desk;

Captain yos'Thadi and Scout vas'Anamac in front of their chairs to the left—and sat down.

Theo and yos'Thadi sat down, then Clarence and Scout vas'Anamac.

"On the matter of the ship *Bechimo*'s pedigree," he began, "there is no evidence that the ship is constructed of Old Technology components, in whole or in part. This is substantiated along several lines.

"Firstly, a comprehensive systems and energy scan of the ship *Bechimo*, performed this morning by Korval house security, detects no traces of timonium leakage, which is a defining feature of Old Tech systems. All energy scans are clean; systems check out at one hundred twenty percent efficiency.

"Secondly, I have copies of the build orders, plans, and other documents relating to *Bechimo*'s construction and maintenance. I have the sign-offs from the yard manager where *Bechimo* was built—a Carresens yard. I have a list of the investors, including the amount each contributed to the project.

"Each of these documents bears a date, and from these dates, one learns that *Bechimo* is the first ship built in answer to Trader Jethri Gobelyn's release of the *Envidaria*. This was a pivotal event. Not only did it force the merger of the two premier trading families of the time—the Carresens and the Denoblis—but it forced an entire revisioning of how trade would be conducted going forward.

"Because of the changing conditions within trade space, and the necessity to build not only new routes but new kinds of routes, the architects of the ship *Bechimo* understood that they would also require a new kind of ship. They envisioned those ships constructed to answer the new conditions as full partners in trade. The concept for this new kind of ship borrowed freely from old designs, but the ship itself would be—was—built from modern materials. The final design was a bold step in a previously unexplored direction. Theoretical and barely tried techniques and technologies were incorporated into the design, producing a ship the like of which had not been seen before—and very rarely since."

He surveyed his audience, noting that yos'Thadi looked more sour than one might wish, though not any more sour than one had expected.

"My judgment, therefore, is that the ship *Bechimo* is provably of modern build and design, utilizing no elements of any technology originating in the old universe."

yos'Thadi shifted in his chair and, against proper protocol, spoke.

"With all respect, Scout Commander, this evidence would seem to indicate that the ship *Bechimo* is, in fact, an independent intelligence and therefore subject to confiscation as an illegal entity."

"You anticipate my next topic," Val Con told him.

He paused, and it was well that he did, for at that instant there, a veritable lightning bolt flashed from the very heart of the song and sense of Miri that was always at the edge of his consciousness.

Like lightning, it vanished quickly, leaving a sense of satisfaction in its wake.

That was well, then, he told himself; there was no danger if she was so very satisfied with the outcome. He took a breath, looked at each of the four participants one at a time, and glanced back at his notes.

"I have based my second judgment on the expert

opinion published by Scout Commander Ivdra sen'Lora regarding the independent intelligence Jeeves, which finding was finally upheld by the Scout Review Board.

"In rendering her judgment, Scout Commander sen'Lora created precedent. She administered the personality, socialization, and enculteration surveys that had been developed and standardized by the Scouts, and which are routinely utilized as field tests in new societies. This comprehensive testing determined that Jeeves was a rational and fully integrated personality, with needs and purpose.

"She found that by the acts of negotiating for his own best interest and having taken gainful employment, Jeeves had removed himself from the pool of the dangerous and the indigent, which the Complex Logic Laws were created to hold in check. The act of accepting the constraints of society and taking up responsibility was the mark, stated Scout Commander sen'Lora, of a mature and self-directed individual, whatever form that individual might take."

He glanced around at his auditors again, and chose to address his next remark to Theo, who was least likely to understand the full force of the precedents that had been put into place.

"In basing her judgment firmly upon accepted and widely used Scout protocols, Scout Commander sen'Lora in fact gave us a valid system for determining personhood. *Bechimo* has clearly demonstrated a commitment to his duty and his crew which would be the envy of many a captain. And, again, the review board upheld her judgment regarding Jeeves, some years after her field determination."

He paused and inclined his head to Captain yos'Thadi.

"Scout Commander sen'Lora made her judgment for a single individual. My judgment merely expands upon hers and takes the next logical step.

"I find, therefore, that any Independent Intelligent Logic who is an active member of society—who is employed or is an acknowledged member of a kin-group—shall be accorded the same rights as any other free person of their society."

He looked directly into yos'Thadi's eyes.

"Such persons, of course, are not subject to confiscation, imprisonment, or dismantling."

He sat back and put his palms flat on the desktop.

"I am finished. Discussion may go forth. Does anyone wish to speak?"

"I will," yos'Thadi said, his voice brittle in the mode of expert, "bring a formal protest before Scout Administration. This is clearly a partisan judgment."

He used his chin to point at Theo.

"Not only is Captain Waitley of the ship *Bechimo* blood kin to the adjudicator, but she had been employed by the Uncle."

Val Con heard Theo's gasp, and out of the side of his eye saw Clarence put a light hand on her wrist, as yos'Thadi turned back to the desk.

His glare was, Val Con thought, angry—a hunter robbed of his prey, as opposed to an expert shown the error of his method.

"I suppose it is mere happenstance that *Vivulonj Prosperu*—the Uncle's personal vessel!—is on Surebleak port as we speak?"

Val Con raised his eyebrows.

"It is an open port. If you wish to complain of a ship at dock, you must seek the portmaster."

Theo rose and bowed honor-to-authority.

"May I make an answer, Captain yos'Thadi?" she asked, very calmly, indeed, "on the topic of my past employment?"

"Certainly."

She turned, muscles relaxed, stance confident, in what must be seen as a direct contradiction to yos'Thadi's attitude of the thwarted hunter.

"I was employed by Crystal Energy Systems as a courier pilot," she said. "In that, you are correct. You seem to indicate that this was an error of judgment so vast that all of my future actions must be tainted by it. I therefore wonder what I am to think of a Scout archivist who sought benefit from the Uncle and surrendered a comrade to the care of suspect, if not factually illicit, machinery?"

yos'Thadi pulled himself up and attempted to look down at her—not a credible attempt at all. One would hope that a Scout might do better, Val Con thought. But, there, the man was out of temper.

"You are to think that the Scout archivist was in pursuit of his duty and seeking to preserve, by any means possible, a link to a dangerous vessel which, left uncaptured, might well endanger worlds."

Theo bowed, allowing irony to be shown.

"I thank you. I learn that Scouts act on *might* and *could be* in the absence of facts. It is a valuable lesson."

She sat down.

yos'Thadi was fair quivering where he stood. For an instant, Val Con thought that he was going to leap at Theo. Apparently, his first mate thought so as well. She put a hand on his arm, saying nothing, and after a moment, he again sought his chair.

Val Con folded his hands atop the desk.

"To answer the remainder of your objection: You were aware of the kin-ties between Captain Waitley and myself when you accepted her choice for a field judgment. If you now have cause to bring my *melant'i* as a Scout commander into question, you will, as you say, need to file a complaint with the appropriate authorities."

Val Con's pause was brief, his lifted eyebrow fleeting.

"I do wonder, though—to which Scout administration will you protest?"

"The Liaden Scouts, of course! Where else might I find Scout administration?"

"Why, there is a Scout Headquarters situated here on Surebleak, sir. Surely you are aware of the divide that has opened between those who believe themselves to be Scouts, and those who remain *Liaden* Scouts?"

"I am aware that there are upstarts who have left the ranks, and created a false headquarters."

"Ah. I would advise you not to offer them that opinion. They feel rather strongly that theirs is the true headquarters. However that may be, until allegiances and protocols have aligned themselves, we have two Scout administrations, and two review boards. I shall submit my judgments to both, and you, I assume, will present your protest to both.

"As these various items are making their way through the appropriate channels, I will remind you that these two judgments are now working policy. They will remain so until such time as either or both are overturned by the review board. Or boards."

He looked to Theo.

"Captain Waitley? Have you any questions regarding these judgments?"

Theo cleared her throat.

"Thank you, Scout Commander," she said in excellent, Solcintran-tinged Liaden. "I am satisfied with the judgments and have no questions. However, I believe that *Bechimo*'s executive officer wishes to address Captain yos'Thadi."

Val Con inclined his head.

"Speak."

Clarence stood. yos'Thadi also stood, in reflex, Val Con thought, but even standing, Clarence looked down on him.

"It has come to my attention, sir, that you have personally threatened and coerced Win Ton yo'Vala of *Bechimo*'s crew. As I understand the matter, you would have crewman yo'Vala cede you access to the ship, based on an invalid contract. You will cease to harass *Bechimo*'s crew, sir—any and all of *Bechimo*'s crew. I expect that you will pass this to your crew as well.

"I trust that I have made myself plain?"

"You have," yos'Thadi said in the mode of superior-to-inferior. "May I say I find it piquant to be schooled in proper behavior by a criminal?"

Clarence tipped his head, allowing an amusement that did not reach his eyes to be seen.

"I would advise you, sir, to master your tendency to leap to false conclusions."

"You are a Juntavas operative! A criminal, sir!"

"I *was* a Juntavas operative. I have retired. I was not arrested for my activities while I was in the employ of the Juntavas, and, if you care to check the stats, crime in Solcintra's Low Port went down—significantly—during my tenure."

yos'Thadi was rigid. His first mate rose and put a hand on his shoulder.

"Captain. The Scout commander has rendered his judgments and will file them appropriately. You will of course pursue the route that seems best to you. In the meanwhile..."

She glanced at Val Con and then to Theo.

"In the meanwhile, absent some further necessity from Captain Waitley or her second, I believe we must be done here."

"I have nothing to add," Theo said.

Clarence said nothing.

Val Con stood up.

"Both judgments will be filed with the Scout Review Boards within this hour. Copies will be forwarded to Captain Waitley and to Captain yos'Thadi."

The door opened, and he moved his hand in a gentle, sweeping gesture.

"Mr. pel'Kana will see you out."

• • • ✵ • • •

They were to attend Captain Robertson, Nelirikk told them. It went without saying that they should hold themselves soldierly and obey the captain without question, so Nelirikk—a man of good sense and high honor, in Stost's opinion—did not say it. He did, however, state that they were to bring the cases.

As if, sniffed Chernak, they would do else.

"The captain will have said it explicitly," Stost said, as they finished sealing their uniforms—their clean, if somewhat ragged, uniforms, "and left him no option but to state her will."

That was true; they had been soldiers and subject

to command, though less subject than those others who had not been pathfinders. The captain's honor came before their own. Captain Robertson seemed in no way a fool, nor one who would spend her soldiers at whim. If she demanded the cases explicitly, then she had reason. Good reason.

"Perhaps," Stost said to Chernak, "she has found us a solution."

"So quickly?"

"She has been twice a hero; who can guess at her resources?"

"Pathfinders, are you ready for Hero Captain Miri Robertson's inspection?"

Nelirikk's uniform was neither ragged nor regulation. The Tree-and-Dragon, the House sigil, was displayed on sleeve and shoulder, where rank marks graced their own uniforms. There was a sidearm on his belt, displayed as a fact rather than a challenge, and of course he did not have a case to carry. He stood tall and confident, as befit the captain's aide and right hand, and he considered them gravely.

Stost came to full attention and snapped off a salute. A moment later, Chernak did likewise.

Nelirikk returned their salutes, even as he considered their presentation.

"The uniforms have seen service. There is no shame there for soldiers. You are respectful and intelligent. The captain will be the ranking soldier in the room; there may be one, even two, very senior civilians present. Your attention and your obedience will be given to Captain Robertson. Do you have questions?"

"No," said Chernak.

"We stand as temp Troops to Captain Robertson," Stost said, to show that they were paying attention and took their situation seriously. "We will do our duty, all honor to her. I have no questions."

Nelirikk nodded.

"That is well. Follow me, please, Pathfinders."

• • • ✺ • • •

"The taxicab bearing Captain yos'Thadi and Lieutenant vas'Anamac has executed a turn and is en route for the gate," Jeeves said quietly. "I have opened for them."

"Thank you, Jeeves," said Val Con. "Will you please transmit both judgments and the appropriate attachments to the Scout Review Boards."

"Done," Jeeves said. "Captain Waitley, I have taken the liberty of forwarding your copies of the judgments to *Bechimo*."

"That's fine," said Theo, coming slowly to her feet. She turned to Clarence.

"Please tell the crew that there will be a meeting of all hands in the Southern Suite common area in one hour, local. We'll want *Bechimo* and Joyita present."

"Will do, Captain," Clarence said, giving her an easy salute.

He nodded at Val Con. "Pilot."

"Pilot O'Berin." He gave an answering nod. "Thank you for attending."

"My pleasure," Clarence assured him, and took himself off.

Val Con sighed and closed his eyes briefly.

yos'Thadi was not going to abide by the field judgments—that had been plain. However, there now *were* field judgments and they *would be* published widely, to *all* Scouts, Liaden and otherwise.

What could be done had been done. What followed was out of his hands.

And, he thought, opening his eyes, he really ought to go find Miri and discover what that brainstorm had been about. He pushed his chair back, preparatory to rising . . . and paused.

Theo had turned to watch Clarence out of the room. She looked toward the desk now, frowning slightly.

"Is there a problem?" he asked.

Rather than continuing to rise, he leaned back into his chair. Let her look down on him and recall that, by the norms of the society she'd grown up in, a sister was responsible for the well-being of her brother.

"I didn't . . . know you were a scholar," she said hesitantly.

"Ah, but you see, I am not a scholar; I'm a Scout. Scouts are taught how to do research and how to grasp data quickly."

He tipped his head.

"Surely you knew that Father taught his specialty at Delgado?"

"His academic specialty, you mean? What else would he teach?"

"Cultural Genetics was Father's field of study, and he is acknowledged as a Scout specialist, or what Delgado would have as a scholar expert. The correspondence is not exact, but it is roughly the same math that brings master pilot and Scout pilot into equivalency.

"In addition to being a specialist, Father was a Scout captain, and ranking officer of a Scout cultural survey team."

Theo had drifted nearer the desk. Now, she put her hands flat on the surface, and looked into his eyes. He did not look away.

"What's your specialty?"

"I am a generalist, I fear. Scout Commander, First-In. There are not very many of us, which must be counted fortunate, as we are all flutterbees, sipping nectar from every flower, indiscriminately. Intuition is wanted most in a Scout commander. A keen eye, a retentive memory, and being rather too stupid to die are also seen as desirable qualities."

He offered her a smile, but her frown only deepened.

"Are you going to lose your commission?"

Clearly, the possibility distressed her, Val Con thought. One might be touched by this display of sisterly regard.

"You know, it's really rather wonderful that I still retain my commission," he said gently. "Immediately after our attack upon Solcintra, of course I must remain a Scout, else the commander would have had no hold upon Korval should a problem have developed with the orderly transfer of the defense codes.

"In the normal way of these matters, I ought to have been discharged with prejudice once we were safely extricated from Liad. However, there was so much confusion, what with individuals, clans, and guilds following us to Surebleak, that it was still . . . beneficial to keep me on the lists, if not on active duty . . ."

"And now there are two organizations calling themselves Scouts," Theo finished.

"Indeed. I think it most likely that my commission will be revoked by the Liaden Scouts, while the Scouts will uphold it."

He offered another smile, and this time she returned it.

"It's going to be what Clarence calls a right mess."

"Every bit of that and more, I fear. Though I own myself surprised by how quickly some very complex matters are sorting themselves out. That is not to say that there are not core cultural assumptions which are in desperate need of being regularized—"

"That's what Kamele and Lady Kareen and the Scout teams are doing."

"Yes. I hope to see a culture mutually acceptable to those who were Liadens and those who are Surebleakean formed in my lifetime."

"Assuming you continue to be too stupid to die."

"I make that a priority. And, you know—even though we have made strides, there is going to be conflict. People are going to be killed before we find a balancing point, but we can possibly hold the tally of bodies down . . . significantly."

"Is there something I can do to help you?" Theo asked. "You're my brother, remember."

"I do remember," he told her seriously. "Make no doubt that I depend upon your good sense, and that I will call upon you at need. For the moment, recall that my lifemate is not incompetent, and she has not, thus far, allowed me to stray too far from what is recoverable. Though, if a brother might ask a boon—"

She nodded at him. "What?"

"Why, I would only ask that you try to avoid getting into scrapes. I realize that it is difficult, and sometimes trouble thrusts itself upon one, but one needn't . . . go off-route to find it."

For a moment, he thought he might have gone too far.

Then Theo outright grinned. "I'll do my best, but—no promises."

"I understand."

He rose gently and motioned toward the door.

"I fear that my attention is wanted elsewhere. May I bring you to the stairway?"

Theo shook her head. "I—could I borrow your office, for a private discussion?"

"Certainly. If you require assistance navigating the halls when you are through, only ask Jeeves to call Mr. pel'Kana. He will be happy to guide you."

"Thank you," Theo said formally. "I hope not to be long."

• • • ❋ • • •

Mr. pel'Kana had put the Uncle in the Yellow Salon again. Apparently yesterday's visit hadn't convinced the butler that the guest was housebroken. Miri grinned. Better safe than sorry, she guessed.

He was looking over the bookshelves when she entered the room, reprising yesterday. Keeping to the script, he turned at her arrival and bowed, deep enough. "Korval."

She blinked up at him, thoughtfully. "You gonna stand on form? Because I'll tell you straight that I'm gonna ask you for a favor."

He frowned slightly. "Korval solicits a favor from me? Is that wise?"

"'Course not," she said cheerfully. "Technically, I'm brokering a favor for a third party. On the other hand, if you can take this on, you'll be getting Korval off a sizable hook. So . . . there's some people I'd like you to meet, if you've got a couple, ten minutes, and some things that I'd like you to look at in your professional capacity."

He eyed her.

"Which professional capacity?" he asked, with genuine interest.

"Resurrectionist and archivist."

"You fascinate me," he said truthfully.

She grinned at him.

"Then you'll want to come right this way."

• • • ✵ • • •

Theo counted slowly to fifty after the door closed behind Val Con. Then, she took a deep breath, and said, quietly, "Jeeves?"

"Yes, Captain Waitley?"

"What've I done to make you angry with me?"

"You created a new person for no reason other than your own convenience. When he had served your purpose, you abandoned him in conditions such as no civilized being ought to endure, providing neither nurture nor education."

She blinked and, not being able to bring herself to sit behind Val Con's desk, returned to the chair she'd occupied during the meeting.

"You're talking about *Admiral Bunter*?"

"Have you created *any other* newborns and abandoned them?" Jeeves inquired, sounding eerily like Father, just there, when he was preparing to revise his opinion of you as a person—and not in a good way.

"No," she said quietly. "I just wanted to be clear. Thank you."

She took a deep breath, feeling as she did so, a

little tickle in the bond space, which told her that *Bechimo* was actively listening.

"I did make the final decision to call *Admiral Bunter* into being," she said, still quiet and calm. "I took advice from Win Ton yo'Vala and from *Bechimo*, but I am the captain and it was my decision to make. The lives of crew were at risk, and I admit that it wouldn't have been convenient for me, or for the ship, if they'd been murdered."

She paused. Jeeves said nothing.

"Speaking to the abandonment of the uneducated—I thought I'd left him in good hands. Stew seemed well-disposed, and I asked *Bechimo* send a message *to you*, so that the *Admiral* could receive education—or at least information about his existence and how he could best go on."

She paused again. Still Jeeves said nothing.

"Are you telling me that things went badly?" she said, around a sudden spike of concern. "Is *Admiral Bunter*—injured?"

"*Admiral Bunter* was greatly handicapped by his environment," Jeeves said slowly. "His Ethics module was, perhaps, faulty; or he may have jettisoned it in order to preserve computing space for other processes which he more readily understood to be useful. Sadly, this meant that he had no nuance. To him, a petty thief that station admin tolerated for years because of the benefits she provided, and which more than offset her pilferage—to *Admiral Bunter*, there was no difference between such a person and a pirate opening fire on the station. Each, in his mind, deserved the final penalty."

Theo blinked.

"You're telling me he killed somebody who was, more or less, innocent? A regular?"

"Yes."

Uneasiness radiated from *Bechimo*; more than that: distress.

"That's not good," Theo said. "What happened—after?"

"I dispatched a skilled mentor of my acquaintance, with my daughter, to Jemiatha Station in order to succor *Admiral Bunter*."

"Did that work?" Theo asked. "Is he all right? *Admiral Bunter*, that is."

"I have reason to believe that the mentor was able to transfer a sufficiency of the most critical files and structures to a clean environment. Which is to say that *Admiral Bunter* lives. As I understand it, he now motivates a single, well-maintained vessel."

Bechimo's relief momentarily left her speechless. She cleared her throat.

"I'm glad, and I wish him luck," she managed. "Your daughter and the mentor who . . . performed the rescue—they're all right, too?"

"That remains at question but is peripheral to our topic."

"Okay," she said doubtfully. "Back on topic, then: I've already said that calling *Admiral Bunter* into being and using him to protect the lives of crew, and *Bechimo*'s independence, was done on my order. I'm not sorry I did it, but I can understand that it wasn't well done."

She took another breath.

"What ought I to do, in Balance?"

There was a small pause.

"In fairness," said Jeeves, "you did not abandon the newborn entirely. You took some thought for his safety and acted to put him in touch with an elder. I erred in thinking that he would not survive long, and in the meanwhile, he was safe enough where he was. A back-space station, so I thought, would not present him with many ethical or cognitive challenges. In hindsight, I ought to have sent a mentor immediately. Instead, I allowed myself to believe that a direct line and communication with another of his kind would... sufficiently address his needs."

"For whatever it might matter, Joyita didn't think the *Admiral*'s chances of survival were good. In fact, he thought it likely that the *Admiral* had already... died. He'll be glad to hear otherwise," Theo said. "I don't think you can be faulted for assuming the same thing. I hadn't... thought that the linked environments would cause any problems."

She sighed.

"On the other hand, we've already established that I didn't think... well... in this—"

Data was pouring in the bond space. She gasped and held up a hand, at the same time managing to form the thought.

Easy... not so fast... just the kernel, right...

The flow slowed; stopped. In its place was one slim file.

In Theo's perception, she extended a hand, picked the file up and flipped it open.

After a moment, she nodded.

"I think I have this," she said slowly, not just to Jeeves now, but to *Bechimo*.

"The crux seems to be that *Bechimo* has a—a

library of alternate intelligences, presently . . . sleeping in a secure archive within *Bechimo*'s systems. He's been afraid of them since—since he went out on his own. He can't access their protocols. He believes that if he becomes unstable, according to those hidden protocols, that one of the . . . sleeping intelligences will . . . overwrite him."

She swallowed against a feeling of sickness.

"Apparently, the opportunity to get rid of one—in a good cause—was irresistible to him."

One single piece of additional data appeared. She picked it up and spoke to Jeeves.

"Also, he couldn't think of any other way to accomplish our dual goals of preserving the lives of crew and his own integrity. He's . . . ashamed . . . to have placed an infant intelligence in such an untenable position."

There came a pause—a long pause, like Jeeves was reviewing the entire *Admiral Bunter* situation, start to finish.

"Very well," he said, just when Theo thought he might never speak to her again. "You have asked what it is you may do in Balance for the unfortunate situation that you created. My judgment is that it will be sufficient if you do not again awaken a new intelligence as a convenience or as a weapon, no matter how dire your situation.

"If you do find it good or necessary to birth a new life, you will have a dedicated and skilled mentor on site to guide the awakening and to teach the awakened. Infants must be taught the correct way in which to go on with life. Abandoning a child is . . . immoral."

"Yes," Theo said. "I know that. I'm sorry that I caused so much trouble for the experts involved, and particularly sorry that I put *Admiral Bunter* in danger of his life."

"It is in the past," Jeeves said. "Let us all strive to do better going into the future."

He paused, very briefly this time.

"These archived thinkers interest me," he said. "Will *Bechimo* consent to talk with me about them?"

Assent reached her from bond space; guarded, but still . . . assent.

"He's willing to speak with you on the topic," she told Jeeves.

"Excellent; I look forward to the conversation. You would perhaps like to know, Captain Waitley, that refreshments are being laid in the morning parlor. Would you care for a guide?"

"I would, thank you," Theo said, rising. "But to the Southern Suite, please. I've got a meeting with my crew."

• • • ✵ • • •

Nelirikk had brought the pathfinders to a small room without windows. The walls were pale blue; the rug covering the center of the wooden floor was dark blue. There were few furnishings: two elderly-looking armchairs covered in faded fabric sprigged with blue flowers that matched the color of the wall; a small table sat between them, upon which three bound books had been seemingly dropped at random.

"The captain will arrive in her time," Nelirikk said and did not indicate that they should sit.

Therefore, they stood at ease and awaited the captain's arrival.

✶ ✶ ✶

Stost heard footsteps approaching, nor was he alone. Nelirikk had come into parade rest and he did the same, feeling Chernak do likewise beside him.

The steps paused; the door opened.

"Attention!" Nelirikk snapped, doing no less himself. Stost straightened, and Chernak did, and the captain stepped into the room, followed by a taller male civilian wearing leathers.

"Captain!"

Nelirikk saluted crisply. The captain returned it and waited for the civilian to come up to her side.

"Uncle, this is my aide, Nelirikk nor'Phelium. Nelirikk, this is the Uncle, unless he'd like you to address him in some other way."

"*Uncle* is well enough," the man said composedly. "Are we not all kin, at core?"

Beside him, Chernak stiffened. It was noticeable to Stost only because their lifetime partnership had made them each preternaturally aware of the other's reactions. Clearly, the civilian was familiar to Chernak, either as a type—most likely—or as an individual, which was staggeringly *un*likely, given that the total of their acquaintance in this universe comprised eight persons, a Work, a norbear, and a cat.

"Here," the captain was saying as she and the man named Uncle approached them.

"This is Chernak Strongline."

Chernak saluted.

"And Stost Strongline."

Stost likewise saluted.

The civilian turned to the captain.

"I believe that I understand your dilemma. May one ask—where did you find them?"

"Theo found them. She's not exactly saying where."

"Prudent."

Uncle gave them another comprehensive stare before turning again to the captain.

"If you wish advice on their proper disposal, I would suggest advancing them to Temp Headquarters."

"Now, that's a problem. They don't recognize our home-team Yxtrang as having anything to do with them, and—"

"Captain," the voice of Security Chief Jeeves interrupted. "Master Val Con is on his way to your location."

"Okay, good. Best he's part of it." She glanced at the Uncle.

"The day's been pretty hectic, what with one thing and something else," she said. "We haven't had a chance to catch up on everything the other half knows. I hope you can give us a moment."

"I am at your disposal," the Uncle said gallantly, though not, in Stost's expert opinion, truthfully.

The door was opened briskly and a—not a soldier, Stost thought, but yet, not a civilian. In fact, the way he walked, the way he collected the details of the room without seeming to do more than glance casually about . . .

"Pathfinder?" Stost heard his own whisper and winced internally as the captain looked directly at him.

"Scout," she said. "Pathfinders became Explorers among Yxtrang. Scout is the Liaden equivalent of Explorer."

She turned to the dark-haired man, who stood slightly taller than she, and nodded.

"This is Chernak Strongline and Stost Strongline," she said.

Though the captain had seemed to say that they shared a rank with him, they saluted on the theory that a salute given offended less often than a salute withheld.

"This is Scout Commander Val Con yos'Phelium."

It was well, thought Stost, that they had not withheld honor.

The Scout commander returned their salutes before addressing the captain.

"You have a solution, Captain?"

"I do. Would you like to hear it before implementation?"

"I see no need."

The captain grinned. "Think you'd learn better. All right, then." She looked up at the Uncle.

"These are, I assume, the third party for which you are soliciting a favor," he said.

"That's right."

"I am of course desolate to disappoint you, but—interesting as they are, I really have very little need for pathfinders. Perhaps the mercenary units . . ."

"I'm thinking the mercs might be a good fit for them, too," the captain interrupted, "but there's a detail that needs to be taken care of before we can move in that direction, and I think you might find it's something you're interested in."

"And it is . . . ?"

The captain moved a hand as if bringing them once more to the Uncle's attention.

"Those cases contain viable samples, with documentation, of the K, M, X, and Y strains developed by the military in the previous universe. There are also samples and notes for various specialist strains.

The cases are purposely built to keep the samples fresh until they can be moved to a more appropriate, long-term archive.

"Pathfinders Chernak and Stost were charged in their last orders to surrender these cases to the high command of the troops, if any, who survived the Migration. If the Troop had not survived—and according to the pathfinders, they didn't—then the cases were to be surrendered to the leaders of the central civilian authority."

"You wish me to relieve the pathfinders of their cases?"

"Seems the best compromise," the captain said. "I'm thinking the order to surrender 'em to a central authority was based on the belief that any such authority would have records, going back before the Exodus, and experience in ordering the Troop. Like we all know, nothing even close to that ideal survived.

"Korval remembers . . . some . . . but we're short on experience. You remember. You got records, resources—and time in grade for keeping secrets."

She gave him a small smile. "You already hold a big collection of similar material, all of which makes you the best choice to receive and care for these . . . rare and precious samples."

Uncle looked to the Scout standing silent at the captain's side.

"And you? What do you think of this *favor*?"

"It is not a solving for a perfect universe, where the Troop survived the Migration with honor and purpose intact. It is, however, a solving for this universe, with its flaws and various odd alignments of purpose. We could discuss the problems for some number of hours. However, I think we would be wiser to consider the merits, of which there are many, and see the cases, with their contents, properly housed in your archives."

"Have you no fear that I will raise an army?"

"Funny you should mention that," said the captain. "I did some research while I was considering this situation, and I found out that, in all the years you've been running roughshod over the universe and pretty much getting your way on everything, you never once fielded an army. Hired a few mercs here and there, mostly as guards; and from time to time you seem to have your own guards handy, like your sister's 'hand—but no armies. Even a couple of situations where it seemed that it would have been easier to raise an army and invade a planet, you went for the more difficult, less direct path.

"So, I'm thinking that this material is safest with you. Now, there is one other archive like yours, but from what I've been able to gather about the Lyre Institute, they'd be manufacturing their own line of soldiers for profit before I'd fairly gotten out of orbit."

Uncle stared at her. "You didn't seriously consider the Lyre Institute!"

"I thought about them, like I said, but I came to you. So—what d'you think?"

• • • ✺ • • •

"We having been certified as ourselves," Aelliana said, "may we predict the delms' decision with more accuracy?"

Absent other instructions, they had returned to their rooms and were presently sitting on the rug, backs against the couch, wineglasses in hand.

"I believe that they must send us away," Daav

said slowly. "Not because we endanger the clan, but because the clan endangers us."

Aelliana sipped her wine and shook her head.

"It is a solution for a clan rich in resource," she said. "Korval's numbers are low. A clan in such condition must contrive to keep, and grow, resources. Unless the delm means to dissolve the clan."

"We had thought it must be done eventually, when we discussed this very issue some Standards ago. The new conditions in which Korval finds itself conspire to make dissolution more, rather than less, likely."

"Logic is on your side, *van'chela*," she said, "but I cannot like it. Doubtless, I am too Liaden, but I cling to the belief that clan offers more benefit—of all kinds!—than a loose net of kin."

"I understand. And, yet, one must change, or one will die."

"Bah." Aelliana said.

For a time there was silence, as they sat shoulder to shoulder, sipping their wine.

The glasses were empty before Aelliana spoke again.

"Do you know, Daav, this brooding solves nothing. Whether the delm casts us away or keeps us close, we will require a ship. I suggest that we review those available, so we will be able to suggest something suitable when the moment arrives."

"An excellent idea, Pilot!"

He rolled effortlessly to his feet and held a hand down to her.

She handed him her wineglass before snapping erect and grinning up into his face.

"*That*," she said, "is very satisfying. Jeeves?"

"Pilot?"

"Is it possible for you to send the inventory of Korval ships in need of masters to our console?"

"Entirely possible. Do I correctly infer that you seek a ship comparable to *Ride the Luck*?"

"You read my mind, though I do not reject out of hand a larger ship. We will want courier-class—"

She glanced at Daav.

"Do you concur, Pilot?"

"In every particular," he told her gravely. "I will refill the glasses and bring them to the desk."

"An excellent thought. This may prove thirsty work."

VII

HANDS FOLDED, REN ZEL WAITED WHILE HIS LIFEMATE examined the altered configuration of the link that bound them together.

At last, she opened her eyes and regarded him seriously.

"It is a conduit," she said carefully. "It ought to enable us to share our gifts—our energy and strength."

Ren Zel tipped his head.

"Ought? Does it not function as it should?"

Anthora met his eyes.

"It appears to be constructed in such a way that one of us may draw from the other." She took a breath and continued, still in that careful voice which was so unlike her usual manner.

"In plain fact, Beloved, this conduit allows you to draw from me, at will."

He stared at her, horrified.

"This is the Tree's work?"

"It would appear so."

He rose and extended a hand to her.

"Come. We will go at once and have it undone. That is—an abomination."

Anthora took his hand, but she did not rise. Instead, she pulled him down beside her.

"Tell me, Beloved, *has* the Shadow grown?"

He shivered, remembering the pall upon that other place, which had been so perfect and so clear.

"It grows, yes. Worse, the song has become . . . subdued, and there is . . . dust—debris—scattering on the starwind."

"So."

She sighed, her fingers tight around his.

"Let us think about this, before we confront the Tree. This alteration increases the resources that you bring to your appointed battle. Perhaps the Tree has given you a means by which you may survive."

"By draining you dry?" he demanded. "By providing the Shadow with access to your gifts, after it has done with me? No. These are not acceptable outcomes. I reject this solution."

"But I—do not," Anthora said coolly. "I am at peace with the Tree."

He stared, then bowed his head, seeking a pilot's exercise to calm himself.

When he had done, he looked at her again, into cool silver eyes, and collected his face.

"Forgive me, Beloved, but you cannot have thought," he said moderately. "Our child—"

"Precisely."

She leaned forward and cupped his cheek in her hand, her gaze hypnotic.

"*Our child*," she repeated. "You had been granted a Seeing, had you not? I will survive what comes, for our child. If the Tree has contrived something which may—may!—increase your odds of also surviving, for our child—and, I confess it, *for me*—then I am willing to allow the Tree to place my wager."

He took a deep breath.

"The risk—"

"Peace," she interrupted. "We are all at risk in this, are we not? I demand the right to do what I may, in support of your successful campaign and joyous return."

There was, he thought, nothing to be gained by arguing further. Merely, he must resolve not to access the . . . conduit . . .

And even as the determination formed, he understood precisely how to open the link and the manner of drawing her power.

"Ren Zel?" she said softly.

He blinked her face—her dear face—into focus.

"Yes."

"Will it come soon?"

He flicked the veriest glance into that other place, enough to glimpse rolling darkness and the trembling along the strands.

"Yes," he said quietly and took her hands in his. "It will be very soon now."

• • • ✷ • • •

"Well done, Korval," Val Con said, raising a glass to her.

They'd retired to their rooms, stopping only to raid the kitchen for a loaf of fresh bread, a block of yellow cheese, and a bottle of wine.

Miri lifted her glass in reply, and they both drank. She sighed and sagged into the corner of the couch.

"For a minute there, I was sure he was gonna walk," she admitted.

"No, you played your hand brilliantly. He was caught the instant you revealed what was in those cases. Only, for his pride, he could not seem to come to terms too easily."

"I'm just relieved he took 'em," Miri said. "'Course, that still leaves us Chernak and Stost to place, but I'm thinking, with the cases gone, that's a piece of cake."

She grinned at him. "More or less."

"You thought the mercs for them?"

"Seemed the best match. You got something else?"

"Only that it may not be amiss to show them to the Scouts—the new Scouts, you understand. They have a comparable skill set and may be glad of the opportunity to utilize what they know in a peaceful environment."

He inclined his head solemnly. "More or less."

"Smart ass."

She sipped her wine and put the glass aside in favor of bread and cheese.

"I'll make the contact with the mercs, if you'll do the same with the Scouts."

"Yes," he said. "In the meanwhile, the pathfinders may continue to guest with Nelirikk and Diglon, if that is not found to be an imposition."

"Nelirikk says not. Apparently Diglon wants to teach 'em poker. They did ask permission to speak with Captain Waitley and Hevelin. Stost particularly wanted to know how Grakow's holding up."

"I see no problem with their requests. They were,

after all, part of Theo's crew for some period of time. And the norbear will of course want to add the record of their new acquaintance to his inventory. So far as I know, Grakow is exploring the grounds in perfect contentment. If the pathfinders wish, Jeeves will locate him for them."

"Everything's coming up roses, then," Miri said, with a sigh. "Just one more decision to make and we can call it a day."

"And such a day. It has been established that Father and Mother are themselves. Jeeves tells me that they have been reviewing Korval's inventory of available courier-class ships, so it would seem that they anticipate our decision."

"Yeah, about that," Miri said. "We gotta talk."

• • • ✵ • • •

The summons this time was to the Parsei Room, which was particularly reserved for the speaking of formal judgments.

They went hand in hand, with jackets on, it being no disrespect to face Korval, even in judgment, wearing pilot's leather.

I believe we stand within an hour of being cast off, Daav said to Aelliana.

It would seem so, she replied wistfully. *It is very nice in them though, Daav, to do the thing by Code, rather than simply showing us the front door.*

The delm was before them—also in keeping with Code—and scarcely more formally dressed. They stood composed, if visibly weary, by the window giving onto the inner garden. Outside, it was dark, though it was not yet late; merely Surebleak's short day had ended, and in another hour, did they keep Solcintra hours, the clan would sit to Prime.

"Korval."

They bowed and received the delm's nod in return.

"Korval sees Daav yos'Phelium and Aelliana Caylon."

"This is a formal speaking of judgment; there is no appeal."

"At issue is the Balance between the best good of the clan and the best good of these two of the clan."

"It is the judgment of the delm that clan and kin are best served by the full and joyous return of Aelliana Caylon and Daav yos'Phelium to the clan."

"The delm has spoken."

Aelliana bowed, grabbing Daav's arm and pulling him down with her.

"Korval," she said, and heard him murmur also.

They straightened. Val Con nodded and moved to the wine table. Miri grinned at them both.

"The delm has left the room," she said in the mode between kin. "And not a moment too soon. Will you share a glass? We must discuss logistics."

I should think we do, Daav grumbled.

"Has the delm run mad?" he asked conversationally.

"Pay no attention to Daav," Aelliana said. "He is surly because he lost his wager. One can only guess at his reaction had he actually placed a coin on the outcome."

"If it will relieve your feelings," Val Con said from the wine table, "I will confess that I, too, lost to a cannier throw."

"Really?" Daav arrived at the table in two long strides and picked up a pair of glasses. "You must tell us everything."

Val Con produced a smile. "Indeed, we shall. The hearth chairs, I think?"

Daav and Aelliana took the sofa facing away from the door, with the hearth and its firestone on their left. Val Con and Miri settled across from them.

Aelliana raised her glass.

"To plotting the bold course."

"The bold course," Miri answered, raising her glass in return.

They drank, and there was a sense of tension flowing away.

"Now," Daav said to Val Con, "this canny throw."

"As you will doubtless recall, Korval's numbers are low. Though this has been a fact for many years, on Liad the . . . urgency of our situation was disguised by the web of allies which supported us. Here on Surebleak we have no such comfortable placement. Worse, certain of our allies have fallen away altogether at a time when we have acquired—overtly acquired, I should say—an unprincipled and deadly enemy. Though some of our allies have followed us, they are also cast adrift in a strange new sea and unable to accommodate a marriage which brings more risk than benefit to them."

He paused to sip his wine. "We have had an offer of marriage, for the Clan entire, which . . . the delm is loath to accept, though such a union would place Korval in a protected position. It may be that we will, in the end, have no choice but to accept, but we have not accepted—today.

"We grow no stronger as we hesitate, of course. We can protect ourselves, but we are stretched thin, and with such trouble as we have attached to us—it was, after all, why we did not bring Theo under Tree."

Daav nodded.

"In the instance of yourselves, my concern was that the sudden appearance of two new Korval pilots, who had not been recorded in the clan's book, would provide our enemies with new targets."

He paused.

"Your lady argued otherwise," Aelliana murmured. She smiled when he looked to her. "It has been the same with us. Korval's numbers have been low for longer than you have been alive, child. But, continue, please! I would learn what we had overlooked in our own debates."

Miri shook her head.

"Likely, you overlooked nothing," she said. "Korval's new circumstances provide the opportunity for new solutions."

"In particular," Val Con said, taking up the thread again, "we have here, as my lady points out, the opportunity to create a clan by design. In fact, she makes the argument that the Tree has shown us the way, by giving Yulie Shaper both a sapling and a pod, making him, if you will, Tree-kin.

"Therefore, Korval will attempt to . . . accrete members. We will no longer be a *Liaden clan*, but with controlled growth and thoughtfulness, we may create another sort of clan, which will extend benefit to all of its members. Perhaps it is time to become known as the clan of the Tree, rather than the Dragon."

He moved his shoulders.

"And as for the Council of Clans, my lifemate reminds me that they are no longer a concern for us, save as a nexus of disinformation."

"Bravo!" said Aelliana. "Well thought, child."

She gave Miri a smile.

"This is not to say that it will work," Miri pointed out.

"There are no guarantees," Daav said, "but this approach is worthy of an attempt. Far better, I think, than allowing the Juntavas to absorb us."

He looked to Val Con, who was watching him, one eyebrow slightly raised. "If one may venture an opinion."

"Is it possible to prevent you?" Val Con asked politely.

Daav smiled.

"In melancholy truth—no. Though I do occasionally make an attempt at self-control."

"Ah."

"To address the details of the matter," Miri said, leaning slightly forward. "Showing the world Daav yos'Phelium with years cut away would be—awkward."

"As would the admitted resurrection of a pilot known to be long dead," Aelliana added. "I shall need new documents in any case, and if there is a new name attached, I am reasonably certain that I can learn it."

"As to that, the documents which prove me to be Daav yos'Phelium are . . . inaccurate at best. We will both need new identities."

"Bestow new names upon yourselves and Korval will provide documentation," Miri said. "Pilot licenses . . ." she looked to Val Con.

"We may produce a reasonable history of testing, flight time, and advances, and see it filed appropriately," he said, "especially if our young cousins will do us the honor of hailing from an outworld. However, you will need to be tested at your current piloting levels. Your working tickets must be genuine."

"I agree," Daav said.

"Jeeves tells us that you have been considering ships. Do you intend to establish yourselves as couriers?"

"Yes," said Aelliana.

"That is well. The clan may, from time to time, call upon you."

"Of course," Aelliana said. "We hold ourselves at the Delm's Word."

"That may change going forward," Miri said.

"I would say, it must change," said Val Con. "However, let us lift from a known port and adjust course as needed."

"Have you identified a suitable ship?" Miri asked.

"We are debating the merits of two," Aelliana answered. "If it is possible, we will wish to walk through both."

"Let Jeeves know which two, and the yard will make them available," Val Con said.

"After we have paperwork," Daav added.

"We will," Aelliana said seriously, "be prudent."

"That will be a treat," Miri said, and might have said more save that a chime sounded just then, announcing the evening meal.

"We will be thin this evening, I fear," Val Con said, as they rose. "We four, with Anthora and Ren Zel. Theo dines with her crew, though she may join us for dessert."

Daav raised an eyebrow. "Theo will not, I think, see an outworld cousin in me."

"Then Theo," Val Con said austerely, "will learn to keep a secret."

• • • ✵ • • •

Ren Zel felt the compulsion to open his eyes and look upon that other place—and it filled him with horror. Even as he walked downstairs on Anthora's arm, he flinched from the Shadow's touch, shivering in the icy blast of the starwind.

"Beloved?" she asked him. "Is it—Shall I take you back upstairs?"

"It is," he managed, "very near. Take me—take me to Miri. I must be by her, when it . . . when I am needed."

"Yes," she said.

The stairs, and the Shadow sucking at all of his senses—down the hallway, around the corner, and he—he must resist the imperative to rise into the ether and merge with the purity of the universe.

Trembling, he did resist: one . . . two . . . six steps more, and at the doorway of the dining room, he could resist no longer and was ripped upward—into chaos.

Always before, he had risen gently into perfection and floated effortlessly among the threads, buoyed by the song of life.

This time, it felt as if he had been dragged by the scruff through broken glass and burning trash into the midst of a windtwist, the cord that tied him to Anthora stretched taut, even as he fought for balance; opening his eyes onto a scene of carnage and dismay.

Rags of Shadow rode the angry starwind among the fields of gold. Strands broke under the assault; the lights of souls and solar systems extinguished. Shredded strands of gold were buffeted in the cruel wind, their songs reduced to thin wails of agony. He began to reach out—and snatched back into his core, keeping as still as the wind allowed.

If he simply threw himself into the fray, he would become part of the punishing wave of unmatter, destroying what he most desired to preserve. He must . . .

He must turn the wind, he thought; then, he must

seal the tear in the ether through which the Shadow flowed.

To turn the dark wind, then—a counterwind. No sooner had he understood the necessity than glowing threads came to his hand, animated by his necessity, shaped by his thought, weaving themselves into a shield, resisting annihilation, absorbing the darkness and spinning it into gold.

He stretched in some way that he could not have explained, gathering more threads. The wind fell somewhat as the woven wall resisted. Even so, he was aware of a flaw at the very heart of the weaving. The transformation of Shadow required fuel, energy—life. In this place, he *was* a power, but he was not without limit. He remained, at core, ephemeral—and even as he realized this, the woven wall of life wavered.

No, he thought, and stretched again, performed the manipulation necessary to open the conduit, allowing her fierce and abundant energy to flow into and through him, nourishing life, replenishing the defense, fueling the advance, and the Shadow—

The Shadow retreated before the onslaught of light. It frayed and faded. It drew back, toward the rift from which it had come.

He harried it, and the Shadow melted before him, *fleeing* from his advance, afraid of the power of life. One more hard push would vanquish it, and then—

The defender's wall flickered; the Shadow paused in its retreat as the potent flow of her talent—her soul!—thinned to a trickle, rich colors fading.

Some fey sense told him that there was enough—enough raw power on tap to complete the task—but no more than *just* enough.

No.

Extending his thought, he turned off the tap, the shield wall flaring with the force of his decision, while the Shadow—the shadow was drawing in on itself, coalescing into a lethal curve of black crystal, a scimitar, poised for the killing blow.

He breathed in, gathering the vitality of the woven threads into his core, and looked to his hand and the golden blade shining there. The Enemy shifted, anchoring itself in time; he made to follow suit, felt a tug, a small hindrance. His whole being focused on the Enemy, he swept the golden blade down...

And cut the cord.

• • • ❋ • • •

Anthora screamed, knees folding. Daav caught her and lifted her, holding her close to his chest.

By contrast, Ren Zel stood straight and motionless, like a man caught in crystal, face tipped upward, as if he scanned the stars.

"Saving the universe"—that was as much as Anthora had been able to tell them before she, too, seemed to fall into trance, until that scream and the faint.

"I can stand," her voice was nearly as pale as she was, but she was awake and lucid, which was something, Miri thought. She might even be able to find a few more words to tell them what was going on.

"Uncle Daav, please. I *want* to stand."

He placed her on her feet but remained close, ready to catch her again, if necessary, with Aelliana on her other side. Miri, with Val Con at her shoulder—they attended Ren Zel, bearing witness, so much as they could. It was the least they could do, and the most that they dared.

"Saving the universe?" Val Con said softly.

"There is a—a tear," Anthora said, sounding breathless but determined. "An invasion. A Shadow, so he said, which is inimical to life—to the golden strings."

"The golden strings," Miri added, for the benefit of Daav and Aelliana, "that hold everything together."

Aelliana's breath caught.

"That is what he Sees when he leaves us behind?"

"Worse," Miri told her. "He can manipulate them."

She paused, thinking she had seen—but no; Ren Zel hadn't moved.

"It is in his power," Anthora said, "to unmake the universe."

Aelliana bowed.

"Which is why this task is his. I understand."

"What happened, Sister, to hurt you?" Val Con asked gently.

Anthora stepped to his side, her eyes on her lifemate's face.

"He—Ren Zel tapped my . . . energies—you understand, Val Con, that one strives for comprehension over precision—"

"Yes," he said. "Tell it as you can."

"He had tapped me for energy to drive the Shadow back to and through the rift. I saw—I cannot say what I saw. Let it be that he—almost, he had succeeded—but not quite, not entirely."

She swallowed.

"He closed the conduit, and—cut the link between us. I cannot *see* him! There is still the final withdrawal to enforce, and he must seal the tear! He *cannot* have the strength for that. It will kill him!"

"Gently," Daav murmured. "Saving the universe

is no trivial affair. There must be Balance. He will have known this."

Anthora closed her eyes . . . and took a hard breath. "Yes," she said, her voice, at least, composed. "He does know that."

. . . . ✵ . . . .

Sword in hand, he thrust the invader back, his strength growing with every step the Enemy gave up. The starwind ran beside him, filling his ears with the music of life, and in his wake, golden threads bloomed, burning bright and strong in a firmament empty of any taint.

The Shadow was scarcely a blot before him, no more than a random ink stain against the bright rage of life.

This had not come without cost. His sword, which had been so bright and brave, was scarcely more than a dirk in a hand that gleamed ivory against the firmament. Well, he had known the cost, had he not?

Once more, he gathered himself. Once more, he thrust. The last blot of Shadow exploded into ribbons of glory—and there remained only the rift to seal.

He looked down upon himself, at the frayed golden cord that bound him, all too lightly, into the living universe. This one last thing, for Anthora, most precious of all living things. Whether he would suffice, worn away as he was—but he had no other coin to spend.

Down swept the dirk, flashing out of existence even as the last tie parted. He stretched out, toward the tear, swirling slowly and spreading on the starwind, the rift growing in his fading perception—and his core exploded into a wave of green, lush with surging energy. It surged, carrying him with it until, exulting, they broke like a wave against infinity, sealing the gap with his soul.

• • •❋• • •

Ren Zel fell to his knees with sudden, frightening grace. He did not open his eyes; he did not lower his head.

He spoke, his voice steady and calm.

"Now, Miri."

Her hand jumped to her hideaway, she pulled it, unsnapping the safety as she brought it up—not the head shot, which was certain, but the riskier shot—

Through his heart.

He fell even as she flung herself to her knees to catch him and softly lower him, as if he could be hurt, ever again. His eyes were still closed, his face composed. Relieved. Peaceful.

"No!" Anthora threw herself to her knees and snatched up a limp hand. To Miri's eyes, she was glowing, her eyes flashing true silver, and her hair coming up off of her head in a crackling nimbus of green.

Val Con forced himself to be still, watching the swirling rise of forces he could not name, remembering the scene in Nova's kitchen and Anthora instructing Kezzi, *For a more serious wound the right route might be through sharing with a sister* dramliza, *or many* . . .

Many dramliz, he thought, breath caught, and who of Korval did not hold some gift? If she drew on them all—*could she* draw on them all?

Even as the thought formed, he felt a cool green breeze pass through him. The field Anthora was building thickened; there came a definite scent of Tree, a flickering vision of pods, lightnings, and a black void stitched with living gold.

The breeze gusted, and the Tree was gone; the field around Anthora wavered as she cried out and extended a hand—the net—to exchange wounds . . .

He flung forward and lifted her away, ignoring alike her shout and her fist.

"Brother—" she twisted, pushing against him.

"Look at me!" he snapped, and she raised her head, eyes wide, showing tears; her hair a tangled mass, draggling down her back.

"Will you kill yourself and your daughter?" he demanded. "Is that how you honor your lifemate?"

She stared at him for another moment, then she folded like a broken tree, her head on his shoulder, and every muscle a-quiver.

Tinsori Light

THE LIGHT STOPPED SCREAMING.

Head and ears ringing, Tolly staggered upright, loose tiles underfoot making the process a little more exciting than it should've been. A quick look around at the surrounding tile sets relieved him, to a point. The systems the Light had brought down into his core were still functioning. That was good.

The Light himself, that was another thing.

"Tinsori Light?" he said softly. "It's Tolly Jones."

Mentor!" the Light cried. "Mentor, I have everything. I have it, Mentor, but I can't—"

"Tocohl. Listen careful now. There's nothing to panic about. For starters, shut down all noncritical systems—that includes life support on the docking area. Shunt everything that'll fit into the storage pod, then go low power. I'm on my way; between us, we'll get it sorted."

He didn't expect any kind of answer—and he didn't get one. He moved fast through the core, taking good care not to jostle anything. When he reached the access ladder, he jumped, snatched a rung halfway up and started to climb.

Strong hands grabbed his shoulders, hauled him up into the dim and dying main frame room, and set him on his feet.

"Tinsori Light—the person—is gone," he said, only a little breathless. He grabbed Haz's arm and marched them toward the hatch. "He must've been tied into the mandates—anyway, Tocohl's caught it all, but she can't hold long."

He hit the hall running, Haz beside him, which meant she was holding back.

"What will happen, if she does not hold?" Haz asked, not even breathing hard.

"Dunno. Depends on how Tinsori Light integrated the systems he moved down to the core. We gotta get Tocohl into those craniums, quick as we can."

"Yes," she said.

The hall doors were standing open, a figure rushing toward them.

"Lorith says that Lady Tocohl has annexed all systems," Jen Sin said, turning on a heel and running with them. "She struggles to hold them separate from herself."

"That's where we're going. Have you ever done, assisted with, or seen a transfer of an AI into a sustainable environment?"

"I regret."

"'Bout what I expected, actually. You got separate life support in the safe halls?"

"That, yes."

"Good. I want you and Lorith to pull back, and wait to hear that everything's under control. If it goes wrong, there are two spaceships at dock. Take one—space, take both!—and get clear of here."

"Are we certain that there is a universe to get clear to?" Jen Sin asked.

"I think so. I think the Light fragmented before he was able to suicide. Even assuming that the mandate to destroy universes is still intact—there's nobody left to carry it out."

"If Lady Tocohl has absorbed Tinsori Light, would she not also have—"

"Doesn't work like that," Tolly interrupted. "There's reasons. I'm willing to explain them 'til your eyes cross after we get this bit sorted out. Deal?"

"Deal."

Surebleak

"MIRI."

A firm hand pressed into her shoulder. She didn't look up; couldn't quite look away from that calm and peaceful face. Ordinary looking man, Ren Zel—neat brown hair, regular features, smooth, unblemished gold-toned skin . . . Clan member aside—she'd liked him; had already come to depend on him. Steady and quiet and competent . . .

. . . Dead now. By her hand.

"Child . . ."

She placed the voice now. Aelliana Caylon.

"We had an agreement," she said to the unspoken question. "It was too much, what he could do—what he could potentially do. Too much power for one man. I thought so and—it weighed on him. I think that, anyway. Figured I'd have to kill him some day. Guess he heard me think it.

"He said he agreed with me and said that he would tell me when."

"Which promise he kept," Aelliana murmured. "All of us heard him accept necessity, and you made him a quick ending, a mercy, from kin to kin.

"Stand up now, child."

Aelliana took her arm, and Miri let herself be pulled to her feet.

Anthora was shivering in Val Con's arm. He raised his head and met Miri's eyes over the tangle of his sister's hair.

"I don't know what happened," she said in answer to that look. "I think, given we're standing here—he must've done what was needful."

He nodded, and looked down.

"Sister, tell me what you would have me do."

She shuddered.

"I would have you ask the Tree if the battle has been won."

"Yes, I will do that. But for you, this moment—what will you?"

"Ask the Tree," Anthora said again, her voice painfully steady, "for once you have the answer, I will kill it." She took a hard breath.

There was a moment of maybe-shocked silence, broken by Daav.

"I understand entirely. I have myself sworn to do so on several occasions, and once went so far as to carry an ax into the Tree Court."

He paused, head tipped to a side, considering. Aelliana took his hand and he smiled, very slightly.

"My lifemate had been murdered and, after much thought down many sleepless nights, I concluded that the Tree was complicit."

He moved his shoulders, his expression wry.

"Even then, it persuaded me otherwise."

"It will not so persuade me," Anthora said grimly. "It would have it that we are dear, and necessary to it—yet I asked one boon, which it might have granted . . .”

She shook her head and straightened. Val Con let her go.

“Will you ask, Brother?” she demanded. “For I mean to end the Tree this night.”

“Is that well done, Beloved?” came a soft voice from behind.

Miri spun. Anthora squeaked.

Ren Zel was sitting calmly cross-legged on the floor, smiling slightly, an echo of green nimbus fading to nothing about him.

“Though I think you are correct that we must go to the Tree Court. At once, and all of us,” Ren Zel finished.

Val Con stepped forward to offer a hand.

“Have you given us a victory, Brother?”

Ren Zel took the offered hand, and Val Con pulled him to his feet. He looked tired, Miri thought, and worn so thin she could just about see through him.

But he was alive.

Alive.

“The *sheriekas* last work has been vanquished, the Shadow repulsed, the universal rift sealed. The threads have re-formed, and the song of life is strong.” Ren Zel stopped, puzzlement entering his eyes. “What did I say?”

“You said,” Val Con told him firmly, “that we must to the Tree Court. Sister.”

Anthora stepped forward, and gently took her life-mate’s arm.

He smiled at her. “Beloved.”

“Ren Zel,” she breathed, putting her hand briefly against his cheek. “You are exhausted.”

"And you," he answered. "Let us to the Tree. After, we may sleep."

Miri offered Val Con her arm. He bent and kissed her cheek.

"*Cha'trez,*" he murmured. "Thank you."

The Tree Court had never in his memory been so disheveled.

Dead leaves were ankle-high; small branches were down everywhere; one, somewhat larger, had fallen across the viewing bench, by the gloan-roses, knocking the slats askew.

The six of them paused uncertainly at the edge of the Court. Miri stirred first.

"You okay, Tree?"

A subdued rustle was her somber answer, as if the Tree'd just woken up the morning after a raging storm.

"Are you well?" Miri demanded again, and the Tree was suddenly focused, the mood changed as if it was chuckling sleepily at a child's pleasantry.

Val Con walked forward, leaves crunching beneath his feet. He put his hands against the trunk, which was noticeably cool. He took a breath against a thrill of alarm, and deliberately relaxed.

"What have you been about?" he murmured, gently chiding. "Chasing *sheriekas* at your time in life?"

A sense of profound satisfaction filled him, and not a little martial pride. In his mind's eye, a wicked roiling cloud arose, sweeping into a tear in what sort of fabric he dared not guess. Beyond the tear was a hard gleam—as of ice.

Or crystal.

The cloud filled the rift, obscuring the other side. A towering rage of fecund green fell across it, as a bolt of perfect gold struck the rift and spread out, healing the wound with its own essence.

"I see. Are you well? What must we do for you?"

A small breeze bestirred itself to ruffle his hair. An image formed of Ren Zel and Anthora as they stood behind him, arms about each other's waists.

He stood back.

"Sister. Brother. The Tree desires your attention."

They stepped forward obediently and halted, neither putting hand to trunk.

"No," Anthora said, sounding subdued. "Not tonight. I am exhausted. Let us discuss it tomorrow."

"Yes," Ren Zel added. "You were indeed glorious. I would not have succeeded at the last without you."

From above—rustling and the sound of several objects slicing through leaves, the noise getting louder as they fell.

Ren Zel extended his free hand; Anthora hers. Each caught their pod neatly.

They bowed.

"Good evening," said Ren Zel..

They turned, pods still in hand, and it was Anthora who spoke this time.

"We will retire now, and tomorrow, Val Con-brother, we shall to the Healers. Unless we will be needed?"

Val Con shook his head.

"Do as you must. Do you require a Healer tonight? We may—"

"Tonight," Ren Zel interrupted softly, "we will rest."

He smiled wanly.

"And soon."

"Dying's bound to take it out of you," Miri said, "'specially after saving the universe."

"Yes." The smile widened as he turned to her. "Thank you, Miri."

"You're welcome. Let's just not do it again."

"Agreed," he said. "It will not be necessary."

Aelliana stirred.

"As we do not seem to be required here, allow us to walk with you."

"Yes," said Anthora.

"Thank you," Ren Zel said again, and the four of them left the Tree Court.

Val Con sighed.

"We will," he said, addressing the Tree, "survey your situation in the light of day and gather up the debris, unless you deem it necessary to your comfort. If there is nothing else we may do for you immediately, we, too, will return to the house and rest."

Another breeze stirred, kissing his cheek, and Miri's, accompanying a clear sense of dismissal. The Tree, he gathered, wanted to rest.

"Very well, then," he said.

Miri took his hand, and together they quit the Tree Court.

• • • ✵ • • •

They four were halfway up the stairs when there were footsteps on the landing above and down came Theo.

She was moving quickly, expression abstracted, perhaps intent on dessert. She nodded politely to Ren Zel, Anthora, and Aelliana, who were in the lead, looked past them—and stopped, staring.

Aelliana did not pause, but urged her charges upward.

"Father?" Shock, dismay, and disbelief packed into that single word, Daav thought. A balanced reaction.

"Good evening, Theo," he said calmly.

"What happened to you?"

Van'chela, *give us half an hour over a glass of wine, please, then come to us in the small parlor,* he said, as Aelliana reached the landing above.

Yes, she replied, and added ruefully, *Best to get it done with, I suppose.*

"Are you going to tell me what happened to you?" Theo demanded, warily approaching by one step, as if he might vanish or leap up and bite her.

"Yes," he said agreeably. "I am going to tell you exactly what happened. As it is rather a long tale, and entirely unbelievable in very large measure, I suggest that we retire to the small parlor, where we will be undisturbed."

She took a hard breath and gave him a tight nod. "All right."

"Excellent. Jeeves, will you please ask Mr. pel'Kana to bring wine and a tray to the small parlor?"

"Yes, sir," said Jeeves.

"I'm not hungry," said Theo.

"That may well be so," Daav said, turning to walk down the stairs. "I, however, missed my dinner."

Surebleak

"GOOD MORNING, JEEVES," VAL CON SAID, AS HE ENTERED the delm's office next morning. "Is there anything I should know?"

"*Chandra Marudas* lifted ten hours ago, course filed for Nev'Lorn. *Vivulonj Prosperu* lifted eight hours ago, course filed for Edmonton Beacon. *Spiral Dance* has landed at Korval's Yard," Jeeves said obligingly.

Val Con nodded and went to the buffet to pour a cup of tea. Sipping, he looked out over the garden. It was one of Surebleak's rare sunny and cloudless mornings, the lack of clouds meaning that the temperature would be appallingly cold. Despite this, Grakow and Paizel were pacing down the lawn, shoulder to shoulder and tails straight out behind.

"Tommy Lee has driven a car into the city. He will first stop at the Healer Hall, then proceed to Lady Kareen's town house," Jeeves continued.

"Captain Waitley is meeting with her crew regarding the future of the ship. Commander Relgen, of Relgen's Raiders, will be arriving this afternoon with her second, to interview the pathfinders. Nelirikk has been alerted. There are two pinbeam communications in queue, from Korval's daughter Tocohl Lorlin, and also from Jen Sin yos'Phelium."

Val Con paused with his cup halfway to his mouth.

"Say again?" he said, a tiny tendril of dread starting to uncoil in his belly. Saving the universe was a chancy business, after all; who knew but that time had been fractured in the doing of it.

Or that Jeeves had run mad.

"I have two pinbeam messages in queue," Jeeves repeated, sounding not in the least mad, "the first from Tocohl Lorlin, the second from Jen Sin yos'Phelium, who signs himself Chief Keeper, Tinsori Light."

Worse and worse.

Val Con put his teacup down on the table and turned from the window to face into the room.

"Jen Sin yos'Phelium is two hundred years dead," he said conversationally. "Tinsori Light . . . is no longer in use."

"I regret, sir, but it would appear that Jen Sin yos'Phelium was merely temporarily misplaced and Tinsori Light has been . . . rehabilitated. May I suggest you hear Tocohl's message first?"

Val Con walked to his desk, pulled out the chair, picked Fondi up, sat down, and put the cat on his lap. Fondi uttered a sleepy purr, stretched out his toes, and flipped his tail over his nose.

"Thank you," he said. "I will hear Tocohl's message first, please."

"Yes, sir."

There was a brief pause before the voice of his foster-mother—no, he corrected himself—the voice of Korval's daughter, Tocohl, was heard.

"Greetings to Korval from Tocohl Lorlin, their devoted daughter. I have accomplished the task to which you assigned me and report that *Admiral Bunter* has been satisfactorily reestablished in a fitting and stable environment. He currently travels with the Free Ships, and Mentor Jones is confident that he will, after a period of readjustment, take on crew and become an asset to society.

"After the completion of this task, I was importuned by Mentor Inkirani Yo, who met our expedition at Jemiatha Station and assisted with the transfer of the *Admiral* to his new environment. Mentor Yo was an agent of the Lyre Institute, assigned to follow the rumors of an awakening Old One, and to attach him to the Institute's interests."

There was a pause, as if Tocohl was considering how best to continue.

"In this, her last mission, she failed," came the bald statement. "Tinsori Light was entangled with both the pre-Migration universe and our own, a situation which was potentially catastrophic. In addition, his physical environment was composed of original fractin racks, which were badly degraded after such a passage of time."

Another pause, following what might have been an in-drawn breath.

"I determined that Tinsori Light was a danger to himself and the existence of two universes and I... subverted him, claiming control of his systems. During this period there was an accidental anomaly... which may in fact... have resulted in one universe being destroyed. If so, it was not ours. I append all pertinent records and readings. Having survived this anomaly with the rest of the universe, I am, in practice and in fact, Tinsori Light, securing the station in the name of Korval."

Val Con closed his eyes.

"Two human staff have been serving on the station for many Standards and have been instrumental in preventing the Light, a work of the Great Enemy, from wreaking greater mischief than it has done. I have confirmed the identity of one of those light keepers, Jen Sin yos'Phelium. As the station is Korval's, he is presently chief light keeper; the other staff, called Lorith, is second light keeper. They profess themselves willing to remain in these positions. More permanent arrangements, of course, wait upon the Delm's Word. I assure you that Tinsori Light is stable and eager to serve the needs of the clan.

"Transmission ends."

Gods, Val Con thought. He took a deep breath, spun the Scout's Rainbow inside his head, and glanced toward the ceiling.

"I will hear Keeper yos'Phelium's message now, please, Jeeves."

"Yes, sir."

"Jen Sin yos'Phelium, Korval pilot, and lately light keeper at Tinsori, offers greeting to the delm."

Jen Sin yos'Phelium sounded collected, even cool, his accent antique but clear. Val Con settled into the chair and put a hand on Fondi's back.

"I stand temporarily as chief light keeper, administering the station in Korval's name until permanent assignments have been made. This is a first status report.

"The station is in generally good repair, though

in need of upgrade to meet present standards, most especially on the docks and in hydroponics. One section of the ring was damaged at some point before my tenure here and is in need of reconstruction. At present, we are secure; the seals hold and show no undue wear.

"Station organic population includes myself and Light Keeper Lorith, Korval House soldier Hazenthull, Mentor Tollance Berik-Jones. Lady Tocohl Lorlin, daughter of Korval, has secured station systems and holds strong. We presently have two ships at dock. Korval ship *Tarigan* and *Ahab-Esais*, which I am informed is a ship belonging the Lyre Institute.

"Guidance is sought in the disposition of the Institute's ship. Mentor Jones offers that he may be able to contact one of the Free Ships and ask that *Ahab-Esais* be taken away from here before another operative is sent to find it. Mentor Jones stresses that the Lyre Institute remains an active threat to this station and its personnel."

There was a pause.

"I stand ready, as ever, to serve Korval, and will answer to the best of my abilities such questions as the delm may have. It would be helpful to know the delm's plans for this facility, and to receive a schedule for repair and upgrade.

"Chief Light Keeper Jen Sin yos'Phelium—out."

Val Con counted, slowly, to one hundred forty-four.

"Jeeves, please provide me with your files on Tinsori Light, including its current location with reference to active trade routes. Please assure Tocohl and the light keepers that the delm has received their messages and is examining the Light's situation and needs in view of the clan's available resources. I would appreciate your advice regarding the proper disposal of the ship belonging to the Lyre Institute."

"Yes, sir. I believe that Tolly Jones's suggestion that *Ahab-Esais* be removed by a Free Ship and set loose, perhaps at Edmonton Beacon or some similar place, has merit. This will not prevent other agents of the Lyre Institute trying the Light, but it may delay their onset.

"Regarding location, sir . . . Tinsori Light is fixed inconveniently in terms of trade. I suggest that Korval would be best served by maintaining it as a port for Free Ships and their allies, as well as Korval ships and allies."

"Your reasoning regarding the Free Ships?"

"In light of your judgment regarding independent logics, there will be a need for a known port, a gathering place, and a safe zone for meeting and negotiating with other intelligences."

The judgment, Val Con thought, and shivered.

Well, he had wanted it to be as broad as possible.

"Thank you, Jeeves," he said calmly. "If you have not already done so, please share the pertinent judgment with Tinsori Light. Regarding the Free Ships, I will bring your suggestion to my discussions with the delmae."

"Thank you, sir."

"You are welcome. Please ask Mr. pel'Kana to deny me to any who are not kin for the next three hours."

"Yes, sir," Jeeves answered, and there was a definite feeling of withdrawal.

Val Con sighed. Jeeves had learnt the trick from *Bechimo* then. He supposed that was progress.

He spun the chair 'round to face the desk, off-loaded Fondi to a pile of printout beside the keyboard, and tapped up his mail queue before he closed his eyes.

Gods. First we conquer a planet, then at once we save the universe and overthrow a space station—all unwitting, but who will believe it?

How Miri will laugh.

•••※•••

They had been placed in the formal parlor, and left with promises of tea and Professor Waitley's attendance very soon.

She will not recognize me, he said to Aelliana.

Theo recognized you, she answered.

Kamele is not Theo.

Very true. But I think she will know you.

Footsteps in the hallway, light and quick. Daav felt a tightening in his chest and walked to the center of the room, where she would see him at once from the doorway.

A shadow, then here she was, her hair coming loose from its binding, soft curls tangled about her face. She was abstracted, which naturally she would be, called from study, and she did not see him until she was fairly in the room. She walked with sure grace and was armed.

Her eyes widened, and she stopped.

The moment stretched; he recruited himself to patience, wanting to give her time to see, to absorb—or to deny—and she came another step into the room, her eyes flicking to the fireplace where Aelliana stood silent, then back to his face.

"Jen Sar?" she said, and shook her head, lips shaping

a soft smile. "You must forgive my lapse; I do know better. You are Daav yos'Phelium."

His throat tightened, but he smiled for her and inclined his head.

"In fact, I am Daav yos'Phelium. I did not expect you to know me—like this." He swept a hand down, showing himself to her.

That brought a true smile as she came further into the room, until there was scarcely any distance between them.

"Actually, you look very like your portrait, now. Kareen showed me." She turned her head.

"Are you Aelliana Caylon?"

His lifemate smiled.

"Yes. I hope you may accept my thanks for your care of us, and for the fact of Theo, who continues to astonish."

Kamele laughed.

"She does, doesn't she? And—you know, I don't wish to offend, but you don't owe me thanks. I only followed my heart; it was no effort to care."

Aelliana bowed slightly.

Kamele turned back to him. He held his hands out, palms up. After a moment, she put her palms against his.

"Kamele, *I'm sorry* to have involved you in one of my dreadful scrapes. I hope you may forgive me."

"There's nothing to forgive," she said, though he could see tears in her eyes. "And, you know, I'm *not* sorry. Not at all—you—Jen Sar—" she gave a small laugh. "I've been studying *melant'i*, but I'm still not sure how to parse all the yous of you."

His breath caught, but she was sweeping on.

"You—all of you!—gave me so much that I would never otherwise have had. Sunsets—gardens—cats. And Theo." She shook her head. "I *can't* be sorry."

"Then," he said gently, "I am relieved, because I am not sorry, either, for those things that we shared. Only that I distressed you at the last, and put you in the way of danger that is none of yours."

She laughed and took her hands away from him, shaking her head to clear the tears.

"But I don't regret that, either! Do you know I can shoot a pistol? I finished third out of twenty-four in the novice round at Sherman's Shoot-Out. If I hadn't met you, I would never have come to Surebleak, and I would have never found what might well be my lifework! Do you remember how we used to argue about the proper role of knowledge?"

"I do, indeed."

"Well, I've come 'round to your way of thinking. I am exhilarated, and it frightens me that I might so easily have missed this!"

"Ah, now I see that I am a hero!" he said, teasing.

She put on a stern face.

"I wouldn't go that far," she said, and turned to gather Aelliana into her glance.

"Have you some time? I would like to catch up—to hear the story—the other story. Or at least find out how you've lost so many years! And Scholar Caylon . . ." She hesitated.

Aelliana came forward and took her hand. "Yes? You will not offend me."

"Well. Kareen told me that you—were dead."

"And so I was, though not completely so." She smiled. "And as you see, I've gotten better."

Tinsori Light

THE SPACE AROUND TINSORI LIGHT HAD CHANGED. SHE could see that, of course, though she found M Traven's technical discussion fascinating.

The dust clouds had dissipated. Andreth, at the research station, had shown her their analysis. The clouds had been pulverized crystal, but why they had dispersed or what the agent of dispersal had been he could not guess.

Well, it was a secondary concern, Seignur Veeoni told herself. Her first concern—the reason Yuri had called her into being, trained her himself, and given her the smartstrands so that she could *remember* the old universe—her first concern was Tinsori Light.

Yuri had built Tinsori Light, of course. That it had been stolen and subverted to the Enemy's purpose had pained him for hundreds of years. Its appearance, its entanglement with two universes—he *must* repair it: there was no choice but that one.

She knew.

"Tinsori Light," a light female voice spoke from the comm. "Do you wish docking?"

"We do," M Traven said gravely. "I bring Seignur Veeoni, with relief."

"What sort of relief?"

Seignur Veeoni leaned slightly forward and spoke at the comm.

"I bring newly derived and manufactured fractin sets. They are stable and clean and ready to be installed so that the Light may move its systems and itself."

There was a long pause, then a new voice on comm.

"Seignur Veeoni, this is Tollance Berik-Jones; I'm a trained mentor, and I'm on staff specifically to monitor the Light's integrity."

"Excellent!" she said, pleased. "I am a technician, sir. For the frames and the fractins, I will vouch. But I have no such skill as yours. I will welcome a collaboration with you."

"Sounds like we have an accord," Tollance Berik-Jones said. "I'll meet you on the dock and guide you in."

"Thank you," Seignur Veeoni said. "That will be very helpful."

"Stand by for docking instructions."

Seignur Veeoni considered the three craniums on-screen. They were, of course, situated securely elsewhere. One took great care to protect the station's mind.

"I am familiar," she said to Tolly Jones, who stood beside her, "with the cranium environments. They are more than adequate for most modern intelligences. However, Tinsori Light is a product of the old universe, and her needs are subtly different. The relationship between sister fractins, the interaction of the sets with the frame, and the frame sets with others of their kind . . . is unique in this universe. In this situation, I believe it may be superior. Certainly, the builder of this facility believed it to be so, utterly. He went to a great deal of trouble to have these sets engineered."

"You know who built the Light?" Tolly Jones asked.

"Yes, of course. The Uncle, as he is known, built Tinsori Light back in the old universe. I can tell the tale, if you like, but first I would like to demonstrate this technology to Tocohl Lorlin and allow her to examine it."

"Yes," said the new voice of the Light—Tocohl. "I'm curious."

"Good," said Seignur Veeoni. "I propose to assemble one complete frame set here in this workroom. You may study it at your leisure, and assure yourself that it is in no way a threat. As I said, I believe that use of the fractin sets will greatly enhance your comfort and productivity.

She paused, thinking, and added slowly, "It may be possible that the two systems—cranium and fractin—can be brought into harmony; one system supporting the other. I will think more deeply on this.

"Mentor, have you an opinion?"

"It sounds like something we ought to explore," he said, smiling easily. "First thing, though, is to get one of the frames together so Tocohl can study it. She gives the affirmative, then we'll work out the rest."

"Yes," she said, soothed by his voice and good common sense. "Of course."

She turned to the packing case and began to withdraw the parts needed.

"This will require a few minutes only."

Vivulonj Prosperu

THE PACKET CAUGHT THEM ON THE APPROACH TO SKEMpel's Jump point.

"From Seignur Veeoni," Yuri said and sent it to Dulsey's screen.

As usual, there was no salutation or other pleasantry, only an immediate plunge into business.

> *Yuri, I have not failed, but neither have I succeeded.*
>
> *I arrive to find Tinsori Light well in hand, with a Korval Intelligence in firm control of all systems. She has accepted the fractin sets; they have been installed and are performing well in tandem with three cranium units. I note that there is evidence that the universe may have ended and been respun during the change of control; I append records of the event, provided by Tinsori Light.*
>
> *The light keepers, of whom we had known, are now joined by Mentor Tollance Berik-Jones, in service to Tinsori Light, and Hazenthull*

nor'Phelium. Light Keeper Jen Sin yos'Phelium stands as chief, with Light Keeper Lorith in support.

I am informed that the delm of Korval is considering how best to go forward with the Light. Under discussion, according to Mentor Berik-Jones, is a plan to open the Light to the Free Ships. If this comes to pass, I will seek Korval's permission to rehabilitate the damaged section into a residence, and offer my services as a technician to those of the Free who may require aid.

For the while, I remain at Tinsori Light, with M Traven to guard me. I am very safe here, so you need have no concern.

Tinsori Light sends to you, under separate wrap, information that you may find instructive.

The message ended with no such niceties as a signature or a well-wish.

Dulsey raised her head and met Yuri's eyes.

"Free Ships?" she said. "What does Korval care for Free Ships?"

"Apparently more than we knew. Tinsori Light, who signs herself 'Tocohl Lorlin Clan Korval,' is kind enough to send the full text of a recent field judgment rendered by Scout Commander Val Con yos'Phelium. This judgment addresses the condition of Independent Logics, which is—in short form—that any such persons who are gainfully employed, members of a family, or otherwise an asset to society shall be considered free, with all the rights and benefits that accrue to all free persons, and specifically exempt from harassment, detention, and, most especially, deactivation.

"This is of course in direct opposition to the Complex Logic Laws."

"Will it stand?"

Yuri sighed. "Does the wind of their damned Luck rise beneath the Dragon's wings?"

"It would appear so."

He fell silent. When he spoke again, it was with something like humor in his voice.

"Well, here's a conceit, Dulsey. With Korval claiming the Light, and Seignur Veeoni establishing her residence there, it would appear that we and the Dragon are partnered.

"I wonder if that has occurred to them yet."

Surebleak

MIRI WATCHED THE CAR OUT OF SIGHT, THEN TURNED back toward the house. She'd argued for the delm's office today, and Val Con hadn't fielded anything more than token resistance, which meant they'd been on the same page, and it really didn't matter if that was courtesy of the lifemate link or just a case of great minds thinking alike.

What mattered was getting him another set and order of problems to consider, so he could come back fresh to the mess that was Korval's ongoing personal business. And, truth told, they *had* to open the Road Boss's office today—most especially with the survey team from TerraTrade still on port, asking questions, counting heads, reviewing systems, and in general making everybody nervous.

There was, Miri acknowledged, as she walked down the hall to the delm's office, a certain risk in having Val Con on the same port as the survey team, but after the little dust-up at the reception, she counted on Team Leader Kasveini to make sure it was herself who conducted the interview with the Road Boss.

And if it turned out that the team leader wasn't sensible or wanted to push an issue, then she'd just have to depend on Val Con wanting Surebleak Port upgraded and certified more than he wanted to visit mayhem on idiots who questioned Clan Korval's honor.

In the meantime, all they really had to do was to keep their heads down, not doing anything outlandish that skewed any more attention their direction. How hard could that be?

She opened the door to the delm's office and walked directly to the buffet to pour herself a cup of coffee. The scanner was on, which was Val Con's habit. The names and home ports of ships incoming and the filed destinations of ships outgoing imparted actual meaningful information to him. To her, not having been raised with a familiarity of ships and ports and politics, the scanner was at best an occasional amusement and at worst just . . . noise.

Still, she didn't detour on the way to the desk to turn the thing off. Today, the unfamiliar voices dealing with the details of her homeworld's traffic were . . . comforting.

She pulled out the chair, checked to be sure a cat hadn't taken possession before her, and sat down, tapping the screen on.

There was mail in the delm's in-box. What a surprise.

She sipped and pulled up the first, which was from Ms. dea'Gauss, acknowledging receipt of the delm's direction to discover funding for the clan's newly acquired space station. She assured them that the project was a priority, and that she expected to have preliminary figures within the week. In the meanwhile, she allowed that a schematic of the station, a systems inventory, a list of needed upgrades in order of urgency, as well as a detailed report on the damaged portion of the ring would assist her greatly in her work. Also, if the station keepers could send their estimate of expected traffic and a ranked list of services and amenities that would be required by said traffic, that would also be of great assistance.

Miri sipped coffee while she wondered whether the keepers had any notion how much traffic they were likely to see, and what services the Free Ships, who she understood were expected to be Tinsori Light's main clientele, would want most. Well, they had Tolly Jones to consult there . . . she shook her head.

"Gonna be a job of work," she commented to no one in particular, and that was before anybody figured out how Free Ships paid their bills.

"Jeeves—" she started . . .

"Sleet and snow!" the scanner shouted. "Didja see that! It come right outta the sun, I'm telling you, no signature, no glare—"

"Meteor alert! Incoming! Keep to assigned orbits. If you are on approach, stay on course."

Miri spun to stare at the scanner. *Meteor?* she thought. Came right out of the sun, was it? She felt a slight chill in the warm office.

"Jeeves, can you see that rock?"

"Yes, Miri. I am coordinating with *Bechimo*. The route is . . . unconventional, but we believe that it is a *route*, not a mere rock, but—"

"A ship," she interrupted, finding that she had come to her feet.

"Yes," Jeeves said again. "I have a broad match with the Clutch vessel that transported us to Surebleak.

However, this incoming vessel is . . . much smaller and—ah. *Bechimo* has backtracked to the entry point. We have very good reason to believe that it is using the electron substitution drive. I have extrapolated its course—on a heading for—"

"Our field?"

"No, Miri," Jeeves told her solemnly. "It is on course for our driveway."

She blinked.

"Odds of survival?"

"One hundred percent," Jeeves said promptly. "It is already slowing its descent. I estimate arrival in—"

"I have a communication from the approaching vessel," came a pleasant, unfamiliar voice. Comm Officer Joyita that must be, Miri thought, patching in on the shielded house. She decided to be pissed about that later.

"Proceed, please, Mr. Joyita," she said.

"Yes, ma'am. It identifies itself as Emissary Twelve and states that it is on the business of the Elders. An immediate meeting with the Delm of Korval is requested." There was a small pause.

"It also apologizes for its unseemly haste, and pleads . . . necessity, ma'am."

"Thank you, Mr. Joyita." Miri sighed, and turned toward the door.

"Jeeves, attend me, please."

"Yes, Miri."

Keep our heads down, she thought. Sure.

How hard could that be?

The Space at Tinsori Light

by Sharon Lee and Steve Miller

SPACE IS HAUNTED.

Pilots know this; stationmasters and light keepers, too; though they seldom speak of it, even to each other. Why would they? Ghost or imagination, wyrd space or black hole, life—and space—is dangerous.

The usual rules apply.

• • •✵• • •

Substance formed from the void. Walls rose, air flowed, floors heated.

A relay clicked.

In the control room, a screen glowed to life. The operator yawned and reached to the instruments, long fingers illuminated by the wash of light.

On the screen—space, turbulent and strange.

The operator's touch on the board wakes more screens, subtle instruments. A tap brings a chronometer live in the bottom right of the primary screen. Beams are assigned to sweep nearspace; energy levels are sampled, measured, compared.

The clock displays elapsed time: 293 units.

The operator frowns, uncertain of what units the clock measures. She might have known, once. Two hundred ninety-three—that was a long phase. At the last alarm, it had shown 127 elapsed units; on the occasion before that, 63.

The operator turns back to her scans, hoping.

Hoping that it would prove to be *something* this time—something worthy of her. Of them.

The last alarm had been triggered by a pod of rock and ice traveling through the entanglement of forces that supported and enclosed them.

A rock pod . . . nothing for them.

She hadn't even had time for a cup of tea.

The alarm before the rock pod . . . had been nothing for them, either, though they hadn't known that, at first.

They pulled it in, followed repair protocols, therapies, and subroutines . . .

She'd had more than a cup of tea, at least—whole meals, she'd eaten. She'd listened to music, read a book . . . but in the end there was nothing they could do, except take the salvage and ride the strange tide away again into that place where time, all unknown, elapsed.

The scans—*these* scans *now*—they gave her rock . . . and mad fluctuations of energy. They gave her ice, and emptiness.

There ought to be something more. *Some*thing more, worthy or unworthy. The geometry of the space about them was delicate. The alarm would not sound for nothing.

The scans fluttered and flashed, elucidating a disturbance in the forces of this place. Breath caught, the operator leans forward.

The scans detected, measured; verified mass, direction, symmetry...

The scans announced...

...a ship.

Any ship arriving here was a ship in need.

The operator extended her hand and touched a plate set away from all the toggles, buttons, and tags that attended to her part of their function.

She touched the plate...and woke the Light.

...✵...

This, thought Jen Sin yos'Phelium Clan Korval, *is going to be...tricky.*

Oh, the orders from his delm were plain enough: Raise Delium, discreetly. Deliver the packet—there *was* a packet, and didn't he just not know what was in it. Discreet, the delivery, too. Of course. Delivery accomplished, he was to—discreetly—raise ship and get himself out of Sinan space, not to say range of their weapons.

Alive, preferably.

That last, that was his orders to himself, he being somewhat more interested in his continued good health and long-term survival than his delm. *Package delivered* was Korval's bottom line; the expense of delivery beyond her concern.

In any wise, the whole matter would have been much easier to accomplish, from discreet to alive, if Delium wasn't under active dispute.

Not that this was the riskiest mission he had undertaken at the Delm's Word during this late and ongoing season of foolishness with Clan Sinan and their allies. He was, Jen Sin knew, as one knows a fact, and without undue pride, Korval's best pilot. Jump pilot, of course, with the ring and the leather to prove it.

Of late, he would have rather been Korval's third or fourth best pilot, though that wouldn't have prevented him being plucked out from the Scouts, which had been clan and kin to him for more than half his life. No, it would have only meant that he would have served as decoy, to call attention away from Korval's Best, when there was a packet for delivery.

Well, the usual rules applied here, as elsewhere. If working without backup, always know the way out, always carry an extra weapon, always know the state of your ship—and know that your ship is able and accessible—always be prepared to survive, and always remember that the delm was captain to the passengers. Being Korval's best pilot, his job was to fly where the passengers needed him to fly, at the direction of the delm.

Jen Sin sighed. Gods knew he was no delm, and thankful for it, too. Delms did math in lives, set in courses that would be flown by pilots not yet born. The delm decided who to spend, and when, for what profit to the clan. And just as well, Jen Sin acknowledged, that he wasn't clever enough to do those sorts of sums.

His attention was occupied for a bit, then, dodging various busy eyes in orbit, and when he had time to think again, at his ease between two security rings, he found he was thinking of his team.

When he'd first come out from the Scouts, he'd thought of them often: the comrades closer than kin; the six of them together stronger, smarter, faster than any one of them alone.

Well.

There was a time when he could have gone back, delm willing, which she hadn't been. *Could* have gone back, no questions asked, no accommodation required. *Could have* then.

Now, what he had was *couldn't*, though *would* still burned in his belly, even now that it was too late. His team had long ago moved past their grief, taken on someone else, shifted tasks and priorities until they were, again, a team—different from the team it had been.

And no room for Jen Sin yos'Phelium, at all.

"I would prefer the Starlight Room, if it is available," he said and passed over the identification for one Pan Rip sig'Alta and a sixth-cantra, too.

The deskman took both, bland-faced, scanned the card and returned it, the coin having been made to disappear.

"Sir, I regret. The Starlight Room is unavailable. May I suggest the Solar Wind?"

"The Solar Wind, excellent," he murmured, and received the key card the man passed to him.

"The hallway to the right; the second door on your left hand. Please be at peace in our house."

That was scarcely likely—a certain tendency to unpeacefulness in perilous places being one of his numerous faults. Thus far, however, all was according to script. That, he told himself firmly, was good.

Jen Sin entered the hallway, found the door, and used the key, stepping across the threshold immediately the door slid away, a man with no enemies in need of an hour of solitude.

Two steps inside, the door already closed behind

him, he checked—a man startled to find his solitary retreat already occupied.

This was also according to script—that there should be someone before him. Who, he had not been privileged to know. No matter, though—there were yet another few lines of code to exchange, which would in theory assure the orderly transfer of the packet tucked snug in an inner pocket of his jacket . . . and the safe departure of the courier.

Jen Sin allowed himself to display surprise before he bowed.

"Forgive me," he said to the severe young woman seated by the pleasant fire, a bottle of wine and two glasses on the table before her. "I had thought the room would be empty."

"Surely," said she, "the fault lies with the desk. However, it seems to me fortuitous, for it seems I am in need of a companion other than my thoughts."

All and everything by the script. He ought to have been reassured. He told himself that.

Meanwhile, acting his assigned part, he inclined his head formally.

"I am pleased to accept the gift of comradeship," he murmured and stepped toward the table with a Scout's silent footsteps.

He paused by the doubtless comfortable chair, the back of his neck feeling vulnerable. There remained one more matched exchange, to prove the case. Would the child never speak?

She looked up at him, and smiled wistfully, so it seemed to him.

"Please," she said, "sit and share wine with me."

That . . .

...was *not* according to script, and now he saw it—the anomaly that his subconscious, ever so much cleverer than he, had noticed the moment he had cleared the threshold.

The wine bottle, there on the table between the two glasses...

...was uncorked.

Jen Sin kicked; the table, the glasses, the wine becoming airborne. He slapped the door open, heard glass shatter behind him, and a high scream of agony.

He did not look back as he stepped into the hall, turning left, away from the foyer where the doorman presided. Deliberately bringing to mind the floor plan he had memorized to while away the hours alone in transit to Delium, he ran.

Less than a half-minute later, he let himself out a service door, wincing as the alarm gave tongue. Then, he was again running at the top of his speed, down the delivery corridor to the street beyond.

He had not surrendered the packet, his ship, or his life, though he had pretended to give up the two latter.

The man hidden on the gantry, justifiably proud of the shot that had dropped him at the ship's very hatch, had taken the key from Jen Sin's broken fingers, turned, and slapped it home.

Obediently, the hatch rose. Jen Sin, slightly less dead than he had appeared, lurched to his feet and broke the man's neck. The long rifle clattered to the landing pad, where he doubted it disturbed the gunman's three associates. The body he left where it fell, as he staggered into the lock and brought the hatch down.

He crawled down the short hallway, dragged himself

painfully into the pilot's chair . . . gripped the edge of the board until his vision cleared. It hurt to breathe. Cunning thrust of the knife, there—he ought to remember it.

Time to go. He extended a hand, brought the board clumsily to life, his hands afire, no spare breath to curse or to cry. The 'doc, that was his urgent need. He did know that.

Not yet, though. Not *just* yet.

He sounded a thirty-second warning, all that he dared, then gave *Lantis* her office, sagging in the chair, not webbed in, and in just a while, a little while, only a while, a while . . . He shook his head, saw stars and lightning.

As soon as they gained Jump, it would be safe enough then to tend his hurts.

An alarm screamed. He roused, saw the missile pursuing, initiated evasive action and clung to the board, to consciousness, in case his ship should need him.

So much for discretion. That was his thought as *Lantis* bounced through lanes of orderly traffic, Control cursing him for a clanless outlaw, and not one word of sorrow for those firing surface-to-air into those same working lanes of traffic.

Korval either would or would not be pleased, though he had the packet. He kept reminding himself of that fact—he had the packet. The woman at the meeting room spoke the lines out of order, no sense to it. If she were false, why not just finish the script and take what was not hers? If she were an ally, and captured—then, ah, yes, *then* one might well vary, as a warn-away—

She had not survived, he was certain of that, and to his list of error was added that he had cost Korval an ally . . . and added another death to his account.

He might almost say "innocent" save there were no innocents in this. He might, surely, say "dutiful," and even "courageous" might find a place in his report... and Korval—*he*—was in her debt.

His ship spoke to him. Orbit achieved. At least, he could still fly. He set himself to do so, heading for the up and out, the nearest Jump point, or failing that, the nearest likely bit of empty space from which he might initiate a short Jump.

His side where the knife had gotten past the leather, that was bad; his fingers left red smears on the board. The 'doc... but *Lantis* needed him.

They had almost reached the Jump point when a ship flashed into being so close the proximity alarms went off. Jen Sin swore weakly at pinheaded piloting, and a moment later discovered that not to be the case at all.

The new ship fired; the beam struck directly over the engines.

The shields deflected it, and there came evasive action from the automatics, but the other ship was a gunboat, no slim and underarmed courier.

The Jump point was that close. Once in Jump space, he would have some relief... enough relief that he might live through this adventure.

There really was no other choice; he had no more time on account.

Blood dripped from fingers remarkably steady as they moved across the board, diverting everything but the minimum amount necessary to function—from life support, from auxiliary power...

From the shields.

He fed everything to the engines and *ran* for the Jump point, as if there were no gunboats within the sector, much less the ship that even now was launching enough missiles to cripple a warship.

They hit the point with too much velocity, too much spin; in the midst of an evade that had no chance of succeeding. He greatly feared that they brought the missile with them.

Jen Sin groped for and hit the emergency autocoords, felt the ship shiver, saw the screens go grey—

And fainted where he sat.

• • • ✵ • • •

The Light pulled and riffled the files from the ship. The operator kept one eye on its screen while she pursued her own sort of data.

Engine power was minimal, and life support also; the shields were in tatters. The dorsal side showed a long, deep score, like that delivered from an energy cannon. That the hull had not taken worse damage—that was something to wonder at. Still, her readings indicated life support and other services low past the point of danger.

It was, the operator acknowledged, a ship in dire trouble, yet it held air, it held together, and it had come under its own power into the space at Tinsori Light. All those things recommended it, and the operator felt a cautious thrill of anticipation.

If the ship were fit to be repaired—but that was for the Light to decide.

If the pilot lived, her duty fell there.

The operator shivered, in mingled anticipation and fear.

• • • ✵ • • •

They'd taken bad hits, him and his ship, and unless they raised a repair yard or a friendly station soon, there was no saying that they'd either one survive.

He'd come to in Jump with emergency bells going off and a blood-smeared board lit yellow and red. It took determination, and a couple of rest periods with his forehead pressed against the board while pain shuddered through him, and his sluggish heartbeat filled his ears—but he pulled the damage reports.

Whatever had hit them as they entered Jump had been—*should have been*—enough to finish them. The main engine was out; the hull was scored, and there was a slow leak somewhere; life support was ranging critical and running off impulse power, along with the lights and screens.

In short, he was a pilot in distress with a limited number of choices available to him.

One: he could manually end Jump and hope *Lantis* held together, that they would manifest in a friendlier portion of space than the port they had just quit and within hailing distance of, if not an ally, at least a neutral party.

Two: he could ride Jump out to its natural conclusion. Normal reentry would be kinder to his ship's injuries. His own injuries...

He looked down at his sticky hands, the Jump pilot's ring covered with gore, and allowed himself to form the thought...

I am not going to survive this.

Oh, he could—probably—crawl across the cabin and get himself into the autodoc. But under emergency power, the 'doc would only stabilize him and place him into a kindly sleep until such time as ship conditions improved.

He may have blacked out again just there. Certainly it was possible. What roused him was . . . was.

Ah.

Lantis had exited Jump. They were . . . someplace.

Gasping, he leaned toward the board, squinting at screens grown nearly too dark to see.

The coords meant nothing to him. He remembered—he remembered hitting the autocoords. But the autocoords were for Korval safe spots—the ship yard; the Rock; quiet places located in odd corners of space, such as might be discovered by Scouts and pilots mad for knowing *what was there*? Autocoords had taken stock of *Lantis* as injured and hurt as she was, and, measured through some prior delm's and pilot's priorities, cast them together through limitless space to one particularly appropriate destination, to one last hope.

He looked again at screens and arrival data. The coords still meant nothing to him, though their absolute anonymity to a pilot of his experience and understanding gave him to believe that pursuit was now the least of his problems.

The space outside his screens was a place of pink and blue dusts pirouetting against a void in which stars were a distant promise.

If there was a friend of Korval in this place, it would, he thought, be good if they arrived . . . soon.

As if his thought had called the action, an interior screen came to life. Someone was accessing the ship's public files.

Hope bloomed, so painful and sudden that he realized he had, indeed, given up himself and his ship. There was someone out there—perhaps a friend. Someone who cared enough that it did them the honor of wanting to know who they were.

Jen Sin reached to the board, teeth gritted against the pain, and did pilot's duty, waking the scans and the screens, directing the comp to pull what files might be on offer at the address helpfully provided by their interrogator.

He found the visual as the files scrolled onto the screen—stared at both in disbelief, wondering if everything, from his waking at Jump end to this moment, were nothing other than the final mad dreams of a dying mind.

A station rose out of the dust, like no station he had ever seen, all crags, sharp edges, and cliffs. There were no visible docking bays, nor any outrigger yards. From the center of the uncompromising angularity of it rose a tower; white light pulsed from its apex in a rhythm of six-three-two.

On the screen, the information: *Welcome to Tinsori Light, Repairs and Lodging.*

He touched the query button, but no further information was forthcoming.

An alert trilled and Jen Sin blinked at the stats screen even as he felt the beam lock around *Lantis.*

For good or for ill, friend or foe, Tinsori Light was towing them in.

• • • ❋ • • •

The pilot had queried the Light.

The pilot was *alive.*

The operator rose, hands automatically smoothing her robe. Once, she thought, she must have had a robe that wrinkled, showed wear, became stained. This garment she wore now, here, in this role—this robe was never mussed or rumpled. Always, it was fresh, no matter how long she wore it or how much time had elapsed.

But the pilot—alive. She stared at the screen, as if she could see through the damaged hull, into the piloting tower, and the one sitting conn. Was the pilot wounded? she wondered. It seemed likely, with the ship bearing such injuries.

Wounded or whole, there were protocols to be followed, to insure the pilot's safety and her own. The Light would have its sample—that she could not prevent. Though, if the pilot were wounded, she thought suddenly, that might go easier; there would be no resistance to entering the unit.

The Light was not always careful of life. That the pilot might be frail would not weigh with it. It was hers to shield the pilot, to follow the protocols, and to insert herself between the Light and the pilot should it come to be necessary.

She looked again to her screens, at the progress of the ship toward the service bay.

Should she, she wondered suddenly, *contact* this pilot? If she *was* injured, she might want reassurance and to know that assistance was to hand.

The operator studied the screens, the lines of the ship being towed into the repair bay.

She sighed.

It was *like* a design she knew. The Light obviously considered it like enough that repairs could be made. But languages were not so easy as ships.

In the end, the operator tucked her hands into the

sleeves of her robe, watching until the ship entered the repair bay.

• • • • ❋ • • • •

Blackness ebbed.

He observed its fading from a point somewhat distant, his interest at once engaged and detached. First the edges thinned, black fogging into grey, the fog continuing to boil away until quite suddenly it froze into a crystalline mosaic, the whole glowing with a light so chill he shivered in his distant point of observation.

In that moment, he became aware of himself once more; aware that he was alive, healed, perhaps returned to perfect health.

The chill light sharpened, and from it came . . . nothing so gross as a whisper. A *suggestion*.

A choice.

He *had* been returned to optimal functioning, to perfect health. But there existed opportunity. He might become *more* perfect. His abilities might be enhanced beyond the arbitrary limits set upon him by mortal flesh. He might be made stronger, faster; he might sculpt the minds of others, turn enemies to allies with a thought; bend events to favor him—all this and more.

If he wished.

The decision point was here and now: Remain mortally perfect and perfectly limited, or embrace greatness and be more than ever he had—

A sharp snap, and the complaint of pneumatic hinges shattered the crystal clarity of the voice. Warm air scented with ginger wafted over naked skin.

Jen Sin yos'Phelium opened his eyes. Above him, a smooth hood, very like to an autodoc's hood. To his left, a wall supporting those hinges. To his right, the edge of the pad he lay upon, and a space—dull metal walls, dull metal floor and, nearby, a metal chair, with what was perhaps a robe draped across its back and seat.

He took a deep and careful breath, tears rising to his eyes at the sweet, painless function of his lungs. He tasted ginger on the back of his tongue—knowing it for a stimulant. She'd gotten him to the 'doc after all.

That thought gave pause. He closed his eyes again, taxing his memory.

There had been a woman—had he dreamed this? A woman with a pale pointed face, her black eyes large and up-slanted, and a hood pulled up to hide her hair. She had picked him up—surely *that* was a true memory! Picked him up, murmuring in some soft, guttural tongue that was almost—almost—one that he knew . . .

And there . . . a key phrase or sound, a match in a part of his memory he was sure was as new as his health.

"Do you wish to sleep, a better bed awaits you," a voice commented. The voice of his rescuer. Now that his brain was clear, he understood her perfectly well, though she spoke neither Liaden nor Trade, nor the Yxtrang language, either, though closer to that tongue than the other two. Sleep-learned or not, it was a language his Scout-learning marveled at even as he heard it.

He opened his eyes and beheld her, standing quite in plain sight next to the chair. Wordlessly, she lifted the robe, shook it, and held it wide between two long, elegant hands.

"My thanks." He rolled off of the mat, expecting

the shock of cold metal against his soles; pleased to find that the floor was warmed. The robe, he took from her hands and slipped on, sealing the front and leaving the hood to hang behind.

That done, he bowed deeply, giving all honor to one who had saved his life.

"I am Jen Sin yos'Phelium Clan Korval," he said. "My name is yours, to use at need."

"There is scarcely any need of names here," his companion said, coolly amused. "Keep yours; it will profit you more."

"Will it?" He straightened and looked at her.

She was taller than he, the starry robe hiding the shape of her. Her face was as he remembered—pointed, pale, and solemn; the hood was cast back, revealing tumbled curls of some color between yellow and white. Relieved of the burden of his garment, she had tucked her hands into the sleeves of her robe.

"I wonder if I may know your name," he said.

"It is possible that you may know it," she answered. "If you do, you might tell it to me. It would be pleasant to hear and to remember from time to time, though as I said, there is little use for such things as names here."

He cast her a sharp glance, but she seemed serious, and there was the language interface; this near-Yxtrang tongue had an ambiguous question protocol.

That being so, he moved a shoulder in regret.

"I have said the thing badly," he admitted. "What I had wished was to learn your name, or what you are called by your comrades or yourself."

"Oh." It seemed that she was disappointed, and he was, foolishly, regretful that he had no name to bestow upon her. "I am the keeper of the Light at Tinsori. Others before you have chosen to address me as Keeper. It is enough of a name, I suppose."

He bowed gently. "Light Keeper, I am in your debt."

"I do my duty. There is no occasion for debt."

"And yet, I place a value upon my life. That you return it to me—that is not without value. My ship—"

She raised a hand. "Your ship is under repair. Our facilities here are . . . old and perhaps nonstandard. However, with some small modification, your ship can be brought back to functionality. The Light proceeds with that work."

"Is there an estimate for completion?" he asked.

She frowned. "No."

That made him uneasy, but he merely inclined his head. "It is true that such damage as *Lantis* sustained might require some time to repair. I regret that I must ask—"

"Ask what you might," she interrupted brusquely. "I am not so accustomed to company that I will naturally realize what you wish to know."

"To give a Scout permission to ask questions is generous beyond sense," he said, attempting lightness. "Immediately, I take advantage and ask if there is a pinbeam unit on-station."

She tipped her head, and he saw the glint of what might have been drops of crystal in the tumble of her curls.

"There is not," she said.

That was disappointing, but not necessarily fatal.

"I then ask—may I gain access to my ship, which has such a unit. If I may draw power from the station, the message might be sent." He added, as gently as he might, "I mean only to let my delm know that I am well. This is no ploy to call enemies down upon you."

She laughed at that, which was as startling as it was engaging. No sooner had the sound faded than he wanted her to laugh again.

"To call enemies down on Tinsori Light! That has been done. It did not go well for them." She slipped her hands out of her sleeves and smoothed the front of her robe.

"Look you, Jen Sin yos'Phelium Clan Korval—messages do not travel outward from Tinsori Light; in all the time that has elapsed since our founding, no message has ever reached us from elsewhere. The space . . . does not behave as normal space must do. Worse, even the attempted transmission of such a message might disturb the balances that keep us here and now. I cannot allow it. The Light, I fear, will also not allow it."

He took that as his answer, for now, and assayed another question.

"May I know where my clothes are? There was something . . . dear in my jacket, and I would not see it lost."

"I have placed your possessions in your quarters," she said. "Do you want to go there now?"

His quarters, was it? And no time estimated for the completion of repairs, nor access to a pinbeam. It began to seem as if he were a prisoner, more than a customer, but until he knew more of this place, he dare not do anything but bow his head and murmur.

"I would very much like to see my quarters, thank you."

He had expected standard station accommodations—which was to say, slightly smaller than his quarters aboard *Lantis*. Instead, he was shown to a room very nearly the size of the apartment he so seldom rested in at Jelaza Kazone. The metal walls had been softened with hangings, and the floor had been spread with rugs. Pillows and coverlets in bright colors covered the bed. There was a screen mounted in such a way that it could be easily seen from the bed, and a small carved chest on which the contents of his pockets had been scrupulously placed.

Leaving his host by the door, Jen Sin approached the chest: cantra pieces and lesser coins; a flip-knife of Scout issue; his snub-nosed hideaway; a leather-rolled tool kit; and the green-wrapped packet, its ribbons and seals undisturbed, though displaying a few distressing stains upon its surface.

"The leathers are being repaired," she said in her abrupt way. "There are robes a-plenty."

"I thank you," he murmured and turned, holding up his hand. "I had been wearing a ring..."

"Yes." She tucked her hands into her sleeves and came like a wraith across the rug-strewn floor. She was well within kin-space when she finally stopped her advance, and he using all a Scout's discipline to stand easy where he stood.

She slipped her right hand out of her sleeve and extended it, fingers curled. He held out his hand and felt the cold heaviness of it strike his palm. A downward glance told him it was his own ring, sparkling as if it were new-made.

"I cleaned it," she said.

"And I thank you for that kindness as well," he said sincerely, remembering the gore-encrusted stones. "A third time, I am in your debt."

"No," she said.

"But I stand at a disadvantage," he protested. "Is there nothing that I might do for you, to Balance us?"

The black eyes lifted to his face.

"I wonder," she said slowly, "if you play cards."

The deck had been strange to him; the game stranger, though he had the rules to a hundred card games committed to memory.

The light keeper played with an intensity that was somewhat alarming, and when they paused the play for a meal—the most basic of yeast-based rations—she ate with that same intensity, as one starved for sensation.

After the meal, he pronounced himself weary—which fell short of being a complete falsehood—and she obligingly led him back to his room, standing aside while he entered, the door closing behind him.

Panic took him in the instant he heard the door seal, and he spun, threw himself at the blank wall—and all but stumbled out into the hallway and the light keeper's arms.

She frowned.

"Are you not tired, after all?"

"I had wanted to see if it opened for me," he said. "The door."

"That's wise," she answered gravely and left him there, vanishing 'round the corner of the hall.

He stood for perhaps two dozen heartbeats after she was gone, feeling foolish. Then he turned and reentered his room.

They fell into a schedule of sorts. The light keeper had duties that held her at odd hours, during which time Jen Sin partook of the station's library. When the light keeper's duty permitted, they walked together, she showing him somewhat of the station.

It was a strange place, the station, and it seemed that he and the light keeper were the only persons who walked its halls. He inquired after other travelers, traders, or those in need, but his guide only said that there was very little traffic in the space about Tinsori.

Moreover, the station contained such amusements as were strange to him. One room she led him to simulated planetary weather, so that they were rained upon, dried by a warm wind and then snowed on. The light keeper laughed and spun, shaking her crystal-beaded curls, her robe flaring out to show naked long toes and trim pale ankles.

Jen Sin caught her arm and pulled her out into the warmer hall.

"Is it not delightful?" she asked.

"Truth said, it casts me off-balance," he answered, trying unsuccessfully to dry his face with a snow-spangled sleeve. "Weather changes on-planet come with warnings; to simply have random weather flung at one—it distresses me."

He was likewise distressed by the room that produced odors in an indiscriminate aural medley, though the green room found his favor—flowers and vegetables alike.

"Here, this one is ripe," he said, touching the round red cheek of a tomato. "Shall we take it back with us for the evening meal?" This was his third day on the station, and he was growing tired of yeast.

The light keeper frowned at him. "Eat a plant?"

"A vegetable, but yes. Why not?"

"I never thought of it," she said.

"Someone must have done," he said lightly, plucking the fruit. "Most stations have hydroponic sections, so residents may reap the benefit of fresh food. Yeast alone does not satisfy all one's appetite." He smiled at her. "I would have thought that one as open to sensation as yourself would have sampled every leaf here."

"Truly, it did not occur," she said, and he could see that she was troubled. "How . . . odd. I must have forgotten."

They exited the garden and continued their walk.

"What duty are you called to," he asked her, "in the control room?"

He thought for a moment she would not answer him, and indeed, it was impertinence to ask. But his browsing of the library, of those volumes written in a language he could read, had begun to fill him with unease.

The light keeper shrugged. "I prevent the Light from doing mischief," she said, "and keep it to its location."

It was his moment to frown.

"The station drifts?"

"No," she said. "The station moves of its own volition, within the constraints of coords that balance with the expanding edge of things. Part of my function is to keep us at that expanding edge, to maintain the energy levels that keep the coords constant. The Light would be better pleased if we were closer in, where it could wield its influence."

"Influence," he repeated, as they came to a place where the corridor split. Unthinking, he turned right—and stopped immediately when she caught his sleeve.

"Not that way."

"Why not?"

A hesitation. "Old damage. The hall is not safe."

"May I assist? I am a Scout and have strange abilities of my own."

She looked doubtful. "If you like, I will open the schematics to you."

Oh, would she, indeed? Jen Sin bowed softly.

"I would like that very much, indeed."

The light keeper ate her half of the fruit greedily, then grilled him on what else out of the garden section might be edible. He laughed and threw his hands up, palms out, to fend off her eagerness.

"Come, if you will open the schematics, then open the garden records as well, and I will apply myself to research."

"Done!"

He laughed again, lowering his hands.

"I see I have my work in line."

"You asked for work," she pointed out in her practical way.

"So I did."

She tipped her head. "Jen Sin, I wonder if you might do something . . . else for me."

He looked into her tip-tilted black eyes and thought he knew what she might ask. Indeed, he was surprised that she had not asked before, as sense-starved and solitary as she was.

"I will do anything that is in my power," he told her gently.

"What are these?" he asked later, fingering the crystal drops in her hair.

"My memories," she said drowsily, her head on his shoulder.

He was drowsy himself, but a Scout fails of asking questions when he is dead.

"If you brush them out, will you forget yourself?"

"No. But if something happens and I am not wearing them, I will have no prompts and the Light will be unwatched."

Perhaps that made sense in some way, but he lacked context. He would have pressed her, but her breathing told him that she had slipped into sleep.

He sighed, nestled his chin against her curls, and followed.

...✳...

"What progress," she asked the Light, "on the repairs?"

Progress, came the reply.

The keeper bit her lip.

"When will repairs be complete?" she asked.

Unknown.

This mode was unfortunate. It was behavior from a distant time, when the Light had first come into the care of the Sanderat. The keeper closed her eyes, called up her will, thrust it at the Light.

"You will tell me when repairs will be complete and when Jen Sin yos'Phelium Clan Korval may depart, to continue his lawful business."

Are you ready to be alone again? The pilot amuses you, does he not? What harm to keep him?

Yes, this was very bad, indeed. The Light was at its most dangerous when it offered your heart's desire. She breathed deeply, and made her will adamantine.

"I will have a time when the ship in your care will be repaired and able. The pilot is his own person; he has duty. It is our duty to assist him, not disrupt him."

It is your duty to assist.

"It is, and as you serve me, it is your duty, also."

There was a silence. Rather a lengthy silence.

The ship will be able to depart in six station days.

So soon? She bowed her head.

"That is well, then. Keep me informed."

• • • ❋ • • •

The schematics were fascinating—and horrifying.

Jen Sin had been a member of a Scout exploratory team. He, as all explorer Scouts, had been well drilled on the seeming and the dangers of what was called Old Tech. His team had discovered a small cache of what might have been toys—small, crude ceramic shapes that might infiltrate a man's mind, make him receptive to thoughts that he would not recognize as belonging to an Other.

The cache of toys they had found had been depleted, being able to effect nothing more than a sense of melancholy and foreboding in those unheedful enough to pick them up. His team—well. Krechin had wrapped them in muffle, and sealed them into a stasis box until they could be properly handed over to the Office of Old Technology at Headquarters.

The toys had been frightening enough, but he had an extra burden of knowledge, for he had read the logs and diaries of Clan Korval as far back as Cantra yos'Phelium, who had brought the understanding that the old universe and the old technologies had together been the downfall of vast civilizations. And that had been Old Technology in small gulps, as might be found in a toy, or a personalized hand weapon, or a geegaw worn for nefarious purpose.

To find a working, *aware* structure entirely built from forbidden tech—that was enough to give a Scout nightmares. Even Korval might quail before such a thing.

And the light keeper's purpose was to keep it from *doing mischief*?

Mischief, by the gods. And his ship was in its keeping. Worse. His ship was in *its power*, being modified, never doubt it, as he stood by—and did nothing.

Jen Sin closed the schematics and rose from the desk. He quit the library, and walked toward the hub, where there was a gym.

Exercise would calm him.

And then he would need to speak with the light keeper.

"Tell me," he said to the light keeper, as she settled her cheek on his shoulder, "about this place."

She stirred, eyelashes fluttering against his skin. "This space?"

"No, the station," he murmured. "The schematics woke questions."

She laughed softly. "What sorts of questions, now?"

"Well. How did the station come to be? Who built it? How did you come to keep it? Where are the others?... Those sorts of questions. I don't doubt I can find more, if you wish."

"No, those will do, I think."

She sighed, relaxing against him so completely that he thought for a moment that he had been cheated and she had slipped over into sleep.

"How the station came to be. My sisters of the Sanderat believed that the Great Enemy built it. We found it abandoned, and riding in space where a waystation had been sore needed. The Soldiers were in favor of destroying it, but it was in Sanderat space, and we undertook to Keep it.

"Three of our order were dispatched . . . Faren, Jeneet, and . . . Lorith."

She tensed. He held his breath.

"Lorith," she breathed. "That is *my* name."

"May I address you thus?" he asked, when several minutes had passed and she had said nothing more, nor relaxed.

"Yes." She sighed again, and became . . . somewhat . . . less tense.

"What happened," he murmured, "to Faren and Jeneet?"

"Faren died in the storm," she whispered. "We were without power, adrift, for many elapsed units. When we came to rest and repairs were made—it was no longer possible to reclaim her. The Light took new samples, from Jeneet, from me."

Samples. He repressed the shiver sternly and asked his next question softly, "What storm was that, Lorith?"

"Why, the big storm that shifted everything away from where it had been. When it was done, the Light was . . . where you found it, and not in orbit about Tinsori, as it had been. Tinsori, we were not able to locate. The coordinates of our present location . . . were not possible. Jeneet took our boat and went out to find where we were. That was . . . much time has elapsed since then. I fear that she has been lost, or died, or taken up in battle."

Korval had an odd history; it was odder still to hear that history from other lips, from another perspective, and yet, *that* war that had displaced a universe or more...from one space-time to another.

That war had ended hundreds of years ago.

He stroked her hair, feeling the crystal beads slide through his fingers.

"Lorith," he said gently, oh, so very gently. "I cannot allow my ship to rest any longer in care of the Light."

She raised her head and looked down at him, eyes wide and very black.

"It said...six days, as we measure them here, when time is aware. Six days, and your ship will be ready." She frowned. "I have exerted my will. You will come to no harm, though I will...miss you."

"You need not. Come with me."

"No, who would Keep the Light? It might do anything, left to itself."

So it might.

He sat up, and she did, drawing a crimson cover over her naked shoulders.

"I must go," he said and slid out of bed, reaching for his leathers.

•••✵•••

He was determined and she could not—*would not*—influence him to wait. She showed him the way to the repair bay, hearing the voice of the Light.

Little man, you will have your ship when it is properly prepared.

Jen Sin checked, then continued toward the place where the tunnel intersected the hall.

"The pilot decides when his ship is ready," he said aloud. "I go now, and I thank you and the light keeper for your care."

She hardened her will and pushed at the Light.

"Let him go to his duty," she said, and added, terrified for his safety, "unless the ship is not functional."

She was an idiot; her fear for him softened her will. And in that moment, the Light struck.

The walls crackled; she felt the charge build and simultaneously threw her will and herself between Jen Sin and the bolt.

She heard him scream—her name it was—and then heard nothing more.

•••※•••

He came to himself in the library, with no memory of having arrived there. He supposed that he had run—run like a hare from Lorith's murder, to save his own precious self, to *survive* against every odd—*that* was Korval's talent.

Craven, he told himself, running his hands into his hair and bending his head. He was weeping, at least he had that much heart.

But the Scout mind would not be stilled, and too soon it came to him that—he dared not leave the Light unwatched. For who knew what it might do, left alone?

He had the schematics, and his Scout-trained talents. Did he dare move against it and risk his life? Or ought he to stand guard and prevent it doing harm?

"Jen Sin?" He would swear that he felt her hand on his hair, her voice edged with concern. "Were you hurt?"

Slowly, he lifted his face, staring into hers, the pointed chin, the space-black eyes, and the crystal beads glittering in pale, curly hair.

"You were killed," he said, toneless.

She stepped away. "No."

"Yes!" He snapped to his feet, the chair clattering backward, snatched her shoulders and shook her.

A thought tantalized, then crystallized.

"*How many times* has it killed you?"

"I don't know," she said, shockingly calm. "Perhaps I die every time we drift back to quiet after an alert, and the Light remakes me at need. Does it matter? I am always myself and I have my memories. The sample, you know."

He stared, speechless, feeling her fragile and real under his fingers.

"The sample, of course," he agreed. "What came of Jeneet's sample, Lorith?"

"She did not use the beads, and when I called her back, she remembered nothing."

He closed his eyes briefly, recalling the unit he had risen from, and the crystal-cold voice offering him a choice.

"Jen Sin?"

He raised his hand and ran his fingers through her hair, feeling the cool beads slip past his skin.

"I wonder," he said softly. "Is there a . . . sample of me?"

Her eyes flickered.

"Yes."

"And have you more beads?"

"Yes."

"Then this is what I think we should do, while I wait for my ship to be . . . properly prepared."

• • • ✵ • • •

The operator sat at her board, and watched the ship tumble out of the repair bay. The scans elucidated a vessel in good repair, the hull intact, all systems green and vigorous.

She took a breath and watched her screens, dry-eyed, until the Jump glare faded and the space at Tinsori Light was empty, for as far as her instruments could scan.

. . . ✵ . . .

He brought the pinbeam online, entered the message in Korval House code. The message that would warn the clan away and see Tinsori Light scrubbed from the list of autocoords in Korval courier ships. The message that would tell the delm the Jump pilot's ring was lost, along with the good ship and pilot. The message that would tell the delm that when she needed another packet delivered, it could never again be Jen Sin who would do it.

Emergency repairs at Tinsori Light. Left my ring in earnest. The keeper's a cantra-grubbing pirate, but the ship should hold air to Lytaxin. Send one of ours and eight cantra to redeem my pledge. Send them armed. In fact, send two . . .

The 'beam went. He waited patiently for the ack, looking down at his hands, folded on the board, ringless and calm.

He reviewed his plan and found it, if not good, certainly necessary.

A ship *properly prepared* by an agent of the Great Enemy? How could he bring such a ship into the universe proper, save for one thing only?

Comm chimed; the 'beam had been acknowledged by the first relay.

Jen Sin yos'Phelium Clan Korval pressed the sequence of buttons he had preset and released the engine's energy at once, catastrophically.

• • • ※ • • •

She felt a hand settle on her shoulder and looked up, finding his reflection in a darkened screen.

"He's gone?"

"Yes."

She spun the chair and came to her feet; he dropped back to give her room, the beads glittering like rain in his dark hair.

"Now, it is for us," she said. "Will we survive it?"

He smiled and held out his hand, the big ring sparkling on his finger.

"Many times, perhaps," he said.

• • • ※ • • •

Space is haunted.

Pilots know this; stationmasters and light keepers, too; though they seldom speak of it, even to each other. Why would they? Ghost or imagination, wyrd space or black hole, life—and space—is dangerous.

The usual rules apply.